Poison Kiss

〜ⓥ〜

EARTHSIDE

ANA MARDOLL

POISON KISS by Ana Mardoll

Copyright © 2016

All rights reserved.

ISBN: 978-1-5480212-2-1

Published by Acacia Moon Publishing, LLC

Cover illustration by James, GoOnWrite.com

Books by Ana Mardoll

THE EARTHSIDE SERIES

Poison Kiss (#1)
Survival Rout (#2)

REWOVEN TALES

Pulchritude

To Kristy and Thomas,
for rekindling my joy in writing
at a time when only embers remained.

CONTENTS

CHAPTER 1

"**R**ose, can you tilt your head for me, please?" The pale young woman who has been assigned to braid my hair whispers the words, her voice so soft that I can barely hear her over the crash of hail that pounds the mansion roof and sends icy pellets skittering noisily across the marble floor.

Obediently, I lean forward to facilitate her task. Her nimble fingers continue their work, twisting and looping my long pink hair into the elaborate style that our mistress has commanded for tonight's festivities. I wonder numbly how many more hours my grooming will take; we've been at this since my morning bath. I'm curious also to know if this girl is as bored with braiding my hair as I am with sitting motionless. Not that either of us would dream of complaining; the May Queen's temper is lethal, and there are far worse assignments to be handed out.

Our shared silence is all the more oppressive against the contrast of the morning's torrential downpour. Hailstones strike the land with a relentless rhythm, the icy missiles large enough to beat the life out of any escaped servants or skulking assassins. Hot summer air, unrelieved by the rain, invades through floor-to-ceiling windows which let out in all directions onto the vast gardens that carpet our mistress' estate; gardens which are now thoroughly soaked. I nurture a satisfying mental image of elegant guests coated in rain-churned muck, but I know better than to hope. Despite the current violence of the weather, the land will be as cool and dry as a bone in just a few hours. Anything less would ruin the May Queen's gala ball.

There is a sudden soft gasp behind me, and then the sharp clatter of things spilling to the floor. I freeze, holding perfectly still as I count the seconds in my head and try to steady my breathing. Did the May Queen enter the room without my hearing her? Is she even now hurting the young woman assigned to wait on me, for some perceived infraction? I keep my head facing straight ahead, my spine stiff. There is nothing I can do to help the girl; if our mistress is angry, my interference would only make things worse for her. I force myself to remain calm and I wait.

"Sorry! I'm so sorry!" The frightened whisper comes from behind me. Yet there are no furious words to follow the apology, no sense of our mistress' tangible rage occupying the same space as us. I turn my head cautiously until I can see my hairdresser out of the corner of my eye; we are alone. She kneels on the cold floor, gingerly picking tiny rosebuds from the white marble and piling them back into their small wooden bowl. Tension eases from my shoulders with the realization that the May Queen was *not*, after all, the source of the cacophony; the girl had merely dropped the decorations she is meant to be twining into my pinned braid.

She senses me staring at her and looks up with a pained wince. "Please don't tell?" she pleads softly.

I shake my head at her, but the sensation of my hair trying to work free from its unfinished bonds reminds me to remain still. "I wouldn't," I promise quietly. Some of the other servants tattle, hoping to redirect our mistress' anger from them, but I never have. I like to believe I never will, but I know it is easy to think so when I am one of her favorites. I haven't yet been truly tempted to resort to drastic measures for survival. The May Queen is cruel, but she is kinder to her Nightshades than she is to the Fragrants and Ornamentals who wait on us.

"Thanks," my hairdresser whispers softly, continuing the task I can't aid her with. I sit motionlessly and scrutinize her as she rescues the little rosebuds, trying to guess her name. Her skin is pale, almost a papery white but with soft freckles sprayed liberally across her cheeks and nose. Maturity is difficult to guess among the Flowers, but we might be the same age; her complexion is smooth, but with tiny lines around the corner of her eyes and between her eyebrows. Her purple hair, worn loose and wavy in the style of the Fragrants, is a sister palette to the candy-pink of my own. Is she Lilac or Veronica or Wisteria? We've been through so many Fragrants since I first awoke that I can't keep track of them anymore, yet I'm sure I've seen this one's face before today. She's not a new acquisition.

When she stands from her kneeling position on the floor, her hair shifts and I catch the tattoo branded on her right shoulder. Three single sprays, the tiny flowers spaced evenly up each stalk. *Lavender*, I realize. No, she isn't new; the last Lavender was killed over two dozen balls ago, which makes this one's term about half as long as mine. She's a survivor if she's lasted this long. Many of the servants don't live more than a few parties. I've been fortunate enough to last as long as I have, though there are nights when it feels more like a curse.

"They say the ball tonight will be a long one," she whispers, resuming her place behind me. Her words are almost inaudible over the crashing rain, as soft as her cool fingers in my hair. I do not respond; I don't want to be drawn into conversation. It is not forbidden, but the May Queen is fond of creating arbitrary exceptions to use as a cudgel against us. Worse, if she saw me becoming close to one of the others, she might send her to me to be killed. She has never yet sent me a woman, but there's always a first time and she might find it amusing to do so.

"The chefs have been told to prepare forty courses," the young woman continues in a dogged whisper. Although I have reassured her I won't tattle on her, her determination to speak with me is unusual; but if her information is correct, it was good of her to warn me.

There is no reliable method by which to measure the length of the parties we attend, and so the number of courses has become the necessary standard. If we are truly in for a forty-course night, many of us will end up falling asleep on our feet, and anyone who does so in full view of the lords and ladies will risk becoming an object of humiliation or worse. I will need to conserve my energy where I can, and perhaps slip away for a brief doze in the hallways; anything to stay awake and on my feet for our mistress.

"We haven't had one nearly so long in over a dozen balls," she continues, her fingers still working at my hair, the touch gentle and lulling. "Have we?" she prompts.

I sit silently, weighing the options before me. I don't want to be caught socializing when we are supposed to be focused on the work assigned to us: the dressing of my hair for tonight's ball. Nor do I want to make friends with someone I may have to watch die, or may be forced to kill. But it would be unwise to be rude, or to make an enemy of this woman. Not all the stories tattled to the May Queen are true ones, and my favored status can protect me only up to a point.

Taking advantage of the privacy the storm offers, I murmur as softly as I can: "No." Having gone this far, I feel I might as well go all the way and add, "I don't think we've had a full forty-course dance since before you were brought here."

She moves in front of me, holding her wooden bowl in one hand as she bends to place flowers carefully into the thick braid wrapped like a crown about my head. "You've been here longer than me," she whispers. Her mouth barely moves when she talks; if I couldn't hear her myself, I'd never realize she was engaging in clandestine conversation. "I remember you were here when I awoke. I thought your shade of pink was wrong for your name, Rose. Your hair should be darker." A pause stretches between us. "I'm sorry; was that a bad thing to say?"

"No," I whisper, quick to reassure her. "I don't like the name either."

As soon as I blurt out the hasty words, I realize I have now entrusted my life to her. I had intended the confession to put her at ease, but the May Queen does not tolerate criticism with regard to her garden specimens.

We accept the names and roles we are given as her Flowers, or we die. Fortunately, Lavender's gaze softens with sympathy, and I don't think she means me ill. "It's not a bad name," she says, her voice gentle.

I'm touched by her unexpected pity. "It's not a bad name," I agree quietly. I know I ought to stop talking, but I've already dug myself into deep trouble. Maybe if she likes me she won't turn me in, or perhaps the loneliness is starting to get to me. "I just don't think it fits me. Not only because of the pink, though you're not the first one to feel my colors should be different; the May Queen agrees." I laugh softly, retreating to the cold comfort of grim humor. "I'm told the one before me was pale, with white hair and bloodless lips. The one before *her* had fiery curls and a face much darker than mine. I suppose I'm a compromise between the two."

Pink hair, the middle ground between red and white, which always looks faintly wrong to me in the looking-glass. I don't add the belief I privately nurture: that my skin, my arms, my hands were mine to start with, and not a gift from the faery queen who woke me. I don't know how I know this—not a single one of us has retained conscious memories from the time before waking to her command—but I feel it instinctively. I know my skin is mine in the same way I know the brand on my shoulder is a rose and the fish on our tables is salmon. I just know.

Lavender nods in understanding. "They told me about the Lavenders before me," she says, "and how they died."

I wince in sympathy, remembering how much I hadn't enjoyed hearing of my precursors' deaths. There had not even been any discernible reason for their weeding, the May Queen seeming to prune her garden at random. She's been through three different Lavenders in the time I've been here, each of them almost identical to this one: sweetly-scented Fragrants with soft purple in their hair. Her Ornamentals are replaced even faster, as I've counted almost a dozen Bluebonnets in my time here. Nightshades tend to last longer, though not always; the Red Rose died during her sixth gala.

"Rose?" she murmurs, her voice dropping lower than before. I look up, shaken from my recollections, to find her staring down at me with a pleading expression. "Rose, have you ever thought about escaping?"

Suddenly the room is too close. I can smell her, a dizzying fragrance of honeysuckle and hope. From anyone else the question would be a trap, yet the scents emanating from her body betray her true feelings. She's serious, and she's going to get herself killed. "Of course I have," I counter in a strained whisper, my lips barely moving. "But you've been here long enough to know what happens to those who try."

Lavender's face remains composed, though her eyes turn miserable. Her fingers continue to work at my hair, and I'm relieved she hasn't thrown all caution to the wind. Anyone who glanced in on our chamber would see that she is working and I am being still, and all is well. "I know what happens to the ones who get *caught*," she argues in a soft counterpoint, circling around to work on my hair from the side.

"You only see the ones who are punished in public," I correct her, my whispered voice steely. "They deal with the others in secret; you just don't hear about them."

"How can you know—" she starts, but I cut her off with a pained hiss.

"Some of them are sent to *me*."

She blanches at this reminder of the lethal kisses of the May Queen's Nightshades. There is silence for several long minutes while the tension has a chance to dissipate and she finds her voice again. "You've been off the estate," she murmurs. "I've seen you go."

"Yes," I affirm, my voice cold in my throat.

Nightshades are occasionally sent out on assignment. Sometimes on foot, but other times in the carriages made for the Ornamentals: giant gourds pulled by garden pests as large as the horses the faery lords ride. The Ornamentals are sent to the courts and beds of those the May Queen would ally with; the Nightshades are, less frequently, sent to those she despises. Two faery men have died under my kiss, though the last one survived.

That episode with the third lord was two galas before tonight, and I've only just managed to stop wincing at every reminder. Lavender would have heard about my misadventure. I was delivered to the May Queen's door, a messy heap of blood and flesh. She decided to salvage me, healing me until not a single physical scar remained, but throughout her ministrations I prayed only for death.

The Fragrant girl strokes her cool fingers gently over my brow, comforting me under the guise of smoothing an errant hair. "You've been off the estate," she repeats softly, her urgent voice seeking to break through my frosty response. "You could guide someone. You must know of hiding places, of a way out..." Her voice falters, and I can't help but pity her again. She's never left the mansion, only ever seen the green hills from the windows. She doesn't know.

"Lavender," I say softly, "there's no way out." I hate to break her spirit like this, but I don't want her to die from foolish hopes. If she really can't live here any longer, there are easier ways to go than a reckless dash for freedom. Still, I'm guessing her desire to try stems more from false hope than from an impulse towards self-harm. "You've seen the lords and ladies who come to the dances? Their estates border our own. Even if you got away cleanly, you'd just be running into one of their territories. And they're all as brutal as the May Queen."

I had expected her to be deflated, but her mouth sets in a stubborn line. "We aren't born here," she counters softly. "We must come from somewhere else. Maybe we can go back there."

I blink at her, suddenly lost in another memory. *We come from somewhere else.*

Those same words had been spoken to me by one of my recent victims. He'd been before the third faery lord, but not long previously—only about three balls ago. He had been a sad, gentle man who knew as soon as he was sent to me that I was his executioner. He did not fight his fate, however, but lay in my arms and spun a wondrous tale which he said was his confession.

I hadn't known how much credence to give to his words. Some of the servants believe incredible things, and others have minds that go bad in captivity—indeed, I am often uncertain of my own lucidity. I had no reason to believe there was a single germ of truth in his wild story, yet a part of me now desperately wants his words to be true. If we can get out of the mansion, away from prying eyes and ears, maybe Lavender would know what to make of his tale.

"Even if we found a way out, we'd be missed almost immediately if we ran," I point out, my voice less firm than before. "It's one thing to doze in the hallways where she can send a servant to check on us; it's another thing entirely to just *disappear*."

Lavender seizes on my uncertainty. "Not at a ball," she insists softly. "Not if there were good reason for us to be away for a long while. Not if she expected us to be gone and we had a head-start. And with guests here, even if she suspected something, she would lose face admitting someone had run off in the middle of a party. She'd let us go rather than suffer a blow to her reputation."

Her honeysuckle smell is now so strong that I'm forced to take quick, shallow breaths through my nose to stave off the raw hope that assaults my concentration. It isn't her fault; the Fragrants can only control their emotional aromas with great effort. Yet the swirl of perfume around her makes it difficult to separate my own thoughts from her soft words, and I have to consciously exhale several times to clear my head.

"It's not a bad plan," I admit, working my way through her logic. "But what excuse do we have to leave the ball?"

The Fragrant girl doesn't dare beam a smile at me, holding her expression calm and steady even now in case an intruder might burst in on us; her green eyes, however, are bright and triumphant. "Leave that to me," she whispers proudly, her fingers redoubling their efforts in my hair.

CHAPTER 2

The rain stops just when I suspected it would: right before the first chime of the seventh evening hour. Tonight the chimes are a cue for us to line the walls of the vast ballroom, where we will stand perfectly still while the guests arrive.

We stand and wait, and the seventh hour chimes again. I wonder how many times it will chime tonight before it moves on to the eighth hour, or if it will instead retreat to the sixth. The gala before this was a backwards one, the setting suns slowly traversing the sky in reverse until the party concluded on their dipping just under the horizon. If the festivities tonight turn out to be a day-party, it will be too dangerous for us to run; we will need darkness as a cover if we are to get any distance at all.

As we are organized by function, Lavender doesn't stand near me against the wall. The Ornamentals are clumped closest to the great doors, painfully lovely to look at. Some of them change color over the seasons, their hair or skin cycling through different hues and shades; others maintain an unchanging ethereal loveliness. Of us all, the Ornamentals come closest to approximating the beauty of the May Queen but it is they she weeds the most often. They are the lowest of us Flowers, though they still outrank the gnarled tree-people who grow as guards along the edges of the estate, line the vast gardens as exotic fruit-bearers, and will serve tonight as coat-racks in the mansion's entrance chambers.

After the Ornamentals come the Fragrants, with Lavender among their number. Grouped so closely together, their scent is dizzying even in the cavernous space of the ballroom. Their emotions are identifiable through the heady aromas: the lemony tartness of fear, the sharp green apple of simmering anger, the overpowering stench of anxious spicy clover that coats everything around us. I purposely avoid seeking out Lavender with my gaze, but spot her out of the corner of my eye. Her skin is pale under the cap of her loose purple hair and the spray of freckles across her face and bare shoulders. I wonder again if this plan of hers will work, and if she can manage to be near me at the exact moment necessary in order to pull it off.

Lining the far end of the hall, away from the giant doors that open onto the main lawn, are the Nightshades. We are less beautiful than the Ornamentals and less alluring than the Fragrants. The lords and ladies assume we are the lowest of her servants, not realizing that we are cultivated for our hidden thorns. Lokelani stands at silent attention on my left, her warm rosy hair a sister to my own. To my right is Violet, her hair a brilliant cloud of dark purple corkscrews, her lips begging for kisses. Across the hall are the twins, Heather with her soft lilac curls and Hyacinth with his wavy blue locks. There are a good forty of us Nightshades in all, the rarest of the May Queen's flowers.

I feel a stab of guilt for my brothers and sisters around me. How can I escape and leave them behind? Yet there's no way I could take them with us; if Lavender can pull off her plan to get the two of us excused for even an hour, it will be a miracle. Perhaps if I escape, they will be treated better for a time, as the favored few who did not run away. I pray that at least they will not be treated worse.

Our mistress stands in the center of the hall where we wait, her exquisite face watching us with unreadable emotion. Tonight her hair is as dark as loamy earth and her eyes match our uniform bright green. She is otherwise colorless, her skin and lips so pale as to be almost translucent. She is moonlight striking a fertile garden as it waits to be tilled; she is a ghostly will-o'-the-wisp floating through a freshly-dug cemetery; she is the embodiment of death waiting to strike us. When the faery lords and ladies arrive, she smiles brightly at them but her white teeth are bared like fangs and the delight on her face utterly fails to reach her eyes.

The visiting faeries are as beautiful and dangerous as she. One lord is as bright as the sun and dazzles my eyes so I have to look away or be blinded. A dozen manservants follow behind him, each more handsome than the last. The men are pretty toys which the May Queen may assign one of us to break; their lord may suspect his hostess of ordering the mischief, but courtesy forbids more than token complaint. The lady beside him is wrapped in a dress of auburn leaves, each rustling in an invisible wind. A small cream-colored monkey creeps behind her on a silver chain, casting about the room with eyes which look terrifyingly human. I remind myself as I stare into those wide eyes that there are worse things than being a killer for our mistress.

Twenty faeries arrive in the first wave of guests, each of them trailing servants in their wake. More guests will trickle in as the night stretches on, especially if this really is intended to be a lengthy forty-course event. As it is there are already several hundred bodies in the ballroom: the faeries who have come to be entertained; the dancers such as myself and Lavender; and other sundry servants who set out the food, provide the light, and perform a thousand menial tasks for their masters. As tonight's hostess, the May Queen will supply the majority of these servants, many of whom are those not awoken as Flowers.

The first course of food is served by the silent vine-limbed people who scurry about the edges of the hall. Already tonight they are sweating profusely from their work, for the cavernous ballroom comprises an entire wing of the mansion that they must repeatedly walk. The garden doors have been thrown open to provide cool relief, but the night breezes barely penetrate the crushing heat of so many bodies. Above us, dim light is provided by the fireflies held aloft in their delicate wire cages. Their soft glow trickles down from the high ceiling, as they watch us from afar with lonely eyes, their thin hands grasping the cage bars.

This party is entirely for the benefit of the lords and ladies. They will laugh and flirt with each other, they will gamble and drink rowdily, and they will sometimes remember to eat the food that has been placed before them. A few servants—mostly the pretty Ornamentals—will be called upon to dance with our masters and mistresses, and none of us envies them their task. But the vast majority of us will dance with our fellow servants, putting on a show of civility. This is theater for them, and we are the entertainers; our roles are to be merry and our performance must be perfect. The May Queen's reputation hinges on the behavior of those who serve her.

Lavender's plan for us involves a subtle manipulation of these dynamics. If I refuse to perform my role, or if I perform particularly badly, I will be punished—and that punishment may well become the centerpiece for tonight's entertainment. The lords and ladies find our torture very amusing. Yet if I can fail in a tiny way, just enough to be sent from the room for a few precious minutes, then we have a chance to escape. The May Queen will notice when we do not return, of course, but it is not in her best interests to reveal to her guests any failure to control her household. If we are careful, we could have hours of privacy to safely escape her sprawling estates and find a way out.

If we are careful, and if we are banished from the room together, when in truth there are several dozen Fragrants, any of whom might be called upon to escort me to the dressing rooms. Then, out on the estate, we must hope that the wild stories of a dying man turn out to be true.

I look up into the face of my dancing partner. He's a beautiful man, with skin the color of warm bark and soft black scruff covering his chin just below the lips. He looks as though he were created for kissing, the edges of his mouth turning up in a wry grin as he leads me easily around the dance floor. If I stay, if we don't run tonight, he might be forced to kiss *me*, and I don't want him added to my long list of victims. I don't want to see his face contort in pain or his eyes glaze over in death.

Lavender is right. I cannot do this any longer; better to risk everything for freedom than to stay another night.

Smiling warmly up at the man, I drop my rose-branded shoulder suggestively as I draw him into a faster tempo for the dance. My partner grins with every evidence of pleasure and follows my quickened step with easy grace. My mind is full of questions I will never be free to ask him: does he genuinely enjoy this sensual charade and the pretty woman in his arms, or is he simply another consummate actor hiding misery? The desire in his eyes does not seem counterfeit, but I suppose the mirroring desire I have feigned to draw him into this dance seems no less real to him.

The thin gown clinging to my skin in the oppressive heat of the room flutters softly with the exertion of our efforts, the fabric lifting in the air and providing more freedom of movement to my legs. We dance with frenetic energy, whirling and dipping through the empty space that appears on the floor as the other dancers discreetly make way for us. I can sense their retreat, their fear of sharing in whatever punishment may befall us for breaking decorum in this way. I feel a sudden pang of guilt at the realization that my partner may be punished for his share in my deliberate disgrace. Yet still we dance on, his strong fingers gripping mine as I drop my head backwards into a deep dip, held from falling only by the strength of his warm hands.

When I raise my head again my hair pulls loose from its pinned restraints, and I feel the thick braid brush against my bare shoulders. The plaited crown on which Lavender worked so hard this morning has come loose, and is weeping tiny rosebuds like droplets of water onto the marble dance floor. I move instantly away from my partner, my hand reaching up to catch at my falling hair, my voice laughing and apologizing and thanking him all at once in a profuse babble. He lets me go with a reluctance that sends a painful sliver of fear through my heart, and I turn my back on him with a finality that I hope will prevent him from following me. Tripping shamefacedly over to my mistress, I pray I haven't signed his death warrant—or my own.

The May Queen stands on the outskirts of the dancing, and the cold expression on her face does nothing to quiet my fears. Reaching her, I curtsy deeply, brushing my lips through the air above her offered hand. My heart still pounds with the adrenaline of the dance and I feel a wild temptation to dive through that thin layer of air and press her hand to my poisonous mouth, but I know this is just a hopeless fantasy. Our talents do not work against those who first bestowed them, and she has kissed me countless times without being harmed in the least. There are tales of lethal servants who tried to turn their gifts against their masters; the only detail on which the stories disagree is which manner of horrific death they suffered.

"Enjoying the dance, Rose?" The May Queen's voice is high and clear, her emotions difficult to read. The shadow of a smirk on her beautiful face might be wry amusement or it might be the harbinger of a lethal temper tantrum at my indecorous behavior.

I keep my face carefully displaying bashful chagrin. "Yes, Mistress," I lie with smiling embarrassment, pushing soft rueful laughter into my voice and keeping my eyes humbly downcast. "He danced very handsomely."

"Mmm, very pretty." Strong fingers grip my jawline, and her thumb presses firmly against my chin, tipping my face so that my eyes meet hers. I stare obediently back at her with wide eyes that I pray convey only dutiful submission. *My only failing tonight is one of etiquette, in dancing too wildly in the arms of a pretty boy,* I remind myself repeatedly. I'm trembling with the effort to convincingly etch this fiction onto my face. Most of all, I must not look like someone plotting a breakneck run for freedom through the dark gardens.

"Shall I get him for you, Rose?" she asks, the pleasant innocence of her ethereal voice masking the harsh cruelty of the question. "I'm sure his master would deal with me. Or perhaps I should send you to lure him into the back passages? You're always so good at arranging assignations, and I do enjoy watching you work."

My face doesn't move, but my eyes drop like a stone to the floor. "Whatever you wish, Mistress," I whisper softly. I nod my head, causing more of the tiny roses to shower to the ground, hoping against hope that the indecorous remains of my hairstyle will outweigh her desire for intrigue.

Her thumb strokes my chin, tracing mocking patterns just below my lips. I stand like a statue under her teasing touch and I find I can't breathe. I hadn't felt this intense need for freedom until Lavender planted the idea in my mind. Now that hope has taken hold, the withering of my dreams feels intensely painful, like harsh frost on naked skin. Fears rise in my throat: that the May Queen will not take her eyes from me tonight; that she'll force me to kill another one for her amusement; that all this will continue on unbroken until she tires and kills me as she has done with every previous Rose.

Fortunately her mercurial nature works in my favor this time when I most need it, for she turns away from me, suddenly bored and blessedly neglectful. "Get cleaned up," she orders coolly, gesturing with distaste to my mussed hair, my braid still swinging freely down my back and shedding tiny flowers in my wake. "I won't have you looking like that before my guests." I curtsy silently in acknowledgment of her command and back away.

Only then do I smell Lavender, the familiar presence at my elbow emitting a soft, wafting honeysuckle scent. She must have been watching me and timed her own dance to end with mine. She hovers obediently nearby, silently waiting to do our mistress' bidding, anticipating her needs as a good servant should. I hold my breath again, and I can feel Lavender doing the same.

If the May Queen notices our anticipation, it doesn't show on her perfect face. "Go with her," she orders curtly. "Do up her hair properly this time, and get back down here before the third course." She sweeps away from us in harsh punctuation of her commands, heading towards the tables. Delicate confections I have no words for sit alongside vile-smelling dishes I cannot stomach. Whether we succeed or fail in our escape tonight, I take cold comfort in knowing that I shall not be forced to choke down raw carvings from the deer-man that one of the lords brought with him as tribute, the killing arrows still protruding from the poor creature's lifeless hide.

I look at Lavender and we breathe a shared sigh of relief. We nod in humble obedience to the May Queen's retreating back, then turn and disappear silently through the passages at the rear of the mansion. Our quick, furtive movements lead us away from the oppressive crush of the dancing hall towards the living areas where Lavender's brushes lie—along with the exits to the back gardens.

CHAPTER 3

I n contrast to the noise and glitter of the ballroom, all is quiet and
serene on the May Queen's lawns tonight. The sprawling gardens and
twisting hedge-mazes that cover the estate seep soft perfume into the
evening air, promising a welcome cloak for the honeysuckle-scented girl at
my side. I don't know if there is an escape route for us to find, apart from
the clean death that the rain-swollen river may offer us, but if anyone is
sent to track us at least they won't be able to sniff us out.

I take Lavender's elbow in my hand and guide her through one of the
open windows that stud the mansion walls at regular intervals. In a few quick
strides we are in the gardens, slipping silently into the hedge-maze, trusting
the leafy walls that stretch over our heads to hide us from view. The grass
beneath our feet is soft and spongy after the morning's rain; not so muddy as
to leave tracks when we walk, but fortuitously gentle under our thin dancing
shoes. Blooming night-flowers create soft splashes of color in the moonlight
and mark a path through the mazes for those who know how to read them.

Lavender follows me through the twists and turns with a quick step. I'm
surprised to find her so willing to be guided. Inside the mansion she had
been an instigator, urging me into this escape plan which almost certainly
won't succeed; yet now that we are in unfamiliar territory, she defers to my
experience. I had pegged her earlier as foolhardy, plunging ahead with no
apparent forethought, but now I find myself reconsidering that opinion.

I wonder what else I might have been wrong about. She knew me before today, knew that I am one of only a few dozen servants who have traversed these twisting garden paths. Did she plan to spill those flowers, trusting me with her hopes when I swore not to betray her? Yet whether or not her confidence in me was spontaneous, I have no regrets being here with her. Even if we don't escape, I cling to this newly-kindled conviction that dying in a failed grasp for freedom is more appealing than staying here another night and killing another man.

Lavender's voice at my elbow, soft and nervous, floats like a whisper on the breeze. "You *do* remember the way, don't you?" she asks, her head twisting to peer doubtfully at a dark trail that stretches off down the maze to our left. "I mean, you've been down these paths? They all look the same," she frets, the honeysuckle scent around us turning sharp and lemony with her fear.

"I've traveled them twice," I answer in a matching low whisper, trusting the dense foliage to muffle our voices. "The third time I rode in a carriage, over the river. That's where we're going, except through the maze rather than on the open road where anyone could see us." I take her hand, more out of a desire to reassure than from a need to guide, and draw us around a tight right turn, keeping our walking pace fast as we brush against a brilliant spray of red hibiscus. "It's not about memorizing the paths. The pattern is the important thing. Turn right at red flowers, go straight at white ones. Yellow means left, but you have to watch because some of them have stripes on the petals. Everything else is meant to be ignored."

I can feel Lavender shaking her head behind me. "Simple to remember," she murmurs, a little incredulous, "and simple to share. It's a wonder she doesn't worry more about people getting in and out. And that pattern will take us to the exit?"

"One of them," I say. "There's an outer ring of hedge-wall that surrounds the entire maze, with exits at regular intervals. Which exit we come to depends on keeping the right direction."

I glance up at the sky, my eyes searching the darkness for a possible guide. Tonight there is only the big moon, which comforts me; I have never liked the sight of the smaller ones. Of course, none of the moons are reliable as compass points—despite a nagging feeling that they *ought* to be—because they move in such unpredictable ways in order to chase the two suns. Yet since we haven't been outside long enough for tonight's celestial body to stray far from its chosen path, we can use it now as a fixed reference. "When we left the mansion, the moon was rising over the west wing of the estate. We're heading south, to the river. Watch your step; the ground is rocky here."

Lavender is silent for a moment as we pick our way carefully; speed is crucial tonight, but we can't afford to twist an ankle or break a leg. "And when we get to the river?" she eventually queries, her voice suddenly small. "We cross it and... then what?"

We didn't have the chance to talk about this part of the escape before, not when our afternoon planning had to be swiftly conducted and concluded before anyone could overhear us. She doesn't know the extent of my knowledge, nor the limits where there is only conjecture and suspicion. I find myself choosing my words as deliberately as my steps, not wanting to crush her hopes now that we've come this far. "You said we must have come from somewhere," I murmur, repeating her words from earlier.

"Yes," she agrees firmly, conviction leaping into her soft voice. "We don't remember, but it's the only thing that makes sense. We're fully grown, not like the little ones that the Ornamentals sometimes have. We know how to do things, like wash and sew and cook. All of that has to come from somewhere," she insists. "That means we could go back there, somehow, if we walk far enough."

I nod, hesitating. "I don't know if it's a matter of walking," I say slowly. "I had an... assignment." My mouth stumbles a little over the innocuous description of such ugliness. "Three galas ago. He had an older face, with silver hair and kind eyes, but he seemed tired and sick at heart." My voice trails away, lost in painful memory.

"I remember," Lavender says. I look at her in surprise, my eyes wide. "I was on body-cleanup," she explains simply.

I shudder at the thought, remembering his mottled purple face, lips stained with vomit and blood. It's a privilege of my position, I suppose, that I am forced only to spend a night with the rapidly-cooling corpse in my room. I've never before thought about the people tasked with clearing away the evidence after the morning comes.

"His master sold him to the May Queen for a song," I whisper, my throat tightening unexpectedly. "He'd grown sloppy in his work and wasn't deemed useful anymore. She bought him for me to kill. I think she wanted him dead before his master could change his mind and put him to work again." My voice turns bitter now. "I don't know which are worse: the ones she buys to die, or the ones we're sent to lure during the balls. Flirting and fishing, kissing and killing, all to break a rival faery's toy."

"They do it to us, too," Lavender says softly. "Marigold was killed by a visiting servant, five parties back. No one ever found out who did it, just that all her blood was taken. We found her lying in the hallway afterwards, the floors spotless and not a single drop left in her."

I'm silent for a moment, digesting this. I've never feared the servants who visit during the balls, having rather been afraid *for* them. If I'd been a Fragrant like Lavender, or one of the Ornamentals, the shape of my fears would have been entirely different. "I'm sorry," I say numbly, the apology sounding empty and hollow in my ears, almost laughably insufficient for what this girl has been through.

"It isn't your fault," she murmurs, squeezing my hand gently in the dark. "I interrupted you," she prompts, and there's a kindness in her voice, almost cheering despite the painful subject. "Silver hair and soft eyes?"

I squeeze her hand back, and pull us carefully around a hard left turn, skirting dark thorns that are almost invisible in the weak moonlight. "He somehow knew what I was," I tell her, my mind drifting back to the memory of him waiting in my bed, the rueful smile he'd given me when first I entered. "They usually don't. Half the time, I don't have to do a thing; they initiate the kiss that kills them." Other memories threaten to flood in: the violent ones, the ones driven with lust and anger, the ones who thought I was prey for them and not the other way around. I drive the memories away, push my breathing down, maintain a deliberate calm.

"He said he was a hunter," I explain quietly, trying to keep my voice detached. "Not like the ones who hunt animals for the feast, but a people-finder. He would go to another world in order to hunt. I don't know how else to describe it," I say, looking back at her with apology in my eyes. "I didn't understand it all. But he went there to get people, and brought them back here to be servants; regularly, he said. He was good at it, but it made him unhappy," I add. "He said he was willing to confess his sins and die. When he kissed me, he knew exactly what would happen."

Lavender is staring at me with wide eyes, hardly remembering to look down at the treacherous ground that threatens to tear at our slippers. "Did he say how to get there, to this other world?" she breathes, excitement and hope suffusing her voice. Her need to believe his tale—told second-hand, with none of the beautiful flourishes of the original—stabs through my heart with almost physical pain; how can I bear to destroy her hopes if it turns out he was wrong, deluded, or lying?

I shake my head, feeling helpless. "Crossings. Borders. He said there were soft spots in the world here, places where you could pierce through to the other side if you knew they were there and were concentrating when you passed from one side to the other."

She nods her head, accepting this as somehow perfectly sensible. "And that's why we're going to the river," she says, "to cross from this world to the world on the other side."

"That's *one* reason why we're going to the river," I say, biting my lip, wanting to be honest. "The north, east, and west borders of the estate are ringed with guards; living willow trees." She's walking beside me now, no longer at my elbow, and I have to pull her gently away from a wrong turn.

"No, not left; see the darker orange stripe on the yellow? They're hard to catch in the darkness, I know."

She frowns at the flower and then grins at me as we hurry on. "Not as easy as I'd thought, even when you know the signs," she says, wry amusement in her voice. "I'm lucky you're here, Rose." I blink at her, amazed by her resilience, and find myself smiling at her compliment. "Sorry—living trees?" she says, prompting me.

I turn back to the task of navigating, picking up the pace again, along with the threads of old memories. "Well, all trees are living, I suppose," I correct myself sheepishly. "But these are different; they *move*. They have these long thin vines that brush the ground. They wrap around people— trespassers, escaped servants, or would-be assassins—and restrain them. Occasionally the mistress goes out to collect them, but some of them starve to death out there, or the trees throttle the life from them."

I close my eyes briefly at the memory of thin vines, deceptively strong, snaking around my ankles to pull me down, twining around my neck to constrict the air from my lungs. "I only got through because she'd ordered safe passage for me, and even then it needed to be... convincing."

"Convincing?" Lavender whispers. The excitement has fled her voice.

"She'd, uh, sent me out those times with the intention of killing a faery lord," I murmur. "They needed to be caught off-guard, to think that sleeping with me was their idea and not hers. I was sent out on foot, playing at being lost and lovely. That's when she taught me the secret of the maze, so that I could dawdle at the edges of the estate away from the main road."

I take a deep breath. "I 'accidentally' ran afoul of the willow guardians, and both times a lord saved me. It was very romantic for them, I'm sure," I add, my voice suddenly tight. I hadn't had a choice to participate, not when it was my mistress' will. And neither of the two men had asked my permission either. They never did, these faeries. We were toys to be played with, nothing more. It was perhaps a miracle that either had bothered to kiss me at all, save that the embrace played into the chivalric fantasy they were acting out.

Lavender's hand grows warm in my own and she squeezes me again, comfortingly this time. I look over to see her sympathetic eyes studying my face and I smile for her, suddenly ashamed of my own weakness. I clear my throat softly, feeling my cheeks burn in the cool night air. "Anyway, that's why we're making for the southern river; no willows there, only water too deep for us to ford easily. When she sent me out on the last assignment, we drove over a bridge. I think I can find it again."

"In the pumpkin-carriage," Lavender comments quietly, her tone subdued as she watches my face.

"Yes. The third time, I was sent out in the carriage," I confirm, keeping my voice low and steady with some effort. "I was being loaned out as a pleasure toy, pretending to be one of the Ornamentals. That might have been why he was more on guard than the other two: because the Queen had arranged the tryst, rather than it being all his own idea."

I sigh quietly, pushing aside a thick branch that has overgrown the path, ignoring the scrapes it leaves on my hands. "At least the carriage saved my life, in that he sent me back in it." Broken and bloodied and more meat than human, sent as a testimony to his strength and a warning to the May Queen, but he did send me back.

"Rose, I'm so sorry," Lavender whispers after a long moment.

Her voice is low and soft in the darkness, full of sympathy undeserved by a murderer like me, suffused with sorrow that would be better saved for herself. She's the one who has been compelled to clean up the broken bodies I leave behind, the one who has been forced to dodge assassins who visit with the intention of breaking the May Queen's toys. Nothing that I have suffered can compare to the dangers she's had to endure.

I'm turning my head to face her, the words already forming on my tongue—that she doesn't have to be sorry, that it isn't her fault, that she's the one who deserves to be safe and happy, that she smells so beautiful in the moonlight, all honeysuckle and hope and warmth—when our hurried pace takes us through a tight archway of vines and white roses and suddenly the path opens up around us. No longer a maze, the hedge-walls widen into a long curving hallway, the outer ring of the rambling estate garden. And there, shining in the moonlight, is an opening in the foliage; silver leaves and silver vines forming a frame, and beyond that the rush and babble of a wide river, flowing fast with the largesse granted by the morning's torrential downpour.

"There it is," Lavender breathes, the excitement in her voice contagious. "And we just cross it? From one side to the other and then we'll be in the world we came from?"

"I-I don't know," I say, hesitating now that our goal is in sight. Navigating the maze was the easy part of our escape; I knew the paths and patterns and could guide us by the light of the moon. But the hunter had taught me no magic words, no special key to memorize and repeat. He'd said it was a matter of will and concentration, of knowledge and trying. I don't know if that's something I can replicate, even if his story was true. "If we continue southeast for a while, we should come to the bridge," I say doubtfully. "It would be safer to try there—"

My words are cut off by a sound that turns my blood cold and sends shivers of fear down my back: a long, low howl of gleeful fury and dark hatred that rings out from the center of the estate behind us. I can feel a lump of terror forming in my throat, even as my breathing quickens with anxious energy.

"The mansion," Lavender gasps, her face turning ashen in the darkness. "They're hunting us."

CHAPTER 4

At the sound of the howl Lavender and I whirl to face the mansion, glowing behind us like a bleached bone in the moonlight. The hedge-walls of the maze stretch up towards the sky, reaching higher than the tallest faery. Yet from this angle beside the swollen river it is possible to see the source of the scream: a giant spider, black as night and big as a carriage, frantically climbing over the walls in a scrambling chase to reach us.

For precious seconds I am frozen in place, staring with unseeing panic at a creature that my mind insists ought to be no bigger than the size of my hand. This behemoth isn't one of the May Queen's creatures, I am sure; she never keeps predators so near her pretty flowers. It must belong to one of tonight's guests—a steed or favored hunting pet—and if the guests have been alerted to our absence, then there will be other dangers out here beyond this most obvious one.

We need to flee; yet still I stare, watching the creature blot out our view of the mansion each time it reaches the apex of a climb. In those brief moments, moonlight splashes down to illuminate the arachnid, its myriad spindly legs black and shiny and wet as they cling to the vines that make up the maze walls. Then it disappears back into the maze, traveling in dips and peaks, not bound by the twisting paths; our pursuer will be on us in a fraction of the time it took us to navigate by foot. There is something else, too; a speck of white color on its back, like a predator's marking or a piece of armor, but I can't quite make out the edges of the lighter shape from this distance.

Beside me, Lavender smells of sour lemons and sharp fear. "Rose!" she hisses, breaking through my stunned paralysis. Her voice is quiet and low, drawing me to face her so that I can read her lips over the rushing water behind us. "Rose, what do we do?"

I blink at her. She looks so pale and fragile in the dark night. I'm struck with a sudden desire to lean through the short space between us and press my lips to hers. A single kiss, a moment's painful thrashing, and she would be free of all this; no longer a captive, and safe from whatever elaborate torments and creative execution methods await us back at the mansion. Her lips would be as soft as her hands were when they worked gently through my hair, and she would taste as sweet and eager as she smells.

She takes my arms in her hands, her sharp thorn-green nails digging into my skin, and shakes me twice, hard. "Rose!" she says, her voice louder now, snapping me out of my mental fog. "Think! How did the hunter pass between worlds?"

I shake my head, trying to concentrate, failing to block out the howls of inhuman rage that echo over the garden lawns. It's impossible to chase from my mind the image of the spider coming closer with every passing second, one corner of my brain uselessly obsessed with trying to work out which is worse: watching it close the distance between us or turning away from the sight only to imagine that every second may be my last one. "I-I'm not sure," I stammer. "He said the crossing was important; border-places, concentration, and intent and—Lavender, I'm not sure!"

I've failed her. I've failed us. I look around wildly in the dark night, but there's no escape that I can see. The bridge is visible from here if I squint, maybe a hundred yards south down the river, but there's no way we could get to it in time. Even at a full run, we can't hope to outdistance a spider the size of a horse. Beside us, the river roars at full strength; its banks engorged with fresh rain from this morning's torrential downpour. "Can you swim?" I ask her, my voice high and urgent in my ears.

She stares at me for a moment, not liking the question even though no other options present themselves. "I don't know," she finally admits, the air around her twisting with a fresh infusion of lemon. "I can hold my breath in the bath."

I feel my teeth grit tightly together. I don't know if I can swim either; I have an ardent belief that I can, a sense that it can't possibly be hard, but no memories to corroborate that stubborn certainty. We don't have time to vacillate, however, not when the creature pursuing us is getting closer by the minute and with no other choice available to us. "Hold on to me!" I tell Lavender, grabbing her hand in mine. "We don't get separated, okay?"

She nods, her hand gripping mine tightly, and we wade into the fast-flowing river. The coldness of it shocks me into heightened alertness, then sets my teeth to violent chattering. Almost instantly I realize what a terrible idea this is; the currents pull hard at my dress, threatening to knock my feet from under me and drag me away. I can feel Lavender fighting the same losing battle, and I wonder whether I'm helping or hindering by holding fast to her hand.

Concentrate, I think, the voice in my head high and panicky as we wade deeper. We aren't going to escape by crossing the river or swimming downstream; the lands on either side are owned by faery lords just as brutal as the May Queen. This will be for nothing if we can't cross to the other world, the one Lavender believes in and that the hunter said he'd seen so many times.

But I don't know what to concentrate *on.* With my head just above the rushing water and pursuit so close behind us, the effort required to stay on my feet occupies all my available thoughts. I still have a grip on Lavender's hand, yet I can no longer feel her fingers twined through mine; my extremities are becoming numb in the icy river. Despite the panic throbbing through my veins I feel sleepy, a stumbling introspection that leadens my every step.

I'm supposed to be remembering the hunter's words, but I only see his face in my mind, weathered with sun and sorrow. I wish he were here now, escaping with us. He'd been gentle with me when he didn't have to be, and I'd have liked for him to have a chance of gaining freedom. I can feel the softness of his graying hair as I'd held his head in my lap and listened to his whispers in the darkness of the room. The whiteness of his scalp had surprised me, forming a sharp contrast to the soft brown of his face. I'd known somehow that sunlight had caused his face to darken like that, which made no sense. The suns don't have the power to do that; our colors are set by the whim of the May Queen, and only she can alter them.

Was that why a part of me believed him, enough to risk our lives out here? Because he had lived under a sun that made more sense to me than the only ones I know? As confused and muddled as I am right now, I'm sure I remember a bright yellow sun that burns those under it. I know that it is steady and dependable, that the seventh hour chimes only once per evening, and is always followed by the eighth hour, never by the sixth or fourth or ninth. And I know that there is only one sun in the sky and only one moon, that they chase each other yet never meet or dance or collide. I don't know how I know these things, only that I know them in the same way I know words, or how to breathe.

A strange white mist is forming on the water around us, hovering on the surface and wrapping tendrils around my arm as I fight to stay upright. I stare at it in confusion, my thoughts lethargic as I try to work out when it arrived and what it could signify. The May Queen has strangling vines, and I wonder if one of the guests brought a sentient fog to bind us with misty tendrils. If we're dragged from the water, we really will be lost. "Lavender, do you see that?" I ask, shouting to be heard over the roar of the river.

Beside me, she nods her head, her long purple hair sticking wetly to her face as she moves. "Is it because the river is so col—" Her question is cut off suddenly as she loses her footing on the rocks, disappearing with the tiniest of splashes as the current drags her instantly under. I feel the yank on my hand, the shock of the impact shooting up my arm. Bracing my feet, I dig into the stony bottom, my free hand flailing around to reach her wrist. I still have a grip on her, just barely; if I can get her standing again, we have a chance.

"I've got you!" I shout loudly over the roar of the water. No, not the river; when my numbed brain catches up with my ears, I realize that I'm shouting over the howls of the giant spider. Its furious screams echo closer now but I can't focus on that; there is only enough space in my mind to concentrate on holding Lavender's arm. She's thrashing wildly, trying to get her feet under her. I pull as hard as I can, upwards and towards myself, trying and failing to lever her upright against the rushing current.

I can feel the cold sapping my strength even as inhuman eyes bore into my back. If I were smart, I would let go—not of Lavender, but of the rocks beneath my feet. I could hold her as the river carries us to a cleaner death than any our mistress will offer us.

Yet now that it really matters, I can't seem to let go. I'm not brave enough to lose Lavender, to accept failure, to give up on the memory of a sun that burns and a moon that cools. My eyes dully register that the mist is thicker now, so opaquely white that I can barely see Lavender's head as she breaks the surface briefly for a gulping breath, still holding on against the current that won't let her stand. Maybe the mist is a boon, if it hides us from pursuit long enough for the cold to take us instead.

"Lavender, I'm so sorry," I whisper, and her green eyes meet mine with understanding before being pulled back under the water.

"Here! I've got you, keep hold of her!" A voice, sharp and commanding, cuts through the icy haze. I feel strange tendrils pulling me towards the far side of the shore, reviving the terrifying memory of strangling willow vines. I struggle uselessly for a moment before looking down to see a thick coil wrapped around my chest—yellow rope brighter than any Marigold's hair.

"C'mon, Pink, hold on to her," orders the voice again, tense and strained from the effort of pulling me towards the shore.

My hands tighten on Lavender's arm, instinctively obeying the voice before my brain has a chance to wonder whether this is a bad idea. If I am caught, the kindest thing I can do is to let Lavender go. I've seen the May Queen's tortures, those she puts on for entertainment and instruction, and they are a far worse way to die than slipping under frigid water to sleepily drown. I strain my eyes to find my captor, following the line of the strange sunny rope that digs into my skin and tears at my thin gown.

There she is, a dark shape outlined against the white mist, a lone woman; not a faery lady but a human like us, judging by her movements. For a moment, I take her for one of us Flowers: her hair is a dark loamy brown, her skin is the soft warmth of dark tree bark, and she seems almost designed to blend into the deadly forests that line the May Queen's estate.

But her bare arms flex with wiry muscle as she hauls us in, the rope obedient in her skilled hands. No Flower was given strength like that or allowed to be anything other than delicately frail. Her clothes, too, are wrong; leather boots that cling to her legs like a second skin and a sturdy green tunic that doesn't tear when the bright yellow rope scratches against it. She looks confident and strong, entirely accustomed to being in charge.

"Hold on, I can almost reach you," grunts the woman on the shore, hauling me closer. She pulls hard, yanking me several feet and causing me to stumble on the loose rocks. My fingers slip on Lavender's skin and I grasp her wrist more tightly. I pull upward with the last of my strength and Lavender kicks hard, shooting forward into me, breaking free from the current for a split moment.

Instinctively I wrap my arms around her, pulling her close to me and leaning back to maneuver her into standing. Here by the shore, the water is shallower and the current just a bit weaker. Lavender stumbles twice on the treacherous rocks before regaining her footing. She stands against me, gasping for air and choking up water, and my arms tighten their hold.

"I've got you," I tell her, wishing I had a free hand to massage her back as more water comes up from her throat to splash our gowns. "I'm not letting go."

"Up you come, Violet," our rescuer orders, planting her foot on the shore and reaching down to help haul Lavender up. She pulls and I push and Lavender scrambles, and between the three of us she flops onto the shore, laughing and crying as she kneels on her hands and vomits more river water.

"You next, Pink," the woman says, gripping my arm with a grasp like an iron vise. I shouldn't trust her, I remember belatedly; we were supposed to be evading capture, not cooperating with it. Yet as brusque as this woman is, her expression strikes me as honest, even kind. I clamber onto the bank with her help, knowing my legs are too weak to run. If I am going to hope for a miracle, it may be that this woman can save us.

"There's a—", I stammer weakly, my hand flying out to point. I'd meant to gesture at the far shore, at the spider I expected to see stalking impotently there, but my eyes widen at the sight of our pursuer stepping onto the raging river, spindly legs carefully balanced on frothing waters that should not support them. The mist surrounds it and us, a dome of white cutting off the moon, the mansion, and everything except this little bubble of the four of us; three women and a spider the size of the carriage that carried me to hell and back.

"I see him," the woman says, her voice tight and cold. When I look back to her, wondering how we can possibly flee this monstrosity, her dark eyes are focused not on the spider but on a point just above it. I twist my head back to the river and see what she sees: the shape I'd seen earlier, pale and white in the moonlight, watches us from the spider's back with bright, triumphant eyes. A faery lord grips the spider's hair tightly, riding his mount with gleeful abandon, savoring the hunt. He carries a spear or javelin in one hand and, as I watch, he prepares to throw the weapon.

Eyes bright with cruel intent, he takes aim. I only have time to scramble uselessly backwards on my hands and feet, a cornered crab trying to scuttle away from an elephant. I see our rescuer drop her shoulder, slinging her arm around in a single smooth motion, her other hand moving up to her back. His javelin adjusts as he switches aim from me to her, his eyes tracking the more interesting target. Her hands come around to a center point in front of her body, and my eyes belatedly register that the woman is carrying a bow; I can see the quiver of arrows resting at the small of her back. She draws, the string taut enough to set my chattering teeth on edge, and his own hand pulls back to throw.

I want to stop her, to yell a warning; she won't hit him. I've seen faeries dodge the fastest of projectiles. Yet before I can draw a breath, her arrow lets fly, shooting sure and true—but not into the faery. The missile buries itself deep into the body of the spider, the shaft instantly coated with dark ichor splashing from the wound. The creature screams a terrifyingly human sound of torment, stumbles on the water, and sinks like a stone, its careful equilibrium upset. The white face of the lord, furious and shocked, disappears beneath the water, churned to a dark froth by blood and the death throes of his steed.

Our rescuer stands there for a moment, a second arrow already nocked and waiting. I notice slowly that the sound of the river is fading, the thick mist evaporating from the air around us. Impossibly, the world around us has changed, as if the mist had rearranged everything it covered. The May Queen's mansion is gone, the hedge-walls of the maze have faded, and the southern bridge no longer exists. Indeed, there is no river left for a bridge to span; the water beside us has thinned to little more than a babbling creek, barely deep enough to wet my ankles.

Lavender stares with me, taking in the long pale grass, browned and dry rather than the May Queen's customary lush emerald green. Then our eyes widen at the sight of something flat and bleached gray in the moonlight: a road, I remember. Not a road like the packed dirt roads between estates, but a real street, made from melted tar and tiny stones and yellow paint to guide carriages. *No, not carriages,* I think, blinking at the sight of the cherry-red truck that sits idly on the side of the faraway road. I can see its lights from here; the driver must have jumped from the vehicle as soon as it came to a stop. Its headlights paint the street a warm yellow; the light inside the cabin is white and stark.

The woman shoulders her bow as the last tendril of mist evaporates, and comes to help us stand. "Up we go," she says again. Though her voice is still commanding, there's more of the kindness I'd sensed earlier and her touch is gentle. "You did good, making a portal like that. Remembered something out here, did you? The river helped, the fae magic is always thin at the estate-borders. And of course there were two of you, and more is better. Good odds, but still very ballsy. Wounded? No? Just scrapes? I have a first-aid kit in the Ford. Come on, here we go."

Her actions match her soothing words, helping us up, moving us towards the car, gentling us with the matter-of-factness of her tone. "Welcome earthside," she continues warmly, slinging Lavender's arm over her shoulder and gesturing for me to take other side so that we can help her limp to the truck. "Don't you worry, the worst is past for now; there's always a rest period before another portal can be opened in the same place, and we'll be long gone by then. We'll get you some food, a place to sleep, and then we have a lot of catching up to do. I'm Celia, by the way. You two have names? Doesn't matter if you don't like them, we can change them later."

I stare at her, my heart still pounding, the cold fabric of my torn gown slapping wetly at my bleeding legs. I have no idea what cut me; the current must have carried stones from upstream. "I'm Rose," I stammer, my lips still numb. "This is Lavender. We're Flowers from Thistle."

THREE MONTHS LATER

CHAPTER 5

The morning sky is a blend of dark denims and inky blues when I jolt awake from my nightmares. My eyes fly open in panic but I force myself to lie motionless, concentrating on slowing my rapid breathing. *I mustn't be heard, I can't cry out, the May Queen will hear me if I do.* Thoughts come in a chaotic jumble before my sleep-blurred vision registers the fact that I am in our apartment. I'm still earthside, which means I'm safe and free. The nightmares were only memories, not new horrors.

Even so, I turn my head nervously to take stock of my surroundings. My eyes flit over the small bedroom and the few belongings that fill it: cellphone, alarm clock, a travel guide to the Dallas-Fort Worth metroplex which I borrowed from Athena. Everything is where I left it, and the apartment around me is silent. The faint dawn light seeping in through my cracked plastic blinds tells me the night is gone. Lavender ought to be home from work already and asleep in her own bed. I sit up slowly, pulling my legs to my chest and burying my head between my knees. Shards of dream still cling stubbornly to my consciousness, making me feel nauseous in the closeness of the room.

I dream of dying men now—every night, all night long—their faces mottled and red, choking for air as my poison kills them. Some of them gush blood from their eyes and ears; others claw helplessly at their throats as their windpipes swell and close. Some merely stiffen and die, the heat seeping slowly from their bodies. Each time I killed someone I'd forced myself to watch until the end, not thinking it right for their deaths to go unwitnessed. Now I behold them nightly, over and over again. While nothing could ever make me wish to return to the otherworld, I am acutely aware that the nightmares came only when we were far enough away from our mistress that I could safely break down.

I can't dwell on this right now. I take as stern a tone as I can muster, trying to still the trembling in my arms. I can't miss another day of work. Athena wouldn't be upset with me for calling in sick, at least no more than she usually is, and Celia would understand, but the principle matters. Rent day is always around the corner and Lavender is depending on me to bring in my fair share.

She rarely calls in sick to her job, even though I know she has nightmares of her own. I've heard her cry out in the night once already this week, after I had woken from my own dreams. I'd splayed my fingers protectively— though uselessly— against our shared bedroom wall as though I could send comfort through the thin barrier between us. Yet she's always bright and strong and cheerful again the next morning. I don't have her sharp glossy coating, but I can try for her sake.

With an effort, I push myself up off the mattress and head for our shared bathroom down the hall. The soft white night-lights we keep plugged into every wall socket illuminate a path for me, mingling to combine with the gray Texas dawn. I move with careful slowness, treading softly in order not to wake Lavender. She works nights and tends to sleep late into the morning, so I jump with genuine fright when I'm brought up short by the unexpected sound of her voice coming from our dimly-lit kitchenette. "You're up early, Ravs," she says, adding contritely, "Sorry; didn't mean to startle you."

I've already spun on my heel to face her, my heart pounding in my throat. She's sitting on a barstool at the kitchen counter, eating cold cereal while reading the back of the colorful cardboard box. "It happens," I tell her dryly, embarrassed. "You're up earlier. Or are you up late?"

"Early," she announces. "I couldn't sleep."

Her eyes glitter with amusement, and again I'm struck by the similar markings which were stamped upon us by the May Queen. The vibrant green in our eyes and tracing through our veins is identical, trailing thick raised vines over our arms and up our necks. To altered eyes, we undeniably hail from the same mistress. The similarities are mostly invisible to normal humans, but Elric gave us the same surname anyway. Lavender could never pass for my sister, being shorter, paler, and smaller-boned than me, but Elric explained at length just how much that wasn't his problem and told us call ourselves cousins.

"Cereal?" she asks, picking up the box and waving it at me.

I recognize the bright yellow colors, even from the back: it's the one with the sea captain on the front. Yesterday she had the one with the rabbit. "No, thanks," I say, rolling my eyes at her. She knows I won't eat any of them, nor the oatmeals, not after I got into that fight with Elric when I asked where the girl-cereals were and he laughed at me.

"We're out of Pop-Tarts," she warns, looking back at her cereal box and smirking to herself. "You ate the last of them yesterday, remember? We need to go shopping."

"Aw, Lavs, don't say that," I beg, feeling my stomach growl and desperately needing her to be wrong. The scent of her this morning—apple cider and marigold and, yes, lavender—is enough to make me ravenous. I flick on the harsh yellow lights and stomp over to the pantry, rummaging around for a few moments before I have to concede that she is right. My breakfast pastries are gone, along with most of the rest of our staples.

She chuckles and I turn to face her, squinting against the overhead glare. With my eyes screwed up like this, half-closed against the light, I can see her the way normal people do, those who haven't been taken to the otherworld. The green in her veins recedes and softens to a paler blue, and her purple hair turns silvery blond, with only the tiniest hint of dark lilac streaking up from the bottom few inches of her curls. I like both versions of Lavender, the faery-altered one and the human-looking one, but if it were to come down to a choice, I prefer the girl with soft lilac hair and bright green vines encircling her skin.

"You're staring again," she says, giving me a soft smile as her eyes flick up from the cereal box.

I feel myself blush as I turn away. "Sorry," I mumble at her, "you're making me hungry." Immediately I wish I hadn't said that; it sounds stupid, like a come-on that Elric might use. I duck my head and give up on the question of breakfast, choosing instead to retreat to the safety of the bathroom. "I'll just, uh, get some donut holes on the way in to work. Maybe some sausage rolls for Athena, to cheer her up a bit."

Lavender snorts at this. "I don't know how you put up with her," she says with a laugh. "You have the patience of a saint. Can you give me a ride?"

I check my step, instantly confused by the *non sequitur*. "What's wrong with your car?" I ask automatically, before guiltily adding, "Yes, sure, of course I will. But is your car okay? Are *you* okay?"

"It's fine," she says airily, swallowing the last bite of cereal before hopping up to dump the residual milk down the kitchen drain. "Work was slow last night, so they let a bunch of us off early. We girls went club-hopping. I ended up carpooling home after the second or third club; I was a bit tipsy. I'm fine now, Ravs."

I shift uneasily on my feet, not wanting to get into another fight about Lavender's outings with mundane humans—'mundies', Elric calls them, even though Mina scolds him—and the many warnings Celia gave us about getting drunk with them. Lavender isn't like me; there isn't the omnipresent danger that she might forget herself and accidentally kill someone with her lips. My issues aren't hers, and I try to remember that. Anyway, she can hold her tongue along with her drink, and even if she got completely blotto and spilled everything, I can't believe anyone would lend her story any credence.

"Well, um. Which club is it?" I ask, dredging up in my mind the names of the ones she's visited in the past, and calculating how far they are from the bookstore.

"I'm not sure," she says matter-of-factly, flashing me a smile as she squeezes by me on the way to her room. "We went to several and I can't remember which one we started at. But we can check them all, it's fine. C'mon, Rose; you know you'll feel bad all day if you don't, so we might as well get it done and over with."

I snort at this. "I'm pretty sure I wouldn't feel bad for more than a couple hours at the most, Lavs," I tell her dryly, but that smile of hers is impossible to resist. "Let me shower and change, okay?"

She grins at her victory and ducks inside her room, only to stick her head out a moment later. "Um. You could come with us next time, Ravs. You do know that, right?"

I blink at her, thrown off-balance by the invitation. "Sure, I know," I respond awkwardly. "Thanks." I dart into the bathroom and lean against the closed door, steadying my breathing.

The bathroom has a mirror, which I try to avoid looking at. Neither of my reflections look right to me: the one with bright pink hair which Lavender sees, nor the one with dark brown hair and rosy highlights that the humans remark on. Every morning, I register with increasingly dulled disappointment that my hair is still stubbornly pink. Even though Mina warned me not to expect my appearance to change, I keep telling Athena not to get used to what she calls my 'pastel nonsense'. I'm unable to shake the superstition that if my green eyes one day turned brown, or if the profusion of rose-pink in my hair dulled to a more natural color, then the memory of who I am and where I came from might return alongside the physical alterations.

Nor can I find a sense of self within the few fractured memories which have returned to me since our escape. I have little flashes sometimes, quick glimpses of a previous life, yet all of unidentifiable relevance: the sensation of lying on Berber carpet, the flickering light of a candle and the soft smell of wax, the feel of an iron skillet in my hands. None of this tells me who I was before the May Queen altered me. I do have instincts, but few conscious memories to bolster them. I knew how to drive a car when Elric let me sit in the driver's seat. The cellphone was a little more complicated, but I was able to pick it up in about a week, with Lavender guiding me. Sometimes when music comes on the radio I know the words to sing along, even though I don't remember ever hearing the song before. Celia calls it our subconscious, and says that's how we knew to make our human appearances when we crossed over.

Yet I can't seem to piece together these sparse memories and instincts into a recognizable identity. I feel stuck in this limbo with Lavender between who we were and what the May Queen made us, unable even to decide upon new names. Mina told us indecision was normal and that probably half of the altered never manage to give up the only names we know. There was no rush to decide, she assured us; if ever we tire of being 'Rose' and 'Lavender', everyone would gladly switch over to whatever names we choose. Mina had run her soft full fingers gently through our hair and reassured us that we had the rest of our lives to decide who we are.

I sigh and hop into the shower, remembering that I don't have time to dawdle. If we're going to drive all over the city in search of Lavender's car, I need to rush or I'll be late for work. I should be annoyed, but in a weird way I'm grateful to have an excuse to spend time with her. Lavs is out as often as she's in, busy with her waitressing and clubbing and doing all the things she wasn't allowed to do before. When we are together—shopping or cleaning or just hanging out watching movies on our days off—there's a distance between us, a gulf caused by neither of us being able to forget what I can do. I can't even hug her when she has nightmares; I'm too afraid I'll touch her with my lips by accident. We'll have this morning, though, and there's no danger of such accidents in the car. We can talk and catch up on our lives. I'll tell her stories about Athena and the customers at the bookstore, and she can tell me how waitressing went last night.

I'm almost excited at the prospect; I miss talking. Athena is kind at heart but determinedly abrasive, and Jing is sweet but so quiet as to almost be unnoticeable in the store, besides the fact that she works the evening shift alternating with mine. Lavender and I could have stayed longer at Celia's house after she picked us up that first night, and Mina would happily have taken us in for as long as we desired, but we'd wanted our own place to make a stab at being independent. I think we made the right choice, but I hadn't expected to feel so lonely. I don't suppose my newfound depression helps; it's hard to find the energy to call Mina for a coffee date when I wake from nightmares that leave me more tired than I'd been before I slept.

But maybe my isolation is for the best. I need to remember to be careful around others; Mina, especially. The raw sexuality she exudes is on a whole different level from anything an Ornamental could muster. Visits with her always carry the risk that I might give into temptation and kiss her lovely lips, and my dreams are haunted by images of the pretty Indian girl dying in one of a dozen different ways.

Nor has Mina made my abstinence pledge easy. Early on, she tried with her unwavering gentle cheer to talk me into experimentation: we could make the attempt with doctors on hand, she suggested, as there were several good altered healers in the metroplex area. And if I didn't want to try with her, there were plenty of nice boys and girls whose powers might lend themselves to romantic exploration with someone like me; why, there was the prettiest undead zombie boy in Arlington, or she could introduce me to this darling snake-girl she knew, because Mina could personally vouch for the value of a forked tongue. I'd thanked her, demurred as strongly as I knew how and fled back to the safety of our apartment.

She was right that I was lonely, but I couldn't let someone take a risk like that for me. Celia had shared my concern, explaining that some of us came out as safe as newborn lambs, but many retained all or much of our previous powers. Often there was no way of knowing our limits until *after* someone had been seriously harmed. She'd made me promise that I wouldn't try any 'experiments' without talking to her first, and said that in the meantime she'd speak to some of the healers about my situation. I wasn't getting my hopes up.

After a quick shower, I throw on a white spaghetti-strap blouse with layers of ruffled lace over a denim skirt barely longer than a mini. I kick on a comfortable pair of flat sandals and pray that the air conditioner at the bookstore will behave itself today. If it does go out again, at least I'm dressed for the Texas heat.

"Lavs, are you ready?" I call, and she pops out of her bedroom looking as fresh as a rose despite the fact that she hasn't slept tonight.

"After you," she teases, springing in step behind me. "Are you sure the RAV will start?"

"It had better," I mutter, catching up my purse and keys. Elric hooked me up with a used Toyota RAV4 a month after we came over, an elderly relative to the model he'd found for Lavender after he'd learned the nicknames we'd given each other. The vehicle ran, but unreliably, and the days were numbered before it inevitably died on me and I would need to go to him for another. "You have your keys?" I ask her. "We don't want to find your car only to—" My sentence ends in an abrupt halt as we step over the threshold.

We're standing on a front porch that ought to be bathed in bright rays of orange sun. Instead we're faced with a mass of thick fog. Mist suffuses the parking lot, spreading into impenetrable walls of opaque white that surround us on all sides. Amongst the cars and the aluminum shelters which the apartment complex provides as protection against summer hail, insubstantial trees flicker hazily in the dim light, looking for all the world like shadowy illusions I could pass my hand through. The trees are much too tall and thick to be native to Texas, and I know we are looking at the landscape of the otherworld.

"*No*," I breathe quietly, my panicked eyes flicking to Lavender. If she doesn't see what I see, then I'm either hallucinating or still having nightmares. If she *does* see it, then we're in serious trouble.

Her bright green eyes stare anxiously up at me, as unsure as I am whether to run or hide. "Rose, why is there a portal in our parking lot?"

CHAPTER 6

Summer in Texas is hot and dry, the morning air usually much warmer than the ground beneath our feet. Mist should not be covering our parking lot, and certainly not forming white walls that reach to close high above our heads. Tendrils of fog engulf the parking lot with thick clouds that obscure vision and muffle sound. The atmosphere feels charged with electricity: heavy and dangerous and full of magic potential.

The towering trees brought over with the mist are shadowy and insubstantial, their trunks poking out of the cement and pushing through the rooftops of nearby cars. In many cases, the bases of the trees are wider than the cars they so impossibly superimpose. In the distance, by the manager's office, I hear a babbling brook that I know shouldn't be there. We are two worlds caught within an enormous dome of white fog, like the snow globes they sell to the tourists.

Beside me is the strong scent of bitter lemons, Lavender's sharp fear infecting the air. "Rose," she hisses, clutching my arm with her sharp green nails, "what do we do?" Her voice is as terrified as her scent, and I waste precious seconds stupidly wondering why she's asking me when I was hoping *she* would know what to do.

I bite the inside of my cheek against the pain of her nails, grateful for the sharpness of sensation to clear my thoughts. *There is a portal in the middle of our apartment complex.* That means we're in danger, because hunters and faeries travel through portals.

I wrench my gaze away from the misty landscape before us, and turn my head to catch Lavender's eyes with mine. Silent communication passes between us: a quick gesture, a nod, a tug on her arm—gently, so as not to scrape her with my own thorny nails. We pull backwards into the meager shelter offered by the brick walls of our apartment porch and my lips hover near her ear, as close as I can come without touching her.

"Can you tone down the scent?" I whisper, fighting to stay calm despite the wash of lemon-soaked fear forcing its way into my nostrils. She frowns and slowly the scent dissipates, though it is still stronger than I would like. I know Lavender can't shut down her emotions on a dime, but her magic heightens my own fear and makes it harder for me to think. If anyone is looking for us in this fog, they'll have a direct bead on us if they have a sense of smell.

"Back inside?" she asks quietly, gesturing towards our door.

I hesitate. Either this portal is targeted at us specifically, or it is coincidence. If someone is escaping as we were three months ago, they might need help—or they might be chased by dangerous creatures. Lavender and I aren't armed and ready the way Celia was on the night we escaped, and I know we would never stand a chance if it came to a fight with faeries. In which case, we should follow our instinct to scurry back into our apartment and hide under a bed or behind a strong door. Of course, this supposes that rampaging faeries or a hunter on the prowl for fresh goods couldn't sense us through solid walls or smell our magic; we don't really know the limits of their powers.

Yet we have to assume the worst case: the portal has landed on our doorstep for a reason, and something is here for us specifically. If a hunter has come to kill or recapture us, a simple retreat inside our apartment isn't going to stymie them for long. If they were able to locate our parking lot, then narrowing down our residence isn't an overly challenging proposition. Better to stay out here where we can run or drive away, rather than hole up in a trap and wait for them to extract us.

"Get ready to run," I hiss at Lavender, crouching slightly in preparation for a spring.

She mimics my crouch as I scan the fog and consider our approach. Once we leave the shelter of the porch, we will be visible and vulnerable. My eyes sweep the parking lot, straining to identify a spot where something might have emerged from the otherworld, while my ears prick for the smallest sound of approach. There is nothing; no spot of color, no flash of movement, no footfall on the cement. Either we are alone or something is lying in wait. I feel a sudden stab of doubt; if our attackers are watching for movement, will it be foolhardy to flush ourselves out by making a run for it?

Lavender presses closer to my side, her lips finding my ear. I'm momentarily startled by her touch, but of course she isn't poisonous and has no fear of hurting me. Her mouth is warm against my skin and I waste precious seconds wishing we had other, less terrifying reasons for her to touch me like this. "Do you think they're here to take us back?" she whispers. I don't have an answer for her—or perhaps I simply don't want to turn my head because that would dislodge her lips. Her closeness is comforting right now, despite the fresh rush of lemon-scented fear she brings. I slide my hand down her arm, lacing my fingers through hers and squeezing her hand in a manner that I hope will be comforting.

Has someone come to take us back? Celia warned us that sometimes people are recaptured, although no one is ever certain when it happens. There are never any witnesses left behind, and an altered could leave town unexpectedly for a thousand mundane reasons. Yet there is undeniably a portal here right now, threatening to draw us over. And if they take us back, they'll separate us. The sudden realization knots my stomach. If they don't kill us outright, will they wipe our memories again? We'll forget we ever knew each other.

The thought of standing here indecisively waiting to be taken away from Lavender is far worse than the fear of being caught while trying to flee. Even if we can't get away, can't drive through the thick white walls, we have to try. I squeeze her hand again, harder this time, and turn to look at her. A fresh rush of fear stains the air as our eyes meet, and I know she understands. I crouch again, straining to listen. There is only silence around us, and my heartbeat pounding in my ears. Praying that we're not making a mistake, I kick off from the porch at the quietest sprint I can manage, Lavender hot on my heels.

My car is fifty feet from the porch, parked under one of the open aluminum shelters. I dart for the driver's door, keys clutched tightly in my hand to muffle the jingling of metal. I pull Lavender along with me, not daring to separate from her. She can crawl into the passenger seat from the driver's side; it'll be a tight fit to slide in, but she's nimble enough to manage.

We're almost there; I can actually *feel* the nearness of the car as my body aches to slam to a halt against it. Then a flash of light catches my peripheral vision. "What's that?" Lavender hisses softly beside me. I twist my head in time to see something emerge from the fog just as we skid to a frightened halt near the car. My hand automatically gropes for the lock, but my movements are clumsy without the benefit of sight. Frantically, I study the creature who has stepped out of the mist, my eyes straining to gauge this newest source of danger.

It is a person, or at least he is person-*shaped*. He seems almost like a decoration, looking exactly like a man who has been dipped in molten silver; a walking metal mannequin or statue come to life. The flash that first caught my eye was the glint of sunlight from the contours of his shoulders. Now that he has emerged from the fog, every curve of muscle and outline of sinew on his body reflects the tiny traces of light that filter through the dome. He stumbles towards us across a parking lot that has been temporarily transformed into a grassy lawn.

His approach would be more frightening if his movements were not so unsteady. He walks as though he were wounded or very drunk, unevenly

47

meandering through the mist. He looks nothing like a hunter capable of determined pursuit, nor does he seem to be actively fleeing any immediate danger. His gaze is wobbly and unfocused; his feet shamble in our direction more from a lack of alternatives. That doesn't mean he's not dangerous, of course, but it might mean we're faster than he is.

"I don't think he's a faery," Lavender whispers beside me, her own nervous concern echoing my own. "Is he escaping?"

"Maybe?" I whisper back to her, not turning my face from his approach. I wish I could have a breath of clean air to clear the pounding fear from my head. "There could be something behind him, though," I point out, my hands still gripping the car door. We need to reach safety; I want to be sure that Lavender is beyond reach of anything in pursuit of the man.

"We've got the car right here," Lavender whispers, the air around her shifting subtly to the scent of warm honeysuckle on a hot summer day. "He's so close. We can't just leave him; Celia didn't leave us."

I draw a shaky breath and grit my teeth. She's right, and if we're going to help him we need to move fast. Anything could come through the portal after him, and if we're not long gone we'll all be lost. I press the keys into Lavender's hands. "Get in the driver's seat, but don't turn the engine over yet," I whisper, and she nods.

With a courage more faked than genuine, I leap forward across the slick grass, grabbing the silver man gently around the waist as he stumbles drunkenly into me. "Careful! I've got you," I hiss, my head swiveling around to look for signs of a pursuit that fails to materialize. "Are you hurt? Can you speak English?" My voice is a steady stream of reassuring murmurs as I guide him as quickly as possible to the passenger side of the car.

"Am I out of Avalon?" he mumbles huskily. His voice is thick and warm, like dark buckwheat honey, with a hint of an accent I can't quite place. The words don't make a lot of sense; there's an Avalon in Ellis county about an hour away, and my unreliable memory pops up to helpfully supply that Avalon is also the last resting place of King Arthur, but I very much doubt he's referring to either of those places. I can hear the sharp fear underlying his exhausted voice, and it's not hard to guess what he means.

"You're out. You're free," I murmur as we reach the passenger door. He's panting as I struggle to guide him, leaning over to brace himself against the car so that he can gulp in air. I fumble with the door handle, my movements awkward with him slumped over me like so much dead weight. "Hold onto the car, okay?" I slip my arm away from him and manage to pull the door open before he can collapse to the ground. "In you go. We need to get out of here."

The parking lot around us is still covered in silent mist. While I'm grateful that we haven't been set on by hunting dogs or screaming spiders or homicidal trees, I'm deeply unnerved by the continued presence of electric magic in the air. Why is the portal not yet dissipating? None of the possible answers are good ones, so I shove the thought from my mind, struggling to guide him into the car seat. He doesn't seem to understand what I want him to do, or maybe he's too disoriented to think straight, because when I put my hands on his waist to move him, he just stands there looking woozily at me.

"Into the car," I hiss, urgency making my voice sharp. "Can you sit down?" If I can just get him halfway into the car, I think Lavender could pull him the rest of the way. But the metal that comprises his body is smooth and cool to the touch, and it's impossible to get a good grip on him. He feels heavy in my hands, and when I push against him to demonstrate how he should move the pressure doesn't even seem to register with him.

He stares down at me with silver eyes that shouldn't be able to see and yet clearly have working irises and pupils, differentiated from the surrounding sclera by subtly darker shades in the metal that coats him. He studies my face with dizzying intensity, blinking softly in the misty light. At this short distance I can see that they've even given him silvered eyelashes, as thin and delicate as wire filaments. "Clarent," he whispers softly.

My ears don't catch the word at first, and it takes a moment for my mind to grasp the fact that he's trying to introduce himself. He's dehydrated or drugged, I can see it in his eyes, or perhaps just exhausted from running for goodness knows how long and how far. I nod my head, anxious to get him into the car.

"Clarent," I repeat quietly. "I'm Rose and that's Lavender there in the car. Can you sit right here, Clarent?" I'm almost gritting my teeth with the strain of being reassuring and cheerful when all I want to do is to shove him into the car, slam the door shut, and throw myself into the backseat so that Lavender can step on the gas.

"Rose," he murmurs, warmth infusing his thick honey voice. Before I can react he leans down, closing the inches between our faces in an instant, and brushes his lips against mine. There is the strange sensation of cold silver against my skin, but then the metal melts and flexes into a warmer softness that presses against me in a gentle kiss. I freeze, partly taken by surprise and partly from long practice in the May Queen's service; I'm not *supposed* to pull away when they kiss me.

"Nice to meet you, Rose," he whispers quietly into my skin, and his lips flutter softly against mine when he speaks. The sensation of his metallic kiss is not unpleasant in the least, though oddly surreal; I can feel his softened skin molding to the curve of my own.

This detail alone brings me back to the danger of the moment. I gasp and pull away from him, expecting him to collapse at any moment. But he merely stares at me with the same unsteady expression on his gentle face, his confusion deepening slowly into a more focused chagrin at my reaction. "Am I not here to rescue you?" he asks.

"Car. *Now*," I blurt out, shoving all my fears aside. He ought to be dead from my poison right now, or at least convulsing; instead, he seems content to remain half-dead from exhaustion and dehydration. Either way, we need to get him out of here and to Celia; she'll know what to do. My grip on his waist tightens, and he finally allows me to push him into his seat; Lavender's small wiry hands reach over to help yank him inside. I slam the door closed behind him, no longer bothering to be quiet, and fling myself into the backseat.

"Celia's," I gasp at Lavender, who starts up the engine with a deafening roar. As she peels out of my parking space I stare anxiously through the windows at the fog, still seeking pursuit. None materializes, and the fog is now quickly clearing. Trees fade slowly away and the white walls scatter under a sudden breeze, and once again the morning is exactly as it should be. I check my watch and note with a twist of my stomach that we were only in the fog for five minutes. I could have sworn much more time had elapsed.

"Rose." Lavender's quiet voice breaks through my thoughts. "Is he gonna be okay?"

"I don't know." I'm panting for breath, trying as hard as I can not to dwell on all the ways I've seen men die, trying not to think about the fact that the silver man has slumped over in his seat and isn't talking or moving. "Match the speed limit, Lavender," I caution, distracting myself with more practical realities. "We don't want to have to explain a naked man in the car."

"A naked man made of silver," she elaborates, frowning at me in the rear-view mirror. The tone of her voice, and the lemon scent that accompanies it, causes me to look sharply at our passenger. Blinking and focusing my eyes, I slowly realize she's right: he hasn't got a disguise covering his metal body. My eyes widen as I wonder how we're going to prevent normal humans from seeing him. I've never heard of an altered coming earthside without a disguise. *Did my kiss do this to him?*

Digging out my cellphone, I frantically pull up Celia's number. I have to warn her that we're coming so that she can get a healer out to her house. He's not dead yet, but his breathing is slow and shallow. Whether he's poisoned or ill or just exhausted I can't be sure, but Celia will know someone who can.

CHAPTER 7

Celia lives in a small three-bedroom house in a suburb outside the metroplex, and shares the cramped space with whichever new foundlings she's picked up recently. We were her last guests, Lavender and I, and I'd found it peaceful to watch for mice and rabbits in the undeveloped field behind her house, their movements causing the knee-high grass to sway in telltale patterns. I'd wondered then if Celia hunts them, but except for the night she rescued us I've never seen her use her bow anywhere other than the range.

Lavender pulls us into the driveway and her hand hesitates over the wheel, unsure whether to honk the horn to announce our presence. To my immense relief our unexpected passenger is still breathing, but he hasn't regained consciousness despite my attempts to wake him. He needs the attention of a healer immediately, but we mustn't draw the notice of Celia's neighbors. The morning is still early enough that many of them won't yet have left for the day, and some might work from home as Celia does.

We're saved from decision as the front storm door slaps open and Celia calmly strides out to us; she must have been listening for our engine. She carries a thin blanket draped over her arm and walks directly to the passenger side to peer in the window at Clarent. Her step doesn't falter when she sees him, but the dazzling silver coating his entire body does elicit a sharp raise of her eyebrow. "Well, you weren't exaggerating," she says, her authoritative voice carrying clearly through the car windows. "Covering him won't be enough; pull around back."

She gestures at the yard gate, which has been propped open with a heavy potted plant. Lavender nods nervously at the command, the spicy scent of clover filling the car; neither of us has taken our car off-road before. But the path is wide with plenty of clearance, and the Texas earth is packed almost as hard as the concrete we usually drive on. She shifts the car into gear and slowly pulls through the yard, managing to look like she's done this a million times before—and perhaps, in her previous life, she has. I twist my head to watch Celia through the rear window, where she follows us on foot after moving the potted plant and latching the gate.

When we're parked as near as possible to Celia's porch, Lavender hops out of the car and I pile out the back. She tosses me the car keys before leaping forward to hold open the back door to Celia's house. I'm already circling around to the passenger door, wondering how on earth we'll get Clarent inside. Even if he weren't covered in slippery silver, he'd still be too bulky for me to carry. Behind me, I can hear the crunch of Celia's boots on the dry grass, her quick stride purposeful and unhesitating.

"Hold this and cover him once I've got him," Celia orders, pressing the blanket into my hands. Before I can react she calmly grabs his arm, bends her knees, and slings Clarent easily over her shoulders before straightening to her full height. I stammer out an inarticulate sound of surprise before registering Celia's impatient look; shaking out the blanket, I toss it over Clarent to prevent the rays of morning sunlight from glinting off his naked body. "C'mon, then," Celia says brusquely, leading us into the house.

All the shades in the house have been drawn closed, and it takes a moment for my eyes to adjust to the cool darkness when we first walk in. Celia carries the unconscious silver man to the couch in her living room, though in the dim light I have to rely on memory and imagination to picture her shrugging him onto the sofa. I almost overlook the bony hands stretching out from the darkness to probe Clarent, and when I catch sight of them my heart catches in my throat in an instinctive shudder. I should feel relief that Celia was able to get a healer here so quickly, but those emaciated hands look better suited to stirring a cauldron—probably one containing small children or adorable talking animals.

"You kissed him?" The voice that emerges from the living room shadows is as insubstantial and papery as the withered hands, the whisper of something that lurks under beds and scuttles through tiny cracks.

"Yes," I answer tightly, not liking the curiosity in the voice or the way I suddenly feel like someone's science project. "I'm poisonous, and he got a mouthful. Or," I stammer, increasingly unsettled, "I *was* poisonous, over there."

"And *he* kissed *her*," Lavender corrects tartly, the tang of green apples filling the air. "It isn't Rose's fault if he hurt himself." She gives me a scolding look for accepting guilt so readily, stepping closer to me in a protective stance.

Celia's expression is as dispassionate as always, apparently uninterested in assigning blame. "He's not breathing too shallow," she points out, studying Clarent with a detached expression. "And the fact that he's still alive is a good thing. Think you can patch him up, Joel?"

Shuffling movement allows me to define the edges of the healer. He is thin and gaunt, his skin stretched over a painfully tall frame. He's at least a head taller than Celia, but his back is doubled over in a stooping posture that puts him effectively on her level. Wherever his skin doesn't stretch it wrinkles into deep pools under his unsettlingly blue eyes and in thick patches at his neckline where his scruffy white beard stops against a knit blue shirt.

"Alive isn't everything, Celia," he whispers. He steps awkwardly into a stray crack of light filtering in from the corner of the closed blinds and I see that the shirt is actually a hooded jacket, a strangely youthful choice in stark contrast to his advanced age. Though it is almost as warm inside the house as it was outside, he has the hood pulled up high over his head and the long sleeves pulled down to his wrists. The skin on his face and hands is mottled and patchy; whiter than Lavender's in some spots, darker than my own in others.

"It's a damn sight better than instant death," Celia counters in a mild tone. "Rose said that's how it was over there, when she had to kiss them. I'd say this is a marked improvement."

"You know the portals sometimes change us when we come over, Celia." He bends to examine Clarent, his lips puckered into a sour expression. "She could have a slow-acting poison now, or one that builds up in the system." His sibilant voice dwindles away as his bony fingers brush exploratory trails over Clarent's metallic chest, moving over his collarbone and broad shoulders, up his neck and over a single silvery-smooth cheek.

"Hey! Hey, what are you doing?" I'm blinking rapidly as I watch him, unsure if my eyes are playing tricks. But I hear Lavender's gasp at my side and I know it's not my eyes and it's not the light; everywhere the man touches with his gnarled hands leaves a trail of drained color. Clarent's lovely silver face is now streaked with patches of darkness, looking as though he's been oxidized by the old man's touch.

"It's okay, Rose," Celia says, but I step forward regardless, reaching out to shove the old man away from Clarent. I don't want to challenge Celia in her own living room after all she's done for us, but I know poison when I see it and I won't stand by and watch another man die.

"Rose, no, look!" I smell Lavender before I feel her touch on my arm, peppery confusion as she holds me back. I narrow my eyes in the dim light, slowly registering that whatever has been done to Clarent is already rapidly healing: the black spots are fading, his skin returning to the flawless polished silver it had been prior to the healer's examination.

The old man doesn't even acknowledge my outburst. "Well," he whispers, his voice like the crackling of autumn leaves, "as far as I can manage, the boy is fine. Exhausted, dehydrated, poorly-fed; the usual. Fluids and food for treatment. Some internal bleeding that wasn't doing too well, and which would account for his unconsciousness. I fixed him up, along with a dislocated shoulder which will want some ice when he wakes up. That was very recent, Celia; I think you may have exacerbated an old injury when you carried him."

She shrugs at this, unconcerned. "It happens," she says simply. "I'll switch sides the next time I need to lift him. Cause of the bleeding?"

His fingers flutter against his stomach before disappearing into the front pocket of his hoodie. "Anticoagulants. Thins the blood and prevents clotting. Even a small stumble or fall presented a danger to him. I removed what I could; time will take care of the rest."

Celia raises an eyebrow, looking thoughtful. "No poison?"

"None that I can find," he admits reluctantly, turning to consider me. His blue eyes sweep over me, lingering on the rose tattoo branded into my shoulder. "It's possible that poison can't affect his metal body. Or maybe just not *your* poison."

"It affected everyone else," I say, and I'm surprised by the defensiveness I hear in my voice. His gaze is disturbingly intense, putting me on edge; he looks at me as if I were a puzzle he'd like to take apart and solve.

"I believe you," he whispers. "But I suspect any poison produced by a green-veined girl named 'Rose' to be organic in nature, probably plant-based. Just a guess, mind you." His blue eyes glitter in the darkness. "The boy is made of metal, and as such may be immune to biological venoms. Give him mercury or polonium or another toxic metal, and it might be another story."

His crackling voice trails away, the final word so hoarse I'm not sure he hasn't simply lost the power of speech. Then he looks at me with renewed intensity and I flinch, grateful for Lavender's hand on my arm. "On the other hand," he murmurs in a soft hiss, "you may have lost all your poison in your portal coming over. I won't really know until I get my samples."

"Wait, what?" I'm not sure I've heard him correctly. I blink at his sharp gaze, feeling a strong urge to back out of the house and drive away, not lessened by the lingering lemon-pepper tickle at my nose.

"Samples of what?" Lavender demands, clutching my arm tighter and holding me fast. She smells like apprehension and anger and curiosity all at once, the mixture of emotions muddying my own.

He doesn't answer us. Celia's dark eyes narrow as she sweeps her gaze from casually surveying the patient to staring intently at the old man. I shiver, even though the sudden sharp focus is not directed towards me. She was like this the night she shot the spider to rescue us, and I've seen her the same at the archery range—and once during the group meeting where she introduced us, when she had to break up a fight between two of the men. I'm struck each time by the sudden change in her demeanor, as she morphs in an instant from a relaxed host to an intense fighter.

The old man manages to meet her gaze without flinching, though his hand flutters with anxious energy at his side. I almost sympathize with his nervous tic; between Celia's withering gaze and the rush of wary sunflower sweetness that floods the room from Lavender, my throat tightens with the need to flee. He stares her down for the space of a dozen heartbeats before his eyes drop away to study his feet. "You know I'm right, Celia," he mutters, sounding sullen under his crackling whisper.

She gives him a long look, one eyebrow raised. An uncomfortable moment stretches out in the darkness, then the edges of her mouth quirk up into the hint of an exasperated smile. "We need to work on how you ask for these things, Joel. If you want a sample, you don't just get to take. You need to explain it to her, and I'm not doing your work for you." She folds her arms over her chest and leans back to watch.

His gnarled hand reaches up to stroke the wiry strands of his beard while his bright blue eyes seem to pierce right through me. "I need a sample from your lips," he explains. His rough whisper is tinged with excitement he can't suppress, an enthusiast having found a pretty new butterfly for his collection.

"I can't." I'm not trying to be terse; I want to sound reasonable. But my mind races with objections that I don't know how to voice: this man is a stranger and I don't know what he wants to do with my venom.

"It's only a little bit," he argues, looking perplexed. "You can always make more. I won't need more than a single vial from you, much less than the blood I'll need from him." Suddenly distracted, he rounds on Celia. "I'm going to need a bag of his blood. The 500-milliliter ones they use at the clinic where Worth works. You'll have to tell him to be patient while I work out how to store it; if it's metal, it might solidify once drawn."

"I can't," I repeat, struggling to keep my voice level and calm. "I can't let anyone else have my poison." I feel my stomach twist inside me; above all, I don't want to be responsible for any more deaths.

Joel purses his lips, the mottled white-brown skin around his mouth set in a stubborn line. Before he can respond, Lavender breaks in. "Rose, if he promises not to use it for anything bad—", her eyes search out Celia, waiting for her nod, "—maybe he can help you? Maybe you're really not poisonous any more, and wouldn't it be good to know that?" She stares up at me for a long moment, her gaze eventually dropping away when I can't find my voice.

"She's right, hon," Celia says gently, despite her avowed determination not to get involved. "Since you're going to be living in this community, it's best if we can figure out a way to keep everyone safe. Even if you have got some poison left, there's a good chance Joel can whip up some antidotes, maybe even cure you. And Joel," she adds, her voice settling back into her usual stern calm, "you do need to promise her you're not gonna do any harm with anything you get off her."

"Of course," he says, his voice almost rising above a whisper, thick with enthusiasm. "I'll do no harm. And I'll share whatever I learn with you."

I haven't agreed but he steps towards me anyway, pulling a silver penknife and a small glass vial from a battered leather pouch he wears on his belt. I dance back a half-step, but Celia frowns at me and I hold my position. "It really is okay, Rose," she says softly.

I look to Lavender, breathing in her warm autumn cider and a shade of frustration I can't define at the moment. She simply shrugs her shoulders, looking up at me with shared uncertainty.

I don't like this at all, and still don't trust this strange man. Yet I trust Celia, and I really do want to help Clarent. He's still alive but I don't know if he's safe. Even though I didn't kiss him on purpose, I don't want his death to be my fault. So I take a deep breath, squeeze Lavender's hand and plant my feet, pretending to be a tree. I don't shy away when Joel's fingers brush my face, not even when the numbness sets in and I realize why his touch darkened Clarent's silver to that bruised blackness.

The healer's touch is poison. His fingers leave a numbing iciness wherever they make contact with my skin, the sensation burrowing and spreading until I can't feel my face. Joel traces a long circuit around my mouth, and I notice how careful he is not to make contact with my actual lips; he isn't sure if he is immune to me. "Hold still," he whispers, his papery voice gentler than before. I couldn't do otherwise; his intense blue eyes hold me paralyzed in place like a cobra with its prey. His knife touches the corner of my lips and I feel hard pressure, though no pain penetrates the numbness. There's a trickle of liquid, and cool glass is pressed against my cheek to catch what my lips have to give.

"That's plenty," he says a moment later. His eyes release my gaze, dropping down to the vial he still holds against my cheek. "Press with your hand there to stop the flow," he orders quietly. I press a thumb to the cut on my mouth, pulling sluggishly away from his draining touch.

"Should it look like that?" Lavender asks, sharp worry in her voice.

The stuff in the vial isn't quite clear and isn't quite milky; I have a vague recollection of separated paint that needs remixing, or milk shot through with egg white. A tiny thread of pink runs through the substance, a drop of blood that crept into the sample.

Joel replies only after he's stoppered the vial and shaken it experimentally a few times, his words confirming my fears. "It doesn't usually." I feel my shoulders sag as hope drains away.

Celia is the one who breaks through my melancholy. "Rose, this boy here is covered in solid silver. Milk in your lips instead of blood isn't even close to the weirdest thing I've seen today. Wait until Joel has had a chance to study it properly." She jerks her head at us. "Now I'm going to get some ice water for him. Lavender, you come help. Rose, you stay here and stop bleeding. Joel, go ahead and wake him up so you can take your sample from him. Then we've got to do something about that silver."

She strides out of the room in the direction of the kitchen. Lavender follows her after a quick backward glance at me, and I'm left alone with the sleeping silver man and a poisonous healer who sends shivers up my spine.

CHAPTER 8

Joel stares at me after Celia and Lavender leave the room, his eyes lingering intently on my lips. "Keep pressure on it," he rasps. I mumble something unintelligible and press my thumb with renewed force into the cut on my mouth.

I don't want to think about the white fluid in my lips, so instead I look at Clarent. He's breathing more steadily now, peacefully sleeping. "What does Celia mean, that we'll do something about his silver?" I ask. "You're not going to cut it off, are you?" I don't like the thought of Joel slicing away all of Clarent's bright skin to be stored in vials.

"No." He shakes his head gravely. "I would if I could, but his metal is as much a part of him as your green veins are of you. Only a faery could restore his flesh now." He puffs an unhappy hiss of air. "The best we can give him is privacy. He should have crafted a shroud when he passed over. Celia will have to help him create one when he wakes."

"A shroud?" I ask, startled by a word my memory associates with death. "Do you mean a disguise? That didn't fix when you healed him?" I screw up my eyes again, hating the unfocused feeling. My sharp green nails recede into blunted ovals; Joel's patchy skin evens out to the color of old leather. Clarent is still bright silver, distractingly abhuman.

"Shrouds, veils, cloaks—call them what you like," Joel whispers in his papery voice. "We craft them to hide our deformities from human eyes."

His hungry eyes flick back to me, a collector assessing a rare specimen. "He's lucky you two found him. If you or I had come through without a shroud, its absence would have been merely inconvenient. Your pink hair is odd, but as long as you had clothes over those veins, you wouldn't attract much attention in the city. And while they would stare at my vitiligo, I wouldn't have been picked up for questioning."

At the mention of his skin condition I realize I have been rude, staring as intently at him as he has been at me. My gaze drops to my feet and my cheeks burn. "But Clarent?" As I ask the question I realize how foolish it sounds, but it fills the awkward silence. "They'd pick him up?"

"Wouldn't you, if you were them?" His whisper is a flat deadpan. "I would."

I look up at him, blinking at what sounds like an unexpectedly earnest attempt at a teasing tone from the withered old man. "Because he's silver or because he's naked or because he's...?" I leave the sentence unfinished, searching for the right word. As alien as he seems, coated in metal and devoid of hair beyond his fine eyelash filaments, Clarent is still painfully beautiful.

The silence stretches between us for longer than my question would seem to warrant, before the corners of his mouth quirk up into the tiniest hint of a wry smile. "Here, girl, help me with this," Joel whispers softly. He draws a plastic bag from his pocket, the other hand still clutching his penknife. He's wiped the instrument off with a handkerchief, a cleaning method which strikes me as dubious. "Getting his blood is the highest priority."

"Shouldn't we wake him first, like Celia said?" I protest. "We need to talk to him, to explain the situation properly. He doesn't know us. If I were in his position, I wouldn't want my blood taken while I slept." It had been hard enough to give my sample with Celia and Lavs there to reassure me.

"Healer's orders," Joel insists, a little petulantly. "I need a sample as quickly as possible, before any lingering poisons have a chance to dissipate. Here, give me a hand— no, not the knife, girl!" He yanks his hand away as I reach for his penknife, his other hand shoving the plastic bag at me. Our limbs tangle for a moment, and I feel a shock comparable to numbing ice water dousing my skin.

"Sorry!" I dance back from his leaching touch, fumbling to keep hold of the plastic bag. "Are... are you okay?"

His piercing blue eyes soften slightly. "I'm fine, girl. Are *you* okay? My touch burns, I know." He heaves a hissing sigh. "The price we pay for healing."

"I'm fine," I answer quickly. It's almost true; the feeling is already returning to my ice-burned hands. Then I hesitate, wary of all his talk of slow-acting poisons. "I *think* I'm fine?"

He smiles at the question in my voice. "You are or soon will be," he whispers, turning to bend over Clarent. "My touch burns magic as a catalyst for the healing process, but if I don't burn too much, you replenish yourself naturally." His fingers brush the inside crook of Clarent's elbow, the silver skin bruising under his draining touch. "I don't know if we could cut him otherwise," Joel mutters, angling the knife in to slice his skin. "It's a strange metal; softens at the touch, almost like melting solder."

I feel an unexpected rush of pity for the older man. His talent is like mine; he's unable to turn it off. I step forward, holding his plastic bag and trying to look helpful. "That's good," he whispers. Liquid metal bubbles out of the tiny knife wound and I kneel on the carpet beside the couch to catch the flow, bracing at the unexpected heaviness in my hands as the molten silver pools and collects.

After a moment, however, the bag feels lighter. I tear my eyes away from the fresh silver stream to stare at the collection of blood I've caught. "It's turning red," I blurt out in surprise.

"What? No!" Joel's whisper is a harsh rasp of frustration. He snatches the bag from me and I pull quickly away to avoid touching his burning hands again. "No, no, no," he repeats, poking at the bag with a bony finger. The liquid inside swirls in spirals of half-silver and half-red, continuing to change as we watch.

Glancing up at Clarent, I see his blood is still flowing from the cut on his arm, staining the couch. I press my fingers to the wound, exerting pressure to stop the flow, and he stirs under the force of my touch. I find myself looking up into silver eyes, flecked with the prettiest specks of gray.

He blinks at me with a soft expression, showing none of the fear I had expected. He seems entirely at ease here, lying on a strange couch in a dark house with a pink-haired woman staunching his bleeding arm with her bare hands. "Hello, Clarent," I whisper softly, not wanting to startle him.

"Rose." His voice is like a warm spring breeze whispering my name, and suddenly his free hand is reaching out to my face to cradle my cheek, brushing dangerously close to my lips. I pull my face back in alarm, tensing to leap to my feet.

Celia chooses that moment to stride into the room with a glass of ice water, Lavender trailing behind her. Her dark eyes take in his extended hand, my wary crouch, and the blood seeping into her sofa. Stalking forward, she takes his offered hand firmly in her own, her grip strong enough to cut through his hazy distraction.

"Celia," she says by way of introduction, shaking his hand. "This here is Lavender, and over there is Joel. You've met Rose." Her voice has taken the stern tone she uses at gatherings to remind everyone to behave themselves. "You're used to touchy greetings?" she observes. "Handshakes and kisses? I can understand that. But I'm gonna have to ask you to dial back the kisses and touching without asking first," she says firmly. "Rose here has a thing about people touching without permission, and she's not the only one. Unless it's a medical emergency," her eyes flick to Joel in exasperation as he wrestles with his bag of blood, "you be sure to get clear consent from folks around here before doing any of that, you hear?"

Her intense eyes hold his gaze for a long moment before letting go of his hand with pointed deliberation, clearly expecting him to withdraw the offending limb and keep it to himself. He meekly does so, his expression confused but subdued, and she nods her approval.

"Good. Now, first things first; excuse me." Her eyes flick to the withered healer still muttering obscenities at the plastic bag which is now entirely devoid of silver. "Joel, you doing okay?" she asks calmly, unperturbed by his quiet fury.

"I am *not*," he hisses, prodding angrily at the bag. "Celia, his blood turns! It won't stay metal! He's one of those whose magic doesn't sustain out here once it's been separated from his core." He's fuming now, though he stuffs the bag into his pocket regardless of the color of its contents. "Like that petal-fingered one out in Briar. She pulls them off and they revert right back to boring normal fingernails—useless as specimens!"

Celia nods briskly, looking unconcerned. "Well, he'll be easier on the septic tank if he's not passing ingots, Joel. Thank heaven for small mercies."

"Wait, stop." Lavender interjects from the kitchen doorway, balancing water glasses in her hands and watching me with worried eyes. The sharp scent of pepper fills the air around her, tickling my nose. "You said he was immune to poison because his blood is metal. Does this mean Rose isn't poisonous, if his blood is really the regular kind?"

"It's not regular blood *inside of him*!" Joel explodes in a furious whispered hiss. "It only *becomes* regular blood when I draw it in order to see if we can learn anything *useful* from it, that's all. Her poison wouldn't be—oh, god!"

His hands fly frantically to his pockets, digging out the vial he took from me; his tense posture only relaxes once he's held the glass up to the dim light to verify that the sample is still white. "Well, at least *hers* doesn't change," he says, sagging with relief. "Though I'll have to test her sample from scratch if I can't use his metal blood as a comparison point."

"Well, you knew you'd have to run more than one test," Celia says mildly, before giving him a sudden sharp look. "Just don't run them on yourself, Joel. That's what the rats are for."

"I know, I know," he grumbles. "But someone may have to kiss her at some point to be sure." He passes a weary hand over his eyes. "Go on, Celia, give him his shroud. I'm done with him."

Celia nods curtly, and turns away from Joel to hand Clarent a glass of ice water. "You're thirsty," she says simply. "Sip on that. Rose, can you sit down for this? Lavender, you too."

I've been quiet through the discussion of my poison, trying not to get my hopes up at Lavender's question or to let old fears rear up at the prospect of further experiments. At Celia's prompting I rise from my kneeling position on the carpet, only to realize that there aren't many places available to sit. Joel has collapsed in a petulant sprawl on the only easy chair, and Clarent still lies across the full length of the couch. The blanket covers him from the waist down, but I doubt that Celia expects me to sit *on* him.

Less hesitant than I, Lavender pushes his feet unceremoniously aside so that she can perch on the armrest; an act which Clarent accepts with aplomb. After a moment's hesitation, I sit on the edge of the couch beside Clarent's leg and try to ignore the feeling of cool silver skin seeping through the thin blanket that separates us. Celia leans against the wall, watching all three of us with intense interest. "Clarent, right?" she begins, her voice softer than before. "Rose and Lavender brought you here to get patched up; you weren't doing too well. On the run from faeries, right?"

His face clouds over, his hand beneath the blanket clenching into a tight fist."Faeries—yes. But I-I wasn't running." His rich golden voice struggles to find the right words. "I was being carried somewhere. Then there was a sharp shift, and I was alone and human again." He looks up at me, his gray eyes soft and warm. "I saw color and stumbled towards it. Thank you, Rose."

Beside me I smell a hint of bright marigold, and I sympathize with Lavender; it really is impossible not to be fond of his gentle politeness. "You don't have to thank me," I insist, my eyes dropping away from his warm gaze. Now when I'm no longer focused on saving his life, I'm suddenly very aware of how naked he is under his blanket. "Lavender helped too. We all help each other out; ask Celia."

Clarent looks between the three of us, unsure how to respond. "Well,

66

I'm grateful you were there to help me, Rose—and Lavender." His eyes flick to Celia and then back to me. "I'm sorry about the kissing. I'll ask next time."

I feel my cheeks burn at the idea of a *next time*, but I'm saved from answering by Celia. "Glad that's settled," she says in a brisk tone. She peers at Clarent with renewed intensity. "Now, you say you were *carried* through the portal? You weren't actively *trying* to escape?"

He frowns, working through the words. "Yes, I was being carried. I-I wasn't thinking very clearly at the time. I'm sorry I can't tell you more."

Celia gives him a sharp look. "That's... unusual," she replies, "but it does explain the lack of a veil." She studies him for a moment longer and then brushes her hands together. "Okay, I'll explain. You came over in a portal; that's what all that mist was that you and the girls saw. Portals require magic to power them, which usually includes an element of intent. In order to cross from one world to another, you need to *want* to leave. Most altereds have an idea—if only a subconscious one—of what's on the other side and what they should look like."

She runs a hand over her long braid. "That self-image is crafted from an unconscious image of what you were before, bits and pieces of your memory that the faeries couldn't burn away. When you walk through a portal, you shape that veil around yourself as you pass over to earthside." She gives him another sharp look. "If you were carried through, it seems you skipped that step. Which means we're gonna have to make a portal here in the living room to take you halfway over and bring you right back."

The rush of lemon-tart fear hits me almost as soon as Celia's words do. "You can't be serious!" Lavender protests, hopping down from the armrest.

I reach out instinctively to take Lavender's hand. "Celia, there could be anything on the other side," I point out, trying to sound reasonable despite the rush of emotions. "It's not safe, surely."

"There could be," Celia agrees calmly, unperturbed by our outburst. "But it won't matter. I'm not going to make a full connection between otherworld and earthside. I'm only going to take him halfway, just long enough for him to form the intention of crossing back." Her dark eyes study us seriously. "I know what I'm doing," she says, her voice gentler now.

I look at Lavender, who still grips my hand tightly. Her lemon scent is fading reluctantly, souring to a softer worried clover. Her green eyes meet mine with the air of an uncertain shrug.

I've never known Celia to lie to us. I've trusted her once already today, letting Joel take a sample from my lips over my misgivings. Now she says she knows what she's doing when it comes to portals. We can either trust her or leave. *And then what happens to Clarent?* I glance down at him and realize he's staring at Lavender and me, as though waiting for our decision. We're the ones who saved him, I realize; as far as he's concerned, we're the experts and Celia is the stranger.

"Celia takes good care of us," I tell him gently, wanting to be honest with him. "If she says this is safe, then it probably is." Lavender squeezes my hand at this, nodding slowly in agreement. "We have to do *something*; you can't walk around looking like this."

He nods seriously, turning to look at Celia. She strides forward to take Clarent's hand in her own. "Hold still," she murmurs as a bubble of mist springs up around us. I have just enough time to shoot one last glance at Joel, who is watching us with a bored expression, before thick fog cuts off the living room and we are lost in a tiny world of white.

"We're in portal-space now," Celia says softly, her voice tight with concentration. "I want you to choose to come earthside with us now, Clarent. Look at Rose and Lavender. Relax your eyes. See how they look? Concentrate on looking human, as they do. Come back with us."

His soft gray eyes stare up at us from where he lies, watching our faces. I shiver at the sensation of magic building in the air, a feeling of static electricity that itches at my nose. Unfocusing my own eyes with effort, I watch and wait for the disguise to build.

Color begins to seep into Clarent's face, a warm tan that spreads from the center of his brow. Warm sandstone pigment replaces the smooth silver on his head and arms, real human skin with rough texture rather than impossibly smooth metal. Pores erupt; lines appear in the whorls of his fingers and strong hands. His knuckles and elbows become dusted with a network of dry cracks, the arms of a man who works hard for a living.

I see his body spasm with the effort of concentration. With my free hand, I reach out to grab his. He blinks up at me in surprised gratitude, and I grit my teeth in a determined smile as his hand squeezes mine painfully. "It's okay, you're okay, it's gonna be okay," I whisper fiercely at him, trying to soothe him with my voice.

Lavender gasps in sympathy as another spasm wracks through his body. Painful memories rush unbidden into my mind, tearing my breath away and causing my heart to pound in a panicky staccato rhythm. His thrashing resembles the death throes I've witnessed so many times before. I don't want to draw attention to myself—Clarent and Celia are concentrating on their own magic, and Lavender doesn't need to see me cry—but the tight constriction in my chest is making it hard for me to breathe.

A low, keening moan erupts from his lips—like a scream, but without the air to carry it. With a final burst of magical electricity, dark hair sprouts along his body: a thick thatch of tight curls on his head, a dusting of shadow along his jaw, a trace of soft downy hair that trails down his stomach. His eyes close with relief, the magic and mist evaporating quickly from the air.

Celia straightens, taking a step back. Her face is still a picture of calm but she looks weary and drained. "That was a rough one," she says mildly. "You okay?"

He nods, panting softly for breath. I swallow hard, pushing down my own panic with effort, my thumb stroking gentle patterns over his hand in an attempt to reassure us both. My eyes flit over him, examining his new disguise. When I unfocus my eyes at him, I see what normal humans will see: warm brown skin and short dark hair. But when my eyes are relaxed, I can still see his lovely silver, the bright metal that will always cause him to stand out to altered eyes.

Lavender peers closely at him, brushing her fingers lightly over his toes. "If you don't cross your eyes, he looks the same as before," she observes, her eyes alight with curious interest.

"I already said that," Joel rasps, standing to offer Celia his place in the easy chair, forgetting that Lavender wasn't in the room for his earlier explanation. "He has merely shrouded himself in an illusion of mundanity." He tilts his head then, giving me a private smile. "Well," he corrects, "he doesn't look *mundane*, obviously. But he looks unaltered to the humans and that will have to suffice, even if he still turns heads."

"It's a good veil," Celia murmurs, out of breath as she settles into the chair. "We need to get you some clothes, kid. I keep a stash of secondhand stuff, and we should be able to find something that fits. And then we're gonna take you down to talk to Athena."

I'm lost in thought, sitting closer to him than I should and still holding his hand. This talk of clothes reminds me that Clarent is in a state of undress, but it is her next words which send a jolt through my spine. "Wait, what? You're taking him to see Athena today? Now?"

Celia digs in her pocket and tosses me the gate key. "Yep. Go on and head out, Rose. If you get there first, you can get her in a good mood for us."

CHAPTER 9

There are a dozen reasons not to leave Lavender or Clarent alone right now and at least one good reason not to leave them alone *together*, none of which I want to admit to myself, let alone to Celia. I tell myself I'm being irrational and needy, and it's not like I can avoid my job forever. But the truth doesn't make me feel any better as I pull out of Celia's neighborhood alone, and I take a small measure of petty revenge in leaving her gate propped open for someone else to close later.

I've got just enough time to stop at the bakery for donut holes and sausage rolls, piling the bags carefully into my passenger seat so as not to crush them. Once I have a warm meal ready to offer Athena, I feel somewhat better. She's always so much easier to deal with when she arrives at the bookstore to find food waiting, and now I won't be forced to skip breakfast. My heart sinks, however, when I pull into the parking lot only to find her car already there, despite the fact that I'm still early for my morning shift.

I'd hoped to arrive first so that I could go through the tedious opening chores by myself, saving her the trouble. Athena doesn't actually want to sell books and would happily consign all opening tasks to a metaphorical bin, but occasionally she soldiers through the motions so that she can complain afterwards. If she's spent the morning counting register tills, she'll be in the deepest of funks. I hop out of the car praying that she's forgotten, or at least decided to leave the work for me again. If she hasn't, not even my breakfast offering of salt and sugar will be enough to put her in a cheery disposition.

I push open the glass door gently, wincing at the jangling shop bell that announces my presence. "Athena?" The store is dark; she hasn't opened the shutters or turned on the overhead lights yet, which is a good sign. Maybe she only got here a few minutes before me and hasn't had a chance yet to work up a mood. "Athena? I brought donuts and sausages. Where are you?"

There's no response, but I'm used to her extended silences. I lay the bakery bags on the counter, and set about tidying up the front while I wait. I leave the "closed" sign in place on the front door, but I don't lock the door behind me; Celia should be here soon with Clarent and Lavender, and I don't want them to have to knock and wait.

I pull open the front shutters, letting bright morning light stream in. Athena hates the sun, hates the way it burns the colors from the book spines, but Celia has told us that the bookstore must at least *try* to turn a profit. Customers won't enter a store that looks and feels like a cave on the inside, so that means natural light. Athena likes to go around behind me and close the blinds anyway. Celia—who actually owns the store—hired me to run interference on that kind of behavior. Yet even after the windows are open and the hated sunlight streams in, Athena fails to materialize to scold me. I frown; sullen silence at my arrival is one thing, but not to storm up and demand her share of the food is another.

I head towards the back of the store, wincing when I see the unholy mess that has been made and the books that litter the aisles. Whole shelves have had their contents stacked in precarious piles on the floor, several of them teetering dangerously as I walk past. I didn't work last night, but it couldn't have been this bad when the store closed. Jing works the evening shift after her classes, and she wouldn't have left things in this state. And if burglars or vandals had broken in, they wouldn't have bothered stacking the books. The chaos must have been caused by Athena, after Jing closed up and left for the night.

72

The extent of the mess indicates that Athena has probably been here all night. That's not good for her. In the otherworld, she was installed as a librarian in an imitation Grecian temple by a faery with a penchant for book collection, trophy displays, and living decoration; the stone columns of the massive building were crafted from transformed human women. "Living caryatids," Athena had called them. She herself had not been carved into stone, but soon envied the women who were; as librarian of the temple, she was forged into a sleepless living reference source for her faery and its guests.

While she was over there, Athena's mind was altered so that she perfectly remembered everything she read, and her body was warped to endure years of grueling wakefulness. When she passed through her portal to earthside, most of her talent was stripped from her. Her perfect memory is gone, and now she works her way from one side of the store to the other, over and over again, recommitting to memory the passages she's lost. She's supposed to remember to get regular sleep, but there are nights when she forgets and spirals into a captivity flashback. Staying up all night surrounded by books won't have been good for her mental state.

I locate Athena in the mythology section, which is the category she loves above all others and by far the largest of our selection. She's slumped into a corner and snoring softly in the dusty silence, her head tilted back against two bookcases where they meet at an angle. In her pastel purple blouse and knitted gray cardigan, she could be a doting silver-haired grandmother.

"Athena?" I call her name softly from a distance, not wanting to get close enough for her to touch in case she's having a nightmare. "Athena, did you sleep here? I brought breakfast."

One bright gray eye flies open when I say *breakfast*. "Rose, what are you doing here? Are you still Rose? You keep saying you're going to change your name and you never do. I was just resting my eyes. I want to reorganize the sections today; you have to help me." This last is said with urgent enthusiasm, the kind of tone that demands reciprocation.

"I can see that," I say, keeping my voice as mild and non-judgmental as I can. "I really wish you'd organize the sections one at a time, though. We could chart it out on paper first and it'd be less messy." I shrug, trying not to look combative. "I brought donuts for me and sausages for you. They're at the front; do you want to come eat first?"

Then I hesitate, torn between sharing the news and keeping it secret so that Athena won't be able to protest. Celia will be here soon enough, so I decide I might as well prepare her now. "Celia is bringing in a new altered," I add, keeping my voice calm and even, "so you'll want to eat before they get here."

"What? No!" Both eyes snap open at this unwelcome news, and she struggles to rise. I step forward without thinking, my arms outreached to help her, but she swats me away with the flat of her hands. Despite looking so old and frail on the hard floor, her gray hair scraggly from sleep and the deep wrinkles around her eyes creasing as she squints against the light, she's anything but helpless. "No! Rose, you're just going to have to tell Celia I'm too busy. They can come back tomorrow."

"Athena, you know it'll take more time to get rid of Celia than it would to deal with him in the first place," I coax, trying to sound reasonable. "And I brought donuts *today*. I'm off tomorrow, and then you'd have to face Celia on an empty stomach." This isn't strictly true, as we don't have anything as structured as actual schedules at the Athenaeum, but if I say there won't be any donuts tomorrow then there won't be—and we both know it.

Now that she's awake and standing, Athena eyes me with suspicious interest. Her burning curiosity rivals Celia's intimidating hyper-focus, and I don't like being subjected to either. I shift anxiously on my feet, wondering what I've done to earn her scrutiny, and whether it would be easier to just fess up to something now or endure her prodding at me until she finds whatever she's looking for.

"You said 'he'," she says, accusation in her tone.

I consider this. "Actually, I said 'him'."

"Celia isn't a 'he' or a 'him'."

"She is not." I try to keep my agreement as neutral as possible.

"The newly-escaped altered is a 'him'."

"You have deduced correctly. Can I treat you to a donut?" I dangle the word in front of her like a tattered and over-used cat toy.

"You don't usually fight so hard for Celia's strays."

"Athena," I say, in a reasonable voice, disliking the direction this is taking, "we haven't recovered any fresh escapees since Lavender and I came over, remember? This is my first rescue. The other altereds I've helped you with came out before me. So I'm still feeling my way with this rescue and rehabilitation stuff."

Her eyes sparkle as she pounces for the kill. "Did you feel your way through anything else?"

"I will eat all the donuts, I am completely serious," I warn sternly.

"Oh, okay, okay," she grumbles, looking petulantly at me for hauling out the serious threats. She's capitulated, but I don't know whether she's done so because I've won or if she's curious and wants to poke at me some more. Knowing Athena, it could easily be both.

We make our way to the front of the store, picking a careful path through the detritus of books scattered during last night's frenzy. I'd like the luxury of tuning her out, but she's got her claws in a mystery now and she isn't going to let go. "You're always afraid of the boys, Rose," she muses. "Either this one is special enough to overwhelm your better judgment, or you think he's immune for some reason. Don't tell me Celia is bringing me another undead one; I'm sick to the teeth of them! It's not a corpse, is it?" She works a foot-stamping motion into her stride. "I won't see him if it's a corpse. I will go home right this instant."

"It's not a corpse, Athena." I'm distracted as I step over a particularly large pile of paperbacks, placing my feet just so and trusting to my dance training not to misjudge and sprain an ankle. "I mean, *he's* not a corpse," I amend.

"But he *is* undead," she announces triumphantly, pouncing on my lack of a broader denial.

I sigh, torn with indecision. If I withhold clues from Athena, she'll be more interested in the mystery Clarent presents when he arrives. On the other hand, the more she knows about him in advance the faster she can process him. Speed is essential; it gives her less time to nurture a good sulk to drop mid-visit as a prelude to storming off. I decide to aim down the middle. "He's not undead."

"Is he immune?" she demands.

I consider asking, "Immune to what?" but she'll be annoyed if I pretend ignorance. "Maybe," I confess. "The healer, Joel, isn't sure. He kissed me and didn't die. Hasn't shown any ill effects yet." I hesitate and then decide to offer a lure, hoping she'll bite. "He's metal."

Athena considers this. We've reached the front of the store and her deft fingers hover over the sausage rolls, seeking the one she deems plumpest. When she settles on her choice—identical to the others, as far as I can tell—her fingers dive in like a hawk to grab it, and she bites half the sausage off in one go before chewing with delicate daintiness. "He's not bronze, is he?" she asks archly. "I won't see him if he is; I have an allergy to bronze."

I give her a sharp look, fairly certain this is untrue. I'm saved from argument by the welcome sight of Celia and Clarent pulling up in her car. Less welcome, I notice with a sudden frown, is the realization that they seem to be alone; I'd expected Lavender to come with them. Maybe she decided to find her lost car first and then follow them out here, in which case she might be quite some time. My heart sinks.

"He's not bronze, and they're here," I say, my tone a little sharper than I'd intended. "Please be nice; Celia will blame me if you're not."

This doesn't evoke her pity. "Don't you want me to run the boys off, like Jing does?" She squints into the dawn light, peering at Clarent through grimy windows. "Ooh, he's a pretty one, Rose. I don't like the look of all that silver, though. Bleh! Ridiculously ostentatious of him. You can't have him!"

76

She pauses for a moment, considering as she watches them approach. "Not unless you get another for working-days," she decides, amending her previous edict. "He's too costly to wear every day! But I suppose that girlfriend of yours was the one born in a merry hour. You're too depressed to be Beatrice, Rose. You're just pretty enough to be Hero, but her part is so very dull." I make an irritated face at her nonsense, but she chews on her sausage roll in a cheery fashion and ignores my glare.

I look back at Celia and Clarent as she leads him up the walk. It's slow going; his wide eyes take in every detail of the parking lot and shop front. The strip mall we're located in is bland and boring, with most of the properties either empty or rented out as offices. But I remember that feeling of vulnerable wonder marked by the nervous half-smile around the corner of his mouth. I want to wrap my arms around him, promise I'll show him around town, and reassure him that he'll manage just fine.

We all look like that, those of us who have been altered and had our memories stripped away, yet somehow the expression seems more poignant on him. I realize with a sudden start that I wish Lavender were here to see his first day out, to witness those vulnerable eyes with me. I had thought I didn't want her with him; a pang of loneliness accompanies my mental image of the two of them together, yet disappears when I imagine myself with them both.

I shake away the tangle of my thoughts and glance back to Athena. Her bright gray eyes study his approach with an intense curiosity which her affected grumpiness can't entirely hide. "You really don't like the silver?" I ask skeptically.

She frowns at the question, glaring at Clarent as Celia opens the shop door and leads him in. "No, no, it's not silver," she announces. "That's very slippery of you, Rose. It's some kind of melting alloy. I wouldn't know what to call it at a glance; it's entirely unfair of you to expect me to. Did you give a sample to Worth? Nee would know better than I. Better than Joel! Does he give samples? Where are you from, boy?" This last querulous question is directed to him.

Clarent gives me a helpless look, his gray eyes soft. "I-I don't remember," he stammers quietly, abashed by Athena's gruff personality. "Ma'am," he adds in an attempt at placation.

"No!" she rejoins sternly, "over there! In the otherworld. What did your faery call it?" She frowns, but her ire isn't directed wholly at him: her hands are digging through the sausage rolls again.

Quietly, I step forward and take the bag of donut holes from the counter. I pop one in my mouth as a silent demonstration, relishing the crystallized sugar glaze as it dissolves in my mouth, and then offer the bag to Clarent. "You said 'Avalon' earlier?" I prompt gently, nodding reassuringly as he takes a number of the pastries in his large hands.

He nods at this, his expression changing to wistful half-remembrance when the sugar hits his tongue. "Yes, Avalon is where I was."

"Avalon!" Athena's exclamation is dismissive, almost angry. "No. No, I've no time for Avalon, Celia, that's utter nonsense. Some faery's idea of a joke." She turns sharp eyes on Celia, patiently leaning against the door, watching us with quiet detachment. "Bring me someone from Atlantis or Shangri-La for once; that would at least be interesting," Athena demands. "Where are the escapees from pleasure-domes and ice-caves, hmm? Even Rose's little Thistle garden was amusing, but not Avalon! What did they use you for, boy? Why on earth are you metal?"

Clarent blinks in surprise, realizing that questions are being peppered at him even though Athena is still glaring at Celia. "I... I was a sword-smith sometimes," he says carefully. "I was supposed to use my blood to repair the swords and forge new ones." He looks down at his smooth arms, rubbing a hand over skin that bears not a single scar.

I feel a pang of sympathy for him, as well as a rush of fresh guilt; I can't imagine being bled regularly as a source of raw materials, and now Joel and I have bled him while he slept, without his consent. *I have to apologize to him later,* I vow silently.

"And mostly I *was* a sword," he adds in a soft whisper, not meeting our eyes.

Celia's head jerks to stare at him, drawing her gaze away from Athena. Her stern eyes soften, and she steps forward to place a steadying hand on his shoulder. The gesture surprises me; she's not usually very touchy.

"Ah!" Athena's triumphant exclamation cuts through the moment. "A sword, huh? Named Caliburn, were you?" she asks with a satisfied nod. "Or Caledfwlch, if he was especially pretentious? Killed a lot of people on the battlefield, wielded by your master's hand?"

Confusion is etched on his face. "No, ma'am," he says, shaking his head tentatively. "My name was— *is* Clarent. And he didn't— I didn't—" He shudders softly. "He, ah, used me while he was holding court. He would stab me into the captives." He gives Celia a plaintive look. "But they didn't die. They screamed, and they hurt, and they *changed*, but they didn't die."

Celia tightens her grip on his shoulder, preventing him from drifting into a flashback. "Clarent. Changed how?"

His eyes drop away, not meeting her gaze. "Sprouted fur. Grew hooves," he mumbles. "Became boars and beasts for the lords to hunt. The women—" His silver eyes lift to linger sadly on me, plagued with familiar guilt. "The women turned as beautiful as you, Rose. They were installed in the towers to be rescued, or sometimes banished to the nunneries when he was in a stormy mood. I rarely saw them again. He never kept ladies at court for long."

His guilt is so similar to my own that I can't stop myself from reaching over the counter to take his hand. I don't know whether it's appropriate for me to touch him or whether he wants this from me right now, but I can't *not* make the offer. His cool metal softens slightly under the warmth of my touch, just as his lips had earlier. He smiles at me, a rueful smile expressing gratitude without lessening his guilt.

Celia frowns, looking as though she wants to say something comforting but lacks the right words. "Clarent—" she manages finally, but she's interrupted by Athena.

"Wait, child. Wait." She's still rummaging through the food I've brought, but now her brow is furrowed with deep wrinkles. Shaking her head every few seconds, she looks like a dog worrying at a bone. "No, that's not..." Another shake of her head, slower this time. "Not Caliburn, *Clarent*." It's his name, but she says the word as though it has another meaning for her entirely: the difference between *Rose* and *rose*. "You, boy, come with me."

Her bony hand shoots out like a snake, grabbing his wrist in a vise-like hold. As she drags him to the back of the shop, he barely has the necessary reflexes to remain on his feet stumbling after her rather than fall flat on his face. I smile encouragingly at him as they disappear into one of the aisles, and then turn to Celia. I'd expected her to follow them, but instead she digs a cellphone from her back pocket and frowns at it.

"Rose, this has been vibrating my butt off for the last five minutes, and I need to go check on someone," she says. Her usually mild voice has a strained tone. "Can you stay with Clarent? Make sure Athena doesn't bully him too much." I nod, but she doesn't even seem to notice; she spins silently on her heel and ducks out through the shop door without another word.

"We'll be fine!" I call after her retreating back, wondering whether I'm trying to reassure her or myself. I watch her climb into her truck and drive quickly away; the thought then occurs to me that perhaps I ought to be more worried than I already am.

I realize that in the disarray with Athena, I haven't had a chance to ask why Lavender wasn't with them. Pulling out my own phone, I feel a rush of panic, even though I'm fairly certain Celia would have told me if her emergency had anything to do with Lavs. There are no missed calls, but to my relief she's sent a text: *Sorry, Ravs, I'm going to crash for a nap at Celia's. She says it should be safe here. Find my car tomorrow?*

I breathe deeply again, cradling the phone to my chest in relief. I don't know what has rattled Celia, and the empty storefront has no answers to the dozen questions fraying my nerves, but at least Lavender is all right. *Sleep well*, I text back before locking up the shop and closing the shutters again. If Athena is going to be involved in altered research right now, we don't need any normals coming in.

CHAPTER 10

Athena and Clarent aren't hard to locate in the dusty silence of the bookstore; all I have to do is follow the sounds of her sharp scolding exclamations and his low apologetic murmurs. It helps that I have a good idea where they will be; sooner or later we all end up in the mythology section with Athena, giving half-remembered answers and receiving exasperated lectures in return. Athena has never been as patient with the newly-escaped altereds as Celia is.

The community we've built in the metroplex revolves around helping the escapees that Celia finds. She recovers us from the portals for which she seems to have a sixth sense, and keeps us in her home until we can get our feet under ourselves. Lily, a golden girl I've yet to meet, is supposed to give us a starting point for researching our pasts—though I was warned not to get my hopes up. Mina, with her warmth and easy optimism, and Elric, with his talent for acquisition, give us a future. Athena, acerbic as she is, has the job of giving us the context of our captivity.

I take my time following them to the back, pausing to try to correct some of the sprawling mess. I hope I can get everything back in order before Jing comes on for the evening shift. Right now, Athena will be grilling Clarent relentlessly about his time in Avalon while she digs through her books for context to hand him. She's quite certain that the faeries don't have a culture of their own, preferring to mimic their idea of ours. The scenery and customs of their realms seem to be based on the snippets of myth and memory that they rummage from our minds, or corrupted from the books they steal from the earthside.

I was one of the lucky ones: Athena took a special interest in me. She's told me the tales of vishkanya, the poison maidens of Indian folklore. They were employed to make lethal love to their king's enemies, just as I was used in Thistle to kill the May Queen's neighbors. And she's read aloud to me the full text of Nathaniel Hawthorne's *Rappaccini's Daughter*, introducing me to the story of the poor girl who innocently tended her father's venomous plants and in the process became poisonous herself.

I hadn't enjoyed hearing the stories. They'd instantly elicited memories best left to my nightmares, sending me into a panicked state of heightened breathing and nervous tension. Athena had muttered darkly about depression and post-traumatic stress disorder before calling Mina and demanding that she drive over and take me in hand.

Yet even so, the stories had given me a strange measure of comfort once I'd been able to calm down. I was still a murderer and I would have to live with that, but knowing the reasoning behind my alteration had made the world seem a little less arbitrary. I had poison lips so that I could be used as a weapon in love-making. Unfair, unkind, but something I could understand. I'd kept the books Athena had shown me, persuading her with great effort to let me buy them; if any more Nightshades were to escape Thistle I'd be here to help them, stories at the ready.

When I round the corner to the mythology section, Athena is crouched on the floor in front of the Celtic subsection. Her nose is buried in a book, and she peppers Clarent with questions as she turns pages. He towers helplessly over her, clearly unsure whether to join her on the floor or wait to help her up once she's found whatever she's looking for.

"You're certain you don't remember a name for your master?" she demands, not looking up at him. "Didn't he introduce himself to the new captives? Did he have any large tables that were ostentatiously round?"

Her voice has the exasperated air of one who is tired of coming up with new ways to ask old questions; I can tell she's digging for an expected-yet-elusive answer.

"No, ma'am," he says. "I'm sorry, but I told you: I knew him only as the High King. I didn't have free movement throughout the castle. I was a man when I was in the smithy and I was a sword outside of it, everywhere else." He shifts uncomfortably on his feet, looking faintly embarrassed at his failure to give her the answers she wants.

"Tsk." She clucks her tongue and shakes her head, still flipping furiously through her book. "I don't know what Rose sees in you; you're not very good at research. 'I don't pretend to be a sage, nor have I all the wisdom of the age'—you don't know French, do you? Molière? Have they not taken you to see Lily yet? No matter." She shakes her head again. "The point is: being the living embodiment of an inanimate object is no excuse for unobservant apathy."

He stares down at her, stunned for a moment by the fresh barrage of abuse. I realize he hasn't seen me yet, and I'm surprised when the corners of his mouth suddenly quirk upwards in the hint of a smile; is he actually *enjoying* being harangued by Athena? "Yes, ma'am," he agrees solemnly, his face otherwise perfectly composed. "It's very important that Rose have only the best."

"Quite so," she declares sternly, turning another page. "She keeps the customers from bothering me. That's important work! You may have to learn another name for her, by the way, she keeps threatening to change it. But Rose by any other name will smell just as sweet— No. No, wait, that's her little girlfriend with the freckles. You watch her; she's far too saucy for a lady's-maid. That's Molière as well, you know."

"Lavender?" he prompts helpfully.

She peers up at him, determined not to be distracted by little details. "As for you, we're going to have to improve your mind. Maybe some Sudoku books; I've been meaning to reorganize the puzzles section. You have to read them here, though, and work out the puzzles on rolls of receipt paper. I won't have you taking the books away! I don't trust you not to write in them, and those metal fingers will tear the pages when I'm not watching. Do you have any more of those donut holes? Rose, quit lurking and come help me look for the bit I remember! You're *certain* he didn't use you in battle?"

His head jerks up at the mention of my name, and he sees me watching. A dark blush brushes his silver cheeks. "No, you ate the last of the ones I brought," he says to Athena. "And, yes, I'm sure. He kept me at court; no battlefields. I was only used against his captives."

"Well, you should have brought more donuts. Wasn't there a whole bag? You left it up there with Rose, hmm? That was sly of you; she likes food." Her gray eyes glitter with mischief. "Though I'm not sure it works as well when she *bought* the food you're giving to her. It seems rather crass, now that I consider it. And there's no point in leaving the sausage rolls with her, not when she refuses to eat any pork."

She shifts her gaze back to him. "What do *you* think of pork, eh? Vegetarian or vegan or halal or kosher or just plain picky? They're not the same thing, you know. More pork for me, if you two won't eat it. Still, she's hungry for something else from you or I'm very much mistaken. She hasn't liked any of the other boys. 'Not till God make men of some other metal than earth', eh? At least you're not bronze. She has an allergy to bronze."

"Athena," I say, my voice taking on a warning tone.

She ignores me. "And you're not undead, so I suppose that's something. That ridiculous minx Mina keeps offering to bring undead around here for Rose to practice on, and I've no patience for it. You're not too talkative, either. Look, see? Here you are. Careful with the pages, boy."

Athena spins around the book she's been flipping through and shoves it at him. I frown, stepping closer to Clarent in order to peer around his shoulder. I hear his sharp intake of breath at the sight of the page and then my own eyes widen. There on the glossy paper is a picture of a beautiful

84

blade; an ornamental attempt at a recreation, the caption says. Below the photograph are the words 'Clarent, the sword of peace'.

"One of King Arthur's swords, you know," Athena says smugly, watching our faces. "Not well known, but integral to the *Alliterative Morte Arthure*. They were a pair, the two swords; war and peace, killing and knighting. Clarent was the peaceful brother of Caliburn, or 'Excalibur' if you prefer. Caliburn was the more famous of the two, by far; more bloody, which always makes for better stories. Clarent was the peaceful sword, reserved for ceremonial uses; knighting ceremonies in particular."

Clarent stares at the page in evident shock, and I wonder how much of this is sinking in. His fingers brush gently over the colorful page illustration, almost in awe. "You mean I was a legendary sword, out of some kind of myth?"

"No! Good grief." Athena snaps the book away from us, cradling it protectively to her chest before he can touch it again. "You children," she scolds. "Do you think I'm the actual bloody goddess of wisdom? Do you bring me golden apples and then offer them to Mina instead and act all shocked and appalled when Celia and I make war on you? No, you don't! Not a single one of you even tries!"

I frown at the sharp, emotional rise in her voice. She's getting worked up, frustrated at having to explain the same things over and over again to different members of the community. Her sleeplessness isn't helping with her flashbacks, shading Clarent over into the same category as her library 'patrons' in the otherworld. "Athena," I say as gently as I can, reaching out tentatively to touch her shoulder.

She glances up at me, seems suddenly to remember I'm here. "And do you think Rose killed boys by being an actual flower in a bouquet?" she continues. My hand freezes in midair as I concentrate on remembering to breathe. "Why would boys try to make love to a flower? That would be ridiculous! At least be consistent in your silliness. No, no, your faery wanted to play at being King Arthur, and incorporated you into the alterations of his new captives as part of his game, pretending he was knighting them." She shakes her head in disgust. "There's an Avalon near here, and the faeries are irritatingly illogical; it's entirely possible he got the idea after harvesting folks from there. Don't get me started on Athens. Are you all right, Rose?"

I realize my hand is still outstretched, trembling in midair. I pull it back as casually as I can and force a smile on my face, trying to pretend I'm not shaking inside. "I'm fine," I say and it almost sounds true. Clarent is staring at me with concern in his solemn expression and I clear my throat, casting about for a change of subject. "Does that mean there's another like him, still in Avalon?" I ask quietly, remembering the other Flowers, my fellow Nightshades. "A brother, Caliburn?"

Athena watches us closely, her sharp eyes darting between us. "Very likely," she decides, her voice suddenly light and airy, matching my casual tone. "They would have met on the battlefield eventually. Clarent was the sword of peace, but in the *Alliterative Morte Arthure*, his role is to be stolen by Mordred and used to wound Arthur. It's all very symbolic, you know; father against son, sword against brother."

Clarent stiffens suddenly, jolting as if electricity had shot through him. "Stolen?" he repeats, his eyes widening. "*That's* what he was doing. That's why they took me out of the castle." He slumps against the nearby bookcase, as though the act of standing requires more effort than he can muster.

I grip his arm gently to steady him. "What do you mean?"

His gray eyes fly open to meet mine. "He— the High King, he brought in a new captive, a girl." I nod at him, stroking his arm in an awkward attempt at comfort. "He called her his sister, Morgan. Morgana?" He looks down at Athena, who answers him with a curt nod. "But he didn't stab me into her to change her, the way he usually did. Instead—"

His voice drops to a horrified whisper. "He kissed her. It was as though the life was leached out of her, all the color and warmth draining away. When he pulled away, her body was empty but she was still standing. She'd become a shell without a soul; not properly dead, but just gone."

I gulp air, hating this talk of kissing and killing. Athena looks at me, her eyes sharp, but nods again. "Go on, boy," she says sternly.

He shivers under my fingertips. "The body started to move. The High King spoke to it, called it by that name: Mordred." He shakes his head slowly, trying to jar his memories free. "I was in court, on display. The body, this Mordred, came at night and stole me. Carried me from the castle. He walked for hours. We crossed some kind of border and then—I was a man again."

"Our parking lot," I prompt, my eyes watching him.

He gives me an apologetic wince. "I was confused. I'm so sorry. I thought it was one of their games, that I had a role to play. Then you were holding me, so frightened and brave and beautiful." He blushes, clearing his throat. "I thought you were someone I'd been brought to save; a blacksmith and a pretty maid. I'm so sorry."

I blink at him, feeling heat spreading across my own cheeks. "So that's what you meant by 'rescuing' me."

He looks, if possible, more bashful than before. "I'm sure you're perfectly capable— *He* was the one with strong notions of—" Clarent stops, running a hand over his eyes and pausing to collect himself. "Women were delicate and cherished in Avalon," he begins again, his quiet voice hollow. "When they weren't being run through with magic swords or drained into emptiness."

Athena nods at this. "The faeries play at love, but it's never real," she says sharply. "We're toys and food to them, and they never truly forget that." Her fingers trail gently over the book cover. "They have the power to rearrange the magic in our bodies, altering us from normal humans to what we are now. They also have the power to drain a human completely, sucking the magic into their own bodies for nourishment. Your Morgan le Fay was drained, and the empty shell left over was used as an avatar."

Clarent frowns at this. "She was food?"

Athena pulls herself to her feet, brushing the dust off her pants as she stands. "She was a toy. He wanted to generate a 'Mordred' from the union of his own 'Arthur' with a mortal woman. He could have stolen a baby, of course; they sometimes do. Or he might have tried to make one from his captives. But children are never a sure thing in the otherworld. They age unpredictably and die easily. An avatar from the body of its 'mother' would be so much faster."

"Did she think she was this person—Mordred?" I ask, hearing the horror in my own voice.

She gives me a sharp look. "No. The mind cannot survive the loss of its magic. He was speaking to another faery." She shrugs then. "They can animate the drained bodies for a time before they wear out. Your High King either animated it himself or it was animated remotely by another faery. Probably they were playing a game."

Clarent considers this. "But where was he taking me? And why did he let me escape?"

Athena looks thoughtful. "If the avatar was being animated by a second faery, then he might have been taking you to his own domain, to be used later in an arranged fight between Arthur and Mordred. If he passed over a border, you could have slipped through into a portal. I doubt the avatars can pass like we can; they lack the intent and have no magic of their own to power the crossing. Once you were earthside, you'd become a man again; the physics over here are very strict about that sort of thing."

"The really interesting question," she adds, staring at him with fresh intensity, "is whether you retained that talent of alteration; whether you could do it again out here."

I stare at her. "But, Athena, it wasn't a talent," I point out, glancing at him. "Right? The faery used him in a ceremonial way, you said."

He nods at this, looking uncertain. "I didn't do anything. He just stabbed me into them."

She snorts. "You children: always so argumentative. Who knows more about magic here, you or me? You were incorporated into the process. You may well have been chosen for it; they shop for us specifically, you know. And ritual has a way of intertwining with magic." She gives him another curious look. "You have a lot of magic to intertwine with, I suspect. To open a portal while unconscious is quite a feat."

Clarent looks down at his silver hands, frowning. "I don't *feel* powerful."

"Why should that be any indication?" she says, puckering her lips into a sour expression. "You are, or you wouldn't be here. And you ought to be able to *do* something with all that magic. They always use us for something. You weren't used for killing or healing. He used you for his alterations, which means you probably have a knack for rearranging magic."

He considers this. "I didn't enjoy it, though," he says quietly. "I don't want to hurt people, or turn them into boars or bears."

"Athena, do you really think he could?" I ask her, my voice low and skeptical. In the three months we've been out, I've never heard of an altered who could infuse normal humans with fae magic, making them altered like us.

Uncertainty creeps into her voice. "I'm not sure," she confesses reluctantly. "We don't know precisely how the alteration process works, just that it does. Maybe you should talk to Worth? Nee has a way of bringing details to the surface. But the faeries do align our magic to their will, consciously shaping us, attuning us to their individual desires. That's why we can't turn our powers on the one who alters us, why kissing your May Queen wouldn't kill her."

She shakes her head. "If Clarent was used as a channel in the alteration process, there's a good chance he could do it again on his own—consciously rearrange magic in a body, maybe even align it to himself, as the faeries do when they align us to them." She looks thoughtful. "He might even be able to drain it, permanently and lethally, as they do; not just in short regenerating bursts like that Joel does. He could create his own empty avatars."

I stare at her, blinking quickly as I try to parse her words; even after discarding the options for murder which Athena has flung out in her casual scholarly way, there remains a flood of possibilities. "Wait. Do you think," I say, very slowly, my voice strained, "that he could rearrange someone who's been already altered?"

She gives me a smirk. "Why, do you know any volunteers?" she asks wryly. Then she gives him a sharp look. "Even if your talents aren't lethal—and there's no way to know without experimenting—there's a possibility that any realignment you do might be permanent. Don't practice on anyone unless they're certain they want to be changed." She turns away to examine one of the shelves with a haughty sniff. "Certainly don't try it on *me*. I need to be able to remember all my books if I'm to do my job."

"Wait!" My voice is sharper than I mean it to be, piercing the quiet of the empty store. "You do think so? You really think he could turn us altered into humans again?"

Clarent watches me with a gentle gaze, his silver eyes full of sympathy, but Athena doesn't even bother to look up at us. "We're all human," she says flatly. "Some of us have more magic than others, and our magic is arranged differently in each case, that's all. Could be he can change those arrangements, or remove magic altogether; hard to say." She sighs and shakes her head. "Magic works at an instinctual level. The touch of a hand, a little concentration, the necessary intent to power the process and— *voilà*!"

She looks up then, her eyes glittering again. "Maybe you can pluck the thorns from our little Rose," she tells him. "You two can experiment; see if you can't get her to a point where she doesn't need Mina to bring undead around after all. Watch that Lavender, though, otherwise she'll swoop in; a right falcon, that one."

"But I—" he starts to speak, only to be cut off instantly.

"Just don't do it in the store!" Her sleep-deprived sulk descends like a sledgehammer. "You'll mess up my books! Go away and come back when I'm not so busy. I have reorganization to do and you're going to need legal identification and cellphones and all the other silly things Celia cares about.

Rose, go drop him on Mina or Elric and then come back to help me with the poetry section. I want to sort the books by publishing date. I'm tired of having to continually restock *Leaves of Grass*, and this way everyone will be less likely to find it."

With that, she turns sharply away from us and we are dismissed.

CHAPTER 11

Even without her curt dismissal, I can tell Athena is done. We won't get anything more out of her for today. That we got as much as we did from her is a minor miracle; I can see she's bone-weary from staying up all night, and any more prodding will only end in stubborn refusal and creative invectives.

I take Clarent's hand and draw him away from the mythology section, shaking my head to warn him against any more questions at the moment. "Sorry," I tell him when we're safely out of Athena's hearing, or at least far enough away I won't feel guilty if she does overhear us in the silence of the empty bookstore. "We can talk to her later, if you have more questions. She just needs a break for now."

"I hope I didn't offend her," he says, turning his solemn gray eyes on me. "I may have teased her once or twice, and I suppose that's not very kind. I-I haven't been around company much, not for a very long time, and I'm afraid I don't remember all the niceties."

I give him a grin that I hope is reassuring. "I don't believe you offended her, no. And I think she can handle any teasing you dish out. She's always a little, uh, garrulous at the best of times, and I know she had a rough night. If it's any consolation, I think you two got on very well. I've seen her send newbies off with nothing more than a list of obscure book recommendations, and with more questions than they'd arrived with."

He nods at this, looking thoughtful. "At least I know what my name means and why it was given to me," he says slowly.

"A lot of people find that helpful," I say gently. "It doesn't change what you've been through, I know, but sometimes it's nice to know that it wasn't just random cruelty."

He nods slowly. "I guess it helps to know I didn't imagine it all," he says quietly. "That I'm not crazy, and it wasn't some feverish nightmare I imagined."

"Hey, don't knock 'crazy'," I say, giving him a rueful smile. "Mental illness rates among us altered are pretty high. We don't have a lot of options for counseling, but Mina does what she can. She, uh, thinks I have depression, post-traumatic stress disorder, maybe some other stuff too." I'm rambling; I bite the inside of my cheek to slow down. "So, yeah. Crazy. Sorry."

He nods gently, his expression grave. "I'll remember," he says softly.

I smile and reach out again to squeeze his hand. "But I know what you mean. Whether your brain is perfect or not, it's reassuring to know that our memories are real. Those we have, anyway. I guess you don't remember who you were before?"

He shakes his head. "Not a thing about it. Celia said that was normal?" he says, his tone turning up into a question at the end. "I thought it was part of, ah, being a sword."

"Almost all of us have amnesia," I say, stepping over a pile of books and then turning to help him. "Or, well, we don't know a better word for it, but they drain us when we're taken. I keep hoping my memories will come back, but it's just bits and pieces so far. Sometimes you'll hear a song on the radio and next thing you know you're singing along. Or you'll learn how to do something much faster than you'd expect; driving, for example." I shake my head. "I keep hoping I'll find my real name, though it wouldn't be the same unless Lavender got hers too."

Clarent considers this. "I can understand that," he says eventually, his warm voice thoughtful. "Rose *is* a very lovely name. But I can see why you'd want your original one back."

I feel myself blushing and look away from him. I wonder how many of Athena's insinuations have gone over his head and how many he might have taken to heart. Do I really want him to take any of it seriously? He's freshly earthside, no more than a few hours, for goodness' sake; he needs rest and time to acclimatize. He doesn't need me pouncing on him merely because he might be the one man on earth who can survive my attentions, and also because he's beautiful and kind and his lips curl up into the prettiest smile.

He's staring at me; I can feel it. When I look up, I see his silver eyes watching my face gently. He clears his throat softly, embarrassed to meet my gaze. "Rose, I need to apologize." I look at him in surprise as his words tumble out. "About the kissing—I didn't mean to upset you. I'm so sorry."

I blink at him. "What? No! No, I'm just glad you're okay, Clarent. You didn't upset me." I smile to back up my words. "Really. I'm just grateful I didn't hurt you."

"You didn't hurt me," he agrees solemnly, his gray eyes watching my face closely. "But Celia explained you were worried."

I hesitate at that. Celia has a short version of my poison and my past which has been distilled down to the bare minimum; enough to warn casual acquaintances, but without the gory details. I wonder which version Clarent got from Celia, with Lavender at hand. "Did she tell you *why* I was worried?"

He brushes his hand over his smooth silver head, looking sheepish. "Not exactly," he hedges politely. "But I got the gist. And Athena said—" His voice trails away, almost apologetic.

I nod. I can't look at him, so instead I stare straight ahead at the shuttered shop windows, the painted sign on the door that spells out *Athenaeum*, the scratches in the glass where children drag their toys when they are bored. "Men," I say quietly. "Athena said I killed men."

"You didn't mean to," he says softly, staring ahead with me, giving me some semblance of privacy by not looking at my face.

"No." I shake my head. "I didn't want to, but I killed them all the same.

Our mistress infused my lips with poison, and then sent me to their beds or put them in mine. I was for killing, because it amused her. There were a bunch of us, her Nightshades; she stuck us in with her Ornamentals or Fragrants. We were her secret thorns, and you didn't know until it was too late."

I realize I'm babbling, piling him high with details that he won't understand, that I didn't intend to dump on him. Flailing to a halt, I try to start over. "I don't know that I've ever kissed anyone without bad things happening," I explain, smiling weakly. "The only ones who survived me before today were faeries, and kissing them wasn't nice like with y— wasn't nice," I clarify firmly. "So, yes, I was worried about you."

He nods solemnly and I'm touched by the fact that he doesn't seem judgmental. He's serious, but in a sympathetic way. "May I?" he asks softly and I blink when he offers me his hand, hesitating just inches from mine.

"May you what?" I ask, confused.

A dark blush creeps over his silver cheeks. "Would it be all right if I held your hand? I mean, we've touched and it's safe, so I thought... if you *wanted* to hold my hand, I'd like that, too."

I'm too startled to speak. I have already touched him, of course; little reassuring squeezes because his story was so sad and I'd wanted to comfort him. But I hadn't really considered that he might want to hold my hand just for the sake of holding it.

I nod, reaching out my hand to his, and his cool touch is a welcome balm in the hot summer air already filling the shop. For a moment I simply stand there, holding him, relishing the strange sensation of his hand in mine as it softens ever so slightly under my warmth.

He grins, looking pleased and trying almost bashfully to hide it. "Celia explained how important it is to ask before any touching or kisses," he says solemnly. "We never really had many women at court, and the ones we did have were too important to visit my smithy. The High King had all these rules: ladies were not to be spoken to without a long list of necessary formalities. But introductions were always kisses and I never thought to ask first." His lips twist in regret and he shakes his head slowly. "I won't forget again."

"It's okay," I say softly, not wanting him to feel guilty for something he couldn't have known. "Nobody was hurt and it won't happen again." The words spill out in reflexive reassurance, and I immediately regret my thoughtless choice of expression.

The kiss *shouldn't* happen again; we still don't know if I'm dangerous to him. But if he could undo my magic, if the May Queen's alterations to me could be undone, would he want to try kissing me again? Would *I* want to kiss *him*? I try to imagine being normal and able to kiss anyone I wanted to. Lost for a moment in fantasy, I wonder whether I could possibly kiss him and Lavender at the same time; then I realize that he's staring at me again.

"Penny for your thoughts?" he asks and then pauses, uncertain. "Is that the right saying?"

I smile at this. "It is, actually," I reassure him. "I, ah, was thinking that Athena is right: I really should bring you to see Elric or Mina. You're freshly out, and there's all kinds of stuff that you're going to need."

He gives me an easy smile. "I'm not complaining," he points out quietly. He looks down at the plaid shirt and worn jeans that Celia has outfitted him with, along with heavy work boots that look too big on his feet. "I've got soft clothes and warm food and new friends." He chuckles. "What more could I want?"

I laugh with him and haul out my phone with my free hand. "No, I'm serious! Elric has to meet you so that he can start creating a new identity for you. Until we get you a driver's license and a social security card, your work options are limited. And there's always the threat of legal trouble if the police pick you up..."

My voice trails away as I dial Mina and the phone rolls over to voicemail. I frown and try Elric's number, but that rings unanswered. "Something wrong?" Clarent asks, looking concerned at my expression.

"I'm not sure. They're not picking up." I make a face and shove the phone back in my pocket, looking around the deserted store and the daunting mess that fills it. In the back of the store, over towards the children's books, I hear Athena industriously tipping over the kiosk of children's toys for no reason that I can fathom except that she must have deemed it in her way.

"Elric and Mina aren't really early risers," I explain, resolving to ignore Athena. I don't add that their sleeping habits tend to vary, based on their bedmate of the night before. "Their phones are probably still turned off, which means we'll have to wait awhile before they call me back." I hesitate. "We could go ahead and drive over to Elric's, but I can't promise he'll answer the door when we get there. I might be wasting your time with a fruitless trip."

He shrugs again, casual and unworried. "It seems like I've got plenty of time to waste, now that I'm free," he says easily. "I'd just as soon waste it with you." His gaze travels the store as he realizes that the messy stacks of unshelved books aren't supposed to be strewn about the floor. "If you like, we could wait here for them to call you back," he suggests. "I could help you clean up?"

The store sound system chooses that moment to sputter to life with "Tie a Yellow Ribbon Round the Ole Oak Tree" from the Golden Oldies compilation disc that I know for a *fact* Athena hates. I close my eyes and pray for patience. "Ah, well, I think Athena wants to be alone with the books," I observe dryly, reluctantly letting go of his hand to gather up my purse and keys. I give him an apologetic smile. "She doesn't make friends quickly. It'll be a few weeks before she can remember not to be reflexively surly at you."

He grins at this. "I don't mind 'surly'," he says with a shrug.

I'd be surprised at how quickly he's adapting to his new life except that Lavender and I were like this too, when we first got out. Calm and normal, joking and laughing during the day, until night came and the bad memories would strike. It took us a whole week to realize we were both having similar emotional breakdowns, and after that it was easier even if I didn't dare breach the wall between us. We were in separate rooms, but at least we weren't alone.

The thought occurs to me that I should tell him he's not alone either; that he doesn't need to be emotionally strong all the time, not anymore. We'll understand if he needs to fall apart and have a good cry. He needs to know that he doesn't have to be perfect out here, that he won't be punished for allowing his emotions to show. Yet I don't know how to say that when he's standing there waiting on me, smiling his kind smile. I'll have to take him to Mina's later; she'll tell him everything I can't, without ruining this moment where we're both trying to be normal.

"Okay," I say, my voice as bright and sunny as I can make it. "Since we're not wanted here, we might as well go rustle up Elric and get him started. You'll need identification from him, and then we'll take you to Mina and she'll get you settled into a place to sleep tonight." I feel myself blushing then, a little embarrassed. "Uh, just so you know: Celia is usually the one who does the introductions, but she had to run off on an emergency, and now you're stuck with me."

He looks amused at this, his silver eyes dancing with sudden humor. "Poor me," he says, very solemnly.

I shake my head at his teasing. "Are you still hungry? Do you need to go to the bathroom first? It's a bit of a drive over to Elric's."

His grin widens. "I, uh, went at Celia's," he admits. Sudden mischief gleams in his eyes. "But now that you mention it, I am still a little hungry. We *will* take the rest of the breakfast, won't we?" He manages an innocent look. "Athena won't mind?"

I stare at him for a moment and then give him a wicked grin. "Yes. Yes, we will take all of it," I announce with mock haughtiness, gathering up the bags of leftovers and leading the way to my car. Athena will complain later but, after her tricks with the sound system, some turnabout is fair play.

He's quieter when we get to the car, sitting in the passenger seat and holding the food in his lap with care, occasionally snaking his hand in the bag to pick out a donut hole to munch. He watches with interested eyes as I coax the engine to turn over; a lengthy process of patience and quiet swearing on my part. I must remember to mention to Elric that my car isn't long for this world so that he can keep his eyes peeled for a replacement.

When the car finally roars to life I pull us carefully out of the parking lot and onto the streets. Clarent watches everything with wide eyes. "So," he hazards shyly, watching through the window as the world flies by, "did Lavender— do her lips—?"

I shake my head at this, smiling a little so he'll see I'm not upset. "No. Lavs isn't a Nightshade like me; she's a Fragrant."

Clarent tilts his head at the nickname. "Lavs?"

"That's what I call her," I explain, feeling the blush return to my cheeks. "It was my first week of working at the bookstore, and I was tired when I came home. I sort of thoughtlessly called her 'Lavs' because, after arguing all day with Athena, the extra two syllables were more than I had energy for. I thought for a minute she was going to pitch a fit, but she just laughed and said it was fine as long as she could call me 'Ravs'."

He chuckles at this. "That seems only fair," he concedes solemnly. "What is a Fragrant?"

I bite my lip. "Her job was to make the estate smell nice and fresh. She was—" I pause, looking for the right words. "I guess you'd say half maid and half air freshener to the faeries. Her aroma varies according to her body chemistry and how she's feeling."

He nods slowly. "I noticed the smells. They're very distracting."

"Yeah, her scents can mess with your emotions if you're not careful," I warn. "Athena calls it aromatherapy, only stronger. It's not mind-control," I hasten to add, defensive on Lavender's behalf. "If you know it's happening, you can push back against it."

He considers this. "That makes sense," he says, his voice thoughtful and slow. "And I guess it would be nice to know what she's thinking, if she's your friend. I'd want to know what *my* friends were feeling, so that I could feel it with them." We're at a red light and I take the opportunity to stare at him for a moment, rendered unexpectedly speechless. He notices me looking at him. "Is that wrong?" he asks, looking a little shy.

"No, no," I say quickly, turning back to the road. "I think it's a really beautiful way of looking at it. But, uh, some of the community members were uncomfortable being around her, because they didn't like the idea of emotion-magic messing with their feelings; too much like what some of the faeries do."

Clarent is quiet for a moment. "Well, I can understand that. I just feel differently," he concludes. "Is it a big community?" He looks at me again, his silver eyes wide with curiosity. "Are there many of us?"

I smile at his eagerness. "Maybe about two hundred in the metroplex?" I estimate. "Not very many. I'm not sure anyone has an exact headcount, because people move away or disappear, or worse. Celia says it's a lot of altereds in one place, but compared to the human population it's nothing at all."

Clarent runs a hand over the armrest between us, anchoring himself. "Two hundred," he breathes. "And I've met five! Have you met them all? Do you know their names?"

"Oh, no," I say, shaking my head. "Celia holds scheduled meetings once every month—sometimes oftener if there's someone new to introduce—but not everyone attends. Some people are scared of each other, some of them just want to forget the otherworld as best they can, and some of them have formed human families which they can't get away from without a lot of excuses and lies." I smile wistfully. "But the community is helpful for those of us who *can't* make human connections."

He looks up at me when I say this, his gaze suddenly softer. "That sounds nice," is all he says, but his honeyed voice is gentler.

My cheeks are burning; I hadn't meant to make him feel sorry for me. "It is! It's useful." I nod my head. "Celia does a lot of the organizing, keeping people in the loop. Worth is our doctor; I haven't been to ner as a

100

patient yet, but I met ner once and we got along well. Athena helps people to understand the otherworld and what they were used for, and since she wanted to be surrounded by books Celia got her the shop."

I chuckle and add, "Jing and I help her out, because otherwise she'd drive all the customers away. You'll like Jing; she's quiet at first, but not once you get to know her. She's translucent—if she holds still, you almost can't see her." I flash him a grin, wanting him to know that he's not the only one with unusual skin. "We all end up helping each other out. I make my living with Celia's help, and what little profit we make from the bookstore goes towards helping new escapees get set up with food and clothes and a living space. It isn't a lot and we're not rich, but everyone helps out where they can."

He nods at this. I realize he's committing the names to memory and storing up questions for later. "And the person we're going to see now, Elric?"

"Elric, yeah." I bite the inside of my cheek as we take a hard left, looking for the right words. "Do you remember what a vampire is?"

He blinks at me and disappears into his own thoughts for a moment. I recognize the distance in his eyes, the look we get when dredging minds that don't consciously remember. The flotsam and jetsam of shared culture is in there, like the lingering muscle memory of opening a soda can. It's easier to feel on this side, without the magic of the otherworld clogging our minds, surrounded by the sights and sounds and smells of things we must have known before we were taken; but the memories are still difficult to consciously recapture.

"Y-yes," he says doubtfully. "Why?"

"Okay." I give him a sympathetic smile. "Elric is going to tell you he's a vampire. You really shouldn't argue with him, because no one ever gets anywhere and it just upsets him."

"Why would I argue with him?" he asks, looking more curious than alarmed at this news.

"Well, because he's the most tanned sun-valley surfer stereotype you'll ever meet. He's not allergic to sunlight or UV; he's got standing weekly appointments at three different tanning salons. He doesn't have pointy teeth, or at least no more so than regular folks. Pretty girls—and sometimes pretty boys, so fair warning he might take a shine to you—hang around him and when one of them manifests a bite mark, it's not *that* kind of bite."

I wave my hand in an exasperated gesture. "He's a total pill, but he forges decent legal documents and gets us expensive tech stuff like cars and phones, so it's best not to argue. Just agree with everything he says, and try not to let him seduce you because he's a heartbreaker." I give Clarent a sidelong glance, feeling a blush creep up my cheeks. "I mean, unless you *want* that. I'm not trying to tell you what to do."

Clarent eyes me with a mischievous look. "You think I'm pretty?" he asks, raising his eyebrows at me with a mock-innocent expression.

I blink at him, saved from the impossibility of answering by fortunate timing: Elric's apartment complex is just on our right, and I cut the wheel sharply, grateful for the distraction. I pull into an empty space not far from his duplex door and press the horn to elicit a quick, sharp bark from the car.

"Um. I wouldn't normally honk the horn," I explain, partly to keep Clarent from picking up bad visiting habits, but also to fill the space so that I don't have to answer his question. "But it's late in the morning and most people are already awake." I duck my head, still avoiding his teasing eyes. "We try not to run into Elric's bedmates if we can help it. He sleeps with a lot of humans and sometimes they ask difficult questions, so it's easier to bring him out here to meet with us rather than go in and be subjected to a lot of unnecessary scrutiny."

"Is that usual?" he asks. "Avoiding humans?"

Clarent's soft question trails after me as I hop out of the car. "Well, there's a lot of lying invol—" Brushing my skirt down, I straighten up, breaking off mid-sentence in a gasp as I look up.

102

Thick mist is gathering in the far corner of Elric's parking lot, the air around us crackling dangerously with the second sudden influx of magic electricity to surround us this morning.

CHAPTER 12

I can hear the blood pounding in my ears as I survey the parking lot around us. Not more than a hundred feet away a boiling wall of mist is rising quickly, bubbling like a witch's cauldron. Thick tendrils shoot out on both sides, spreading fast around us and engulfing a section of the nearby street. I twist my head to watch as the last of the cars drive through the mist without seeming to notice it, and then we are alone; no new cars join us in the shadowy silence.

Already the white mist has closed over our heads, blocking out the sun. The fog is so thick that everything on the other side of the dome is completely cloaked from view—assuming that there *is* anything on the other side. I still don't know how the portals work, and all the practice I'm getting today is far from welcome. Can this really be a coincidence, two portals in one day, or is this second one an attempt to recapture Clarent?

Another possibility strikes me, one I don't like at all: am *I* causing these somehow?

"Rose?" Clarent's soft, cautious voice cuts through my panicked thoughts. I look over the roof of the car to where he stands, close to the passenger door, frozen in place. He's the picture of calm, prepared for action with tense alertness etched into the set of his shoulders. "Should I get back in the car and wait, or do you want my help with any escapees who come out?"

He thinks this is normal, I realize. Biting my lip, I watch as more mist boils out from the dome wall to fill the air around us, the swirling fog pooling and spreading in every direction. "I don't know that there will be any," I admit carefully, pitching my voice low to match his murmur. "Clarent, I've never heard of two portals opening in one day. Escapees are usually separated by weeks, if not months."

He frowns, trying to piece together this new information. "Why else would a portal be here, if not because someone's escaping?"

I hesitate, unsure whether to share my fear that something far more dangerous could emerge. My eyes sweep over the empty street, seeking an escape. If we drive through that wall of fog, where would we find ourselves—earthside again, or lost in the otherworld?

"Clarent, they might be trying to recapture you," I say gently. I don't want to frighten him, but he needs to be prepared to run or fight. "Athena said you were important, remember? Maybe your faery is upset and looking for you. We need to be ready for that."

His quiet, calm acceptance of potential recapture is the last response I'd have expected; he merely nods solemnly. "Can I bargain for your safety, Rose?" he asks thoughtfully. "Or do you think it would be better for me to distract them while you get away? I don't know if we can trust the High King to keep his word."

"What?" My voice is too loud; it carries over the parking lot. I duck my head with a wince, eyes straining to discern movement: a color, a shape, anything that might indicate the direction of a threat. "Clarent, no! I— we don't— I'm not— no! I just mean to be ready; we might need to run or drive."

My hand tightens on the roof of the car; we could get in now, start the engine, drive into the wall of mist and hope for the best. But Elric lives so close; I can see his front door from here. If the portal isn't here for me or Clarent, might it be here for him? It would be an amazing coincidence, but I don't want to abandon him to be recaptured. We have to try to collect him first, and then get away—or hide.

I turn to face Clarent, the words colliding in my head. I need to explain to him that we don't abandon each other to the faeries, that I can't leave Elric behind and I certainly can't leave Clarent. Leaving him to his fate would be like committing murder again, and if it comes to someone serving as a decoy, it should be me; of the three of us I've caused the most harm, and I can do the least good for our community. But before I can get the words out, Clarent's head whips round to look at something I can't quite see, a blur of black in my peripheral vision.

"What's that?" he hisses softly.

I twist my own head to look, whirling in an attempt to locate the half-glimpsed streak of motion, but it has disappeared again into a world of disorienting swirling whiteness. I notice as I peer around us that the wall of fog is no longer boiling fresh mist; the portal seems to be complete, the edges sealed and no longer expanding.

Tiny flecks of dim white light filter through the dome above us, but otherwise we are in shadow. Rivulets of thin mist bleed from the dome walls into the parking lot, obscuring our vision further and causing my skin to prickle with the electric sensation of magic. I narrow my eyes, my gaze tracking slowly, and then I see it again: a flash of dark gray against the bright white.

Now that I know where to look, I can see a focal point in the fog, a darkness that I had at first taken to be shadow. As I watch, black smoke seeps slowly from that point, seeming almost to infect the tendrils of white mist that swirl around it. The darkness spreads like an oily stain in the air, and I realize with alarm that it is approaching us at a steady pace.

"Rose, do you see that?" Clarent whispers, and I nod, distrusting the look of the dark vapor. I don't think it's an altered. It's some kind of smoke-themed faery, maybe; a demon or a djinni.

Either way, I decide we're not going to wait here to find out. The approaching black cloud makes it significantly easier to decide whether to stay or go: it's moving towards us, not in the direction of Elric's door; which means we're going to get out of the area now and worry about Elric later.

"Clarent," I order, my voice softer now. "Get in the car, we're leav—"

My voice dies in my throat as the smoke before us parts, just enough for me to see the creature at the center of the black cloud. It's not a faery at all but a little girl. She's gaunt and exhausted, with the bent shoulders and broken eyes of a fellow altered.

"Rose?" Clarent asks softly, the question audible in his voice.

"I see her," I say quietly, my own voice trembling. "She's an escapee like us."

She walks towards us slowly, her eyes wide and confused, as we stand rooted to the spot, watching her. I study her anxiously, my gaze taking in every clue that she's been neglected for a very long time. She's young, barely a preteen, with dusky skin and wide black eyes, wrapped in a dirty black robe that covers her from head to foot. She's small and her face and arms are thin, with the gnawing look of hunger so keen and so long present that the sufferer is no longer consciously aware of it.

My first impulse is to leap forward and catch her up, bustle her into the car as I'd done with Clarent a few hours before. I want to drive her far away from the portal to the safest place I know. But she's a small starving child and I don't want to scare her with quick movements. I haven't known many child-servants, but the May Queen kept a small number in her gardens; they were almost invariably the most damaged among us and easily frightened.

"Hey, sweetheart," I say gently, pitching my voice to carry. I approach her slowly with my hand outstretched, trying to demonstrate with my body language that I'm not carrying a weapon and don't intend to harm her. "Can you come here? My name is Rose. I'm not going to hurt you."

She looks at me with dull eyes; not frightened, but neither does she seem pleased to see me. I can't blame her for her apathy; as I approach, I realize that I'm treating her like an animal. She's not a feral dog, she's a person and deserves to be treated as such. But I'm rushing because the portal is still open and I'm afraid that something else might come through after her. I promise myself that once she's in the car with us I'll apologize profusely, as soon as I'm driving her and Clarent away from this place.

She stands quite still, refusing to move any closer now that she can see me. I take another tentative step towards her, praying that she won't turn on her heel and run. "Honey, are you hungry?" I ask quietly, wishing that Clarent and I had known to save some food. She looks up at this, but I'm not sure if she understands the question. There's something familiar in the numbness of her blank expression and the resigned set of her shoulders.

She doesn't answer me. "Are you escaping?" Clarent asks, very gently, his low sweet voice carrying softly from where he stands by the car. She looks at him with the same blank expression.

I have the sudden strong impression that she's *not* an escapee, at least not in the way that most of us were. When Lavender and I crashed through our portal with Celia's help, we had been running for our lives—our hair matted with icy water, dresses torn from the thorns of the hedge-maze, lungs bursting for breath. But this little girl doesn't seem to have been running, nor is she in a panic. She doesn't look dizzy or tired or out of breath. Her robe is dirty and threadbare, but the sweep of fabric that covers her head and hair isn't disarrayed from hurried movement.

Physical hunger is written on her skinny body, so she might have been hiding on her faery's lands before she could reach a portal boundary. Maybe she's just too tired or weak to run at this stage in her escape. Yet the hunger she carries seems older than that, not something new and recent. The details of how she got here don't really matter, of course; she's a child, one of us and we have to help her. But if she's not being actively pursued, that means we have time to help her understand. It means I don't need to entertain thoughts of grabbing her and shoving her into the car against her will. She needs food and water and shelter, but maybe I can give her those things without further traumatizing her.

"Sweetheart, can you understand me?" I've taken another step towards the silent girl when I feel a nasty scratching at the back of my throat. I cough twice, trying to clear the sensation, but rather than bring relief the spasms cause my throat to burn more fiercely. I cough again, almost choking with the need to clear the pain away. Every wracking breath seems to tear the soft tissue of my throat. My fingers itch to claw at my burning lungs, to rip the pain away if only I could reach.

I look up, choking, to seek her face in the mist, my eyes widening with realization. As my gaze meets hers, I well up with burning tears that have nothing to do with my emotions and everything to do with the chemical storm assaulting my body. *Her face. That expression.* No wonder she looked so familiar to me. It's the expression worn by my fellow Nightshades, the calm broken acceptance of fatality that I wore as a hundred men were sent to me one by one. The little girl stands there quietly, watching with sadly resigned eyes as poisonous black smoke surges forward to wrap around me.

"Clarent! Stay back!" My intended warning is a garbled slur in my ears. I stumble backwards away from the girl, hands flailing behind me in search of the car. But already I've taken several deep breaths of the polluted air and my vision is blurring. My limbs feel heavy and unresponsive, and I can't seem to pick my feet up from the ground. The oily smoke snakes out toward me, like a predator sensing wounded prey, carrying the ugly stench of sulfur, soot, and decay. The smell is like a dying city.

My foot stumbles against pavement and I feel myself falling, though I can no longer see for the burning tears in my eyes. I hit the ground hard, the side of my face slapping into rough concrete. At the force of the impact, my vision clears and I can see her sorrowful dark eyes trained on me. A pang of sympathy shoots through my heart at the sight of her numb grief and I grit my teeth against the chemical burn, determined not to let the pain show on my face. Instead I make my best attempt at a reassuring smile, knowing that she'll remember this moment as I remember all of my own victims. I won't give her more nightmares if I can help it.

"Rose!" Clarent's worried shout pierces my murky consciousness, and I can hear his feet pounding against the pavement as he races around the side of the car.

No, I think. *You need to run.* But my lips can't form the words, and even my thoughts feel blurry now. I can sense him kneeling over me, checking my thready pulse with his cool fingers, pulling back my eyelids, moving on instinct. There's a brief surge of relief when I realize that he's not hurt by the deadly smoke that envelops us; he *is* immune to poison after all.

I want to tell him that I'm sorry, to say that I didn't mean to die on the day we met. This was my fault for being careless and stupid, when I should have driven us away at the first sign of fog. I don't want him to blame himself or to shoulder guilt for something that wasn't his fault. I wish I could tell him that I should have kissed him. I want him to take care of Lavender for me, and to say goodbye to Celia and Athena and Mina and Jing. That I can't say these things to him hurts more than the pain, which has started to ebb away into a sleepy numbness.

He straightens from his stooping position and strides towards the girl. She is motionless as a stone, her dark eyes still locked on my face. They aren't far from me, but when he speaks I hear the sounds as if from a great distance, an incomprehensible babble to my muddled brain. She looks up sharply at him, taking in with sudden shock his close proximity. I wonder how long it has been since anyone has been able to stand so near to her. She doesn't move her head or speak to him, doesn't acknowledge his words in any way, but her silence is helpless; the smoke that billows out of her does not diminish, and I know in my heart that she can't control her power any more than I can mine.

What will Clarent do to her? Icy fear trails down my spine. I know I'm about to die and that she's a danger to others, but I don't want her harmed. I can't imagine how Celia will be able to handle her, whether they can put Joel in some kind of containment suit long enough for him to reach her. I don't even know if he *can* do anything to help her, but surely there's something they can try. I've never heard of an altered emerging this strong, leaking lethal fumes that kill everyone who comes near; but Clarent can approach her safely and maybe they can use that. The burning in my throat and the stream of blood I feel running from my ear tell me that I'm as good as dead, but maybe they can save her.

He reaches out to her then, and I tense in expectation of a blow. But no, he simply places his broad hands on her frail shoulders. It doesn't seem to hurt her; she stares up at him in surprise but no fear. He concentrates on her face, his eyes burning with intense focus and his lips moving in a soft murmur; I can't make out his words for the ringing in my ears.

Then she cries out. I feel my heart twist in my chest. I want to open my mouth to cry out with her, but my muscles feel frozen solid. What is he doing to her? She's still standing, looking up at him, the expression on her face one of shock, not pain. And I think I must be hallucinating, because the dark smoke that fills the air around us seems to be drawing slowly back into her, like bathwater being sucked down a drain. *What on earth is happening?*

"Clarent." I manage to force open my mouth to croak out his name before pausing in puzzlement at the fact that I can speak at all. I pump my jaw experimentally twice, and though the movement is sheer agony the muscles are no longer locked in place. My throat feels like sandpaper, but the burning is lessening; though tears still well in my aching eyes and the raw air stings painfully, my vision is clearer. "Clarent?"

The air whirls angrily around us, faster and faster. Smoke continues to seep out of the air and into her body. The white fog thickens, crackling with magical electricity. I wonder if I should roll under the car in a bid for shelter; I'm shaky and weak and on the verge of unconsciousness, but I might be able to do this one small thing. Yet I can't tear my eyes away from the silver man and the little girl standing in the eye of this magical storm.

There is a sudden release in the air: an explosion without sound or light. Wild electricity sweeps over me, frizzing my hair and making my teeth ache with the power of the blast. In a bright flash of scalding yellow sunlight, the mist and the last of the black smoke disappears, the dome above us dissipating in the space of a heartbeat. The parking lot is back to normal, the sun above us and the noise of the street behind us. Only the addition of a frail dark-haired girl with puzzled eyes indicates that the mist was ever there.

I feel blood on my face and a lingering burn in my throat. I feel dead, but the pain is proof that I'm still alive.

A sandy-blond head appears in the air above mine. His professionally-colored and perfectly-gelled hair frames a face that manages to look both deliciously desirable and appallingly arrogant at the same time. His skin is tanned to a golden bronze, his jaw dusted with a smattering of overnight stubble. It's a face I want to caress and slap at the same time, the sort of face whose owner knows and revels in the passionate and contradictory impulses he provokes.

At least he isn't grinning his usual cocky swaggering smile at me; instead, Elric's beautiful face is twisted in furious irritation. "What the fuck, Rose?" His bright golden voice is pure scorn. "You'd better not die on my doorstep. I *hate* corpses and you know it. Who're these kids and why the fuck didn't you call first? Dammit, Rose, you're bleeding on my fucking parking lot. Where is your cellphone? *Jeezus!*"

He stoops over me and his hands pat perfunctorily at my pockets, looking for my phone. I want to croak out Celia's name, but my throat burns too much to make the effort. Now that Clarent and the little girl are safe, the adrenaline pounding through my system settles down and the pain catches up with me, dragging me into the comfort of darkness.

I slip into the embrace of unconsciousness as Clarent approaches us, concern in his gray eyes and a quiet little girl holding his strong hand.

CHAPTER 13

When I open my eyes, I'm lying somewhere cool and comfortable. The room around me is dimly lit by shafts of bright afternoon sunlight peeking in through closed blinds. The light stings my aching eyes, but otherwise my vision is blessedly clear again.

I'm lying on a small bed; a camping cot, by the feel of the frame beneath me. A shower curtain hangs loosely in the air nearby, affixed to the ceiling in a way that causes my muddled brain to supply the word 'hospital' even though the rest of the room feels like a small house instead of a public building. I attempt to sit up but a dark face appears over me, calm and stern, and I feel strong hands pressing me gently back down. It's Worth, I realize, taking in the serious eyes beneath a wild mop of frizzy hair.

Worth is every inch of six feet tall, so gaunt and skinny that you'd think a stiff breeze would knock ner over. Yet ner hands are like iron holding me down, and ner expression brooks no refusal. "No, child," nee says firmly, "you're not nearly recovered enough to move around yet. Rest and be still. Yes, children, you can stroke her hair now."

Nee moves away from my cot and bustles out of the room, and ner last remark makes no sense for a moment. Then I feel cool metal tentatively smoothing the hair back from my brow, the touch like a balm to my throbbing head. Belatedly I smell subtle hints of lavender and honey, and then Lavender's hand joins Clarent's as she gently touches my face.

"Lavs? Clarent?" I tilt my head back to order to see them, fighting a fresh wash of vertigo. A relieved smile spreads across my face and my voice sounds far away, strangely dreamy to my ears.

"Rose?" Clarent's expression is pained and worried, though I can see he's trying not to show it. "Do you hurt?"

Lavender is more to the point. "Dammit, Ravs, you *scared* me!" Her hand cups my cheek, her fingers touching my throat as if she could heal the damage with just her touch.

"I don't *feel* hurt," I murmur. I feel warm and safe and sleepy, with a light floating sensation in my limbs. "I'm sorry I scared you. Your fingers feel so nice." My voice is a hoarse whisper but there's no pain.

I look down at myself and realize with numb detachment that there's a needle in my arm. Long tubing connects it to a nearby bag of liquid, hanging from what looks like a coat rack. The bag of medicine is presumably the source of the lovely warm sensation that stirs through my veins. I feel a surge of hazy gratitude that Worth would waste ner precious medical supplies on me, and that Clarent and Lavender would sit vigil while I was unconscious. I want to curl up in their arms and sleep for a day, to let someone else worry about mist portals and poisonous children.

Children! My eyes, which had closed, flutter open in fresh alarm. "The girl? Is she okay?"

"She's fine," Clarent soothes quickly, his cool fingers still stroking my brow.

"Celia took her to the kitchen for some food," Lavender adds with a sigh, her lips twisting. She doesn't say any more, but I know she's as upset as I was over the neglect of the little girl.

"Clarent—you saved her, didn't you?" I ask softly, my eyes drifting shut again. "You made her into a normal human, like Athena said?"

"He saved *both* of you," Lavender jumps in, the soft scent of her flaring in the air around us. "You were dying and he saved you, Rose."

I look up at them both, smiling at her agitation on my behalf and taking in his soft gaze. They look so lovely sitting there together, touching me.

"Rose—" he says softly, but another voice interrupts us.

"If you're going to thank someone while you're drugged into a state of gushy gratitude, it really ought to be yours truly."

The sulky tone comes from the foot of my cot, and I lift my head to see Elric sitting in a folding chair impatiently tapping his foot against the carpet. He's still shirtless, even though I suspect he could have found something to wear since my collapse this morning. His tanned stomach muscles are casually on display, and his stonewashed jeans are quite deliberately worn low enough to display the thick Calvin Klein elastic band on his underwear. He's draped in his chair in an obvious pose and, infuriatingly, is no less desirable for his artifice.

"*I* was the one who called Celia, bundled you all into my car, and got you to Worth before you kicked off to the choir invisible. Your boy here couldn't figure out a cellphone if your life depended on it." He waits a measured beat to make sure we've all caught his wit. "And it *did*."

"Most of us come out not knowing cellphones, Elric," Lavender snaps at him.

I turn my head back to Clarent, happy to have someone other than Elric to gaze at. "Don't worry. We'll teach you."

He smiles at me, but Elric isn't done snarking yet. "Add it to the list, Rose; I'm sure you two will be teaching him a *lot* of things." Lavs shoots him a withering look but he just grins at her. "Hey, I'm happy for you guys! I've been saying for months now that the whole Poison Ivy look works for you two. Almost enough to tempt *me*," he adds, grinning provocatively.

Clarent thins his lips slightly, and I get the strong impression that the two men haven't gotten along swimmingly while I've been unconscious. "Generous," he murmurs, his warm voice deepening.

I have to hide a smile at how perfectly Elric has managed to annoy them both. Our golden vampire is a brat, but he's not usually quite this bad; he must have been pretty anxious if he's so determined to make everyone miserable. "You were that worried about me, huh?" I ask weakly. "Elric, thank you for calling Celia. I'm sorry you had to wait for me to come around. Do you need to leave?"

Elric doesn't look fazed in the slightest by either the annoyance or the courtesy on offer. He stretches in his chair and leans his head back against his crossed arms, looking terribly smug. "There are at least a dozen places I need to be, Rose, least of all in Worth's house babysitting a bunch of invalids, but I was told to stay here and watch Kieran. Your boy and girl there only had eyes for you; Celia had the orphan to deal with; and Worth's been bouncing back and forth between the three of you, digging out ner supplies, cooking up a storm, and making sure the little moppet doesn't kill herself by eating anything too rich before she's ready."

I blink at him, working slowly through his litany of cheerful complaints. "Watch Kieran? Why, what's wrong with Kieran?"

A thick sound, more growl than voice, issues from the other side of the shower curtain. "What is *currently* wrong with me is that you four won't shut up."

I tilt my head at the noise, but I can't see anything through the opaque barrier that hangs between us. "Kieran?" I try sitting up again and actually manage a vertical position this time, although my vision spins sickeningly for a moment.

Clarent is instantly at my elbow, arms outstretched to catch me if I fall; thankfully, he doesn't try to restrain me. Lavender frowns, looking alarmed at my sudden movements. "Rose, are you sure you should be sitting up? Worth said the medicine would make you woozy."

"It does," I murmur, shaking my head slowly. "Clarent, give me your arm?" I hop up from my cot, pitching forward slightly as Clarent's arms catch and steady me. Shuffling towards the curtain, trusting him to keep me from falling, I reach out to push away the flimsy material. "Are you ill? *Oh, Kieran!*"

Kieran is a wild boar of a man. He's only a few inches taller than me, but he bristles with muscle from head to toe. Athena says he's a former

116

gladiator and insists on calling him 'Ares', to his endless annoyance. I've seen him effortlessly subdue bigger men than himself without breaking a sweat. Now he looks like he's gone ten rounds with an enraged lion and lost. A mess of blood and bandages, he lacks even the energy to give more than a cursory glance at my intrusion.

I gasp and instantly feel Clarent's arms tighten reassuringly around me. "Worth says he'll be all right," he murmurs, looking understandably unsure. Out of the corner of my eye I see Lavender bite her lip, but she says nothing; any comfort we might offer Kieran would sound hollow right now.

"Kieran! What happened?" I breathe. There's another folding chair on this side of the curtain and I stumble to it, letting Clarent guide me. "What did this to you?" Dark blood is matted in his trim beard and on his shredded clothes. His visible skin is deathly pale from blood loss. Huge claw marks rake his arms and legs, the larger cuts sewn shut with widely-spaced stitches and covered with bandages that are thoroughly blood-soaked.

The wounded man growls at me, closing his eyes in annoyance. "Climbed into the lion habitat at the zoo," he mocks in a low grumble. "Wanted to teach them a lesson for their attitude. Would have had the king, but turns out they don't fight fair: all his girls jumped me. Now go back to bed and be quiet, Rosebud."

"It's Rose," Lavender reminds him, her voice even.

"Same difference," he returns in an equally chilly tone, his eyes sweeping pointedly over my pink hair and shoulder brand. I feel an unexpected surge of sympathy for Athena, along with a strong suspicion that Kieran may have earned his unwelcome nickname by provoking her ire at some point.

"He's just embarrassed that another altered could beat him up so badly, the poor darling," Elric interjects in a sardonic drawl, earning a nasty scowl from Kieran. "Oh, they're going to find out eventually, princess," he smirks, utterly unfazed by the glare. "You know Celia will have to tell everyone."

"Tell us what?" I demand, my voice tight as a fresh wave of dizziness sweeps over me. Clarent reaches out his hands to steady me by the shoulders, his gesture faintly reminiscent of the way he touched the little girl earlier.

I realize with a sudden start that we now know he can remove fae magic from people. He's tried it and it worked; no one died from being drained as Athena had worried they might. He could alter me back at any time, drawing the poison out of me forever. I could kiss him. I could kiss Lavender. Hell, I could kiss Elric; it would eternally confirm my terrible taste and poor life choices if I did, but I could do it safely and enjoy myself.

A blush creeps into my cheeks at the thought of all this kissing, and Elric smirks at my reaction to Clarent's touch. "Celia would tell you, the lot of you, the three of you *together*," he teases mercilessly, "that dangerous shit is coming out of the portals and you should run the next time you see fog."

"That's not actually what I said, Elric." I turn to see Celia enter the room, my head swimming at the sudden movement. She stands in the doorway to our 'hospital room', one arm wrapped around the little girl, while Worth peers at me from over Celia's shoulder.

"Child, what are you doing out of bed?" Clicking ner tongue in exasperation, Worth bustles over to me. Strong wiry fingers check my pulse and examine the needle in my arm; after a moment, nee pinches the tubing closed and gently works the needle out of me. "If you're well enough to stumble around, you're well enough to do without painkillers," nee declares, shaking ner head at us.

"She's going to be all right, then?" Clarent asks anxiously. Beside us Lavender sits a little more stiffly, the air suffusing with honeysuckle hope.

Worth nods easily, bundling up the tubing and medicine bag. "Tox's poison is fading very quickly from her system. I believe their faery made the pollution lethal but short-lasting. I presume he did so that his own servants could run away from them and survive to serve another day, rather than needing to be replaced after a single unlucky chance encounter."

"I do still hurt," I venture sheepishly. I don't want to complain, but I'm not sure if this is something Worth needs to be told. Already I'm wondering if all this moving around was such a good idea, now that the gentle warmth in my veins is fading and the rasp has returned to my throat.

Nee nods at me as nee moves the coat rack away from the cot and, with a firm hand, helps me to lie down again. "You're talking too much," nee warns. "The soft tissue in your throat is going to be sore for a while. And you should limit your eyes to dim lighting for the rest of the day." Nee places a cool cloth on my brow and motions for Lavender to dab at me while nee steps over to Kieran and begins the arduous process of changing his bandages.

I realize that Celia is watching me with intense interest. "Sorry. You were saying?" I prompt quietly, softening my voice to lessen the sting. "About the mist?"

"Three portals in one day, which is a first," she says coolly, studying my face. "All in city limits, which is also highly unusual. And all three popped out altereds who weren't actively *trying* to escape." Her eyes narrow. "In a single morning, we've found a silver man who can undo alteration magic, a talent I've never even heard of before, a child with lethal airborne poison and a bear-woman who jumped Kieran and inflicted serious damage before I managed to get there."

I stare at her, my brain moving sluggishly from the aftermath of the drugs. I feel numb from the fresh pain of using my voice. Lavender voices the question I can't find the words to frame. "How did you know to get there and save him?"

Celia frowns at her, looking grim. "The portal didn't close correctly, so Kieran was able to get out a cellphone signal. The crossing was bad and the woman was confused. Worse yet, there were human witnesses and now we've got to lie low. Someone snapped a blurry picture, and reports are going round about a bear escaped from the zoo." She sighs, looking weary.

Worth looks up from where nee is wrapping fresh bandages around Kieran, who grits his teeth silently against the pain. "When no one presents at the hospital and the zoos find they aren't missing any animals, it'll be written off as a hoax," nee says calmly. "We just need to be careful until then."

Celia nods. "We need to figure out why this is happening, though," she says firmly. Her eyes flick back to me. "I would be looking at you as a possible common denominator in all this, Rose," she says bluntly, "as you were there for both Clarent and Tox coming out. But Kieran swears he hasn't seen you since the last group meeting. Are you sure you haven't seen him, maybe without his realizing?"

My eyes widen and I shake my head, my hair catching painfully on the cot frame beneath me. "I haven't seen him," I protest, feeling helpless. Beside me I sense Lavender tense up, ready to hop in and defend me.

"Mmm." Celia stares at me a moment longer before mercifully relaxing her scrutiny. "In which case we still have no idea why the portals are forming and where they may hit next. That is why I said, Elric," she adds, turning to him, "that people should react to the mist with caution, immediately text their location to me, and try to exit the portal area before it can seal. If they can't get out in time, they should hide and not approach anyone coming out of the portal."

"Is that not the same as running? Little difference, I'd have thought," Elric says with a shrug, though his insouciant eyes don't try to meet her gaze. "But at least you captured your bear-woman and you got a little orphan girl out of the deal—"

"They are a 'child', Elric, not a 'girl'," Celia corrects, cutting in calmly. "And you are not to refer to them as an 'orphan'."

I glance up at the correction, wondering if this means that the little altered child is genderqueer like Worth. They stand silently in the doorway with Celia, clinging to her leg, listening to us discuss them. They are still wrapped in the black robe that covers them from head to toe, their pretty face and wide dark eyes peeking warily out at me.

I try to offer them a reassuring smile, hoping to convey that I'm unharmed and not upset or angry over what happened. The child snuggles closer to Celia, looking a little alarmed by my friendly overtures. I remember how frightened I was earlier when I'd thought I had hurt Clarent, and I can only imagine how much more worried they have been while *I* was unconscious. At least I had known this morning that if Clarent had died Celia wouldn't harm me in retaliation; yet we are all strangers to this little one, and they must have wondered if they would be hurt or punished if I didn't survive.

"You've got a nice child, then," Elric continues smoothly, unfazed by Celia's correction. "And Kieran was overdue for a good beating, anyway—"

"You're going the right way to get a beating of your own," Kieran growls, but it's clear that he's still far too weak to rise from his cot.

"Oh, princess, you're just saying that because you miss me," Elric teases, his eyes dancing. Worth shushes them both.

"Hold still, child," nee scolds Kieran sternly. "Unlike little Rose, the damage to you wasn't designed to be short-term. If you keep wriggling, I'm never going to get these bandages changed." Ner dark hands move with quick sureness as nee wraps fresh gauze around the angry red claw marks. The sheer volume of the work is overwhelming to watch; almost every patch of Kieran's exposed skin is cut or bitten.

"Fuck the banda—" Kieran starts furiously, unwilling to be as compliant a patient as I, but he's interrupted by a loud clatter in the hallway. Worth and Elric look up, startled. Clarent quickly steps between my cot and the door while Lavender leaps from her chair, ready to help him. The little child—*Tox, nee said their name was*—squeezes closer to Celia, their dark eyes clouded with worry.

Only Celia doesn't seem perturbed by the intrusion. "We're back here, Joel, try not to knock everything over," she says idly, patting Tox reassuringly on the head.

"Worth, I've said a thousand times not to leave medical journals stacked on the floor." Joel's voice is a whispered hiss, sibilant and thoroughly annoyed. "Celia, you're going to be carrying someone in here someday and trip, and then where will they be? Dead. Crushed. You should have called me first. The pink-haired one is my patient now. It's just unprofessional, is what it is." He emerges from the hallway then, his piercing blue eyes peering out at us from beneath his hoodie, which is pulled up against the afternoon sunlight.

"We *did* call you first," Elric interjects, sounding genuinely and uncharacteristically angry. "You didn't pick up." He tenses in his chair and for a moment it looks like he might rise to his feet, but Celia touches his shoulder gently and he settles back into his usual slumped posture, studying the floor with bored detachment.

"I was busy," Joel says primly, stepping around Celia and Tox. "Oh, hello; are you the new poisonous one?" he asks solicitously, peering closely at them.

"The child is no longer poisonous," Worth says, looking at Joel with tight-lipped frustration etched in ner face. "The boy there has undone their alteration, and the treatment seems to be permanent as far I can measure. You can confirm that better than I, however."

"What? No!" Joel rounds on Clarent with a burst of fierce energy, though his expression softens somewhat when he sees me lying on the nearby cot. "I mean," he explains, "I *need* the poison if I'm to transmute it into something useful. Good god!" His eyes widen in sudden horror. "You've not done it to Rose yet, have you?"

Elric snickers, which triggers the spread of an embarrassed blush across my face as Clarent glances down at me uncertainly. "I haven't— no. I carried her here when she collapsed, that's all," he says, stumbling under the force of Joel's scrutiny.

"Well, that's fine," Joel says briskly. "Just don't take her poison away like you did with the little girl—"

"*Child*, Joel," Celia corrects smoothly. "And that's really up to Rose; you know that."

122

"No, but look!" Joel darts forward excitedly, and before anyone can move to stop him there's a sudden flash of glass and metal in his hand. He grabs the tubing going into Kieran's arm, angles a sharp needle into a small plastic junction in the tube, and shoots the contents of the syringe into Kieran's bloodstream.

"Joel!" Worth's voice is pure outrage; nee draws nerself up to full height and stares imposingly down at him in tangible fury. Ner glare lasts only a moment before nee immediately turns ner attention to Kieran, hurriedly taking his pulse and examining the pupils of his eyes. "What the hell did you just give my patient?"

"Rose's poison," Joel says, sounding immensely proud of himself.

CHAPTER 14

There's a sudden babble of voices; outraged, frightened, and astonished. I can't pick out individual words over the pounding heartbeat in my ears. *He promised.* I'm stunned by the unfairness of the betrayal. Joel had sworn he wouldn't use my poison to kill anyone, and Celia had assured me I could trust him.

"Kieran, no!" I don't remember standing, yet I'm on my feet. I stumble to him, though I can't think of any way to help except to hold him as he dies. I'm close enough to brush his hand, my fingers clutching his, but the room spins wildly around me and I pitch forward clumsily. Clarent's strong arms catch me before I hit the floor and he holds me to his chest, his expression matching the horror I feel.

"Holy shit! What the—?" Elric is on his feet as well, apoplectic with rage and shouting over the rest of us. But the sudden shock in his voice overcomes the fury, and his eyes widen in surprise as his question dies away. I twist my head to follow his gaze.

Kieran lies quietly on his cot, looking puzzled but not in any pain. He's practically serene, yet my victims always writhed in agony until paralysis and death claimed them. To my utter astonishment, his angry wounds begin to close up as we watch, the shredded skin knitting together so finely that no scars remain in their wake. Worth hesitates for the briefest of moments before grabbing a pair of sharp tweezers; as nee quickly snips and

124

pulls stitches away, the tiny holes heal almost instantaneously.

"Rose, look," Lavender breathes softly. I feel her warmth beside us, one arm at my elbow to help support me, the other clapped around Clarent's shoulder to steady herself. The room is filled with the fragrance of lavender and honeysuckle, the heady scents intertwining with the drugs in my system to send me to fresh heights of vertigo.

"That's not— I can't—" My voice trails away, unable to find the right words. *Have I been able to do that all along since I came out?*

Kieran watches his body heal with sheer amazement in his dark eyes. When Worth has clipped the last stitch, he swings his legs over the side of the cot and stands carefully, flexing his legs and arms to test his range of movement. He peels the bandages away, marveling at the healed skin underneath the streaks of blood that he scrubs away with crumpled gauze. There's not a scratch on him, or at least nothing that hadn't long since healed over from his time in the otherworld.

He looks up at me then with an expression of genuine shock. "If that's your idea of poison, Rosebud, you can kiss me any time."

"No, no," Joel interjects, sounding smug. "No, it has to be treated first. I have a process! If you kissed her directly, you'd die in seconds. Any of us would," he clarifies as Kieran shoots him an irritated glare. "Well. Except Clarent, because of his metal; and maybe the child, depending on whether they've retained their natural immunity to poison." He frowns down at the little altered, looking doubtful, but quickly turns back to us, not long fazed by his own uncertainty.

"Some of the undead altered might also be immune," he admits cheerily. "The zombies, anyway, on account of their different circulation. It's hard to say for sure without further experiments. Of course, Elric here would almost certainly die." He glances at the tanned vampire who still glowers at him. "But once treated properly, her poison has powerful healing properties. That's why I need her to *stay* poisonous," he adds pleadingly, whirling round to appeal to Celia.

"I'm going to need to see your method," Worth breaks in evenly, ner voice still cool.

"Of course, whenever you like." He agrees immediately, and I realize with a surreal sort of calm why he's anxious to please Celia and Worth. *He thinks they'll agree with him if he's polite, thinks they'll make me stay like I am.*

Celia runs a hand over her eyes, looking weary. "We're not going to decide right now," she says firmly. "Rose and Kieran are going to rest here while Worth monitors them. Joel, you're coming down to the kitchen with me and Tox. We need you to check to see if the toxins are still in their system."

The quiet child tugs fearfully on her shirt at this. "It's okay," Celia says gently. "Joel is safe, and I'll be right there with you. He just needs to make sure all the poison is gone so that no one gets hurt. Elric, you stay with Kieran and Rose," she adds in a sharp bark over her shoulder.

"Celia! I have a dozen better places to be—"

"While you wait, you can text everyone about the emergency gathering we need to hold," she interrupts firmly, turning her intense gaze on him.

He bristles under her attention for less than a minute before dropping back into his chair. "You owe me, Celia," he mutters sullenly.

"Of course," she agrees easily, ushering Joel and Tox out of the room.

For a long moment we are quiet. Elric glares at the floor, eventually digging out his cellphone and utterly ignoring us. Kieran eyes me from his cot with disquieting interest blended with a touch of suspicion. Worth silently hauls out ner medical equipment and begins the tedious task of charting his blood pressure, measuring his pulse, and taking samples from him. Nee does not watch me as nee works, but I can guess the unasked questions nee must be saving for a later opportunity.

Only Clarent and Lavender provide something approaching comfort. His cool hands steady me gently, while her worried eyes study my face. "Let's get you back to bed," he suggests softly and I nod agreement. His strong arms guide me back to my cot and Lavender adjusts the thin shower curtain, cutting off Kieran's piercing gaze and affording us a tiny measure of privacy.

My poison healed Kieran. I don't know how to deal with that fact. He'd been so badly injured. For all his gallows-humor, the reality was that he'd have been deeply scarred for life. He might even have suffered loss of function in his arms and legs. Now, in less than a few minutes, it's as if it never happened. If he'd been dying when Celia found him and she'd had a syringe of my treated poison with her— *Could my poison save lives?*

Clarent sits cross-legged on the floor beside me, holding my hand in his. Lavender scoots her chair closer, her warm fingers gently stroking my hair and combing out the tangles. I'm so grateful they're both here for me, even though I feel guilty for monopolizing their time. Lavender ought to be sleeping; they must have woken her from her nap to bring her here. And Clarent should be getting on with the important business of taking his life back.

"I'm so sorry," I murmur, turning my head to look down at him. "I was supposed to square you away with Elric and Mina so you could get settled in. You're free now and you deserve your space."

Warm gray eyes turn to meet mine. "I don't mind," he says with a soft smile. "Please don't feel bad, Rose. I'm glad I was there to help, and I'm happy to be here with you now. I can't think of anywhere else I'd rather be." His cool fingers stroke my hand gently, reassuring me with his touch.

"And it's not your fault what happened," Lavender adds in a dark undertone, still angry with Celia; the sharp scent of green apples swirls around us. "You were very nearly killed."

I lean back into the cot, smiling a little at her fierce protectiveness. "You know she has to consider all the possibilities," I murmur. "Three portals in one day! *I* suspected me, probably before she did."

Lavender takes a deep breath to argue, but Clarent's gentle teasing breaks in. "Maybe you *are* bringing us over," he says softly, eyes dancing. "Both of you. Maybe we're all being drawn over, seeking a glimpse of those lovely green eyes."

I grimace playfully at this, shooting a look at Lavender in time to see her reluctant grin. "Our faces have launched a thousand ships?" I tease back. "What makes you so sure it's us? If anyone has to be Helen of Troy, I nominate you for the role."

He pulls a thoughtful face. "Well, you did say I was uncommonly pretty."

My cheeks burn at the reminder, not helped by Lavender's wicked giggle. "I think I just said 'pretty'," I correct him. "The 'uncommonly' you added yourself."

He chuckles at this, grinning up at us. "I live in hope," he says easily. Then he sobers and his voice drops lower. "Rose, I'm grateful to Celia and Joel and everyone for all their help," he says, a frown creasing his silver brow. "But, I mean, if you want me to remove your magic, I'm going to do what *you* want—not what someone else tells me."

Lavender beams at him, sharp apples turning to warm sweet cider with the force of her approval. "Yes," she agrees in a soft whisper. "Rose, this is what you've been looking for all this time." She leans closer in to us. "We could do it right now before they get back. An accident, you know? There's no reason to think that Clarent has perfect control over his talent yet, right?"

Their faces are so close to mine that I can feel their breath on my skin, gentle and soothing. "No! It's not about their feelings," I hiss softly, shaking my head. "You saw what my poison did! We have so few healers, and none of them can be bottled like that. If they don't get there in time when Celia calls them, people die!" I turn pleading eyes on her. "Lavs, I could save people's lives."

Clarent shifts in place, looking uncomfortable. "Rose, you deserve to be with people," he whispers, glancing at Lavender. "With anyone you choose, not just whoever is immune."

Lavender's green eyes flash with fresh anger. "Rose, don't you dare get all martyr on me!" she hisses, genuinely upset. "What happened over there was *not your fault*. You don't have to live like a pharmaceutical factory as an act of atonement."

I bite my lip. "Lavs, I... no, it wasn't my choice," I argue quietly, knowing she can't really understand what it was like. "But I did it anyway. I didn't refuse—"

"You couldn't!" she explodes quietly, her scent turning sour. "I *saw* a Nightshade refuse, Rose. The May Queen thought it was hilarious. She sat with him—it was the second Hyacinth, I remember—and made him watch while they tortured the poor girl who was to have been his victim. She was begging for death, pleading to be kissed. The Queen took bets on how long it would be before Hyacinth broke down. He lasted a whole damn hour." Lavender is almost spitting with fury. "You *knew* what would happen if you refused."

"I knew," I agree quietly.

"Well then!" If we were alone, I realize, she'd stamp her foot.

"Rose," Clarent breaks in, his voice low, "I was used to hurt people, too."

My hand grips his tightly. "That was different," I whisper, blinking back tears. "That wasn't the same, Clarent. I could have refused. Yes, I could have, Lavs," I insist softly, wiping at my eyes. "I could have killed myself, somehow. I didn't; I played along to save my own life."

"I was made to forge swords which others were forced to use on each other," he says softly. "I didn't throw myself into the forge fires. Rose, if self-preservation is a crime, then we're both equally guilty." His cool thumb strokes the back of my hand gently. "Please. I'd like to give you some peace after so much pain." He smiles warmly and adds, "Maybe even a little pleasure."

I snort softly, my emotions ragged. "You want to give me kisses?" I ask, confused by the offer. Hadn't he just heard the monstrous things I've done?

"I was afraid you'd never ask," he breathes and then his lips are touching mine. His flesh is solid and cool, warming and softening at the contact of my own body, turning pliable and firm, like the illusory flesh draped in disguise around him.

I freeze instantly, a thousand concerns charging through my mind. But he doesn't reel away in pain, and Lavender doesn't draw back in shock. Instead his lips move gently against mine, enjoying the touch of me, all the evidence indicating that he is perfectly safe. And then Lavender is bending over us, pressing quick kisses into my forehead, my hair, and along my cheek and I am melting with sudden heat.

I reach up my hands to touch them: a cool face here, a warm neck there; broad shoulders and soft curls. My fingers trail heat across cool skin; my nails draw soft shivers as I trace over her raised veins. Clarent's fingers tighten gently in my hair, pulling me closer into his kiss and sending a thrill of excitement through me.

Above us, a throat is softly cleared. "Ah, I don't mean to interrupt...?"

Lavender jerks away in surprise and I quickly pull back from Clarent, my hands flying up to cover my lips, cheeks burning furiously. Joel's bright blue eyes peer down at us, looking equal turns amused and apologetic. Worse, Elric hasn't stopped existing despite our best effort to ignore him; he sits in his chair openly watching us with the tilted head and pleased smile of a discriminating connoisseur.

Clarent subtly shifts his position on the floor, moving between me and Joel. "Yes?" he asks in a cordial tone.

Joel manages to contain his eagerness long enough to give him an apologetic look. "Sorry," he rasps in his papery voice. "I need to draw another sample from Rose. Kieran used the last of what I drew this morning, and I have to run more tests. There's a magical binding agent to isolate, and several more experiments to run..." His voice trails off in happy anticipation.

I stare at him numbly, one hand flying up to touch the cut that still lingers from when he took the sample this morning. It stings at my touch, and yet I hadn't noticed the pain when Clarent's cool lips had pressed against it. "Okay."

He hunches over me and produces an empty syringe. "Easier than the knife," he mumbles by way of explanation. He runs numbing fingers around the corners of my mouth before puncturing my lip with the sharp needle. He pulls the plunger back but quickly stops, shaking his head with a deep frown. "Too much blood, not enough poison." I look down at the needle and indeed the sample is almost entirely red blood, with hardly any of the milky white fluid.

"Rose, how long did your faery make you rest between sessions?" Worth's cool voice intrudes gently, and I look up to see ner watching us from around the curtain.

"Um, I don't—" I look at Lavender, faced with the impossibility of trying to measure time in the otherworld. "Maybe a week? It was hard to tell over there."

"A week!" Joel looks crestfallen. "Worth, that's only fifty-two harvests a year."

"That's fifty-two more than we had yesterday," Worth points out sensibly. "Did you get anything from the child?"

"Nothing," he says bitterly. "They're almost completely mundane; some basic immunity left boiled into their biology, but not a drop of poison left to experiment with."

Worth regards me carefully. "Well, we can set up a recurring appointment," nee suggests. "She can come in to give samples, and we can measure the rate of regeneration."

Elric's amused voice breaks in. "You two are planning to check more than just her lips, right?" he asks. "Blood? Saliva? Sweat?"

Joel glances at him, confusion clouding his wrinkled face. "She said only her lips were lethal, Elric. If her touch were poisonous, we'd have noticed that."

Elric rolls his eyes at him. "They're both honey-pots like Mina," he observes. "You only have to look at them to want them, and that means seduction-magic." He levels a knowing look at Clarent, unfazed by the sharp glare he receives in return. "And the floral perfume fucks with your head something fierce. Haven't you noticed?"

Joel gives him a long look, measuring and unreadable. "You seem to be universalizing your experiences again," he remarks, sniffing primly. "But the underlying suggestion of multiple loci is sound." His eager blue eyes swivel back to me. "A full examination, then?"

I shake my head at him, drawing back into my cot. "No, I. *No*. The only magic I have is in my lips." I need to believe that. I don't think I can cope with more of my anatomy being damaged and subhuman.

Worth's expression softens and nee steps closer, patting my shoulder with ner warm thin hands. "A private exam, you and I," nee offers softly, ignoring the huffy sigh that is Joel's response. "Nothing invasive," nee promises."A sample from those green veins, a scraping under your nails. Your touch is clearly benign, but possibly not your scratches." Nee gives me a gentle smile. "We won't know until we test, and after that you can rest easy."

Lavender strokes my cheek tenderly, her touch soothing my troubled thoughts. "Rose, are you sure you want to do this? You don't have to." She doesn't bother to whisper this time and there's a hint of challenge in her voice; I sense she's waiting for someone to object so that she can round on them.

I reach up to touch her fingers. "It's okay," I say softly, trying to convince myself, my breathing unsteady. "It's just a few samples. It might save someone's life, Lavs. I can do this."

"No exams for today, though." Celia appears from around the curtain, brushing her dark hair back from her eyes and looking tired. She levels a long look at us. "I've reserved the church community center for tomorrow night. Told them our bingo caller was going into hospital for a minor surgery and we needed to wish her well and have a big hurrah beforehand. We're lucky they didn't have a basketball game scheduled. I can't really enforce mandatory attendance of course, but I want everyone there." She raises her hand before Kieran can get out more than a guttural exclamation from his side of the curtain.

"I know it's short notice," she says curtly. "But this is close to a state of emergency. Something is opening portals to let through dangerous altereds who aren't trying to escape. Tox was on regular patrol, walking the borders to speed up decomposition on anything that had died trying to get in or out. They didn't even know what was happening until suddenly they were earthside. They're certain they walked that patrol dozens of times without any incident, and that this time was no different. And, Kieran, your bear-woman was just as puzzled to be out here."

"Didn't stop her from jumping me," he growls.

She nods easily. "She was confused, yes. Her portal didn't close properly. We'll have to discuss that, too. Somehow the portals are becoming easier to open. That shouldn't be possible."

Worth looks thoughtful. "The emergency meeting is to convey all this to everyone?"

Celia nods. "And to open the floor for ideas, yes," she says. "We've got a few experts besides me and Athena, and I want to get everyone in the same room for a town hall meeting. Until we can sort this out, we're in danger. Confused altereds need to be approached with care; and if they can slip over here without trying, we have to face the real possibility that we might inadvertently be pulled over there."

The room is deathly silent while we each process the terrifying specter of recapture, then Celia claps her hands and changes the mood. "So it's a buddy-system for everyone, and call it in if you see so much as a lick of fog. Joel, you stick with Worth while you show ner your research notes. Clarent, we were going to put you up with Mina anyway, so I'll take you and Lavender over there. Rose, you're staying with Elric for the night—"

"What? No, she's not!" Elric doesn't budge from his chair, but he looks profoundly shocked at the order. Clarent and Lavender don't look much happier; I note with tired amusement that I had not expected the three of them to find rapport on the subject of my sleeping arrangements. "If I have to babysit someone, why not Kieran or metal-man?"

"Because of the three of those, my money is on Rose being the least likely to murder you," Celia says dryly. "Which really does say something about your interpersonal skills, Elric. Kieran, you're crashing with me and Tox tonight."

"You'd better have something decent to eat in your fridge," Kieran grumbles but doesn't argue.

Celia shrugs. "We'll order in. I have high hopes that we can help Tox remember pizza."

Clarent clears his throat then and Celia turns her head to focus on him. "I'd like to stay with Rose," he says firmly, not flinching from her gaze. Beside him, Lavender nods firmly, the air around her hot with spiced pepper and irritation.

Celia's expression softens. "I know you do," she says gently, "both of you. If it helps, I'm pretty sure she wants to stay with you, too." Her eyes flick to me. "But she's got a lot to think about, and she can't do that if she's surrounded by people pressuring her. If you two care about her, you'll give her a few hours to sort out her shit."

Clarent drops his eyes from her gaze at this speech, and even Lavs can't hold out long. "Oh, for fuck's sake," Elric snaps into the silence. "No one cares what *I* want! Rose, I'll be in my damn car."

I give him a wan smile and manage to sit up with Worth's help. Now that the soft haze of the medicine has passed through my system and the warm glow of Clarent's and Lavender's kisses has faded away, I can feel the old depression washing over me.

They both need space from me. Clarent will meet Mina soon, and he'll spend the night with Lavender. They'll see that they don't need me. They can get everything they could ever need from each other. Clarent shouldn't be with me just because I'm the first girl he kissed out here, and Lavender shouldn't be with me merely because I'm her friend. They'll be happier and better off without me. And I will do the right thing by giving them up, letting them be together, so that I can live a life of chaste healing.

134

Maybe then the nightmares might stop.

"I'll be fine," I reassure them softly. "You two have a good night, okay? I'll get some rest and I'll see you in the morning, I promise." I squeeze Lavender's hand gently, wishing I could do more. I lean forward and kiss Clarent's forehead, regretting that I can't be with them both tonight. With a smile that's warm and carefree and perfectly faked, I allow Celia to help me out of the room and down to the car.

CHAPTER 15

Elric's duplex is as sumptuously posed as he is. Though the enormous effort and expense that has gone into staging his bachelor pad is obvious at a glance, the effect is undiminished: both the man and his home are meticulously gorgeous. The downstairs is open and clean, sparse but not spartan. The carpet has been pulled up and replaced with dark hardwood laminate that is far too expensive for the neighborhood, then decorated in thick shag rugs that look recently dry-cleaned. A black leather couch dominates the main room, facing a sleek entertainment system. Surround-sound speakers that are probably quite expensive peer down at visitors from the corners of the ceiling.

I know I'm supposed to be impressed, even seduced, by the setting but the place feels cold and antiseptic in comparison to the warmth of Mina's apartment. I wish I were there now with Lavender and Clarent, calling dibs on the colorful pillows that decorate her couch and settling in to watch one of her favorite movies. I know I made the right decision in letting them go, just as Celia made the right decision in pushing them together, but that doesn't mean I don't get to be miserable now that it's done.

The company I'm keeping is not helping to alleviate my mood. Elric pushes past me at the doorway, still in a furious sulk, and tromps heavily up to the second floor. His stomping is muffled by the thick carpet on the stairs. "Stay there," he orders, not bothering to glance over his shoulder at me. I scowl at his retreating back and head to the kitchen, determined to find something to scavenge. He hasn't exactly begged that I make myself at home, but I'm not going to bed on an empty stomach.

The kitchen looks out onto the living room via an open counter-top that doubles as a bar. The cooking equipment, such as it is, is noticeably sparse compared to the expensive gadgetry in the living room. Evidently Elric is not in the habit of cooking. Both the fridge and the pantry confirm that impression; save for a handful of sodas, potato chips, and dry cereal, the apartment is apparently devoid of food.

I make a face and dig through the available options. There's a ginger ale brand that I'm partial to, and he has the Kettle chips I like, the ones that feel so familiar on my tongue. I'd rather have a solid meal to settle my stomach, especially after sleeping through lunch, but I've been hungry before. I'll survive.

I'm sitting on the couch with my gleanings, working the sandals off my feet and staring at the blank television screen, when Elric stomps back down the stairs. He's found a cotton shirt to cover his bare chest, which seems strange given that he spent the entire day in ostentatious display at Worth's house. He carries a pillow under one arm, and a blanket tossed over his shoulder.

"You're sleeping on the couch down here," he announces, then does a double-take at the chips in my hands. "What, you raided my kitchen?"

"I haven't eaten all day," I point out, trying to sound reasonable; I don't mention the donut holes, which weren't very filling anyway. I choose not to remind him that I'm no happier about my being here than he is. "I could cook something, if you prefer," I suggest dryly. "Do you have anything that *can* be cooked?"

He curls his lip at me in an expression of personal offense. "No. When one of my lovers wants to cook for me, they bring their own ingredients. How would they know what I have on hand?"

I stare at him. "You're kidding me. What were you going to eat tonight?

You can't live on dry cereal and chips! Elric, there's not even any milk!"

He rolls his eyes at me, and tosses the pillow and blanket onto the couch. "Tonight I was going out on a date, same as almost every night. I eat very well, when I'm not having to cancel because I have a wilting flower crashing on my couch who'd rather be orgying it up with her roommate."

I wince at his pointed remark and munch deliberately on another chip, considering silence and destructive gluttony my best options for revenge at the moment.

With a frustrated sigh at my lack of response, he throws himself onto the couch. For all his flirting earlier, he's sitting as far away from me as the furniture will allow. The bedding he's brought downstairs squats between us like a protective barrier. "Gimme a chip," he demands, sounding resigned to his dinnerless fate.

I shake my head in exasperation, but pass over a single chip as requested, my fingers brushing against his in the exchange. "We could order food," I point out. "Pizza, Chinese, maybe sandwiches? There must be places around here that deliver."

He gives me a sidelong glance, looking a touch mollified. "Mmph. That's not a bad idea. I have a phone book in the kitchen with delivery places circled," he admits grudgingly.

I give him a wry look. "I thought you ate out on expensive dates every night."

Elric shakes his head and holds out his hand in demand for another chip. "Delivery is for nights when we're too occupied to leave the apartment. Jeezus, Rose, don't you know anything?" He peers at me with grudging curiosity. "Have you and Lavender really not been getting it on since you got out?"

I can feel the instant burn in my cheeks. "None of your business," I mutter, slapping another chip hard into his palm.

He turns his head to me then, and I'm surprised to see his expression soften. I'd expected a teasing retort but instead he gives me a tolerant smile, something approaching sympathy in his eyes. "I forget you're not like me," he says. It's not an apology, but it comes close.

I blink and look away, staring at the bag of chips in my lap. It's easier when Elric is a brat, I realize, because then we can forget everything he does for us. Even if he likes his work, he's still at it more hours a week than I ever am. Although I suppose that might change soon, if I stick to my plan of becoming a pharmaceutical factory, as Lavender put it. If that happens, will I envy Elric his sumptuous dinners while I'm being drained of bodily fluids for Worth and Joel?

"Hey," he says quietly, reaching over to snatch another chip from my fingers. "C'mon, don't sulk. That's my job."

"I-Is it difficult?" I blurt out, my voice catching with embarrassment. "All those dates, all those people, and so many of them normal humans who don't understand."

He raises an eyebrow at this, looking a touch puzzled. "What, the mundies?"

"You get us identification, and used cars, and cellphones and computers. You find places for us to live and— and— and just everything." I look up at him, feeling guilty; his sandy-brown eyebrow is raised in amusement now, the puzzlement gone. "None of the stuff you get for us is free, is it?" I reach out without thinking, wanting to give him reassurance or an acknowledgement or perhaps both, my fingers closing around his cool hand.

He smirks and leans forward, closing the distance between us. With his free hand he wraps a strand of my pink hair around his index finger, tugging in a teasing manner. I nearly jerk back from his closeness, instinct telling me to draw my lethal face away from him, but it's just Elric being Elric and I don't want to give him the satisfaction of a reaction. He's flirty and provocative, but not foolish or suicidal.

"My friends do favors for me, Rose," he murmurs, his voice a throaty whisper. "And I do favors for my friends. You seem to think I don't enjoy their friendship."

"Just friends having fun? I'm sorry I misunderstood." I manage to keep my voice casual and bored, but the nearness of him is causing my heart to pound with fear and desire, each sharply intertwined.

I don't want Elric, not really; but Clarent and Lavender aren't here and I've lived such a long time alone—long enough to make even a bratty vampire desirable. He's beautiful and he's confident and I know he would never deliberately hurt me, not when he had been so worried for me earlier. Despite his constant stream of lovers, I think he understands loneliness.

We could make love without kissing, if we were careful. Would that be nice? A fling without any strings attached, just pleasure and a fond parting afterwards? Yet I wouldn't be able to relax, not with the constant fear that my lips might touch him. I know he's not going to do anything stupid, when Joel said less than an hour ago how lethal I would be to him, yet even still his hovering proximity and the arousal in his eyes summon bad memories.

He leans in closer, his breath sweet on my face. His eyes are full of teasing laughter. "Don't you like to do favors for your friends, Rose?" he presses softly, his eyes eating me up with seductive hunger. "Aren't I one of your friends?"

I shiver at how close he is to me, how much trust he's placing in me. If I wished, I could lean forward and kill him in an instant. I don't want this kind of power, and the memories pushing to the surface now far outweigh the pleasant rush of heat. I reach up to push his hand away from my face, but he catches my fingers and twines his into mine.

"Elric," I say firmly, my voice not as stern as I'd hoped, "you already know I like you, and you also know I can't."

"What, because of the dynamic duo?" He chuckles warmly, beautiful and incorrigible. "Don't you know they both just want you to be happy? You should have heard them while you were passed out, nattering on all afternoon like old friends. Rose, you're so deliciously innocent not to realize these things." He leans forward into me, his lips gently parted.

Clarent had taken me by surprise because I'd not been expecting his kiss. Elric, in contrast, has been telegraphing his arousal for a full minute and a half. This time my mind doesn't need to catch up; my body reacts perfectly well on its own. My hand flies up to cover my mouth, smacking him in the face in the rush to squeeze between our bodies; at the same time I lunge backwards, scrambling over the edge of the couch and landing hard on the floor.

"Elric, what are you doing?" I demand, the sharp fear and anger in my voice partially muffled by the hand I've clamped over my mouth.

He doesn't try to pursue me, staying perched on the couch, amused at my reaction. "I was trying to kiss you, Rose," he says with a shrug equal parts apologetic and defensive. "I want to kiss you. I thought you wanted to kiss me." His apologetic eyes slip back into the hint of a smolder. "Do you want me to talk you into it? We have all night, and I can be as convincing as you want me to be, sweetheart."

I stare at him in shock. He can't possibly be serious, but he's carrying this game way too far. "Of course I don't want you to kiss me, Elric! *You* don't want to kiss me!"

"I don't want to kiss you?" he repeats, looking thoroughly amused by the idea. "Why on earth would you think I don't—"

He pauses, a noticeable hesitation in his voice, and his seductive smirk morphs into a confused frown. "No, I don't want to kiss you," he says slowly. "That would be incredibly stupid. Rose, why the hell did I try to kiss you?"

Of all the implausible events that have occurred today, this is the moment that is most causing me to doubt my senses. Elric is brash and arrogant and sexualized from head to toe, but he can read people like a book. He is endlessly infuriating, throwing my desires in my face, but he's good at being annoying precisely *because* he knows what people want. For him to misread me so badly, to pick up only my arousal and not my fear, is wildly out of character. The fact that he's misread himself as well sends the entire night into the realm of the surreal.

141

"You don't want to kiss me," I repeat very slowly, enunciating each word carefully, "because my kiss would kill you." I feel like a broken record but apparently this needs repeating.

"That, too," he agrees, sounding a little dazed. He peers at me as if I'm a riddle he can't solve. "There's a good half-dozen reasons why I don't want to kiss you, Rose; so why I have wanted you since I came downstairs? You're no closer to me than you were in the car on the drive over. Oh, dammit, Rose!"

He leaps to his feet in a fluid blur of graceful motion. I tense in readiness to scramble away from him, but he's not trying to approach me; he paces the living room until there are several steps between us. Then his eyes clench shut in irritation and he pinches the bridge of his nose. "Rose. At what point were you going to tell us that those green fingers of yours cause arousal?"

I blink up at him, then stare at my hands. My fingertips are the same vibrant green as always, the color tapering down to the brown skin of my knuckles. My nails, strong and sharp as thorns, are stained deeper green. "I-I didn't know," I stammer, feeling my stomach twist into knots. Then I rally slightly. "I don't think they do! My hands are just decoration, like our hair colors and the green eyes. Lavender's hands are the same; you've seen them!"

He glares at me. "Oh, yes; clearly the pretty little flower who has emotion-altering perfume-magic couldn't *also* have seductive fingers! How silly of me not to realize." He shakes his head in exasperation. "Rose, I think I know desire better than any of us, and I sure as hell know my own! I didn't want you until after you touched my hand, and then I wanted you badly enough to forget how deadly you are. That's epic levels of stupid." He shoots a look at the bag of kettle chips lying on the sofa, now badly crushed. "Jeezus, and you were touching the food, too. Who knows how it's transferred? Rose, who have you touched since you escaped?"

My thoughts are colliding at high speed, my breath short and ragged. If he's right, then every man who ever kissed me, even the few I tried to warn, must have felt the pull of my magic. They're still just as dead as before, but the idea that I'm even more culpable than I'd thought is horrifying. I shudder, wracked with fresh waves of guilt.

"Rose!" Elric's sharp voice cuts through my thoughts. "Who else have you touched? Concentrate. This is important. You can fall apart later."

I stare numbly up at him. My chest feels tight, every breath hurting my ribs. "Um. Lavender, Celia, Mina, Athena. Never Jing, she doesn't like to be touched. Almost everyone at the gatherings; there was a lot of handshaking. Worth and Joel. Kieran! Oh, Clarent!"

Elric snorts. "Well, at least he already wanted you, from the look of it."

"But he— he kissed me after I touched him and now he—"

"Rose." He rolls his eyes at me. "He was celibate over there for god knows how long, and you're ridiculously pretty. We don't need to haul in boner-magic to explain that just yet. Now shut up for a minute and let me think." He throws himself against the nearest wall, tucking his foot up behind him and crossing his arms over his chest. A minute ticks by and then another, while I struggle to force my breathing into an even pattern.

"Mina wouldn't even notice," he eventually says, his exasperated voice turning thoughtful. "That girl is on all the time for almost everyone. Celia and Athena I've known for years and never seen them hook up with anyone. Joel and Worth both prefer men, though Worth doesn't jump at the chance much and Joel can't, on account of his touch draining people. Can't really say one way or the other with Lavender; you're both eye-fucking each other all the time, but you say you're living like two chaste little nuns, so either you're immune to each other's magic or it's not compulsive."

I stare at him. "You think I'm attracted to Lavs," I say, rounding the words slowly, "just because of her *fingers*." The words feel absurd in my mouth. I'm attracted to Lavender because she's brave and good, and full of bright hope and fierce protectiveness. She trusted me, confided in me, in the May Queen's manor when I was one of the scary Nightshades and she just another lowly Fragrant instructed to braid my hair.

She'd touched me then, I realize, and I liked her—yet it hadn't been like Elric's description. I've never forgotten myself around her, never tried to kiss her. Though I suppose I've been very careful not to allow the situation to arise. We live together, yes, but how many times have I listened to her crying through the shared wall between our bedrooms and chosen not to comfort her for fear that I might hurt her instead?

Elric is watching me closely, his expression unreadable. "Even if it's true," I argue defensively, "I'd have loved her anyway. She's worth loving; it doesn't matter if there's magic behind it or not. And that's *if* it's true. You're the only one who's felt anything."

"Kieran felt it," he says slowly, his voice low and even. "He was definitely thinking about it. At the time I thought he was just impressed by the healing and maybe a little giddy from the speed of it. But I noticed, and that wasn't like him." He smirks at me. "I won't say you're not his type, little flower, but on any other day you'd have to contend with me being in the room."

I stare at him. "*You?*" I'm not shocked to hear that Kieran likes boys as well as girls, but more than a little stunned at the mental image of him with Elric in spite of their bickering. "And you really think he wanted me more?"

"Mmm." The sound is a blend of irritation and lingering arousal. "He definitely wanted you and didn't look too thrilled about it; so it's powerful enough to be noticeable, but not overpowering." His expression turns thoughtful. "Easier to deny, maybe, in a hospital bed with your on-again off-again lover watching you than, say, in a living room on a come-hither fuck-me couch."

Despite the gravity of the situation, I have to resist the urge to roll my eyes at his description of the furniture. "Well, you're resisting me now," I point out, hoping this remains the case.

He runs a hand over his eyes, looking suddenly very tired. "I am. It's not pleasant. If I had my druthers I'd call Celia, trade you in for Kieran and fuck him silly, but she's got the orphan to deal with."

"I could just go home," I point out, hoping he'll agree. A mist portal in my bedroom would be preferable to this entire conversation.

"Celia'd have my teeth," he mutters darkly. "And as much as you're a real kick in the dick right now, Rose, I don't want you dead. I'm going upstairs to get some sleep. You stay down here. Got it?"

"Elric, I'm not going to—"

"I mean it, Rose! I don't care if the place is on fucking fire, you don't come up those stairs."

"I won't," I say, raising my hands in surrender. "I promise."

He doesn't look entirely satisfied, but nods and stomps up the stairs.

"Don't you want any more food?" I call up to him.

"No."

"Can I at least borrow some nightclothes?" I add, dreading the prospect of trying to sleep in my skirt.

"Go to sleep, Rose," he snaps curtly. There's the slam of a door above me and then silence.

I pick myself up off the floor and realize I'm shaking. Perching on the edge of the couch, the back of the stairwell behind me, I feel belated tears running down my cheeks. He'd been so close. He'd nearly died. I'm angry with him for trying to kiss me, and I'm angry with myself for not stopping him sooner. Most of all, I'm angry with the May Queen for doing this to me.

If Elric is right, my fingers have magic. I don't know what to do with this fact. The faces of dead men swim before my eyes, my culpability for their deaths greater than I knew. They're joined by the living, everyone I've touched since coming over earthside. Have I been infecting them with desire all this time?

Athena never mentioned it and she surely would have; tact is not counted among her virtues. Celia, too, would have warned me; she is the soul of discretion about my past, but she's not careless. Kieran desired me but he didn't do more than look. Mina has always wanted to kiss me and has offered to do so many times, but she's never forgotten what that might do to her. Did Elric forget tonight because of something I did, or is this level of attraction unique to him? I've never asked him about his time in the otherworld, being a vampire; maybe I should have.

If my fingers cause desire, what should I do? Wear gloves, maybe? But if it can pass into food or water, what then? Joel and Worth can test me; maybe Clarent can undo all my alteration, not just my poison. I'd have to give up any thoughts of healing others, any chance for redemption, but at least I wouldn't be causing more harm.

How can I look him and Lavender in the eye tomorrow and tell them they only care about me because of fae magic?

There's a noise on the stairs behind me. I turn quickly, still on edge, only to be hit in the face with a pile of thrown clothes wadded together in a bundle. "What the—?"

"Sleep well, Rose."

Elric's voice is punctuated by a slammed door. I'm alone again, wrestling with what turns out to be a baggy cotton shirt, knit terrycloth shorts that tie at the waist, and a pair of thick men's socks, balled up and tucked into the pockets of the shorts.

I stroke my fingers over the clothes for a long moment, relishing the comfortable feel of their well-worn softness. *Even when he's being nice, he still pretends to be a jerk.* I brush my tears away and head to the hall bathroom to change. I don't know if I'll be able to sleep tonight, but this is a good start.

CHAPTER 16

I wake from a dream of Lavender and Clarent and kissing and no death whatsoever. I swim reluctantly towards watery dawn light, wishing I could stay in the dream world a little longer. When I open my eyes, I'm disoriented to find myself on a leather couch in a living room I don't recognize, but then the events of the previous evening slam into place.

I hurriedly scan the room, dreading the sight of Elric's lifeless body on the floor. What if he'd kissed me while I was asleep? But the living room is empty and I am alone. My cellphone lies nearby on the pillow, vibrating noisily as texts pile in. I pull up my messages to see that I've missed three texts from Celia—no, make that four, with more coming in.

Rose, let me know when you get this. Drop by your place to shower and change if you need, then meet me at Dakota's. No need to call Athena; I'll talk to her.

I want Clarent and Lavender there, too. Let me know if you're willing to swing by Mina's to pick them up, or if you need me to. It's your choice.

Rose, Elric isn't picking up his phone and I'm not in the mood for his shit this morning. Tell him to roll out of bed and call me.

Tell him I need paperwork for three new members. Don't let him beg off; he's had plenty time off since doing you and Lavs.

Prioritize Tox and Clarent. I want drafts for both today. The bear-woman is still laid up from yesterday and won't or can't talk yet. Joel is with her.

Lily is here and swears Tox's accent is Iraqi-American. Need full adoption workup. List Dakota as parent. Check with me if it turns out the paperwork is gendered.

And Rose, if you killed him, tell me sooner rather than later. I'll be in a better mood if you're honest. If I have to come over to find out, I'll be annoyed.

I blink at the last text, but nothing follows it. I'm reasonably certain I've never seen Celia annoyed, and I'd like to keep it that way. I sweep my fingers over the screen in a quick response.

I'm awake. As far as I know, Elric is alive. I'll wake him up and then head out. I don't mind going to Mina's. Be there soon.

I sit up on the couch, stretching experimentally. Despite my run-in with Tox yesterday, I don't feel too sore. My throat is a little scratchy but I'll survive. I hop up and make my way to the bottom of the stairs, peering up as I consider my options. Elric had said I wasn't to come upstairs under any circumstances, so shouting seems the best way to go.

"Elric!" My voice seems far too loud in the early morning silence, and I belatedly hope his neighbors are already awake. "Celia says to answer your phone. Elric?" There's not a breath of movement from up there, or none that I can hear. "Elric, if you don't answer me, I'm coming up to check on you!"

His sleep-muffled response filters through the closed bedroom door. "Dammit, Rose, you'd better not! Tell Celia you have succeeded in getting me both up and awake. Now leave me alone!"

"All right. Fine! But she wants to talk to you," I holler back. "She needs paperwork for three. She said she wants to see drafts for Tox and Clarent today. Dakota is adopting them. The little one, I mean, not Clarent."

"Yeah, yeah," he calls back, sounding bored. "Undocumented kids are a bigger risk than grown men. I'm not a fucking *amateur*, Rose. Wait, what?" There's the sound of muffled thumping and his bedroom door flies open. Elric storms out to the landing, looking down at me with exhausted irritation in his face; there isn't a stitch of clothing on him.

"Elric!" I turn my face away but I've already had an eyeful.

He ignores my reaction. "Rose, I can't work up two people in one day, that's entirely unreasonable!"

I shrug helplessly, shielding my eyes with one hand. "She said you've had plenty of time off since you did mine and Lav's."

"Oh, sure," he snaps angrily. "That *might* be relevant if I could prepare birth certificates and licenses in advance, but I *can't*. Celia should know that! She's just getting back at me for calling the kid an orphan to their face."

"She said just drafts today, Elric," I protest weakly. Quickly, I snatch up my shoes, my purse, and my bundle of clothes, deciding to change at home and give back Elric's clothes later. "Nothing finalized. I don't think she's expecting miracles. You should call her! I have to meet her at Dakota's, so I'm going to get moving. I'll see you later!" Hastily, I close the door behind me as he lets out a string of profanity that I'm sure he wouldn't say to Celia's face.

I lean against the duplex door, deeply inhaling the clean morning air, and try to concentrate on looking like a normal adult human and not an emotional mess. I'm not sure how well I succeed, but none of the residents of his complex give me a second glance as they head to their cars. I suppose a sleep-disheveled girl leaving Elric's place with her clothes tucked under her arm is not an unusual occurrence around here. I clutch my purse and clothes a little tighter and head to my car, still parked where Tox came out yesterday.

The drive to my own apartment is blessedly uneventful. Despite Celia saying it wasn't necessary, I decide to leave a message with Athena. I don't have to square my absence with her as she's not really my employer; the bookstore is in Celia's name, since Athena refused to have a legal identity. But she's my friend and I don't want her to think I'm ill or angry, so I leave a voicemail explaining the situation. While I have my phone out, I also jot off a text to Mina letting her know I'm coming, and then I whip through a quick shower.

Celia hasn't said what she wants me for, but I figure a sun-dress in summer can't go wrong. I pull on a cream-colored chiffon dress that stops just above the knees, has a wrist-length sleeve on one side and a bare shoulder on the other to show off my rose tattoo. I push away any thoughts as to why I'm dressing up this morning, managing to keep introspection at bay until I get down to the car. Then the anxiety kicks in.

What will I say when I get to Mina's apartment? Lavender is my best friend and my roommate, Clarent quite literally saved my life, and yesterday the three of us kissed. A simple greeting after all that doesn't seem right, but at the same time I don't want to belabor the point. I need to convey that I'm happy for them to be together, that I'm not upset, and I'm still their friend. I've made my choice and am at peace with being alone.

But that's a lie. I'm not at peace, and I'm not sure I've made my choice. Memories of the previous night with Elric come rushing back, along with the reality I've put off thinking about: I'm not merely poisonous but also a lure. How can I tell Clarent he only likes me because of my touch? If it's true, does that mean he only likes Lavender for *her* touch? Do she and I only like each other because of fae magic? I can't accept that. Lavender is worth loving, and the affection I feel for her could never have come from the May Queen.

So where does that leave me? Either Elric is wrong, or there's something I still don't know about my own body.

150

I pull up to Mina's complex to see that she and Lavender and Clarent are already outside. Her ground-floor apartment has a tiny gated patio with a small glass-topped table; she's made breakfast, and the three of them are soaking up the brief window of cool morning air before the sun gets too high. The sight of them takes my breath away for a moment; they look like something out of a magazine, all three bright and beautiful in the dawn light.

Lavender is her usual casual self, and Celia must have taken them by our apartment so that she could fetch her clothes. Ripped jeans, a gray ribbed shirt with dark purple sleeves, and brown leather ankle boots complement the lavender curls that cascade over her shoulders. Clarent, in contrast, has been coaxed out of his plaid work-clothes from yesterday so that Mina can dress him in a dark sports coat and a crisp white dress-shirt. His shirt opens at the base of the neck, providing a glimpse of bright silver and warm brown, and my stomach turns to jelly at his new confident poise.

Mina, our beautiful seductress, is her usual stunning self, dripping with sex appeal from head to toe. Her dark eyes are dusted with smoky eyeliner, her full lips are a warm dark pink and her fawn-colored skin glows in the morning light. The dusk-rose dress she's wearing is sheer lace over the stomach and above her cleavage, showing tantalizing hints of soft ample flesh framed by glossy black hair. She's big and beautiful and completely desirable; she was surely attractive before she was taken to the otherworld, but now she is nothing short of divine.

As I park the car, I realize they haven't seen me yet. Mina is laughing and telling one of her stories in between bites of naan bread spread with butter and jam. Lavender is curled up in her chair nursing a cup of more cream than coffee, if I know her. Clarent is enjoying Mina's idli, the little steamed rice cakes I used to help her make from a packaged mix. I watch them eat and talk, my heart twisting at how happy they look without me. I'm about to walk up and ruin that.

Damn! I should have let Celia come on her own.

I take a deep breath and step out of the car, pasting a smile on my face. Their heads swivel at the sound of my car door. Mina's face lights up in a grin, always happy to see me, and I'm more gratified than I should be to see similarly bright smiles bloom on the faces of Clarent and Lavender. Before I can reach them Clarent rises from his seat, places his broad hands on the low patio railing and vaults easily over to join me.

"Rose!" His deep honeyed voice is full of happy relief, like he can't quite believe it's me. He wraps his hands around my waist and lifts me in a playful spin, which ends as he lowers me against him into a cool kiss no less passionate for its metallic temperature. Behind him I can hear Mina and Lavender giggling.

"H-Hello!" I manage breathlessly when the kiss breaks. He's staring down at me, glittering brightly in the sunlight, almost painful to look at. Lavender leans over the patio fence, chuckling and shaking her head.

"Don't *I* get a hug?" she teases, grinning brightly.

I swallow hard, wishing my heart weren't beating quite so loudly. "Well, come and get it," I offer, trying to sound casual. She laughs again and leans over to kiss Mina before disappearing inside, having decided not to copy Clarent's vault.

He grins at this but his expression quickly turns sheepish. "Sorry," he murmurs, leaning forward to touch his forehead to mine. "I know I said I'd ask before kissing. I was just so excited to see you."

"I'm glad to see you, too," I hasten to reassure him, feeling myself mellow under his unflappable cheer. "How are you? Are you adjusting well?" My eyes travel over him, taking in his warm, untroubled smile and the easy way he wears his new clothes. "You look amazing," I admit, a warm blush spreading through my cheeks.

An answering dark flush creeps into his own under my gaze. "Thanks." He rubs shyly at the back of his neck. "I felt more normal in the clothes Celia gave me, but Mina said it was important to try lots of different things to see what feels familiar." His smile broadens. "I'm glad you like them. I'm glad you're here! Mina said you were coming, and that we're all going to see Celia? I was afraid—"

The front door bursts open and Lavender springs out with her light step. She must have slept last night, I conclude; she seems much more her normal self now that she isn't suffering from sleep deprivation and adrenaline-soaked worry. The scents of sweet honeysuckle and lavender fill the air around her, hope and happiness trailing on the breeze. "Here I am!" she announces, bounding up to wrap me in a tight hug.

My hands come up automatically and I almost bury my face unthinkingly in her neck. Just in time I remember to jerk my head to the side, preventing my lips from touching her skin. I don't want to cry; I promised myself I wouldn't make a scene, but I can feel the tears well up in my eyes. She's soft and she's warm, and all I want is for Clarent to make me human again. If he changed me I could hold her without fear, I could cover her in kisses and be happy.

Her fingers clutch at my bare shoulder and the smell of her invades my lungs. I want her right now, and the need is so much stronger than any magic. I care about her, yes, and about Clarent, but more than that I *need* to touch someone and to be touched in return. I must have been with people before I was taken, but for what feels like years I've had no real human contact.

Now here I am, being hugged by Lavender and freshly kissed by Clarent. I can choose a life of selfish pleasure with the people I love most, or I can grit my teeth and do something useful to try to make up for all the pain I've caused.

"Here you are," I agree softly, gently letting go of Lavender and taking a step back. I give her a wan smile, trying to act as usual. "I was, uh, telling Clarent how much I like his new clothes."

"Isn't he pretty?" she asks with a wry grin, giving him a shameless once-over. "Mina dressed him up. I'm not any help with fashion, but I know what I like."

His blush doesn't retreat but he looks more at ease now. "I was

153

informed," he says solemnly, "that next on the agenda would be a suit and tie; possibly even a tuxedo." His lips quirk at the edges in a smile that he is trying not to show. "Shall I be pretty then, do you think?"

I bite back my own grin. "You look uncommonly pretty no matter what you wear," I admit, giving up the fight for the moment. "Yes, we're supposed to go see Celia, but let me talk to Mina for a minute?"

He blinks at the echo from yesterday's banter and breaks into a wide smile. "But am I uncommonly pretty when I'm not wearing anything at all?" he teases, his voice a warm purr in the summer air. Before I can respond, he kisses my forehead. "I'll wait in the car," he announces cheerily. "Lavs says we have to see if I know how to work the air-conditioning before she'll consider trusting me to drive."

I stare after him, blinking in surprise. Lavender smirks at me, smelling of fond marigolds; Mina watches us both, her hazel eyes full of laughter beneath her smoky eyeshadow. "You didn't waste any time teaching him how to talk sexy," I observe, clearing my throat and giving Mina a look.

"I didn't do anything!" she protests with a warm laugh. "He's a terrible tease once he gets past his shyness; you'll see. And it's so unfair, Rose, watching you two kiss and not being able to have any of it."

"It is," Lavender agrees in a low murmur, her lips twitching.

I swallow hard. "You both had him last night, surely," I insist weakly. "Isn't that enough?"

Mina and Lavender exchange an odd look, then Mina laughs and shakes her head. Taking another dainty bite of her breakfast, she delicately wipes away a dot of dark raspberry jam from the corner of her mouth. "No, dear," she says cheerfully between mouthfuls, "I haven't had a single kiss from him. It's so vexing."

I glance back at the car where Clarent sits quietly, intently studying the knobs on the dashboard. "He didn't—?" I look to Lavender for help; if she was willing to share Clarent with me, surely she would have leaped at the chance to do so with Mina.

Mina grins and takes a sip of her coffee. "Rose, darling, you must know that not everyone falls for me." She winks at us. "Not that I wouldn't love to try with either or both of you."

Lavender's own cheeks are coloring now, a faint pink under her pallor. "I think I'll go wait in the car with Clarent," she says, beating a fast retreat. I stare after her in some confusion.

"Naan?" Mina offers mildly. She holds out a piece to me and I take it automatically, biting numbly into the soft sweetness.

"So, uh, did they—?" I attempt to ask, nodding towards the car. I know I shouldn't ask; it's none of my business. I'm happy for them, though I wish I could be included too.

Mina gives me a fond look and takes pity on me. "No, dear," she says gently, leaning forward over the railing. She hands me Lavender's cup of coffee to wash down the bread. "We watched movies. He asked a lot of questions about living earthside. We dressed him up in some of the clothes I keep for the newbies. We talked about you an awful lot. They fell asleep on the couch midway through the third movie. I drew a blanket over them and went to bed." Her eyes gaze softly at me. "They missed you."

Tears spring to my eyes, accompanying a thick lump in my throat that the coffee can't wash down. "He's fresh out," I stammer quietly. "She's lonely. They don't need *me*. He barely knows me!"

She gives me a dry look, her lips twisted in that teasing way of hers. "Rose, she's lived with you for three months and you helped her escape, so I think she's allowed a crush on you. And why shouldn't he like you? You're pretty and sweet and you saved each other's lives. He isn't trying to marry you, darling; he just wants some kisses." She gives me a long look over her cup of tea. "As do I, for the record," she teases. "Are you going to argue with me too?"

"I should," I mutter. "I'm supposed to be arguing with them. Everything keeps being so complicated."

Mina nods in sympathy. "It's hard sometimes," she says gently, "deciding how to live your life, when all you remember is being a captive. You didn't have any choice for a long time and now you have too many choices, with no easy way to narrow down what's realistic and healthy and wise." She shakes her head sadly, her silken hair slipping over her shoulders.

"I've made my choice, though," I insist, though the words feel less firm in my mouth than they had in my mind. "Did they tell you? Clarent could cure me, but if I stay poisonous Joel can use my venom to heal people."

She smiles at me, her eyes still sad. "That's a noble choice, Rose," she says quietly. "No one should tell you that you shouldn't do that, if it's what you want." She reaches out very gently to touch my cheek. "But if you go that route, you should do it because it makes you happy and not because of what your faery forced you to do."

"I'm still responsible, though," I whisper, leaning into her fingertips. I'm almost in tears from the sweet relief of being touched by another person and the sharp longing for more.

She's quiet for a moment. "Maybe I'm wrong," she admits. "But, Rose, we've learned the hard way how fragile life can be. My advice is to live your life as fully as you can." She smiles, mischief dancing in her eyes. "And, Rose, there's nothing to say you can't be Joel's petri dish for a few months and then human afterwards. You can do both; it doesn't have to be a permanent sacrifice."

Silently I stand there, basking in the warm morning sunlight and her soft touch. "I'll think about it, Mina."

She chuckles at my reluctance. "You do that, Rose. You deserve to have fun." Her grin widens. "I'm just sorry I couldn't break him in for you!"

My cheeks erupt in a bright burn. "I'll, ah, pass the offer along if you like."

Mina grins. "It's fine," she says, waving her hand airily. "Celia sent a text earlier saying that Kieran could use someone to vent to and that Elric wasn't picking up. I might give him a call." She winks at me. "But, um, Rose?"

I'm already moving back towards the car, not wanting to keep Clarent and Lavender waiting any longer. The tentative note in Mina's voice checks my step and I look back. "Yes?"

She fiddles uncertainly with her teacup. "Well, darling, you're not very— and he's— well—"

I frown, thoroughly puzzled; I've never seen her shy away from any topic. "Mina?"

She fidgets a moment longer before looking up at me with tender concern. "Rose, it's just I was thinking that, if you wanted to practice first, I have a metal dildo around here somewhere that you could borrow."

My eyebrows rise so rapidly I'm not sure they haven't ascended to a higher plane. "Mina! *No.* No, thank you, but no." I dart back to the car, mumbling incoherent farewells over my shoulder, ignoring the intrigued looks from Clarent and Lavender at the sight of my flushed face.

CHAPTER 17

"Rose, did Celia say why she wanted to see us?"

We've tacitly decided not to discuss my conversation with Mina, which suits me fine. Clarent has finished fiddling with the air-conditioning knobs, declaring that he remembers cars perfectly well. I'm a touch skeptical of his confidence, as he needed quite a bit of guidance from Lavender. I make a mental note to offer him driving lessons after we're done at Dakota's.

I shake my head at Lavender, glancing up at the rearview mirror to make eye contact with her. "No, she didn't say why, not exactly. But Tox is supposed to be there; Dakota has offered to adopt them. Celia told Elric that she wanted identities drafted for Tox and Clarent today, so my guess is we'll be doing paperwork together."

Lavender nods at this and makes a good effort at looking game for anything, but I can already smell musty geraniums and spicy clover, mingled apathy and anxiety filling the backseat of the car. Our own paperwork experiences do not bode well for today's activities: long boring stretches of watching Elric work, punctuated by short bursts of frustration and tears when memories refused to come.

I glance over at Clarent, who is looking out the window with his unreadable silver eyes. "Did Mina explain that we'll be making up an identity for you?"

He nods, looking back to me with a solemn expression. "Yes. I need papers out here among the normal humans; licenses and birth certificates, she said, and work and credit history. Names of places I'm supposed to have lived, and of people I've known." He looks a little overwhelmed at the thought. "She made some suggestions, but nothing sounded familiar."

"Sometimes memories come back slowly," I say gently. "That's why we try different things: clothing, food, books. You're not alone; we'll help you. Everyone will. You've met Athena already, but there are others. Celia will want Lily to see you; she's been out of town and we haven't met her yet either, but she's supposed to be a whiz with accents and languages. She's placed a lot of people's hometowns."

"And even if you never remember, that's perfectly okay," Lavender assures him, reaching up to touch his shoulder. "We've been out for three months now and still don't remember who we were. It isn't too bad, you know? More like a fresh chance to be whoever we want, without any baggage."

He nods, looking thoughtful. "That makes sense. I guess I can't go back to my former life anyway, even if I remember it; could I?" He looks down at his metal body, examining the sleek silver of his arms. I wonder if a normal human would feel the unnatural smoothness under his disguise of skin, that slippery satin texture where hair should be.

"No," I agree softly, keeping my voice as gentle as I can. "Most of us can't. Celia says some of us have tried in the past, but it rarely goes well. We have to explain to families and friends why we were absent for months or years, with no answers anyone would believe. And if the authorities become involved, things can get complicated and even dangerous."

Clarent looks up to give us a rueful smile. "I guess if you can't see the silver, it's hard to swallow that I'm a fairytale sword, huh?"

"There are rumors about altereds finding their families and being believed," Lavender says, her tone thoroughly skeptical. "But the stories are always about folks who moved away, urban legends rather than firsthand accounts. And even if you could find a human who would believe what you told them, they'd never really understand what we've been through," she adds, her scent souring to a peppery sharpness as her fingernails grip the seat.

This sentiment surprises me, coming from Lavender. Of the two of us, she's the one with a proper human job: waitressing, where she interacts easily with the normal people. She has human friends, too, for drinking and dancing on the weekends. I hadn't thought of her as lonely, not like me. Have I been wrong all this time?

"But does that mean that there's a family out there somewhere, missing me?" Clarent asks, frowning as the idea occurs to him. "Shouldn't I at least try to send them word that I'm alive, or would that make things worse?"

I hesitate before my answer. "It's possible. We can try to find out. Celia says some folks have managed to track down their families using bits and pieces of memory that surfaced over time. But, well, sometimes humans don't remember us." I bite the inside of my cheek, trying to work out how to break the news. "Some of the altereds seem to have faded out of human memory; not all of us, but quite a few. Physical things are affected, too: they disappear from photographs, and legal records vanish."

"The altereds could be remembering incorrectly," Lavender points out, "thinking they've found their family when they have the wrong people entirely. It's not necessarily some kind of fae magic."

"Celia says it's happened more than once," I say with a shrug, not inclined to argue. "The point is: we'll help you look for your old family if you want, Clarent, but the odds of a happy ending are slim. I'm so sorry."

He's quiet for a while after this, digesting what we've told him. "It's all right," he says eventually, his voice calm. "I wasn't expecting to be free again, so it's not as if I got my hopes up planning a happy reunion with people I don't remember." He stares out the window again, quietly pensive. "I don't know what to put on the paperwork in the meantime."

Lavender squeezes his shoulder gently. "You really don't need to decide anything," she says. "Elric fills out the forms and we just have to memorize the information. Most of the stuff doesn't come up in day-to-day life and

160

he keeps things easy to remember, by which I mean he gives us stupid names because he's a heel."

Clarent quirks an eyebrow at this."Stupid names? How do you mean?"

I snort and nudge my purse at him. "Open the front flap if you want to see my license: 'Rosalie Flowers'. Lavs got the same surname, even though we don't look a bit alike to normal humans."

"He called us 'kissing cousins'," Lavender notes, thinning her lips.

Clarent studies the little plastic card with interest. "How did he find out you're twenty-two years old?" he asks curiously.

I laugh. "I'm almost certainly not. Add another four or five years at the least; but the younger he can pass us off, the easier it is to fill in the gaps in our missing credit history."

He strokes the tiny rectangle that shows my human face before passing back my purse. "What will he name me?"

"Something *good*," Lavender insists, frowning as the sharp scent of green apples fill the air. "We'll make sure he does."

I chuckle at this. "He'll probably go for something phonetically similar, like Claudio or Clement. For the surname, who knows? Probably the Spanish word for 'sword', whatever that is. Don't worry; you don't have to actually use the name he gives you. No one calls me Rosalie Flowers, except the cashiers when they check my license." I give him a warm smile. "I know Elric seems like a jerk, but his heart is in the right place."

He glances back nervously at Lavender. "Rose, about Elric—are you okay? Mina said he'd behave himself, but we were worried."

Hearing the concern in his voice, I look up; he's watching me closely, his expression solemn. Lavender avoids my gaze, looking down at her feet. "I'm okay," I say quickly, blinking in surprise. "Did you think I wouldn't be?"

"He was flirting with you, and you were pretty shaken up," Lavs says defensively. "Celia shouldn't have sent you home with him. It'd be just like him to take you to bed and then kick you out the next morning. You know how he is."

I have to concentrate to keep the car steady and not drift into another lane. Lavender was worried that Elric would break my heart? "I'm really all right," I repeat, shaking my head slowly and gripping the wheel to focus. "It wasn't like that. I mean, we didn't do anything." I can feel my cheeks burning from embarrassment. "You know I can't."

She gives me an exasperated look. "You can't put your lips on anyone," she corrects firmly. "That's not the same thing, Rose."

"And either way," Clarent breaks in gently, "we didn't want you to feel bad. The things he was saying were mean."

I have to swallow back a sudden lump in my throat. "No, it wasn't completely his fault," I tell them. I look up at the rear-view mirror, catching green eyes with my own; then I take a deep breath and steel myself for this revelation. "Uh. Lavender, he thinks that our fingers cause desire; magical desire, I mean."

She surprises me by bursting into laughter. "Rose, you don't believe him, do you?" she asks, the scent of bright marigold tickling my nose.

I shift uncomfortably in my seat, my hands tightening on the wheel. "He made a convincing case, Lavs."

She snorts at this. "He would. Rose, he's a player!" Her eyes narrow, her expression mingling sudden worry and protective anger. "Sweetie, oh my god, please tell me he didn't guilt you into getting him off with your 'magical' fingers?"

My cheeks are on fire, my eyes firmly on the road. "No, Lavs, I said we didn't do anything!" I sound shrill to my own ears, embarrassment raising my voice a full octave.

"Listen to me," I start over, trying to sound reasonable. "I touched his hand. I was passing food to him, and then it was like he forgot what I am. He tried to kiss me, and freaked out when he remembered. I had to remind him— Lavs, it felt like magic," I finish quietly.

There's a flash of sympathy in her eyes, but I can tell she still doesn't believe me—or, rather, doesn't believe Elric. I look to Clarent, embarrassed for him to see us fussing at each other, but detect only gentleness in his expression.

I clear my throat, conscious of how silly this all sounds in the cold light of morning. "I touched you before you kissed me," I tell him with the air of a confession.

He nods slowly. "You did. But I kissed you this morning without touching you first," he points out.

"That's true," I admit. "But we don't know how long the magic lasts. Elric didn't want to risk being alone with me this morning, even after a night's sleep."

He's quiet for a moment. "I'm sorry," he says after a long pause.

I blink surprise at him. "Sorry for what?"

His soft silver eyes look up at me, clouded with concern. "Rose, I like you a lot. Lavender, too," he adds, turning his head to flash her a warm smile. "I'd give you both so many kisses, if you would let me." He turns back to me, looking very solemn. "But I shouldn't kiss you any more if it makes you feel bad about yourself. I'm so sorry; I never meant to cause you any pain."

Tears spring to my eyes at this. "No! No, Clarent," I say in a rush. "It's not your fault. That's... that's the whole point." I glance up at the mirror but Lavender is avoiding my gaze, looking thoughtfully at her own hands. "I like you too," I tell him. "But it's not fair to you if my magic makes you like me."

He watches me with gentle eyes. "It isn't?" he queries, his deep voice thoughtful. "If I like you because of magic, is that different from liking you because you're beautiful or smell nice or have a good heart?"

I shake my head, not knowing how to explain. "It comes down to choice. Free will."

"But you said Elric didn't kiss you," he remarks, his head tilted quizzically. "Doesn't that mean he had free will, and used it?"

"No, he didn't kiss me, but he— most people don't want to feel an attraction they didn't choose to have," I fumble. "Kieran didn't like being attracted to me. He barely knows me and he prefers Elric, and maybe Mina," I add, remembering her earlier mention of calling him. "People he knows and trusts."

Clarent nods. "But I'm not Kieran," he points out patiently, "and I know and trust you."

"Rose," Lavender says suddenly. "Okay. If Elric is serious and not just trolling you, then this is something I'm supposed to have too, right?"

I bite my cheek again. "Yeah, he reckoned that was likely," I admit.

She takes a deep breath. "So, Rose, seriously, why don't we just do it?" Her eyes meet mine in the mirror, wide and pleading. Tentative honeysuckle pulls at me, her hope stirring fresh feelings of guilt. "Clarent can make us human again. I'll miss your pink hair, not gonna lie," she says, flashing a rueful smile at me. "But you won't have to worry about hurting people or luring them, none of that. Everything the May Queen did to us? Gone. We'd have a fresh start, to live the lives we want together."

The road is blurry for the sudden tears in my eyes, and I can't meet her gaze in the mirror. I drive on, wishing I could shield myself from Clarent's sympathy and Lavender's raw emotion.

We ride in silence for the remainder of the short trip. When we reach Dakota's neighborhood, I park alongside the curb in front of his house, pulling up behind Celia's truck and a car I don't recognize. I unbuckle my belt and twist in my seat so that I can face them both. Celia is waiting for us, may even have heard us arrive from inside the house, but this is much more important.

"Cards on the table, Lavs," I say quietly, praying that my voice won't crack. "Yes, I want that. All I've ever wanted since we came over was to be normal again." I can feel the tears coming again and blink them back as fast as I can. "But now I-I have a chance to do something *good*," I whisper, "to make up for all the bad."

"You're already good, Rose!" she explodes, tears in her own eyes. "You work in that damn bookstore and put up with Athena's bullshit. You help

164

with the other altereds, so that they understand what they were and learn what they need to know. You're patient and kind and you don't complain, even when you have every right to!"

"It's true, Rose," Clarent says gently, reaching out to touch my bare shoulder with his cool hand. "You helped me. You've been helping me since I came out yesterday, and you're still doing it now."

I want to melt into his touch, to let him hold us both and whisper those low deep reassurances to me until I can believe them. "It's not the same," I whisper, swallowing back the lump in my throat. "It's not nearly enough."

Lavender brushes furiously at her eyes, swiping away tears. "Rose, how would you feel if it were me?" she demands, reaching out to grab my hand. "Suppose I were the Nightshade and you were the Fragrant? Would you want this for me? Endlessly beating myself up for things I couldn't control in the otherworld?" Her eyes flash with fresh anger. "If I told you right now that I'd killed people, that she'd made me kill people, would you feel any differently about me?"

"No," I whisper, shaking my head. "No; you could tell me you killed a thousand men over there, and I'd still love you. I'd still want only good things for you."

Her hand squeezes mine tighter, her green eyes pleading. "Well then," she says quietly, the soft tone returning to her voice.

Clarent's hand moves gently on my shoulder, blessedly cool metal in the morning heat. "Rose, do you want me to?" he asks gently. "I know how to do it now. I can rearrange the magic, like I did with Tox. You can kiss Lavender all you want then." He gives me a shy smile. "And me, too, if you still want to."

I laugh, but the sound that emerges is more like a relieved sob. "The question is whether *you* will want to, afterwards," I point out weakly. I look at Lavender, hoping she won't notice the trembling in my hand. "You do realize we may feel differently about each other once we're normal, if Elric is right."

She tosses her head fiercely. "Rose, I know how I feel," she insists. "And if that somehow changes, then I'll just fall for you a second time." She tosses her purple curls over her shoulder, flashing me a confident grin. "If not, I think we could base a beautiful relationship on hate-fucking," she teases.

I'm laughing again, a shaky burbling giggle that has nothing to do with the joke and everything to do with my raw nerves. I don't know if this is the right thing to do; I don't know if I'll regret this tomorrow and see this moment as the most selfish decision of my life. But it's a middle finger held up defiantly to the one who took us, and a choice to be truly happy for the first time that I can remember.

"Okay, Clarent," I say, giddy with the suddenness of the decision. "Do it. Please."

He smiles at me, turning in his seat to face me. The hand on my bare shoulder caresses me gently, trailing tiny goosebumps in the wake of his touch. His free hand comes up to touch my covered shoulder, the coolness of him seeping through my thin sleeve.

He's so lovely that for a moment all I can do is gaze at him. I raise my hands to his face, shyly stroking his smooth cheeks. A delicious shiver runs through me when he smiles under my touch; he closes his eyes as I trace my fingers over his softening lips. As I stare at him, I slowly become aware of a strange feeling behind my eyes, a disorientation that isn't quite dizziness.

He shimmers in the morning sunlight, the soft silver of him dissolving before my eyes as his veil creeps into place. He's warm and brown and beautiful, and the sensation of silver smoothness under the illusory stubble of his jaw isn't unpleasant under my fingers, but he doesn't look like himself. Blinking in surprise, I gasp and yank my hands back as quickly as if I had been burned. His eyes fly open in concern at my reaction, his hands instantly drawing back. "Rose, what's wrong?"

I clutch at my head, feeling light-headed as the world swims before me. With his hands gone, my vision slowly clears back to what it should be, what I'm used to: Lavender's purple hair is as vibrant as fresh spring flowers, the thick green veins on my arms are as bright as serpents, and Clarent is once again glorious silver that flashes brightly in the morning sunlight.

"I-I'm sorry," I stammer, feeling ashamed of my reaction. Did I really think that becoming a normal human would be painless, or that it wouldn't have its price? I look up at Lavender, who watches me with wide worried eyes. "It's a funny feeling, seeing only the veils," I try to explain. "It's like a buzzing behind your eyes."

"Do you want me to go first?" she offers tentatively, her hand reaching out to me.

I look up at her, the dizziness slowly subsiding. Yes, she's beautiful in all her altered glory, bright purples and greens against her delicate paleness; but if I cross my eyes and bring her veil to the forefront of my vision, she's no less beautiful. Different, yes, but still Lavender, still lovely.

How long would it take me to get used to seeing her with human eyes—a day, a week, a month? Even the idea of lying in her arms, kissing her, being happy with her for the length of time necessary for my eyes to adjust is a luxury impossible to imagine. I would lie down to sleep next to her at night, knowing that she would still be there in the morning, alive and happy.

"No," I say, smiling in refusal of her offer. "I want to go first. I just freaked out a little; I'm okay now."

I turn back to Clarent, giving him my brightest and bravest smile. "Sorry," I apologize. "Let's try that one more time."

Then I blink at him. For the second time in as many minutes, Clarent looks wrong to my eyes. He's still silver, still beautiful and smooth and cool in his seat beside me. Yet previously I'd had to squint to look at him, my eyes dazzled by his constant reflection of the morning sun. Now there is no brightness to him. His skin is a dull flat gray, starved of the barest hint of light. Puzzled, I turn back to gaze out the windscreen, my eyes widening with a fresh rush of fear. *No! Not again.*

The car, Dakota's house, and a fair stretch of the street and lawn around us are completely surrounded by a thick wall of mist reaching high into the dark sky above us, enclosing the world in a dome of swirling fog.

CHAPTER 18

Lavender is the first to speak, tart lemony fear underlying the anger in her voice. "What even is going on here! How many is this in two days—*four* portals?"

"Celia said we should run or hide if it happened again," Clarent urges, his voice a soft whisper in the car. "Rose, can we just drive out?"

I shake my head, my eyes straining to pierce the mist. The whiteness is thicker than before, swirling in tight clouds that threaten to block Dakota's house from sight. "It closed too quickly. I didn't even see it forming this time," I murmur, half to myself. "We're trapped."

Lavender takes a deep breath. "Even if we could leave, that would mean abandoning Dakota and Celia," she points out in a strained voice. "Tox, too, if Celia brought them over with her."

I frown at Celia's truck, parked at the curb in front of us along with the other car that I don't recognize. Who else is here, I wonder, and can they help us? Then I remember Celia's earlier texts mentioning Lily; I've never met the polyglot woman, but I don't think she's an expert on portals. I peer at the house, looking for signs of movement from the windows, any signal that they're aware of our predicament. But the house is silent and lifeless, with no help forthcoming.

"Where do we hide?" Clarent asks, his calm practicality cutting through my thoughts.

I look around us quickly, suppressing panic. We could crouch on the floor, but we'd have nowhere to retreat if something dangerous were to approach the car. Outside, there aren't many areas suitable for hiding; the street is flat and wide, and there are no trees except the shimmery insubstantial ones brought over with the portal.

"The house," Lavender whispers, her wide eyes watching the dark building. "We can get to it, can't we?"

I bite the inside of my cheek, scanning the fog again. Dakota's yard is a wide expanse of dry crunchy grass without a lick of cover. Moving towards the house could draw attention to us. "It might be risky," I hazard.

"Staying here would be more dangerous," Clarent observes quietly, looking at me with concern in his silver eyes. "Rose, you almost died last time."

"We're stronger as a group," Lavender insists, her fingers gripping the back of my seat. "Clarent can de-magic anything that gets close to us, right? And Celia must know the portal is here. She has her bow; she can cover us."

I frown, still studying the silent house. There are too many variables in this plan; we don't even know if Celia has been carried over into the portal with us. Yet it's true that we're not safe here in the car; Clarent sticks out like a silver thumb, as do we with our cotton-candy hair.

"Okay," I whisper. "Exit on your side of the car. I'll slide over and follow you. Crouch low, try not to move too fast, and head straight for the front door." If no one is there to let us in we'll be in trouble, but alternatives like scaling the backyard gate or breaking a window would attract even more attention. *Worst case scenario, we can hide in the garden bushes out front.*

Clarent eases open his passenger door and for once the aging hinges do not creak. We pause, the three of us holding a collective breath. Nothing moves in the mist. He slides from his seat and drops into a silent crouch on the lawn beside the curb, waiting. I touch Lavender on the shoulder and she follows suit, opening her own door the bare minimum necessary to squeeze out and slip onto the lawn.

Now it is my turn. I slide over the gearstick and into Clarent's seat, dropping onto the ground beside him. The summer grass under my fingers is dry as straw, and I wince in sympathy with its thirst. I point to the house and Clarent nods, pushing off from the ground in a quick crouching walk. Lavender follows, glancing back at me briefly. I bring up the rear, cringing at Clarent's heavy footfalls which are only barely muffled by the thick mist around us.

I feel heat before the blow lands: a bristling sensation in the air behind me, a sudden fierce burning like standing too close to a bonfire. When I turn my head to look, my eyes already watering from the dry sting in the air, a heavy hand lands on my shoulder and I scream as intense pain floods through me. Lavender and Clarent whip around, alarm etched on their faces, and then I'm flung aside by a blow with inhuman strength behind it.

I hit the ground hard, the side of my head slamming into the earth. My vision swims sickeningly as I struggle to rise, propping myself against the ground with my elbow. One leg is twisted painfully under me, and my bare shoulder is burning. I reach up to touch the area gingerly, horrified by the sensation of seared skin already prickling with heat blisters. "What happened?" I hear myself say, too disoriented to remember to whisper.

"Rose! Are you okay?" Lavender flies to my side, kneeling to help me sit up. The sheer terror and raw fury rolling off her send another wave of dizziness washing through me. Slowly, I register that Clarent has moved next to us in a protective stance, watching my attacker with wary eyes.

The newcomer is another altered, unlike any I've ever seen before. He's black as soot and shadow, not the natural dark brown of skin, but rather a literal absence of light, like a black hole taken shape in the misty morning air. Pulsing orange-red veins cover his arms and legs in spidery patterns, weaving together in a thick throbbing mass right over his heart. He looks like living magma, like burning coals poured into the shape of a man.

He stands a few feet away, allowing no chance for us to run or hide. The red eyes set deep into his face glower at us like smoldering embers. Given how frightening he looks and how badly he's hurt me, it's difficult to remember that he's not necessarily hostile to us. Celia had said the bear-woman who attacked Kieran had been confused by crossing the portal; this man may not understand that he's not in the otherworld anymore and we're not his enemies. I take a quick gulp of air, determined to be conciliatory.

"Hello," I greet him. My throat is raw after my scream; I must have reopened yesterday's wounds. "I'm Rose. You're—"

"You're the metal one," he interrupts, staring intently at Clarent. His voice is low and liquid, smooth but threatening. "I thought I was going to have to actually *look* for you. They didn't say you had girls with you." His burning eyes travel over us, his gaze curious and faintly hostile.

Lavender rises angrily, stepping around me to juxtapose herself between us and him. "Welcome earthside," she says firmly, her words polite but her voice tight and protective. "Why don't you come with us? You can meet Celia and—"

His arm sweeps around with sudden violence, backhanding Lavender hard enough to send her reeling. She slams onto the ground beside me, the air knocked out of her in a single pained grunt. His heavy hands throb with the same fiery veins that mark his arms; his attacks are like being slugged by burning stone. Already I can see the burns on her pale face, angry blisters rising and puckering.

I hear Clarent shout wordlessly as he steps forward to deal with the man, but I only have eyes for Lavender. Gulping short breaths against the pain, I pull myself to my knees. My fingers fly gently over her, checking her pulse, looking for anything broken. She's unconscious but breathing. Her lip has been split where he struck her, and more blood dribbles in a thin line from her nostril; the deep red fluid contrasts with the angry pink burns on her delicate skin.

Behind me I hear sounds of a struggle: the scuffling of Clarent's shoes in the dry grass, and then the sickening sound of stone grinding against metal. I whirl to face the two men, my eyes widening at the sight of the altered holding Clarent in a tight headlock.

172

Our attacker hasn't been changed into a human as I'd expected; instead, his thick stony arm is wrapped around Clarent's neck while his free hand grips his own wrist, pulling the hold tighter and cutting off his air. The maneuver pulls Clarent steadily backwards, so that his feet have to fight for purchase in order for him to stay upright and breathing.

Clarent's hands scrabble ineffectually at the arm that encircles his neck, but he can't touch the altered for more than a few seconds before jerking convulsively away from the heat. If Clarent can't touch him, I realize, he can't change the altered man back into a human. Already his silver palms are blackened and burned and the smooth metal on his fingers has twisted and run. I understand with sudden horror that contact with the man is actually *melting* Clarent's soft metal.

"Hey! Hey, let him go." My voice sounds weak in my ears, hazy with shock and pain. "You're earthside now, you don't have to do this." I dig my nails into the ground, swallowing back the nausea that reaches with icy fingers into my stomach. "We're not your enemy. No one is making you do this. Please stop."

The altered man peers curiously at Clarent, completely ignoring me. "You're definitely metal," he observes in a low voice. He tightens his hold against Clarent's windpipe, the heat softening his silver neck so that it bends painfully under the relentless force. "Right size and weight, good color. But they didn't say anything about girls. They should have; I don't like surprises."

They? The icy fingers in my stomach clench harder as his words sink in. He glances at me, his stony face looking mildly amused. "Can't carry three back with me," he notes in a bored drawl. "Only got two hands and they said you weren't optional, metal-man. That means I gotta pick between the pale one and the dark one." He looks back at Clarent. "Do you have a preference?"

Clarent's face is contorted with pain, his eyes bulging as he loses his fight against the chokehold. At the threat against myself and Lavender he grunts angrily and lunges backwards against his attacker. The man barely seems to register the movement, absorbing the impact with a chuckle. "All you have to do is point at whichever one you want," he mocks, tightening his grip.

I have to do something, but I can't see what. I could run for Celia, but the house is still dark and silent; I don't even know if they were caught in the portal with us. I could try to get around the men and back to the car. Two tons of metal slammed into our attacker might give him pause for thought—but he's still holding Clarent and I don't want to hurt him as well.

Can I reason with him? If he was sent by the faeries to collect Clarent, maybe we can convince him to stay here, to be free and join our community. But I don't like the way he looks at me and Lavender, and I'm certain there's nothing I have that I want to offer him.

I see a flash of movement from the corner of my eye, a window curtain stirring as if in a slight breeze. I hear the tiniest click, a sound barely carried through the mist; then an arrow tears through the window screen with a soft ripping sound and hurtles straight towards us. The projectile slams into the side of the magma man's head and shatters uselessly against his hard stone-plating.

"What the—?" He spins towards the house, whipping Clarent around in his grasp. Frowning angrily, he peers at the dark building, devoid of movement save for the tiny tear in the screen which flaps gently in the swirling mist. I hear another soft click, and the man clenches his red eyes shut just in time to protect himself from a second arrow that bounces harmlessly off his left eyelid.

He twists back, hunching his neck and shoulders against any further attacks, and glares daggers at me where I sit. "That's cute, honey, really adorable," he growls angrily. "Got yourself a friend in there who thinks I don't know to protect my soft spots? Like this is my first hunt?" His voice drops to a purr in happy anticipation of more violence. "Time to finish this," he announces.

174

The magma man's hand snakes up under his arm and grabs Clarent by the throat. His arm twists hard, and he spins Clarent around in a tight circuit to face him. A flash of fresh pain crosses Clarent's face and his eyes flutter as he fights to stay conscious. Huge hands grip his neck and raise him higher until he's struggling to remain standing on his toes. The stone hands pulse with heat, and I'm horrified to see liquid metal dripping from Clarent's neck to stain his clothes red.

In a burst of panic, Clarent's hands grip the altered man's arms. His silver eyes clench shut against the pain, and there's a brief moment where everything shimmers like a mirage in the desert. Black stone becomes cool white skin, and I hear the distant sound of another soft click. Then reality slams back into focus and Celia's arrow ricochets harmlessly away from hard stone.

The man chuckles. "They mentioned you have a rare talent. But I don't think you can concentrate through the pain, friend," he gloats, tightening his burning hands. "Nice try, though." His hands squeeze harder and Clarent's eyes flutter closed.

I have to do something. Clarent's magic didn't have a chance to work. Celia couldn't help. Lavender is wounded, stirring but not yet conscious— and what could she do against this creature? I could try to trip him, wrestle him to the ground, but he subdued Clarent easily and he's much stronger than I am. I'm near, though, and I'm fast; maybe I could get at his eyes with my nails, or tear at that mass of veins covering his heart. Maybe I could—

My nails. My fingers. The world slows around me. *My fingers cause desire. My lips are poisonous.* I've been killing men for years, some of them stronger even than this one. I'm an actual biological weapon, deadlier than the heaviest car or sharpest arrow.

Heat distorts the air around him, and my shoulder still burns from where he struck me. He can't really be made of magma and fire, or Clarent's clothes would have burned away, I would be wounded more severely than I am, and he'd have no hope of bringing us back alive. He must have some control over the heat, enough to keep from being lethal. But kissing him will hurt, and if I manage to survive I'll be a murderer all over again; this time by choice.

I leap to my feet, throwing myself at the altered. He ignores me, his concentration entirely on Clarent as he chokes him to unconsciousness. His bored expression implies that I'm harmless to him, just a helpless girl flailing about uselessly in defense of her lover. *Good,* I think. *Underestimate me.*

I duck under his outstretched arms and come up between them, wincing at the intense heat that envelops me. "Hello," I murmur, my voice low in my throat, ignoring the burning limbs on either side of me in order to press closer to his chest. "I'm Rose. You are...?" He blinks, surprised by my boldness, though he doesn't tear his gaze away from Clarent. I lay my right hand against the orange veins over his heart, my touch gentle and nonthreatening. I pray Elric isn't wrong as I will any desire-magic residing in my fingers to invade this man's bloodstream.

It hurts to touch him, the pain much worse than I'd expected to endure. My fingers burn with the excruciating heat, my skin melting to fuse with him. Only now do I realize the uncertainties inherent in this plan. We've never even verified that my fingers work on Clarent, let alone on a man who has liquid fire running through his veins. The poison in my lips and hands may be burned away by his very touch.

Yet there's a stillness in the air, a moment when I can feel his heartbeat under my burning fingers and hear his breath catch. He blinks again, and his red eyes draw reluctantly away from Clarent to focus on me. I nod encouragingly at him, flashing him a coy smile and snaking my left hand around the back of his head. Bracing myself against the imminent pain I touch his neck, drawing him down for a lingering kiss.

It burns. Every ounce of my self-control is taken up in keeping my lips pressed against his. I want to pull away, to howl with the intensity of the pain. Then I feel Clarent tumbling to the ground behind me. Fiery hands come up to wrap around my back, drawing me deeper into the kiss, and I melt into fresh agony. I don't have to force myself to hold still any longer; the desire I've inflicted on him has ensured that I cannot escape.

He holds me close, his lips moving possessively against mine. I feel the searing sensation of my lips melting as he pulls me tighter into him. I screw my eyes shut against the heat, feeling the skin on my face blistering and peeling away. I pray that he dies quickly or that I do; death is preferable to the excruciating torment of being crushed by a pillar of living ember.

There's a scuffling sound in the grass beneath me. My eyes fly open, but for a moment I can see only black stone and red heat. There is a flash of silver near my feet and the blessed smoothness of Clarent against my leg. His hands snake out to grip the altered's ankles; he's too shaky to stand but determined to help. Again there comes that soft shimmer of mirage in the air, the feeling of magic moving, changing, rearranging.

Heat begins to ebb away, though my skin still burns from the damage already done. The stone and fire that fill my vision shift to white skin and blue eyes for a brief moment before shifting back again. He struggles to pull away from Clarent's grip, but I hold him with every last ounce of my strength. My burned lips press hard against his, and I feel the choking knot form in his throat before blood begins to dribble from the edges of his mouth.

He's dead now even if he doesn't know it yet, even if Clarent still struggles to change him. I pull my face back a few inches to view my handiwork, struggling to stay conscious through the pain. He flickers again, stone and skin, but now his skin is patched purple and red and tiny cracks appear in the stone. His eyes widen with fear before flashing with fresh anger. Broad hands move up my back and fasten unexpectedly around my throat, squeezing furiously.

Stone or flesh, his hands are strong enough to choke and I am not made of metal. I feel the clench in my neck as air is cut off, and then the tight inexorable crushing that will take me into death with him. I should have known better; I could have scrambled away from him after the kiss began to take its toll. Yet on reflection, I feel at peace dying here. Being killed by one of my victims feels like justice, and now Clarent and Lavender will be safe.

The man shivers again, the trembling in his arms jerking me back from the edge of unconsciousness. There is one final flash of stone and then he is flesh and blood and fully human. Clarent slumps forward into the grass, releasing his grip around the man's ankles now that he's done everything he can. It's too late to save me, but I'm grateful that he made the effort.

Without any warning the man coughs violently, fresh blood gushing over his purpled lips and splattering my face. He wobbles where he stands, loosening his grip on my neck. My legs give out from under me and I collapse to the ground beside Clarent. Looking up with hazy eyes, I'm stunned to see Lavender. She's standing there bristling with raw fury, in her hand the shaft of the arrow she's buried deep into the man's back.

The life in the magma man's eyes extinguishes entirely and he crumples slowly into the grass. I wonder if it is safe for me to black out from the pain, before I realize that I have no remaining choice in the matter. As darkness claims my vision, I hope that Celia can get everyone inside before the humans see.

CHAPTER 19

In what is rapidly becoming an unwanted pattern, I wake without knowing where I am, what time it is, or how wounded I might be. My consciousness swims toward light and sound, my eyes fluttering open to blink against the bright light washing over me.

A voice I don't recognize pierces my ears. It is clipped and precise with a musical accent I can't place, and sounds extremely angry. "No, Celia, I'm not staying! This is ridiculous! I'm furious that you called me out here at all, if this sort of thing keeps happening around them. You ought to have warned me!"

Celia's voice is as cool and calm as usual, the normality soothing to me. "Lily, you're safer here with us than you would be anywhere else, and I need you here to talk to Clarent when Elric gets here with his papers. The girls would like to talk to you as well; Rose has been especially curious about her past."

"Oh, *fuck off*, Celia." Even when swearing, the new voice is like a golden symphony. "You know perfectly well what to put him down as. He's clearly Hispanic; you can hear his accent as well as I can. English as a second language, thoroughly fluent; probably picked it up as a toddler. He's a local through and through, and almost certainly a rush job nabbed by a finder at short notice. Best explanation for how he ended up in an Arthurian smithy."

"He may be a local," Celia says, her calm voice unperturbed, "but I still want you to check and be sure. His talent is a rare one, which means he may have been specifically sought out. And whether he's local or not, I'll need you here when Elric shows up. We're going to require cities he's plausibly lived in, family names, and so on."

"I've heard him, Celia! 'Help them, help Rose; I'm fine'." The lovely voice deepens into dark honey, perfectly mimicking his soft accent. "That's more than enough to pin him down to the area! Get me a map to draw a circle on if you must, but I'm done and gone. I won't stay here while hunters are prowling around!"

"Lily, you brought your laptop, didn't you?" Celia's voice is as steady as ever but carries an undercurrent of warning. "Why don't you get some work done while we wait?"

The other woman makes an angry noise, but doesn't argue; I hear her sit heavily in a nearby chair, followed by the furious clicking of computer keys. I turn my head towards the sound, my eyes adjusting to the harsh light filtering in through sheer curtains. As my vision swims and clears, I realize I'm lying in a strange bedroom on a big bed full of crisp white pillows and cerulean blue sheets. I've turned to face a beautiful blond woman with gold-dusted skin who sits sullenly in a nearby easy chair.

"Oh, good," the glittery woman says tartly when she sees my open eyes. "You're awake; we can get this over with."

I hear a small gasp of relief, and then someone heavy and cool settles onto the bed beside me, silver arms draping gently over me in a tentative hug. "Rose! Rose, are you all right?" Clarent asks in a voice as soft as a prayer.

"I'm okay," I whisper, testing my voice. I'm amazed to find there's no pain; even less than yesterday when I was on Worth's medicine. I ought to be badly burned from the magma man's rough handling. Instead I feel fine, impossibly whole and well. "Where's Lavender?"

"She's okay," he reassures me quickly. I turn my head to face him, my vision swimming at the movement. His silver eyes are worried and pained as he studies my face, and he's still in his bloodstained clothes but looks otherwise healthy. "She's downstairs with Joel and Worth. They're getting you some water and food."

He's interrupted by music which suddenly floods the small room. Warm piano notes pipe tinnily from laptop speakers, accompanied by a voice like a liquid purr singing in a language I don't understand. Celia is leaning against the wall by the door but looks up sharply at the music. "Lily," she says, her voice a low warning.

The blond woman ignores her, turning gold-flecked eyes to Clarent. "You, silver boy—do you understand the singing?" He nods, blinking at the question. "Congratulations," she says in a clipped voice edged with anger. "You speak Spanish, surprising no one," she snaps. "Welcome earthside. Please enjoy bonding with Celia over your newfound shared language. I'm leaving."

Lily rises in a fluid motion, and I blink when the sunlight catches her. For a moment she gleams as brightly golden as Clarent is silver, but it's just a trick of my eyes. She's not metal as he is; she's flesh and blood, with body glitter grafted into her skin. *A gilded lily*, I realize, and not a real Flower like Lavender and I. She snaps the laptop shut with a flick of her wrist, but the music continues, dancing in the air around us.

"Lily, please sit back—" Celia's stern voice falters as a man's voice joins the singing, thick and high and lovely. He's singing in English about lips touching and sparks flying, about danger and flames; my breath catches suddenly in my healed throat, and the beautiful harmony continues.

Celia's expression darkens dangerously and she rounds in anger on the golden woman. "Lily, shut that off!"

Lily gives her the most innocent of looks. "What, you don't like Hugh Laurie's *Kiss of Fire*? I'll admit he's no Louis Armstrong, but I do love Gaby Moreno."

I'm having trouble breathing, gripping Clarent's cool hand tightly with my own and trying to close my ears to the relentless music. Celia's voice is furious. "Lily!"

"Oh, all right," she concedes, thumbing the laptop open and touching a button. The room falls blessedly silent.

Clarent strokes my hand gently, and I open my eyes to his worried gaze. "Are you okay, Rose?" he whispers softly.

"F-Fine," I assure him, gasping for air. I shoot the golden woman as dirty a look as I can manage. "I'm good. No thanks for that," I splutter weakly.

Lily looks utterly unfazed. "She's a city girl," she observes coolly. "Her accent's muddy. Born up north and then brought down here, I'd guess. Hard to say; she's picked up a lot of faery inflections in otherworld. Never lived in the country, though; not like her purple-headed California girl with the freckles." She frowns then. "Something else. The intonations and the way she releases. Ugh, what a bother. Hang on, I don't have this one memorized."

She plunks back into her seat and pulls up something on her laptop. "Repeat after me," she says crisply, her eyes flicking over the screen. "Baruch atah Adonai—"

The words aren't English, and yet I know them. I can feel the spaces between the sounds, even as she reads them off too quickly to hear. When I open my own mouth to repeat the words, I find that I'm almost *singing*, a soft chanting cadence that fills the room. "Baruch atah Adonai Eloheinu, melech haolam, asher kid'shanu b'mitzvotav v'tzivanu l'hadlik ner shel Shabbat."

Blessed are You, Adonai our G-d, Sovereign of the universe, who hallows us with mitzvot, commanding us to kindle the light of Shabbat. And then, another thought hard on the heels of the first: Have I always known that?

"Congratulations," Lily says dryly. "You're some flavor of Jewish. Good luck sorting that out on your own time." She levels a contemptuous look at Celia. "Satisfied?"

Celia still simmers, though her voice is calm again. "Go downstairs, Lily. Wait with Dakota."

"Oh, goody!" Her golden voice rises in a parody of enthusiasm, although her face remains set in a sneer. "I can bond with the adorable child. What sort of music do you think they'd like?"

Celia grinds her teeth in frustration before running a defeated hand over her brow. "Fine; we'll manage Elric without you. Go home. But call me if you get into any trouble, Lily; I mean it."

The beautiful woman sniffs, looking almost offended by the offer. "I'm safer on my own and you know it, Celia," she says coldly. "And don't look for me at your meeting tonight. I think it's criminally irresponsible to pile everyone into the same room when hunters are prowling around looking for this one." She jerks a thumb at Clarent, gives me one final hard look, and sweeps haughtily out of the room.

"Don't come running to me when you get yourselves killed," floats back, her final parting shot as she descends the stairs.

Celia stares after her for a moment, her expression an odd mixture of fury and softness. She returns her gaze to me. "You sure you're okay, Rose?" she asks.

I nod silently, thankful for Clarent's reassuring grip on my hand. I'm still trembling from the first song, the one about fire and kisses, but my mind whirls with the revelation brought by the second song, the one I sang without consciously knowing I could. *I have a past.* I still don't remember it, but I have a starting point now.

"Try not to let Lily bother you," Celia counsels, noting my shaking with her gently worried eyes. "She's had a rough time of it." She runs her fingers over her russet-brown braid. "Elric will be here in a bit with all the paperwork, now that the healers have the worst of the wounds fixed up."

I clear my throat softly, reluctantly pushing away my excitement about my past to focus on our immediate present. "About that," I start awkwardly. "What happened?"

There's a rough step on the stairs in the hallway and a mottled face appears at the door, shielded by his customary hood. Indeed, I think it's the same hood he was wearing yesterday. Joel's blue eyes alight when he sees me. "Ah! I told you it would do the trick! She's already waking up!" He bustles into the room, coming round the side of the bed to peer at my eyes with a tiny flashlight he produces from a pocket.

Worth follows at a more sedate pace, carrying a glass of water which nee sets down on a nearby table before bending over to touch me with gently probing fingers. "I never said that it would not heal her, Joel; and, if I recall correctly, administering the dose was my idea," nee says, ner voice dignified. "I merely expressed concern that your methodology is alarmingly imprecise. No, child; hold still, please," nee adds to me, as I stir under ner touch. "Half your face was melted before we gave you the injection. You're healing up fast, but we don't want you to strain yourself."

Joel looks aghast at ner skepticism. "Well, clearly it *does* work," he points out touchily. "New skin in a matter of minutes, and she woke up faster than we thought she would; only slept for about an hour." He peers at me. "How is the pain?" he asks, his papery voice eager.

I blink at him. "No pain," I say, shaking my head.

"See?" he says, aiming a triumphant look at Worth.

Nee sighs. "Yes, it works," nee says patiently. "We still don't know *why*."

"I told you: I isolated the binding agent in the venom—"

"You isolated something that you *believe* is a binding agent, via a process you didn't write down adequately the first time and yet managed to reproduce perfectly the second time. All despite the fact that her last batch was full of blood-borne impurities, and you maintained almost no controls in your lab." Worth levels him a dry look. "And we still have no idea *why* the substance in her lips can heal after your treatment, yet kills on contact before it. Nor do we know why the metal boy is immune to her when the body downstairs was clearly not."

"Rose!" Worth is interrupted by the appearance of Lavender in the doorway, carrying a plate piled high with sandwiches. She shoves the plate into Celia's hands when she sees me, surging forward to clamber onto the bed and hug me around the waist. "You scared the daylights out of me," she scolds.

184

"Lavs, your face," I breathe, touching her gently. She's perfectly whole, not a burn or a blemish on her; her freckles stand out against the white of her skin. Her hands, too, are soft and healed. If I hadn't seen it with my own eyes, I'd think the magma man had never touched her.

"I'm fine," she insists, reaching to stroke my cheek. "You were hurt the worst! Joel healed me." She looks up, frowning. "Now that we're both well, can you go back to healing Clarent?" she prompts, her voice insistent.

"Ah, yes, sorry," Joel responds, not terribly contrite as he bustles to the other side of the bed to place his long spindly fingers on Clarent's neck. Clarent winces at his draining touch but submits with quiet grace. "Rose was being interesting and Worth was arguing."

I stare at Clarent, realizing with a start that he is more wounded than I'd first realized. The bright sunlight flashing from his silver skin had blinded me to the lingering indentation in his neck where our attacker had softened and bent him, nor had I seen the blackened burns that remain on his hands. He returns my look self-consciously. "They started on me, but I wanted you two healed first," he admits. "I've had lots of burns before in the smithy, so it wasn't as bad for me."

"Liar," I gasp, knowing it must have been painful for him to wait. I want to lean in to kiss him, but Joel is in my way. Only then do I remember all over again that kissing is for normal people. I, on the other hand, have just killed a man with my lips. *Again.*

"You saved us," Lavender whispers, snugging me tightly around the waist and jarring me from my thoughts. "I heard most of it while I was still dazed on the ground, and Clarent filled in the rest while you were sleeping. That hunter was going to knock Clarent out and carry him back over to the faeries. He'd probably have taken one of us with him, too. You stopped him, Rose."

My laughter sounds weak in my ears. "And you two saved me," I say quietly, remembering. Clarent had been able to turn the man human once he was no longer pinioned and fighting for breath and the hunter was distracted by me. Lavender had then killed him before he took me with him into death. "Thank you," I whisper.

Celia watches us closely from where she leans against the wall. "Dakota and I were able to get you all into the house before the portal dissipated," she says calmly. "Lily called the healers once we could get a signal out." She hesitates. "Rose, I know you aren't thrilled about your poison and don't want to make a habit of killing—I think that's wise—but I want you to know that you three did the right thing."

I nod mutely at her, but all I can concentrate on now is Clarent. He winces again under Joel's draining fingers, his silver skin blackening and bruising wherever the healer touches. "Does it hurt?" I whisper, running my fingers anxiously over his arm.

Clarent offers me a grin between winces. "It's not too bad," he promises. "Better than being bled for the swords."

"It's *awful*," Lavender contradicts, but her tone is cheerful and the air around her is soft and sweet. "You're lucky Joel's magic doesn't work on you, Rose."

I blink at her. "What do you mean?"

"Oh, you very nearly died," Joel interrupts blithely, sending fresh shivers down my spine. "Your magic simply will not catalyze correctly; I could barely heal you at all. Then Worth had the bright idea of using the venom we collected yesterday. We only had a single dose, not nearly as strong as what we used on Kieran." He sighs, the huff of air sounding wistful. "I don't know what we'd have done if we lost you. How would we collect more samples?"

"Joel! For goodness' sake. "Worth clicks ner tongue at him. "Child, we've all of us been worried about you, and not just for your fluids," nee says dryly. Nee leans over me again, brushing my hair from my brow. "We do need to ask you some questions, though," nee says, ner voice apologetic.

Worth's hands feel good against my skin, cool and gentle. I don't know our altered physician very well—we've only met briefly at the get-togethers

186

before all this started happening—but I like ner, and nee has already done so much to help me. Looking up into ner dark eyes I almost feel like we're alone, that I could tell ner anything and the answers would remain between us. I nod, subdued. "What kind of questions?"

Ner voice is gentle. "Can you tell me about your time in otherworld, Rose? I only know bits and pieces."

I nod again. "I'm always honest about it," I say, a little defensively. Lavender's arms grip me tighter around the waist, but she seems far away. "I just don't like to talk about it much. Bad memories. Takes my breath away, makes my heart hurt."

"I know," Worth says softly, still smoothing my brow. "I don't want to trigger you, but this could be very important. Can you remember a little for me now, here where you're safe? You were used to kill other captives, yes? Could you describe a typical encounter?"

My tongue feels thick in my mouth. "If the May Queen owned the man, he'd be brought into my room," I say slowly, my heart already beginning to thud faster. "If he belonged to a party guest, my job was to seduce him and draw him off to a secluded place. I never had any trouble doing so, but I hadn't realized my fingers cause desire until Elric told me so last night. My job was to kiss them, or let them kiss me, and then they died; always." I hesitate. "Well, almost always. One faery man survived."

Clarent squeezes my hand, frowning with concern. Worth nods again, very gently, ner curly hair a dark nimbus cloud framing ner kind face. "Did you ever kiss anyone like the hunter downstairs, made of lava and fire and stone?" Ner fingers tuck a strand of hair behind my ear. "Is that how you knew you could kill him?"

I shake my head slowly. "No, the May Queen never had anyone like that over. She didn't like fire. I didn't know if it would work or not, but I couldn't think of anything else to do."

Nee looks thoughtful, glancing up at Clarent. "Child, did you turn the hunter human before or after she kissed him?"

"During, I think," he says, sounding unsure. "She kissed him and he dropped me. Once I wasn't choking anymore, I was able to concentrate on realigning his magic; before that, I couldn't think straight while I was gasping for breath."

Worth nods again. Nee touches my brow once more and then moves away to sit in the chair that Lily vacated. There nee steeples long fingers and studies me with dark eyes, ner gaze lacking the commanding authority that had been in ner face moments before.

I blink, feeling as though I am emerging from a mental fog. *What was that?* I would have responded to ner questions truthfully without prompting; I have no reason or desire to lie to Worth. Yet there had been a moment when I couldn't even imagine refusing to answer ner.

"What are you thinking, Worth?" Celia says, her calm voice intruding. "We've dealt with desire-magic before. Mina has a dose, though she lost a lot of it coming through her portal." She gives me a blunt look. "Haven't been getting that vibe from Rose, though."

Lavender looks like she can't decide whether to be relieved or annoyed. "I mean, the idea came from *Elric*," she says, rolling her eyes. "I said he was wrong."

"I don't think he was," I protest. "Lavs, I put my hand over the hunter's heart and he kissed me back! He had every reason not to drop Clarent. He knew we had friends in the house, and it was important to finish knocking Clarent out and get back over before the portal closed. Lavs, he knew that and he dropped everything in order to kiss me."

Worth nods slowly. "There's *something* magical about her," nee says, looking thoughtful. "Beyond the lethal kisses, I mean."

"There's also the problem of healing her." Joel's voice hisses softly from Clarent's side of the bed. "Her magic won't catalyze properly. I think that does it, boy," he adds to Clarent, finishing his healing work. He stands, unfolding his gaunt body slowly, and walks with halting movements to my side of the bed. "Worth, you saw. It was like trying to light damp wood.

Her magic didn't want to burn properly. I've never seen anything like it. As for these fingers—"

His long, gnarled fingers reach for my hand. "They cause desire," I warn, my voice pinched tightly with fear.

"So I hear," he says dryly, his voice like brittle paper. His draining fingers grasp mine gently, turning them carefully in his grip, bruising and numbing my green skin wherever they touch. "But they *don't*."

I blink at him. "But Elric—"

"Elric almost certainly desired you before he ever touched you," Celia interrupts calmly, watching us closely from where she leans against the wall by the door. "He has a bad habit of believing that everyone around him feels as he does."

"Kieran and Mina—"

"Are both attracted to girls, child," Joel whispers, amusement spreading through his papery voice. "Presumably the hunter downstairs was also. I am not."

Worth leans forward, ner chin tucked onto ner steepled fingers. "Everyone who has touched you or been touched by you is fond of you in their own way," nee observes with interest. "But not all of them, or even most, are attracted to you. Many have no desire whatsoever to kiss you. If you're meant to be a lure, your faery seems to have failed."

I shake my head, feeling bewildered. I'd been so sure that my newfound desire-magic compounded my crimes. "But if my fingers don't cause desire, what *do* they do? They did *something* to the hunter! It sure looked like desire."

Worth watches my face closely. "It is possible that your magic intensifies the feelings we're already inclined to feel towards you. Someone who is already attracted to you, like Elric, might indeed experience your magic as increased desire. But someone who is more likely to view you as a friend, like Joel, may simply choose to confide in you sooner, with greater intimacy. If that were the case, it would mean that those of us who like you

189

do so with free will, but like you faster than we might otherwise have done. Social interactions sped up through magic, so to speak."

"Makes the seduction more likely to succeed," Celia observes in a quiet tone. "When you lay on the desire-magic thickly, as with Mina, you risk putting a target on guard. Speeding up a naturally-occurring emotional response is a more subtle approach. The target is less likely to question feelings that are their own."

Lavender raises her hand for a question, her lips pursed tight as her green fingers wiggle for attention. "That only makes sense for a Nightshade," she points out. "I wasn't tasked to seduce anyone. Why am I supposed to have magical emotion fingers?"

"And does it work on me or just the man downstairs?" Clarent breaks in, his voice soft and low. We all turn to stare at him, and I realize he hasn't participated in this conversation until now. He clears his throat quietly, looking apologetic. "I don't mind one way or the other," he says, "but Rose was worried."

Worth frowns at this. "I still can't imagine why Rose's lips and fingers would work on a man made of stone but not on a man made of silver," nee confesses, looking solemn. "And yet here you are. Joel swears up and down that there's no poison in your system, and you seem perfectly healthy."

Celia pushes away from the wall with the air of someone exhausted by the subject matter. "Well," she says, "I don't think we're going to solve that one right now. We may just have to accept that Clarent's immunity is a fortuitous accident." She sighs. "I'm going downstairs to check on Dakota, and to see how he and Tox are doing. Worth, Joel, you want to come with? I'll leave these here for the patients so they can rest." She plunks down the plate of sandwiches next to our water glasses and stalks out of the room, her boots tromping softly on the stairs.

Joel looks dejected. "I wanted to take another sample," he says, his eyes lingering on my lips. "She's healed up now, and I think there's more there to harvest."

"Let her rest up for a bit first, Joel," Worth decrees, ner voice soft but commanding. "Children, try to take a nap. We'll call you down when Elric gets here." Nee touches Joel lightly on the back of his jacket and guides him out into the hallway, closing the door behind them.

CHAPTER 20

I slump back against the pillows when the door closes, only now aware of my tension. Clarent lies beside me on my right, propped up against the bed cushions; his presence is as cool and solid and comforting as ever. Lavender, on my left, lies with her head tucked against my side so that her arms can wrap around my waist in a hug she won't let go. If I'm honest with myself, I don't want to ever move from this position.

Clarent turns his head to look at me, gazing down with his usual gentleness. "Have I thanked you for saving my life, Rose—again?" he asks softly.

I snort at that. "I think you did, yeah," I say, looking up at him with a smile I can't quite hide. "But I don't know that the first time counted. I just helped Lavender get you in the car, you know; Joel did all the healing. So I think I've only saved your life the one time. We're even."

He chuckles, reaching down to stroke my forehead. His fingers are soft and gentle, and feel so different to Worth's parental touch. "Well, I count the first time," he says, returning my smile. "You both saved my life yesterday, as far as I'm concerned."

Lavender grins at this and hugs me tighter, but I can smell the spicy clover seeping out of her and I know she's worried. I lift my head to look at her and her green eyes slide away. "Are you okay, Rose?" she asks, her voice almost lost in the emptiness of the big bedroom. "I know you're healed, but... are you okay?"

I stare at her and the impact of the morning floods over me. I've killed a man. I swore when I came out that I would never use my lips to kill another person, and yet I've just done it again without a second thought. The hunter deserved to die, yes, and I only did it to save Clarent and Lavs, but I still don't feel even remotely okay. I'm a murderer, this time by choice, and I'm going to have to carry that knowledge for the rest of my life.

But Lavender doesn't need to hear that. "I'm all right," I lie, trying to work out the best thing to say. "I'll be fine. I've done it before; I've had lots of practice." A weak smile, an attempt at a joke that isn't remotely funny.

She drops her eyes from me again. "You're mad at yourself," she observes, sounding hurt and wounded. "You're mad at me, too?"

I blink at her. "What? No! Why would I be mad at you, Lavs?"

Exasperation flashes in her eyes and the smell of her anxiety grows stronger around us. "Well, I mean you keep insisting on hating yourself for being a killer, Rose, and I'm a member of that group now!" she snaps. Her voice is like a slap across my face and she won't meet my eyes.

I feel my expression fall, my heart squeezing with the intensity of her panic. "No! No, Lavs," I say, lowering my voice so as not to disturb everyone downstairs. I touch her hair, my fingers trailing through her soft velvet curls. I hope I sound reassuring. "Lavs, I don't hate you. I never will. How could you think that?"

"But, Rose," Clarent says, his low sweet voice breaking in gently, "we feel the same way about you." His cool fingers trace the line of my jaw, tipping my face up to him. "What you did in the otherworld wasn't your fault, and what you did today saved our lives. We love you, and it hurts to hear you hate yourself."

Tears well up in my eyes and I blink to clear them. "I don't hate myself for being a killer," I argue, attempting a laugh. I grit my teeth and take a deep breath, steeling myself for my announcement, praying my voice won't crack. "In fact, I'm going to stay this way."

"Stay what way?" Clarent asks, confusion creeping into his voice.

"Poisonous." My voice is a whisper, my eyes downcast.

Lavender jerks her head up to stare at me. "Rose! What are you talking about? We agreed earlier that we'd let Clarent turn us fully human. You can't stay like this; you're miserable!" The worry in the air around us intensifies, tinted with the crisp scent of sorrowful basil. I force my gaze up to meet hers, knowing she deserves the decency of eye contact.

"Lavs," I say quietly, "you were nearly taken back today. You could have been *killed*. You must see that I can't go back to being human now." I swallow the lump in my throat. "If Clarent had finished altering me in the car, who knows what would have happened to you two." I shudder to think of the ugly possibilities.

She grits her teeth, fresh sorrow spreading overwhelmingly through the room. "Rose," she says firmly, each word punctuated with a stern pause. "I do not care at all, period. That hunter is gone and good riddance and we can get back to the business of making you human and happy."

I shake my head at her. "Lavs, please think for just a moment," I beg. "He said 'they' sent him. If that's true, if faeries are trying to recover Clarent, then they'll send more hunters. They may even look for you and me now, since we killed the last one; retribution." I hold her green eyes with my own, silently pleading with her to understand. "I can't give up the best weapon we have for protecting us," I whisper. "I can't."

Her face crumples and fresh guilt washes over me. She manages to wipe away her tears before they fall, but her voice cracks when she speaks. "I want to kiss you," she whispers, sounding utterly miserable.

I cup my hand over my mouth; for once not to protect anyone, but because otherwise I'll sob out loud. "I know." My voice is muffled against my palm, but the admission is easier to make than I'd feared it would be. "I want to kiss you, too. But I can't give away my talent and leave you unprotected. Please don't ask me to, Lavs."

She glares at this. Despite her sadness she suddenly looks herself again, fierce and determined. I'm about to open my mouth to continue the argument, but she startles me by sudden acquiescence. "Fine!" she says firmly, sitting up on the bed. "Keep your talent and protect us. And I won't get any kisses, but damned if I'm not going to make you happy all the same. Up!"

This last word is barked with all the assurance of a drill sergeant and it takes me by surprise. "What?"

"You heard me," she insists. She's kneeling on the bed now, facing us both. Giving me a look, she swats impatiently at my leg. "Up. Up!"

Slowly I clamber to my knees, marveling again at the complete lack of pain from my healed injuries. I face her on the bed, resting back on my heels. I don't know what she wants and that worries me, so I carefully keep a few feet between us, remembering how Elric took me by surprise last night.

But she doesn't try to kiss me. Instead she reaches forward to take me by the shoulders. "Turn around," she orders, guiding me until I'm facing Clarent. My back is turned to Lavender, and her hands still lie on my upper arms. "Now," she says firmly, "kiss Clarent."

My heart skips and I look round at her in shock. "Do what?"

Lavender gives me an exasperated look. "Rose," she says, her voice as patient as if I were a recalcitrant child, "do you like kissing Clarent?"

I glance at him; he watches us with bemused eyes, apparently willing to be the object of this examination. "Well, yes," I admit, my cheeks starting to burn. "The, uh, times we kissed were very satisfactory."

Lavender nods approvingly. "And would you like to kiss Clarent right now?" she prompts.

I stare at him, faced with a question that seems impossible to answer. Thoughts flit through my mind only to dissolve into incoherent confusion at second glance. No, not when I've just killed a man; yet the feel of Clarent under my lips might drive away the lingering memory of heat and pain. No, not when half a dozen people are downstairs waiting for us to join them; yet if he were to be hurt at all by my kisses, surely Worth and Joel could heal him right away. No, because I don't deserve his smooth lips and sweet smile; but yes, when the mere sight of him now causes my stomach to flutter with painful need.

"If he'd like that," I manage, my voice suddenly hoarse. "Yes."

The smile he gives me is pure pleasure. "I'd like that very much," he murmurs, his voice all soft honey and warmth, sending a fresh jolt of desire through my stomach right down to my knees.

Behind me, Lavender nods as if this is all very satisfactory. "Well," she says, her voice brisk and reasonable, "I can't kiss you and you can't kiss me, but you *can* kiss Clarent while I watch."

I blink, not quite following her reasoning. Yet we'd done that yesterday, hadn't we? Clarent had kissed me and Lavender had been there, and it had felt so nice. I nod briefly. "Okay," I say, unsure what to do next.

Clarent grins and sits up straighter. Lavender guides me forward with little nudging pushes and I'm kneeling beside him, facing him, leaning down a little to meet his lips with mine. Cool silver touches my skin, smooth and gentle, and his metal softens and warms under my touch.

That first kiss lasts an eternity, the seconds spinning out around us as I wait for him to gasp, to seize up, to bleed from the mouth. But he kisses me back, gentle and unhurried, and then the first kiss becomes a second and a third and a fourth as my lips move greedily over him. He feels so good, so much like everything I've been hungry for, solid and happy and kind. Whenever our lips part for a breath he smiles up at me, his eyes shining with a joy that makes my heart leap.

There is a touch of warmth at the back of my neck, soft skin that isn't mine and isn't metal. I jump under the touch and feel Lavender's purr in my skin as she trails electricity across my neck to my bare shoulder. "Can I kiss you like *this*, Rose?" she whispers.

Her tone is playful but I hear the fear in her voice, smell the fresh burst of clover in the air. *She's afraid I'll reject her,* I realize, for the crime of becoming a murderer like me; or because I might redetermine to live a life of chastity as sacrifice for my own crimes. And shouldn't I? Depression, my old companion, weighs heavily on my heart, reminding me that I don't deserve to be happy and that Clarent and Lavender would be better off if I weren't here between them.

Yet she smells so anxious and her voice trembles underneath her teasing. I can't bear to hurt her when she's so vulnerable. My desire for martyrdom is weaker than my wish to make her smile.

"Yes," I tell her, my voice raw in my throat. "Please. Please kiss me, Lavs."

I hear her soft sigh of relief and smell the instant change as soft lavender replaces every hint of clover. The scent of her—not afraid, not angry, just *her*—fills the air like a heady perfume. I tilt my head back to drink her in and she dips to kiss my collarbone, her hair spilling over me like a cloak. Soft lips drag electric tingles across my skin, coaxing a moan from my lips. Clarent, smiling, leans back to watch us, but I reach out to him. Cupping his face gently between my hands, I draw him up for fresh kisses.

I am a desert drinking in the summer rain, taking and keeping and still needing more. Clarent's kisses on my lips, Lavender's mouth on my shoulder and neck are the draught of fresh water I've been longing for. I'm breathing hard, little panting gasps for air between kisses, my skin flushed and warm from their touch.

Lavender's fingers move over my body, pulling gently at the tattered rags of what had been my favorite summer dress before the magma man burned away most of it. I hear myself gasp, not quite sure that I want to undress, but another soft kiss from Clarent stokes the furnace in my stomach. "Please," Lavender whispers in my ear, and she sounds as needy as I feel. "Please, can I? I've waited so long."

I choke back a sound that might be a sob, though not one of sadness. "Yes. Okay," I gasp, not sure of the right words. I'm nervous of being exposed, but how can I tell her 'no' when there's such fierce desire in her voice?

Then her hands are traveling over me again, touching where my clothes come away. There's pleasure in her fingers, and I don't know if it's magic and I realize I don't care. I hear my voice moaning, begging softly for Lavender to touch me just a little higher, just a little lower, to keep moving. She giggles softly, her lips pressed against my ear, and I feel electricity shoot through me again as her tongue darts out to flick the soft skin of my earlobe.

"Lower like this?" she whispers. Then her hands dip down over my body, and I have to bite the inside of my cheek to keep from crying out at the unexpected pleasure where she touches. "So tell me, do you still think my fingers cause desire?" she teases, pinching and rolling her fingers gently over the spot she's found.

"*Accelerate* desire," I correct with a gasp, my nails digging into Clarent's shoulder for support. "Worth was— ah!— very clear." I almost cry out and I have to stuff my hand in my mouth to prevent it.

Lavender giggles again, torturing me mercilessly with her touch. "Clarent, if she's being kissed properly then she can't yell," she scolds with a laugh, and he grins and leans forward to take her advice. Cool hands reach up to tangle in my hair, his touch gentle and soft. Lavender maneuvers easily around him, her lips finding my ear again. "Isn't this so much better than being miserable all the time?" she asks, her earlier plea echoing under her teasing.

"Yes," I gasp between kisses, trying not to giggle. "Yes, Lavs! This is better. Laugh at me if you must, but you're convincing." I realize, to my profound embarrassment, that my hips have started to grind just barely against her fingers, a trembling neediness stirring in my stomach.

Blood rushes to my cheeks, burning with shame as I try to rein in my traitorous hips, holding as still as I can under her touch. Clarent kisses the heat away from my face but then looks up at me with fresh worry in his eyes. "Do you need to stop, Rose?" he asks, his voice full of concern.

I shake my head, looking away shyly from his probing gaze. I wish I could bury my head in his shoulder. "I'm fine," I whisper. "I just... it's intense, that's all."

Lavender snorts behind me. "It's supposed to be *more* intense," she mutters, sounding put out, "but these nails are too damn sharp for what I want to do. Fucking May Queen." She pulls her fingers away, drawing a little whimper from me, and begins to pull at the shreds of Clarent's trousers. "Off with these," she says crisply. "I need your help with this part."

Clarent blinks but obeys her without question. He wriggles and she pulls, and I have a front row seat to watch as he strips for me. He's beautiful and silver, his body smooth and hard. For a moment, all I can think of is Mina's offer of a practice dildo and then I'm trying not to giggle for fear he would misunderstand and my laughter might hurt his feelings. "Over and up," Lavender says, breaking my reverie with a sharp smack on my rear.

"Wait, I—" I look back at her, my eyes locking with hers. Questions I don't know how to ask flit through my head. Is she okay with this, with him doing this to me? In front of her while she watches?

Her green eyes soften and her lips twitch with amusement. "You first," she says gently, reaching up to touch my cheek. I try not to cry, fighting the urge to surge towards her and wrap her in a warm kiss—a kiss that would kill her.

"If you're sure," I whisper. She grins and slaps my ass again, her touch gentle. Her hands guide my legs to straddle his hips, and then she reaches down to grasp him and guide him up to me. I gasp again at the touch of him; he's cool and solid but warms quickly at the touch of my skin, softening just enough to mold to my contours—as though he were made for me.

"Down you go, Rose," Lavender murmurs, her lips at my ear. She nips gently at my skin, bringing me near to a yelp again, and I duck instinctively away from her teasing teeth, my movement sliding me down onto him.

He's cool and warm at the same time, hard and soft in equal measure. Clarent's hands fly up to grip my hips, his eyes wide and his mouth open as he pants quietly for breath. "Oh, god, Rose," he whispers, his hips moving slowly under me, unable to hold still. The motion drags another soft moan from my lips, and I have to bite my hand to keep quiet.

I'm moving on him and I remember how to do this. I must have done it before, because this isn't like anything I'd experienced in the otherworld. My hips rise and fall as I drag slowly over him and then slide easily back down. Each time I do, a raw stab of pleasure shoots through me. I can feel my knees trembling beneath me from the intensity of what I'm doing to him, of what he's doing to me with his tiny, gentle movements.

Lavender nestles close behind me, cupping me with her warm body. She moves with me, up and then back down again, undulating with me like a wave. Her hands reach around to slide over my legs, over my thighs, and over the back of Clarent's hands, drawing a fresh gasp of pleasure from him. Then her fingers are moving up, over my hips, over my stomach, trailing pleasure as she cups the curve of my breasts.

I hold my breath, embarrassed all over again to be touched this way while being watched by Clarent's soft eyes, but her fingers feel so good. Her thumb reaches up, sliding over the round curves to caress my nipple. Electricity arcs through me, causing my body to clench tightly.

"Oh, do that again," Clarent begs, gazing up at Lavender like a supplicant.

She grins at him from over my shoulder. "Do what, Clarent?" she teases softly, her eyes flashing wickedly. "Do this?" Her thumb strokes me again, and again I shudder from the intense pleasure of it.

"Yes, god, that," Clarent pants, his cool hands caressing my hips as he moves faster. "Rose, please can she do it again?" he asks, his silver eyes wide as he looks up at me.

"If she does it again," I gasp, my throat dry and raw from the effort not to cry out, "I think I might explode."

Lavender leans in towards my ear again, her eyes dancing. "That's the idea, Ravs," she whispers wickedly. A single green thumb flicks over my nipple a third time, even as its companion slides back down to caress the tiny button just above where Clarent slides in and out of me.

I tilt my head back, pleasure overwhelming my senses in a steady

200

relentless beat as she works. Lavender leans over my shoulder to nibble gently at my neck, murmuring words I can't hear and smelling sweeter than I could ever imagine. As the world explodes from her touch and the hard fullness of Clarent inside me, I have just enough sense remaining to stuff my fist in my mouth, muffling the cries of pleasure that I can't hold back as I careen over the edge.

Clarent holds still as I buck against him, his hands steadying me gently. When I come back to myself, the room is somehow brighter than before. I'm leaning over him, my hands on the sheets on either side of his chest. He smiles up at me, even as Lavender pats my hair gently and trails soothing kisses down my spine. "Are you okay?" he asks softly, his eyes full of warm hope.

I can't help but laugh, my voice shaky. "Yes. Yes, Clarent. I'm better than okay. Thank you." I feel a fresh burn creep into my cheeks as I realize that though he's stopped, he's still hard inside me. I'm sore and embarrassed and not at all sure what to do about that, when Lavender taps me sternly on the shoulder. I look back at her, not knowing what she wants.

"Scoot forward, greedy-guts," she scolds, grinning wildly. "My turn."

My eyes widen at her, unsure if she's serious, but I'm too far gone to argue. Carefully I slide off of him, scooting forward a few feet to straddle his stomach. Behind me, Lavender moves against my skin, and I can see the breath leave him when she envelops him in a single easy motion.

He's so beautiful. I reach forward to touch his cheek, and he closes his eyes in an expression of pure bliss as she rides him. She moves faster than I did, her fingers wrapped around my waist for support as she rocks.

I lean back into her, content just to be held and hugged, feeling her rising pleasure as though it were mine all over again. "You felt so good," I whisper softly back to her. The angle is awkward, but I reach behind me to touch her legs, her hips, anything I can reach as she moves against me. "You feel so good right now. I love the feeling of your skin on mine. Lavender, why did we wait so long to do this? I'm so sorry."

I don't know if my soft babble is for myself or her. I want her to be pleased. I don't know how to use my fingers on her the way she does, how to be gentle without hurting her with my hard nails, but I'm determined to learn after this. I do know how to tell her that I like this, that I'm happy; I want her to know that she's made me feel so much better than I'd have ever thought possible. "Thank you for this, Lavs," I whisper, wishing so much that I could kiss her. But this is good too, I think; maybe this can be enough.

She comes as she grips my hips, pulling me against her in a tight hug as she buries her face in my neck. Little sobbing cries muffle against my body and tears fall wet upon my skin. I caress Clarent's face and chest, coaxing him over the edge with her, leading him there with the pleasure in my fingertips. He almost cries out, my fingers stopping his lips just in time as his cool body bucks under me and Lavender.

When they are both still again, I flop onto the sheets next to him. Lavender lies behind me, spooning me close, her arm draped over me to rest on Clarent's chest. I can feel her breath in my hair, and for the first time in my known life I feel content. I'm safe here, with Clarent's cool solidity beside me and Lavender warming me from behind. *Everything is as good as I could hope for,* I think as I snuggle closer to them both.

Then my eyes fly open in a sudden flash of guilt. "Dakota is gonna kill us," I realize, my eyes taking in the tussle of sheets and blankets beneath us.

Chapter 21

I can't doze after that, my guilt over dirtied linens too great for me to relax. Irrational, perhaps, but it's easier to grapple with than my sudden and unexpected decision *not* to live a life of repentant chastity.

I ought to be happy; I have Lavender and Clarent, without giving up my best chance to protect us and help others in our community. Yet I feel unsatisfied and anxious, depression gnawing at the corners of my mind. I still can't safely kiss Lavender despite dearly wanting to, and I'm terrified that if I become accustomed to kissing Clarent I might forget myself in the middle of lovemaking and end up hurting her. This hypothetical scenario twists my stomach into painful knots.

Lavender seems equally restless, and though I can only guess at the thoughts in her head I smell the soft worry that permeates the room. Is she worried *for* me or *about* me? Whatever is bothering her, I'm too cowardly to ask and she doesn't volunteer an explanation.

Eventually we come to a silent agreement to give up any attempt at sleep and instead drink the water and devour the cold sandwiches she brought up earlier. Clarent partakes in a relaxed fashion, seeming content in the post-coital silence. I don't think he's failed to notice how anxious we both are; his calm seems like a conscious decision, anchoring the three of us through the storm of scented emotions that whirl through the room.

After eating, there is washing following by the conundrum of dressing.

The clothes I'd so carefully picked out a few hours before are now ruined; there's no way to salvage them. Lavender and Clarent aren't much better off than me, their clothes coated with blood and grass stains that I don't expect will come out in the wash. "Your lovely suit!" I can't help but lament to Clarent, mourning the destruction of the beautiful outfit Mina had given him.

He nods in a sympathetic way. "At least Celia brought me more," he says, producing a weathered duffel bag from under the bed. He draws out fresh jeans and a soft sleeveless undershirt. "She said she scrounged them from her hand-me-down stash. I feel more comfortable in these, anyway," he admits bashfully.

Celia must have brought the clothes knowing she would see him again today, I realize, and stuffed the bag under the bed when I was unconscious. I wonder if he guesses that she probably bought the clothes specially for him on the way over, rather than 'finding' more from a bottomless closet. Of course, she had no way to know that Lavender and I would need extra outfits after an unexpected fight with a hunter, and so we are forced to dig through Dakota's closet with the expectation of paying him back later.

The clothes in the guest room seem like older outfits he's put into storage, and some of them appear completely unworn: gifts from Celia, maybe, or from other community members. I eventually find a short spring dress; it's not as pretty as the one I lost and a little more businesslike than I'd have chosen, but soft and comfortable. Most importantly, it fits. "Zip me up the back?" I ask Lavs, pulling my hair to the side so that the zipper won't catch.

She turns to me and immediately giggles. "You just had to pick the most delicate outfit in the closet," she teases. Zipping me up easily, she surprises me with a soft kiss on the back of my neck, just above the collar. "There. All done."

I can feel my cheeks burning, and I busy myself with looking through Dakota's shoes until the blush fades. Unfortunately, I quickly come to realize that his feet are half a size too small. I'll have to wear my bloodstained shoes until we get home again.

When I turn back, Lavender has found a thin long-sleeved shirt and cotton shorts for herself. She's wearing pajamas, and they *look* like pajamas. I raise an eyebrow at her. "Really?"

She laughs. "I just got backhanded by a magical hunter made of fire, Rose," she says, sticking her tongue out at me. "I'm allowed comfort-clothes for a day. It's no worse than what the college kids wear to your bookstore. C'mon, you know they're waiting downstairs for us."

I take a deep breath, allowing her to grasp my hand. Clarent smiles gently at us both and wraps his arms around us. "Ready?" he says softly, and we head downstairs together.

The ground floor is bright and cheery, the late morning sunlight streaming in through open blinds. Elric and Celia stand near the staircase, and by the sound of his cheery voice and her tight one, they are actively engaged in one of his inexhaustible supply of arguments.

He's leaning against the dark wooden banister when we approach, perfectly dressed and insouciantly smiling, the picture of blond beauty. He whirls at the sound of our step on the stairs, a flash of genuine solicitous concern crossing his handsome face for the briefest of moments.

He then takes one look at our borrowed clothes, my bashful smile, and Clarent's arms wrapped protectively around our shoulders, before he explodes in a tantrum. "I haven't had any for forty-eight hours, dealing with all this newbie nonsense, and silver-boy here has been rolling around in orgies! Dammit, Celia, I'm going home for a week and I don't want to be called for any reason at all."

She ignores his outburst. "Ah, there you are," she says to us, her voice a study in unruffled calm. "Rose, Elric was worried about you. I had to ask him not to barge upstairs while you three were resting."

He makes an exasperated face at this. "Well, Celia acted like you were at death's door," he grumbles. "Again." He gives me an arch look. "She didn't say anything about you fornicating with undocumented immigrants. Who are now, thanks to me, sufficiently documented enough to take out on the town. You're welcome."

He pulls out a file folder which he clutches under one arm, shoving a handful of papers at Clarent. "You're going to need to read over these and memorize everything," Elric says tartly. "Your new name is Clarence Smith, which is an obvious improvement on Flower Fucktoy."

Celia levels a stern look at Elric. "Clarence Smith?" she says, not entirely happy. "That's awfully Anglo-Saxon. Did you not get my text? Lily confirmed he's Hispanic; probably Latino."

"Yes, yes. But he was adopted as a baby by a stuffy old English couple," Elric counters airily, waving his hand dismissively. "Like the kiddo. I thought we had a whole adoption theme going."

Clarent's honeyed voice cuts through the gathering storm. "It's a fine name," he says, and although his back tenses a little his tone is still gentle. "Thank you. Is that all? Just memorize the papers?"

Elric looks a little deflated to see the fight end before it can properly start. "No, that's not all. There's more to follow once I put everything else together. I'll have to catch up with Lily and create a list of previous residences, family names, credit history; stuff like that. Maybe a childhood injury or two, just to round out the profile. Then you'll need to sign some stuff. Nothing difficult. But the folder has what you need for walking around."

Dakota takes this moment to stick his head in from the kitchen. There's an open archway at the end of the hall, and now that I'm distracted from Elric's antics I can see little Tox at the kitchen table, shrouded in bright yellow robes and playing with crayons. Despite having acquired a child overnight Dakota seems perfectly calm, with a peaceful smile on his lips that fades only a little at being forced to interact with Elric. Even the soft golden faery-glow that permeates his skin at all times seems a little brighter than I remember.

He gives Elric a look which suggests no love is lost between the two men. "Since you're handing out papers now, I'll take what you've drafted for Tox," he says, holding out a hand in expectation.

"Oh, yeah, sure; I've got you covered," Elric drawls, handing over a second file full of papers. The corner of his mouth trembles with the effort required to keep a straight face.

Dakota scans the papers quickly, his handsome brown face darkening with anger. "You named them 'Annie Orphan'?" he all but yells. Tox's head swivels up and around to us, their dark eyes full of curiosity. Celia frowns, snatching the papers from Dakota to scan them herself.

Elric smirks at the outrage. "Well, Celia said we weren't calling them an orphan in the general sense, but I think you'll agree it's very endearing as a surname," he argues cheerfully. "Anyway, you'll be changing their name as part of the adoption process—"

"I'm *not* changing their name," Dakota interrupts, stepping closer to Elric to stare furiously into his face. "And I'm *not* letting you pull the same naming nonsense that you did with me. You're going to give them a good name that reflects their actual heritage, not some joke of a name that you picked to amuse yourself!"

"But I like it!"

We all turn to stare at the little child, still sitting meekly at the kitchen table. It's the first time I've heard their voice, as warm and sweet as butterscotch. A shy smile peeks out from under the soft butter-colored scarf that covers their dark hair. Dakota looks positively stricken at the pronouncement, and even Elric looks startled.

"Is it a bad name?" The child fidgets in their seat, their gaze dropping away from ours, feeling self-conscious under the force of so many stares and such heavy silence.

Dakota moves quickly to wrap his arm around their shoulders. "It's not the best name," he explains carefully. "We're going to get you a better name, but we'll find something that you like just as much. I promise." He glares at Elric, who seems genuinely at a loss for once. "You are *going* to fix this," Dakota orders in a low undertone. "My study. Now."

Elric makes a face. "Aw, is this going to be like your tribal directory search?" he whines. "You've been at that forever! My way is faster and it's not like Clarence complained. Okay, okay, I'm going!" He yields to Dakota's determined glare. "By the way, I'm glad you're not dead, Rose," he adds over his shoulder in a parting shot. "But, jeezus, you didn't waste any time, did you?"

I watch Dakota haul him off, shaking my head as he does so. I don't know Dakota well, but Celia mentioned once that he doesn't suffer fools gladly. I certainly hope they can come up with a better name for Tox. I glance at Lavender, but she seems lost in her own thoughts.

Clarent is preoccupied with his papers. "There's so much to remember," he murmurs, flipping through the file. I peer over his elbow to see a temporary driving license, the kind they print out on paper until the plastic card comes in the mail. "Is that what I look like, really?"

Peering at the tiny picture, I twist my lips. "Elric's phone doesn't have the best camera," I observe. "Could be worse, though." Idly, I note the age and date of birth Elric has selected for him, and then my eyes stumble when I get to the current address: Elric has listed our apartment as Clarent's permanent residence. *That jerk.* I feel a sudden stab of kinship with Dakota.

But it's fine, really. He has to stay *somewhere*, and Celia and Mina are already overwhelmed. Lavender and I can make room, can't we? I feel my heart skip a beat at a sudden mental image of the three of us rooming together, watching movies and making love whenever we want. That would be a nice change of pace, wouldn't it? Something fun and easy, to balance all the fear and danger we've been living with.

"Why don't we go sit down so you can spread everything out?" I suggest, nodding at the kitchen table, hoping my thoughts don't show on my face.

Clarent nods at the suggestion. We make our way into the kitchen, tuning out the argument that drifts in short bursts from Dakota's study. Tox looks up at us shyly, offering me a tentative handshake. "I'm glad you're better," they tell me in a quiet voice, attempting a nervous smile. I realize with a pang of guilt that I've nearly died twice in front of them.

"I am, thank you," I say. I'm about to accept the handshake when I remember my magic. "Uh, can we wave instead?" I ask apologetically, wiggling my fingers in greeting instead of taking their hand. Their face falls and I rush to reassure them, "It's not you, it's me. Sorry! I have magic fingers. We're not sure yet exactly how they work."

"Rose won't hurt you," Lavender adds quickly, giving them an earnest look. "We're just being extra careful."

The child nods, accepting this explanation matter-of-factly. "Dakota explained about fae magic. I don't have it any more," they announce, choosing a green crayon and offering it to me. "Joel checked."

I take the crayon with a smile and move closer to fill in green grass on one of the drawings, pleased to be allowed to help. In human years, they're too old for crayons—maybe eleven or twelve years old, though it's difficult to be sure when they're so tiny from malnutrition—but who knows how young they were when they were taken and all the things they have missed out on. Celia nods at me and moves away from the table, giving us more room to work while she coaxes Dakota's coffee maker into starting a fresh batch.

Beside me Clarent hesitates, looking grave. "Does that bother you?" he asks, his voice low and concerned. "Being human again?"

Tox shrugs, picking up a brown crayon to start on a tree. "No," they finally decide, their voice calm. "I was lonely. Nobody could come near without being hurt. Now I have people and food and Dakota lets me watch cartoons. I like those." They look up at Clarent with wide dark eyes. "Does it hurt being metal?"

Lavender stiffens at the question. "Can you still see his silver?" she asks, her voice carefully neutral.

The child nods happily. "It looks heavy. Is it heavy?"

He smiles gently at this. "I don't think so. Would you like to feel it?"

He holds out a hand for their inspection, and after a brief hesitation they reach up to weigh him with their touch.

I notice Celia watching us, her heightened attention indicating that she hadn't realized Tox could still see through our veils. She doesn't comment on the revelation, however; she cradles her fresh cup of black coffee and gestures for Lavender and I to join her by the kitchen counter.

"The hunter's body has been disposed of," she murmurs, sipping slowly. "He had just enough magic left to let me open a very small portal and boot him over." She sighs. "You two did the right thing taking him down, but I wish we could have captured him alive."

Lavender's lips tighten. "He didn't leave us much choice," she points out.

Celia nods, unperturbed by her tone. "No, he didn't. And it would have been especially hard to restrain and interrogate him when he could burn through my ropes. Anyway, no use crying over spilled milk."

"What would you have asked him?" I murmur. I lean against the counter and watch Tox and Clarent color while they tell him all about the cartoons they've seen so far. "Surely we can assume that it was Clarent's faery who sent him; the High King?"

She shrugs and sips again. "Could be. But, Lavender, you mentioned he said 'they' sent him? If he meant that in the plural, it'd be worth knowing who else we're up against. And in addition to the question of 'who', I'd still like to know 'how'." She holds her coffee in both hands, staring into the dark liquid as though it might produce answers.

"You're wondering how he found us," Lavender prompts.

"The portal came down so quickly. I assume he did that?" I exchange a worried glance with her.

Celia shakes her head. "All hunters have ways to find their targets, and most of them can track fae magic," she says, her voice dropping. "That's *why* they're hunters. But being able to tune directly into his target's location from the other side? Slamming a portal right down on top of him? I've never heard of a hunter who could do that."

Her words jog a memory. "No. He was surprised," I recall, frowning in concentration. "He said something about expecting to have to search for Clarent."

Celia looks relieved at this. "If he didn't know Clarent was here, that means he *wasn't* an unprecedentedly good tracker with skills I've never heard of," she observes. "Which means we're back to either coincidence or... something else," she admits. "Four portals in two days is improbable. For you and Clarent to be caught in three of them, Rose, is a hell of a coincidence. And a hunter's portal forming right on top of his target?" She shakes her head. "The chances of all that occurring together must be next to impossible."

Ice traces down my spine. "If we can't figure out what's causing this and how to stop it," I observe in a thin voice, "people are going to start dying."

Lavender's eyes narrow with worry. "You've nearly died twice already, Rose," she points out.

"You're both right," Celia says with a nod. She looks thoughtful for a moment, savoring the bitter liquid on her tongue. "Seems like we have two problems. One is Clarent and this High King. I'm not going to lie," she says, giving us a serious look. "Having even one faery after you is a very bad thing. I can teach you ways to hide better, and how to run when you can. The good news is: if the High King fits the usual pattern, he'll lose interest after a while. They're vicious bastards, but capricious—forgetful and easily distracted. That works in our favor, but only in the long-term."

Lavender bares her teeth in a determined grin, pleased to have something concrete to do. "And we can make sure he's never alone, at least not for the first few months," she says. "Rose works days and I'm on the night shift, and there's still plenty of overlap for us to both spend time together," she adds, stealing a glance at me. I feel a blush creep into my cheeks at the open discussion of me and Lavs spending time together.

Celia hides a smile. "It's a good plan; I approve." She sighs and takes another long sip. "Second problem is these portals popping up. That's *not* a wait-and-see situation, as far as I'm concerned. Faeries are a known quantity: they're dangerous and clever, but they rarely chase after an escaped altered for long. We just aren't important enough to fixate on. So whatever is causing portals to pop open is something I don't recognize or understand, and waiting could make it worse."

I bite the inside of my cheek. The portals probably have nothing to do with me, since Kieran was caught in one when I was on the other side of town, but being caught in three of the last four has made me anxious not to repeat the experience. "What should we do? The last one hit too fast for us to escape before it closed, and Clarent's came down while we were in our apartment. We can't maintain a state of constant vigilance, always looking out the window."

Celia runs a hand absentmindedly over her thick braid. "Yesterday I was thinking about maybe taking you three to talk to another altered," she says slowly. "She's only been out for a couple months now; came out after you two escaped. But she's got some information that I don't think anyone else in our community has."

I'm surprised to hear this; I'd thought there hadn't been any new escapees between our own flight and Clarent's appearance. "A new altered? Has she been to see Athena yet?"

Celia shakes her head, frowning. "No. She's... complicated. I've got her in an apartment for now, sequestered away from everyone else. I wasn't sure whether it was safe to take you to meet her, but after this hunter attack I think it would be more dangerous to do nothing at all. She might be able to help, or at least to tell us something useful."

Lavender considers this, reaching out for my hand. "It would be better than waiting around for tonight's meeting," she points out quietly.

I make a face and nod slowly. "Yeah. Okay. I mean, it's either this or try again to get some sleep, right? Celia, what's her name?" I ask her as she polishes off the coffee.

She hesitates and then shrugs, figuring we'll find out sooner or later. "Her name's Oracle. I'll go tell Dakota we're leaving. You two let Clarent know he's coming with us. She's going to want to see him."

CHAPTER 22

Celia drives us to an apartment complex not far from Dakota's house. I recognize the area; the bookstore is only a few miles up the road, and Celia rents a residence here for Athena. I wonder if we're here to pick her up, but Celia instead pulls her truck around to the far side of the complex. The four of us pile out, and she leads us up the open-air stairs to a third-floor landing. She knocks on the metal door of the farthest apartment in the row, and the entrance is cracked open just wide enough to let us squeeze in.

We're fully inside the apartment before our host slips out from where she's hiding behind the door. When I glimpse her in the low light, my heart races painfully and my breath comes in shallow gasps. I stare at her, trying to understand why I have a strong desire to run and hide. She's only a few inches shorter than me and maybe a few years older. She's sickly wan—not white like Lavender, but strangely ashen, with blue veins that stand out in harsh contrast. Her eyes are too pale, strangely cloudy and gray. *She's a corpse,* I realize, my heart beating faster.

I know there are members of our community who look dead. Mina had been enthusiastic in her matchmaking attempts on behalf of a zombie boy I'd never met. I'd dismissed her suggestion at the time, not being interested in pursuing happiness I didn't feel I deserved. I'm now immensely relieved I never agreed to meet him; this girl looks exactly like the bodies that lay overnight in my room, her dead skin and cloudy eyes summoning a storm of painful memories.

"Hello, Oracle," Celia greets her in a gentle tone. "Sorry we're a day later than you wanted."

"It's just as well," the girl says with a quiet sigh. Her voice is a high rasp that tickles the back of my throat; it makes me want to cough on her behalf. "He was cranky yesterday, but today has been better." Her eyes flit over us with obvious interest. "You're Clarent, right? You remove fae magic?"

Celia touches Clarent on the shoulder, preempting his answer. "He does," she answers. "But, hon, I really don't think you should volunteer just yet. We don't know what will happen to you."

Exhaustion and exasperation mingle in the girl's pallid face, the expression of someone who is tired of a familiar argument. "I'm done giving him a ride, Celia," she says firmly. "I want to be free of him. If it kills me in the process, so be it. He should have died long ago, and— mmm."

Her sentence ends abruptly in a low hum, her high voice segueing into a much deeper resonance. Her stance changes, shoulders hunching forward and her fingers steepling thoughtfully as she looks at us. When she speaks again her voice is lower, deeper, and gently accented where it wasn't before. "Mmm. No, I won't die today, girl," the new voice purrs. "Not unless you kiss the pink one, and then we'll both die. The purple one is safe, though. Do keep it in mind when you're piloting us, no matter how much we want them."

Her gaze sweeps back to Clarent. "Is that the boy you've been watching?" Her rasping voice doesn't seem to be addressing any of us. "He doesn't remove magic. He certainly can't remove *me*. Did anyone actually say he could? Was it that silly speckled healer, Joel? He's a child surrounded by babies, and it's gone to his head. Or did you just assume it from watching the boy work? Your eyes deceive you, girl, no matter how sharp your sight."

Celia takes the disconcerting shift in personality in her calm stride. "Hello, Hermit," she says mildly. "Would you like to come sit on the couch with us?"

214

The girl nods. Her expression doesn't change, but her deep voice sounds sullen. "Oracle says not to put your dirty feet on the coffee table," she grumbles. "There, I told them so you don't need to speak. Quiet down. I said, quiet dow—"

There's a pause, a sense of internal struggle, and then the girl's voice returns to her higher soprano. "There's sodas in the fridge where you put them, Celia," she says, resignation suffusing her voice. "You'll have to get your own glasses; he refuses to host properly."

"That's what servants are for," the girl adds, sniffing haughtily as the deeper voice returns.

"We're fine," Celia says stiffly, ignoring the last comment and leading us to the couch.

I follow, intensely uncomfortable. "How do you know us? How do you know Joel?"

"And why do you want Clarent to de-magic you?" Lavender pipes up, frowning at our odd host as we settle into our seats.

"You're one of the avatars, aren't you?" Clarent asks. "Like the one who carried me out. A dead shell for a faery to remotely control." His eyes glint in gentle hope. "Did you get away before they could finish draining you?"

The girl waves her hand in a gesture of annoyance, her deep voice dripping with disdain. "Hardly! A modified avatar, perhaps, but far superior to the original; in no way deserving of the same term. And I am anything but remote, human."

Lavender leaps to her feet. "You're a faery?" she breathes, scented fury filling the air.

"She's complicated," Celia repeats firmly. "They both are."

Oracle's pitch rises again. "He destroyed his own body," she says, her expression glum. "He was trying to make a vessel that wouldn't break down over time, one he could permanently embed his consciousness in. Instead he got stuck in here with me, with only limited control."

"That is a *very* simplistic explanation," the deeper voice of Hermit grumbles. "I acquired this servant because she has a gift for far-seeing, projecting her consciousness to view events from a distance. I believed she would be an excellent candidate for total removal. My experiment yielded unexpected results, and now she is quite stubbornly present despite my best attempts."

His hand snakes out to grab a piece of candy from a bowl on the coffee table, only to fiddle helplessly with the wrapper in frustration. "She wants the boy to exorcise me, without realizing— fix it, girl!" he snarls, frustrated by the candy.

The hands still for a moment as though two drivers are exchanging control, and then she unwraps the candy with ease, a weary expression flitting over her face. "You have to be patient, Hermit," she says dully, eating the newly-liberated candy without gusto.

Celia watches all this with a grim expression. "Oracle phoned me yesterday, Rose, right after you found Tox. Her call came through before Elric's did."

"I saw what he'd done," Oracle says, nodding at Clarent. "I was stepping out for a while, to get away from Hermit. I saw the whole thing and asked her to bring him over." She flashes an apologetic look at me. "After they healed you, of course."

I stare at her. In a few short, panicky moments I've gone from being afraid due to her resemblance to my victims to irrationally wanting to add her to their number before the faery inside can hurt us. I could kill them both right where they sit. Yet she's a victim as much as any of us. "It's no wonder you can't bring them to meetings," I whisper.

Celia nods, her voice grave. "The fewer people who know, the less I have to worry about someone climbing through her window with a knife."

"But we're in danger," Lavender argues hotly. "He could be plotting with them! Sending information back! Especially if she can see us without our knowledge. No offense," she adds to the girl.

Oracle shrugs wearily before Hermit reasserts himself. "Bah! Stupid girl," he grumbles. "To whom would I send information? I'm an abomination to those nitwits. Trapped in a human body? They'd kill me rather than acknowledge such a thing is possible."

He grabs another candy and manages to work it out of its wrapper on his own. "How do you think she escaped? Do you imagine she took control from me long enough to bring us out? Ha! No, I went into exile for my own safety. And you can't have any candy," he adds, shooting a glare at Lavender.

Oracle sighs and pushes the bowl away. "You've had enough already, Hermit," she says glumly. "You'll make us sick." Looking at Celia, she asks, "If you aren't here to bring Clarent to me, what has brought you out? I haven't seen much, but enough to gather that you're too busy for casual house calls, I think."

Celia nods at her. "We've had four portals open in two days. One of them was created by a hunter looking for Clarent, so that one is less surprising except that he defied all probability by opening right on top of him." She gives Oracle an apologetic look. "I was hoping to talk to Hermit."

Oracle's face falls with fresh disappointment before morphing back into the haughty self-assurance of her counterpart. "Portals," he scoffs in his deep voice. "Finicky things; I don't care for them. You're a hunter, Celia. You ought to know enough about them without needing to bother me."

Lavender jumps beside me but Celia pretends not to notice. "Humor me. Talk Rose through the mechanics," she requests.

He gives me a curious look. "Why Rose?"

I lean forward. "The portals keep forming on top of *me*. Am I doing something to cause that?"

"That depends," he says with a chuckle. "It is well known that humans yearn to return to the human world, while faeries desire their own homeland. Are you a secret faery princess, little Rose?"

I widen my eyes at him. "You know she's not," Celia says firmly. "Don't lie to us, Hermit, or I'll shuffle everyone right out the door."

His face twists briefly back to the resigned expression of Oracle. "I'll step out for the rest of the day if you drive them off," she threatens him. "You'll be all alone."

He flinches. When his haughty expression settles back into place it is slightly subdued, his tone sullen. "Very well. Our world and your world overlie each other, but only the portal-space allows passage between them. When conditions are right, two points are joined to make a third. For that moment in time, three separate locations exist in the same space; for example: your apartment in the human world, a forest in the fae world, and a portal which imperfectly attempts to combine the two."

I nod at him. "Okay. What about the people?"

He steeples his fingers again. "The portal-space can copy inanimate objects and some aspects of the scenery: trees, grass, and so forth. More complex life forms, no. Anything living at either of the two points will stay where they are, often unaware of the portal, or will slip into the portal-space. For faeries or humans, slipping requires an act of will, which is quite a hurdle for humans who don't know the fae world exists. But altereds slip easily, often without meaning to. You brim with fae magic, yet you are neither fully faery nor fully human; you exist in a state between two worlds."

"You said 'when the conditions are right'," Lavender repeats with a frown. "What are those conditions?"

Hermit makes a face. "Sufficient power and the will to expend it," he says, his tone suggesting this should be perfectly obvious. "Portals require magic to power them, human or faery, it doesn't matter. The only real variable is the amount of power needed, which depends on the conditions at the two points. The border of a faery's estate or the edges of a human city have less magic worn into them over time, and are therefore easier for the portal-space to copy."

"That's why the portals tend to open on the outskirts of town, not smack in the middle," Celia says calmly, resting her hands on her knees. "Which is partly why it's so alarming that the three yesterday popped out where they did."

He shrugs at this. "Location merely increases the amount of magic the portal needs to power it."

Clarent leans forward, listening intently. "Where does the magic come from?"

Celia is the one who answers. "That's the other problem," she says, her voice tight. "The magic comes from us, from the person or people opening the portal. There is power in our intent, in the will to cross. If our will isn't enough, the raw magic in our bodies can make up the difference. A hard crossing can leave an altered weakened for days, or even strip some of their magic away permanently."

She shakes her head at Hermit. "All three of yesterday's altereds lacked sufficient intent to power a portal. Nor did any of them lose their raw magic, so far as I can see. There's a deficit of power to explain their crossing."

Hermit frowns at this. "Why would they lack intent? Humans escape because they *want* to escape, because despite our best efforts some part of them remembers there's another world they belong to. That's why there's rarely any point in recovering the ones who get away."

"I didn't want to escape," Clarent says softly. "I wasn't conscious enough to want anything."

"You're sure?" Hermit rounds on him, looking extremely dubious.

"None of the three intended to come over," Celia repeats firmly. "Clarent was a sword, Tox didn't have the slightest memory of our world, and the bear-woman was brought over in a broken portal. The edges didn't close, and there were human witnesses. I've only ever known that to happen when one party wants very badly *not* to cross. It's why hunters drug their prey unconscious. Are you still going to tell me she powered a portal with her intent?"

He's quiet for a time, mulling this over. "Portals require power," he repeats slowly. "But some portals require less power than others. Just because they weren't weakened by the crossing doesn't mean they couldn't have paid a small toll." He frowns. "You'd need to know the conditions on both sides. You cannot solve the equation when you only have half the facts. That the portals opened in the middle of the city is odd, but if the fae side was particularly barren—"

"There were trees," I pipe up, anxious to help. "Grass, too."

He glares at me. "Barren of *magic*," he explains impatiently. "If the magic were particularly thin in the fae world where your three crossed, then the portal would not need much power to open. One of the deserts our parents sometimes leave behind, perhaps; a coincidence, but no longer an unbalanced equation."

"You have parents?" I frown in surprise. Never once in otherworld had I heard of a faery giving birth. That was something only humans did, and even then very rarely.

"We call them that," he says, his deep tone turning dry. "The Elder Fae are foci of magic. They absorb power from the land and air around them, creating deserts in our world. When they have sucked an area dry, they move on in search of greener pastures. They vary in size and strength, but it is from them that we are spawned and to them that we return. We may be merely a by-product to them, like shed scales or fur."

"Or shit," Lavender adds in a soft voice.

He ignores her, his tone turning lofty. "I choose to believe we evolved as part of their metabolism. Our job as their children is to acquire food for them. We are very willing to oblige, for when they become hungry enough they eat us. They say the first children were quite frantic until they found humans to offer as tribute."

"You made portals," Celia breathes. "The will to find food was strong enough to channel a crossing."

Hermit nods, looking smug. "Yes, we crossed to hunt, though it is uncomfortable for us in your world. The first children only hunted when they were hungry, but that was risky and our parents were rarely obliging enough to give sufficient warning of their needs. We learned to keep humans as cattle. Later, we decided we no longer needed to do the hunting ourselves, and we acquired finders to visit your world and replenish our herds."

"Didn't you care that they were people?" I breathe, feeling a lump form at the back of my throat. "That *we* are people? You're looking at us, talking to us! Don't you care that you take us away from our homes?"

"Not particularly," he says with a careless shrug. "Do you worry whether your steak left a family behind? You aren't all cattle, of course; we do keep quite a few of you as pets. Pretty playthings for our beds and parties; tailors to clothe us and our favorite toys; musicians to play while we dance. We altered the humans to be more useful and pleasing to us, and so you might last longer in our world. Your culture, too: we took what we liked and adapted our society around it."

I bite the inside of my cheek, steadying my breathing. I don't want to listen to any more of this; yet I've been searching for answers since we escaped, only finding guesses and speculation. *Vishkanya. Rappaccini's Daughter.* Our best attempts to piece together the May Queen's motives for making me a murderer, for plaguing me with a lifetime of nightmares.

"Why do you turn us into assassins?" I ask, my voice low. "If you're all serving the same parents, why do you kill each other? Shouldn't you cooperate?"

He arches an eyebrow at me. "Our own parents kill us when they are hungry and our herds are too small to satisfy them. Can you think of a better way to double your flock than to acquire your neighbor's?" He lunges for another candy before Oracle can move the bowl away. "The desire to survive didn't evolve in us the same way it did in you; but we learned. Now we cultivate thorns in our gardens: assassins to kill our neighbors and guards to keep them from killing us."

Lavender stiffens, the air around us full of sour anger. "If you live and die by the size of your 'flocks', why do you waste so many of us?"

Hermit shrugs. "Do you waste nothing? Many of us are bored. We're born fully grown, you know; we are given a selection of knowledge from the memories of our parents. As we no longer spend our time hunting and the existence of servants has given us leisure time, there is little to do between birth and death. We take our amusements where we can."

"The humans she made me kill meant nothing to her," I whisper. I'd guessed as much, but it hurts to hear the confirmation. "I was given my magic to kill her rivals, and everything else was just to pass the time."

"No," he snaps, correcting me. "You were not *given* magic. All humans have magic, just as all faeries do. We merely arrange you to resonate with our own, like a magnet polarizing a steel needle. To actually *give* you magic would require losing some of ours, a luxury we cannot afford. Faeries who weaken themselves in that way are quickly killed off by their neighbors."

He peers at us, his eyes narrowing. "Tracing the pattern left by another faery is difficult, but from the looks of you two she was quite a budding alchemist. Different humans have different magical strengths but we have guidance over your shaping, like a potter with clay. You are both powerful and were probably specially selected for your potential. The snotty purple one is designed to influence and ingratiate; the little pink one carries a unique taint."

Lavender growls at him. "Her lips are poison," she says firmly, "that's *all*. She's not 'tainted'."

He laughs, the sound unpleasant and grating. "Her lips are harmless. The resin she produces is a magical binding agent designed to restore cohesion within a damaged system; I used a similar substance to heal my own wounded servants. When she kisses someone, the fluid disseminates rapidly through their bloodstream, arresting damage and boosting regeneration. But since she is infected, her taint clings to the binding agent and the virus spreads within seconds, killing her victim faster than they can heal. If you were to draw the fluid from her lips, the virus would die instantly without a living carrier and the resin would once again be beneficial."

Celia sucks a surprised breath of air against her teeth. He looks confused at her reaction and then laughs. "Oh, you knew that already, did you? Did you think her fluid gained its healing properties because of something *you* did?"

My heart is pounding. "What virus are you talking about? I don't understand. I'm not sick."

"Your whole body is infected," he states flatly. "You were made to kill any faery who could be coaxed to consume you. The magic in your fingers increases our hunger and makes you seem like a particularly tasty morsel. Once your target is infected, the virus spreads quickly via the binding agent, corrupting and destroying all magic from the inside." He studies me, his eyes eager. "I wonder if her eventual goal is to create a weapon for use against the Elder Fae."

Lavender stares at him, outraged. "The May Queen expected Rose to *kiss* one of your faery parents?"

Hermit shakes his head, looking thoughtful. "No, I doubt that was the plan. The mouth as a point of infection was probably an interim step to test the process as she refined her methods. She can't experiment on Elder Fae without being found out, but she can test on faeries and humans. Nothing can live once their magic has been destroyed, after all. She probably intended to serve up a whole bouquet of edible flowers," he muses. "Pretty sights and smells, and one deadly Rose in the very center."

"I've kissed Rose and my magic wasn't affected," Clarent points out. "Joel said that indicated a biological poison, one that didn't affect metal."

Hermit laughs at him. "You didn't survive because you're made of metal; you survived because of your unique talent. You have an instinctive control over magical alignment. When her virus enters your body, you simply realign the invasive magic to match your own. Very few faeries would be able to accomplish what you seem able to do without conscious thought."

I feel panic tightening my chest, irrational fear building. "No. You're wrong," I whisper. It was bad enough when I thought only my lips were deadly; to have my whole body soured by the May Queen is more than I think I can bear.

Hermit gives me a dry look. "Oh, you don't have to believe me, little flower," he says. "Here, boy, I'll show you. Take their hands, both of them."

Clarent hesitates but takes my hand gently, his other hand reaching over my lap to touch Lavender. She looks displeased to be asked to relinquish her grip, but reluctantly releases me in order to take his hand in hers.

"Focus," Hermit says, his voice dipping lower. "I know you can see the web of magic around them. Study the arrangement around their fingers, the changes around their hair. You're not just looking for the marks of fae magic, but the subtle individual variations that make them different from each other."

Clarent's breathing slows, his silver pupils widening as he studies us both for markings that the rest of us cannot view. "I can see it," he murmurs, his voice softer now. "I can see where the web thickens and changes. But I don't—" His voice stops; his eyes widen as he looks at me.

"What? What do you see?" I stammer, feeling my heart clench.

Out of the corner of my eye, I can see Hermit smirking. "You see it now, don't you, boy?"

Clarent shakes his head at me, trying to find the words to soften the news. "Rose, I'm so sorry. Yes, you're different, but it's not *bad*. I thought it was just because you had a different faery from everyone else. But Lavender—" His face falls as tears well in my eyes. "I should have told you," he whispers, sounding miserable.

"Not your fault," Hermit says cheerily, reaching for another candy. "It's a nice little piece of work. Subtle, really; wouldn't expect most faeries to pick it up at a glance, which of course is the point. I could probably recreate it if I had enough time to study it, though I imagine it's specially designed for exclusive use in her flowers. No point in letting another faery steal your research, is there. Candy?"

CHAPTER 23

After the first flush of tears, my sadness ebbs away to be replaced by a numb emptiness. Around me, I hear raised voices as Hermit and Lavender and Celia argue, but their words feel distant and disconnected, not important enough to hear or remember. Clarent holds me to his chest, his solid weight sheltering me as he tucks his chin protectively over the top of my head.

"Come outside with me?" he whispers softly, his voice warm in my ear. "Get some fresh air?"

I don't want fresh air but neither do I want to stay here with so many people, so I nod. Gently, he helps me up. Lavender jumps up with us, her eyes worried, her hands outstretched to steady me. Clarent jerks his head towards the front door in explanation, and after a brief hesitation she nods her approval.

"I'll be out in a minute," she says, her voice tight. "Stay with Clarent, okay, Rose?" I nod again, not meeting anyone's gaze.

He leads me out to the landing, where the only sound is the nearby traffic and the air doesn't smell of emotions that aren't mine. The sun blazes brightly off his silver skin but his arm stays cool around me. I clutch the nearby railing and stare at the faraway ground, wondering if I'm about to be sick.

"You're still you," he murmurs, gazing over my shoulder at the traffic below us, the cars driving by. "You're a little different from everyone else, but you're not bad."

I shake my head slowly, unable to find the right words. I wish I could feel my sadness again or shed some tears, but instead I feel empty. "I'm tainted," I whisper, my voice hollow. "Not just my lips, every inch of me. Dirty."

He wraps his arms more tightly around me. "I don't think you're dirty," he says, his voice gentle. "I've seen you and your magic, touched you and kissed you." He nuzzles my hair with his nose, the gesture lightly teasing. "I'd do it again, if you'd let me."

I almost snort at this; it's not a laugh, but it comes close. "I've wanted to know for so long who I am and where I came from," I admit, my voice low. "Why they took *me* and not someone else. I wanted to know what they did it *for*, what was worth ruining my life over." I shake my head again to try and dislodge the numbness clinging to me. "Then I find out I was nothing more than poisoned meat. They could have kidnapped a roast from the grocery store instead."

Clarent listens to this in silence. The way he holds me, the way he breathes beside me is warm and tender, accepting everything without judgment. "They took our history away from us," he agrees solemnly. "They made us forget that we speak other languages. How many more might we know?" He hugs me closer to him. "But we're still ourselves," he says firmly. "You're still you and I'm still me, no matter what happens."

I twist my head to the side, trying to catch him in my peripheral vision. "How do you know?" I ask quietly, feeling tears prick my eyes. "When your body has been altered and your memory locked away, how do you know you're really *you*?"

He smiles down at me. "Well, sure, there are things I don't remember right now that I want to discover again. And they've done things to my body that make life different than it would have been otherwise." He leans down, nuzzling my ear. "It isn't fair, and we've got every right to be angry.

But maybe I can make something good out of this; maybe I'll end up knowing myself better because I won't take anything for granted. Every memory I can pull to the surface is precious." He kisses my cheek softly. "And the new memories are pretty good, too," he whispers.

I choke back a cry in my throat, turning in his arms to bury my face in his chest. The sorrow slams back down, flooding the numb emptiness of my mind and drawing tears from my eyes. "But there's so many bad ones," I mumble into his cool skin. "So many bad memories. So many dead faces and constant worry!"

My voice rises in a high whisper as he holds me, my words punctuated by sobs. "Clarent, I'm afraid I'll hurt Lavender if I stay this way, but that I'll fail to protect her if I change back! I don't want to be fae, but I'm afraid that turning me human might make things even worse."

"I know. I'm sorry. I'm so sorry," he repeats, stroking my hair and holding me through the sobs. He hesitates, and a long minute spans out as the worst of my tears subside into hiccups. "Rose," he says, his voice very tender, "may I look again?"

He takes a half-step back from me, holding me steady with his hands on my arms. I look up at him anxiously. He's staring at me, the way he did before when Hermit was guiding him. His eyes move over me, studying invisible details that don't correspond with anything in my mirror. "It's bad?" I hazard, my gaze dropping away from his scrutiny.

His voice is low and reassuring. "No. No, Rose, absolutely nothing about you is bad. Your magic is different, that's all. The way it moves over you, the patterns; Rose, you're beautiful and unique. It's not dirty."

"It kills people," I remind him, my eyes still not meeting his.

"It does. But, Rose—" He hesitates again, frowning in concentration. "I think I understand the pattern of your magic, what makes it different from Lavender's."

His frown deepens, his eyes tracing the curve of my shoulder, following an invisible eddy. "He acted like it was so difficult," he muses, almost to

227

himself. "But if the flow changed in this direction, the virus would be stronger; counterbalance it the other way and your magic would be more like hers."

"You can see my magic in that much detail?" I ask, my eyebrows rising in surprise. Hermit had said very few faeries could accomplish what Clarent does by instinct; I'm astonished at how he seems to master his talent more every time he uses it. *What would he be able to do by now if his faery hadn't kept his mind muddled as an inanimate sword?*

His eyes return to mine, roused from his musings. "Rose, it might take me a little time, but I believe I could remove the poison. If you don't want to be a normal human, I think I could make you like Lavender. You'd still be able to protect us; Hermit says she can influence people with her emotions. If I made you like her, you'd be able to do the same."

"Clarent—"

We're interrupted by the door opening behind us. Lavender slips out silently, leaning her back against the wall and looking weary. For a moment, I feel a surge of guilt at being caught crying in Clarent's arms. We've been discussing my magic and our future, topics that she deserves to be included in.

Yet if she's upset with us, nothing shows on her face or in her perfume; her smile is tired, but she seems relieved to join us. "Celia has the keys to the truck, otherwise I'd take us home right now," she explains, running frustrated fingers through her hair. "He positively refused to apologize for being a jerk, and now that she's said we're leaving he's throwing a tantrum. I don't think we're going to get anything useful from him."

"So we still don't know why the portals are forming or how to stop them," I murmur, feeling dejected. "His best guess was that the three altereds yesterday passed through a kind of magical desert, making the portals easier to form. We're back to taking shifts of looking out the windows and being ready to run, while we wait and see whether or not it keeps happening."

"Which is untenable, yeah," Lavender agrees with a nod. "But, look, I've been thinking. Celia keeps saying we have four portals to explain, but we don't; we really only have three. We can set aside the magma one. He's explained already that he was coming over to look for Clarent."

"She said it was an amazing coincidence for him to tumble out right on top of us," I point out.

Lavender nods. "I have a theory for that, though. The hunters have a sense for fae magic, right? There were seven of us in the area: you and me and Clarent in the car, and Dakota, Celia, and Lily in the house with Tox. That's a lot of altereds gathered in one place. If the hunter was looking for Clarent but didn't know where he was, wouldn't that be a logical place to check?"

I frown, considering this. "You think he chose his portal location based on the concentration of fae magic on the other side?"

"Yes! Even if Clarent hadn't been there, it was still a good place to start. If any of the altereds knew Clarent—which we did—they would have been able to tell the hunter where next to look. He was strong; it would have been easy for him to take the information he needed. Maybe resources, too; a cellphone with Clarent's number in it, or a car to drive around in while hunting him. That's a more efficient hunting technique than just traipsing randomly around the city, isn't it?"

"That makes sense," Clarent agrees, giving her a warm smile. "So now we're down to just the three?"

She flashes him an approving grin. "Yup. And the big mystery with those three, besides their sheer number, is that Celia and Hermit said the portals have to be paid for in magic. Right?"

Clarent nods at this. "Either from the mind or the body or both, as long as it all adds up."

Lavender nods briskly, her green eyes intense. "So who is to say that the magic isn't being paid for by a faery? Celia keeps saying that the three yesterday didn't seem to pay. They didn't have the necessary intent and didn't lose their magic. So why couldn't someone *else* have paid?"

"You think a faery is helping people to escape?" I ask slowly, my eyes widening with disbelief.

Her gaze softens. "Rose. Sorry, but... do you remember when we over there, how the May Queen would use you Nightshades to get rid of another faery's favorite toys? They'd visit and one of you would be sent to take out the head valet, or the best guard, or their handsomest lover?"

A lump forms in my throat and Clarent hugs me closer. "I remember," I whisper.

Lavender looks pained at forcing me to relive old memories but she continues. "Okay, so what if a faery wanted to get rid of their rival's best servants, but for various reasons those servants couldn't be easily killed? An assassin couldn't get near Tox, and that bear-woman was pretty dangerous. Maybe it was easier to just spend a little magic and dump them over here."

Clarent frowns. "I don't think that I'm particularly hard to kill," he admits, his voice solemn.

Her lips quirk in amusement at the admission. "Maybe not, but you were locked up safe and sound in your castle. Then, the minute you're taken outside, boom! You're sent over, and the High King is poorer for it."

She turns bright eyes on me. "And then this faery pops them out near one of us; you and me, Clarent or Kieran or whoever. What's going to happen? We kill each other or we become friends. In either case, the faery who's just lost a servant is going to have a harder time recovering them."

"So the theory is," I say slowly, catching my breath as I roll the idea around in my mind, "that one or more faeries are providing the magic necessary to power these portals, and they're sending powerful altereds over as a sort of... industrial sabotage? If they can't kill the altered, or steal them for themselves, they can at least put them out of the reach of their master?"

Lavender claps her hands. "*Yes*. And if that's the case, then we don't really need to 'stop' the portals. We have to be careful, because we don't want to get hurt by a dangerous or confused escapee, but it's a *good* thing that they're being sent over. And since we won't need to kill anyone, you don't have to stay deadly. Clarent can change you—"

The door opens again and Celia strides out, her face an unreadable mask. Behind her, Oracle lingers on the threshold, looking forlorn in the dim loneliness of her rooms. "I've got your number," Oracle reminds Celia, nodding when she sees us. "I hope you can come again sometime," she adds sadly to us. She closes the door and the four of us are on our own.

"Well?" Lavender demands, shooting Celia a hostile look.

Celia remains unruffled. "Hermit announced he was going to take a nap," she reports in a mild tone. "Either he doesn't have anything more to offer, or his need for secrecy outweighs his desire for social contact. There's also the possibility that he knows more but can't remember; I think his extended stay over here is affecting his mental state. Oracle promised to call if he lets slip anything important."

Lavender doesn't back down. "I'm more interested in *your* secrets right now," she says, her tone blunt. "You're a hunter? And you're letting faeries run around town?"

Celia runs a hand over her long braid, leaning against the metal door. "Hermit and Oracle are a unique case. When he destroyed his body to take over hers, he lost everything: his estates, his servants, and potentially his life, if the other faeries find him and realize what he is. Above all else, he wants to survive, but she's making that very difficult. She's depressed and suicidal. Right now he's the only thing keeping them alive, by virtue of making sure food gets into their body."

Lavender blanches but stands her ground. "He's also a faery," she points out. "They're dangerous."

Celia fixes her with a weary look. "Hermit has been rendered harmless," she declares firmly. "He's rude and annoying, but his magic has been reduced to a fraction of what it once was. I won't kill an innocent girl simply because she's been possessed by an asshole. And I don't dare integrate them into the community for fear that someone with fewer scruples will consider her acceptable collateral damage. So I'd take it as a kindness if you didn't spread the word around."

Lavender looks away in frustration, unable to meet her eyes any longer.

Clarent clears his throat softly, still holding me in his arms. "Can I ask what's all this about hunting?" he says, his low voice polite and casual.

"You kept it a secret from us?" I ask Celia, looking up at her. The numbness has returned, edging out my earlier sadness and holding Lavender's anger at bay.

"It's not a secret," Celia says. Her calm expression doesn't change but her eyes are suddenly very sad. "It's just not something we volunteer to everyone fresh out of the otherworld. No reason to spook people right off the bat."

"That's why you know so much about the portals, isn't it?" Lavender asks, her voice bitter. "That's how you're able to find them when they open and to track down fresh escapees for the community. You used to do the same kind of hunting for the faeries."

Celia runs a hand over her braid again. "Mmhmm. The finders took me because they sensed I had a knack for it. They shop around like that sometimes; pick people on the basis of specific latent talents they want to draw out. Hunters are special, because they need us to navigate the human world while searching for escapees to bring back. They're more selective about which memories they take, and they set us up with seed money to fund hunting expenses."

She's quiet for a moment, lost in her recollections. "Pretty sure I had just turned thirty when they took me. Pulled my name, my family, and most of my childhood out of my head. Set me to hunting for a few years. Didn't enjoy it," she adds with a glance at Lavender.

"Couldn't you run away?" I ask, my voice barely above a whisper. The faces of dead men flash through my memory, the sensation of being trapped rising in my chest. "*We* didn't know there was anywhere to escape to, but you were earthside when you were hunting. Why didn't you just... not go back there?"

Celia closes her eyes. "They're not stupid," she murmurs. Her voice is

232

as calm as ever, but pain flashes over her face. "We're assigned buddies, held in chains against our return. If we escape, our counterpart suffers for it. It's a very motivating system, especially when they select someone they know you care about."

I drop my gaze from her face, feeling intensely guilty for prying. *Who am I to question what she's done in the past?* She's only ever been kind to us, and it isn't my place to demand to know her personal demons. Removing myself gently from Clarent's embrace, I step forward and wrap my arms around her in a tentative hug.

Her eyes fly open in surprise, and one hand comes up to pat my hair awkwardly. "Uh, thank you, Rose," she says, disentangling from me after only a moment.

Lavender watches her with wary eyes but slowly the air around us turns softer, touched with the sunny hints of marigold and fond amusement. "Okay, okay," she concedes, a wry grin tugging at the corners of her lips. "I guess we all have pasts. Sorry I got touchy with you; I think Hermit took all my patience for the day." She doesn't hug Celia but she offers her a friendly fist-bump.

Clarent watches all this with gentle patience before clearing his throat again. "Ah, sorry," he says politely. "I asked because if you were a hunter once, does that mean you can tell us how to avoid them?"

Celia gives him an approving nod. "Yeah. I was telling these two earlier, though I reckon that was when you were entertaining Tox. Hunters aren't invincible or omniscient. They're good at tracking fae magic, but they can be tricked or outrun or killed just like any other altered."

Lavender leans against the nearby railing, more at ease now. "We killed the last one," she points out reasonably. "And you mentioned that the faeries usually lose interest pretty soon. So how long do we need to lie low for—a week? A month? How many more do you expect they'll send?"

Any lingering pain in Celia's face is pushed away to make room for more practical concerns. "Well, it'll partly depend on how many hunters they have," she muses calmly. "A lot of them don't bother keeping even one hunter, let alone multiple. You have to understand: they don't *like* losing their property, but most of the time it's not worth it to bring anyone back. It's a question of investment."

She extends her hand, ticking off costs on her fingers. "First you've got to acquire a hunter. You can pick anyone off the street, but if you want a *good* one you'll need to find somebody with a latent ability for sensing and manipulating fae magic, so they can open portals and track their targets. Then you feed and clothe and keep your hunter on standby against the statistical probability that one altered in dozens will eventually make a successful run. Then you send your hunter out and hope they come back; even if you've taken every precaution against their own inclination to escape, you can't be certain they won't get shot or stabbed."

Lavender's eyes flash with grim amusement. "Oh, I do hope the hunter we killed was expensive," she murmurs.

"Very likely," Celia says, her voice dry. "And when they do bring an escapee back from our world, what do you *do* with your newly-retrieved property? Whether you put them back to work or punish them as an example to the others, the rest of your workforce learns there's somewhere to escape *to*. More people run, because now they know there's somewhere to run to that isn't the same old nightmare ruled by a different faery. And more of those runners are able to open portals now that they know there's another world out there. You're not just dealing with unconscious intent at that point; you've got a potential riot on your hands."

"So why do they keep hunters at all, then?" I ask. "If the system is so inefficient, why not just accept the loss when one of us gets away?"

Celia shrugs. "Some of them do," she says simply. "But they aren't any more inherently logical than we are. Some want revenge and are willing to pay for it; for others it's an expensive sport or a hobby, something they subsidize with their time and resources. It depends on the individual faery. What do you think, Clarent? Did your High King go in for much hunting?"

He considers this. "He liked to hunt deer and foxes," he says slowly. "Boars, too, and the occasional bear. I don't know that he ever hunted out here, though; but of course I didn't know earthside existed."

I imagine the High King on a horse, hunting animals in his forest. Unless his earthside hunters could supply them, neither the horse nor the hunted would be real animals; they'd be humans he'd changed, using Clarent as part of the process. I frown at the mental image of red foxes and brown deer, something not quite adding up. "Doesn't it seem strange that an Arthurian faery would employ a man made of magma?" I look at Celia. "You said hunters have to be kept, right? Does living stone and fire really fit that aesthetic?"

Lavender's brow furrows, considering this. "Maybe he was supposed to be a demon?" she asks. "Like Christian quests and holy grails and medieval imagery?"

Celia looks thoughtful, tapping her boot against the wall. "I've seen better demons," she mutters. "And we still don't know if the High King is the one who sent that hunter. It's just a guess." She sighs. "All of which adds up to this: I don't know how many hunters might be sent after you, nor how long you might need to lie low. I do know that your best defense right now is in numbers. The next hunter might be forewarned about Rose's poison and my arrows, but might not be prepared for some of the tricks the rest of us have up our sleeves. We're stronger as a group."

"We've got that meeting tonight," Lavender says, looking thoughtful. "Could we ask for volunteers? People who might be willing to stay with us for a few days, in some kind of rotation?"

Celia nods. "I think that's a good idea," she says, turning it over in her head. "We've got quite a few folks who are good in a stand-up fight, as well as some sneaky bastards and the occasional faery-killer like you, Rose. No offense."

I manage a wan smile, trying to be strong for Clarent and Lavs. "None taken," I murmur. Trying to turn the pain into a joke, I add, "Though you've hurt my ego. I thought I was special."

She gives me a rare smile. "You're reasonably special," she affirms solemnly, not quite teasing me. "We've got a couple of hundred altereds in the area, and I'm hoping we can pull in at least half of those for the meeting tonight. Out of that, maybe a dozen or so have taken down a faery. It's a fairly exclusive group."

"The more the better," Lavender declares, setting her teeth and looking grim.

Celia kicks off the wall, gesturing for us to follow her down to the truck. "I'll probably ask Kieran to help," she muses as we walk. "Elric is gonna pitch a fit, of course. I think they're due for another reconciliation after he saw Kieran wounded like that, so he's not going to be thrilled at my yanking his boyfriend to ask that he move in with you kids for a few days. Oh well. I pity the next altered he has to name, though; you got off lucky, Rosalie Flowers. And I still can't believe he thought *Smith* was clever."

"Out of curiosity, what did he name you?" Clarent asks, tilting his head at her.

She fixes him with dark, serious eyes. "Cecily Hunter," she growls.

The fact that Celia does *not* look like a 'Cecily' hangs unspoken in the air around us. "Yeah," she says shortly, acknowledging our expressions. "So I don't feel too bad interrupting his playtime when it's necessary. Shame for Kieran, though."

CHAPTER 24

There is a little church on the northern outskirts of the metroplex, roughly equidistant from everyone so that the gatherings are equally inconvenient for us all. The building is big, with an attached gymnasium, but the church membership is small and dwindling: mostly elderly couples whose children have grown up and moved away. Celia is allowed to rent space for our meetings, as the church needs money to keep the lights on and the water running. She's told them we play bingo, which is apparently traditional enough to allow us the use of the gym but scandalous enough to keep the conservative congregation away from any hint of gambling.

Very rarely, a stray human will show up to attend the event despite our complete lack of advertisement, but Celia has guards posted outside checking everyone in as they arrive. The guards have a variety of compelling excuses for refusing entry to the humans: our seating is limited, reservations must be made in advance, and the interloper wouldn't fit in with our tight-knit group anyway. Since the guards are an assortment of escaped sirens, rusalki, and loreleis, the humans tend to believe what they're told and rarely come back. Once the meeting begins we lock the doors and pull down the shades, and for the next few hours we can enjoy just being ourselves in a community.

The church sign labels itself a tabernacle but the reality is less grand.

The building is old and neglected, the grass neatly trimmed but dying. The red brick is faded and chipped, and the stained-glass windows on the front are in dire need of cleaning. I think the windows are supposed to cast pretty rainbows but the pictures are depressing, the stylized depictions of torture triggering bad memories. At any rate our rental agreement only covers the gym, which is far from the colorful windows and faded carpeting; we can eat and drink there without worrying about the occasional spill.

When we walk in there are already tables set up with snacks, and hundreds of church folding chairs placed in neat rows. A podium has been wheeled to the front of the room alongside a single row of chairs that face the audience. Celia gestures for us to take a seat at the front, then immediately finds herself moderating a fierce argument between Dakota and Elric.

"Ugh, I don't want to sit up front," Lavender grumbles, echoing my own thoughts on the matter.

"You know it'll just be worse if we argue," I point out.

"Is it always so crowded?" Clarent asks, staring around the room in mild astonishment at the people milling about; a hundred at least, so far.

I twist my head with him, counting up who I know and who is still a stranger to me. Kieran drifts around the nearby buffet table, one eye constantly on Elric without making his interest too obvious. I notice that the burly fighter now has a sharp-looking machete strapped to his back. He ought to look ridiculous but considering that the last time I saw him he'd just been mauled by a bear, I suppose he felt a few extra precautions were in order.

Tox isn't here, but the meetings sometimes run rather late so I imagine Dakota has procured a babysitter for the night. Lily isn't here either, but of course she'd said not to expect her. I also don't see Joel or Worth, which is rather odd; I'd have expected Celia to include them in the discussion, since they were witnesses to a lot of the events of the last two days. I wonder if she's had a chance to call them since our meeting with Oracle and Hermit, and if they know now that my lips heal without Joel's special 'treatment'.

238

Mina *is* here, holding court in her 'good chair'. The flimsy little folding seats are uncomfortable for her, so Celia always makes sure one of the office chairs is wheeled in. Mina radiates sex appeal tonight, her low-cut lace dress only barely containing her cleavage. She gives me a warm smile from within the circle of admiring men and women who've claimed the area around her—one of whom seems to be regaling the others with an amusing story—and I wave back.

"There you are!" A sharp voice behind us causes me to jump. I twist around to see Athena nearby, peering suspiciously at us. She's accompanied by Jing who hovers nervously at her elbow, trying not to make eye contact with anyone. Under the harsh overhead lights, the young woman is almost translucently clear.

I smile at her, ignoring Athena's gathering ire, and tilt my head to indicate the silver man by my side. "Jing, this is Clarent," I say by way of introduction. "Clarent, this is Jing. She works at the bookstore with us." I offer her an apologetic smile that Athena is welcome to consider her due as well, should she so choose. "Sorry I haven't been pulling my weight lately. Did you two close up the store and drive here together?"

Jing nods. "Yes. Well, kind of." Her eyes flick up to meet mine and she shimmers nervously, looking skittish. "We drove here together, but we couldn't close up properly. Joel and Worth were there when we left, digging through the medical texts. They didn't want to be disturbed, so we let them stay and just locked the door behind us. They said they'd be here for the meeting, but they looked pretty distracted."

"They're *touching* my books, and I'm not there to supervise," Athena fumes, crossing her arms over her chest. "I'm going to have to order new copies of *everything* just to be safe, and Celia will fuss at the expense." She narrows her eyes at me, taking in the three of us and the way we stand so close together. "At least you've stayed busy, Rose," she announces sourly. "If it will get you back into the shop, the metal-boy can come work the registers. He has to promise not to touch anything, though."

Lavender snorts softly and I can see her struggling not to roll her eyes; her few encounters with Athena have not gone very well. I step in quickly. "I'm sure Clarent appreciates the job offer," I assure her, knowing the bookstore can't possibly support another employee at this time but that it would be futile to argue with her. "We'll talk about it later, after the meeting, but we should take our seats now." Indeed, in a miracle of good timing Celia is striding to the podium, carrying the cordless microphone that she'll tap for attention.

"But I wanted some of those cupcakes," Athena protests, her gaze swiveling to the table full of snacks. Then she frowns mightily, her eyes narrowing as she glares at something behind me. "Oh, that's not good at all. Rose, are you causing all that mist outside? It will make me sneeze."

Her words are slow to penetrate my brain. Then I whirl to stare at the windows that line the walls. Most of them have been covered, the shades drawn against prying eyes, but one of the shades hangs askew, providing an unobstructed view. Outside the grass lawn is liberally covered with fog, and the orange rays of the setting sun have disappeared under a gray haze.

"Celia!" My tongue feels thick in my mouth, but I'm able to force the word out.

Her head whips around at my cry. "*Shit*. Mina, get folks into the main offices," she barks, her crisp voice cutting through the nervous murmurs springing up.

Mina doesn't waste a moment, rising in a single fluid motion and gently herding the nervous and frightened among us to the offices at the north corner of the gym. The offices are small and the halls narrow; if there is a hunter in the area, the weaker community members can hide there while one of the fighters deals with the threat.

"What do we do?" Clarent asks, his low voice full of concern.

"Jing, you and Athena need to go with the others." My hand reaches out to touch the translucent girl, but at the last moment I remember her triggers and my fingers veer away.

240

She nods, her translucent eyes wide with worry. "Okay. But, Rose, won't you come with—"

"No, I'm not going anywhere," Athena declares, planting her feet stubbornly.

"We should all go," Lavender urges, ignoring Athena. "Rose, it'll be easier to protect people away from the windows."

"You go with them, Lavs; and you too, Clarent. I'll stay out here with Celia, in case she needs me."

"No, we shouldn't split—"

There's a flicker in the air around us, the sharp crackle of magic like a shockwave converging on the center of the room. With an ear-splitting shatter, every window in the gymnasium bursts inward. Flying glass shards cut the faces and arms of those huddled near the walls, and the sharp fragments skitter across the floor to rest at our feet.

"What's happening?" Clarent asks, his voice full of tension. "The portals weren't like this before!"

Mina is still urging the crowd through the north doorway. "This way, come on. No, I know it's bleeding but it's shallow; we'll patch you up inside."

Lavender tugs at my arm. "Rose, we need to go!"

I'm frozen in place, watching with wide eyes as mist seeps into the gym through the shattered windows. Clarent is right; this isn't like any of the portals we've been in. The magic in the air is almost tangible, causing my hair to frizz at the ends and setting my teeth on edge. The color in the room drains away, replaced with a dull haze that renders everything in gray light and dark shadows. In the very center of the room, the electric sensation of raw magic gathers like a storm.

I hear Celia gasp—a strangled, inarticulate sound of alarm. In that moment, the space in the center of the room folds in on itself. A flash of blinding light illuminates the area, sending spots dancing across my eyes. My hands reach out for Lavender and Clarent, steadying myself from falling as I blink watery eyes, attempting to coax back my vision. Then I see them: framed in a circle of charred ash, three men stand in the center of the room where a moment before there had been only empty chairs.

They are fae. They are bright and beautiful, burning with inner light, the only splashes of real color in this strange gray portal-space. They scan the room with their haughty gazes, considering us as if we were no more than ants. One of them is a haggard older-looking man with bronzed skin and dark curly hair; he locks piercing blue eyes on Clarent, who stiffens beside me. "*There* is my property," the faery says, his deep voice stern and cold.

The tallest of the three men towers almost a full seven feet. He is thin and gaunt with warm ginger hair and burning red eyes, his skin as pale as death. His voice is breathy and quick, and his fingers can't seem to stop moving, drumming against each other in a beat only he can hear. "Ah. See? You said I lost him. I didn't lose him. I knew he would be here, where they were all gathered; so many pretty morsels. Some compensation is in order though, yes? I lost my hunter; very vexing. He'll have to be replaced."

"Scavenge whatever Father does not eat," the older man suggests. His tone is contemptuous, but when his eyes flick to the third member of their party his demeanor is wary, even frightened.

The third man is small, shorter even than Lavender and very young. If I had to guess his age, I'd place him in his late teens. He is beautiful but uncannily so, like a plastic mannequin. His skin is shiny and stretched smooth, and his eyes are as white as the mist that fills the room. His blond hair ruffles in a breeze that doesn't touch the rest of us, and he gazes around him with naked hunger in his face.

His eyes come to rest on Elric, who is edging nervously towards the north exit. "Mine," the young man declares, his voice soft and high, almost childlike. He steps over the ashen circle, eyes locked on our vampire, hand already outstretched to grab him.

"No, he damned well is *not*," Kieran bellows. The burly man leaps forward, his machete already in his hand. Folding chairs scatter in his wake, clattering to the floor as he shoves past, and the shining steel in his hand glitters as he raises his weapon high for the strike.

The little blond faery entirely ignores him, completely focused on his goal. Elric stands perfectly still, frozen with fear or perhaps not wishing to endanger others by drawing nearer to the huddled crowd. Kieran's blade strikes down with unerring aim and severs the faery's outstretched arm in a single smooth stroke.

We each hold our breath. There is no howl of pain, no shout of anger or gush of blood. A smooth arm, perfectly severed, flops to the ground and then stills, seeping a thick viscous fluid that looks more like green sap than proper red blood. The young man glares at his wound like one contemplating an annoying inconvenience, as if he had noticed a broken nail in need of filing. "I'm going to have to eat that," he complains, gesturing with his stump at the fallen limb.

Movement catches my eye and I stare at the cross-section of his arm, my stomach tightening in apprehension. There are no bones or muscle showing at the cut, only a slick inky darkness that writhes and grows. Tendrils shoot out of the oozing stump, curling over his skin and continuing to grow like some monstrous plant. The blond hair on his head lengthens and darkens, spilling over his face in a mass of writhing black-green vines that grow at an impossible rate.

He's a tree, I think, recalling the unluckier servants of the May Queen, but this designation falls woefully short. His legs widen to the size of tree trunks, yes, and his skin darkens to the color and consistency of bark, but he doesn't stay upright like a tree. Instead, he stoops to crouch on all fours even as his back hunches and thickens and grows ever larger. Within seconds, he is neither man nor tree but a four-legged giant beast towering over us, covered in dark earth and writhing vines. He is a living mountain, his size constrained only by the gym walls around us.

"Mine," the creature repeats, but his youthful voice is now rasping and ancient, a deep bellow as old as the earth.

He lunges at Kieran, his movements ponderously slow but undeniably powerful. Kieran's eyes widen but the ex-gladiator leaps aside without pause for thought, rolling easily and coming up with machete still in hand.

Around us, I see more weapons being drawn. Celia already has her bow in her hands, aiming an arrow at the space where the creature's eyes had been. Others hold knives and guns, hesitating whether to take a defensive position or join the fray. Even Jing brandishes a tiny can of pepper spray on her keychain, her last defense against recapture.

"Rose, look out!" she cries, grabbing Athena by the collar and dragging her back away from us.

I whirl around to see that the older faery, the High King, has left the ashen circle and is only an arm's length from us. Taking advantage of the confusion caused by his father, he reaches out and grabs Clarent by the upper arm in an iron grip. Clarent gasps from the pain, twisting ineffectually in an attempt to escape the man and his punishing grasp.

"You've been lost long enough, sword," the faery man observes in a low grumble as he drags Clarent back towards the center of the room where his tall companion watches and waits. "I have prisoners in need of alteration, and the Fiery Lord and I have a battlefield to arrange for Father. We were fortunate that he granted us a reprieve and agreed to help recover you; he is very hungry."

"No!" Lavender screams at him. She seizes Clarent's free arm, helping him to brace himself against the inexorable pull of his master. "You can't have him! He's not yours! Fuck off!" Raw fury shoots through the air around us, her own invisible tendrils assaulting my senses and making my heart race faster.

With her help Clarent plants his feet hard, grunting with the exertion of resistance to the much stronger man. He doesn't say a word, doesn't waste a single breath, and I know he thinks we can't bargain or argue our way out of this.

The High King narrows his eyes at Lavender's objections. "The smithy is no place for a lady," he observes sternly. "Say goodbye to your swain. I will allow you to stay here and weep for him from afar."

He thinks he's a gentleman. The realization flashes through my mind. He's as cruel and cold and bad as the rest of them, but he wants to believe his own fiction. His world is an Avalon where he is king, where Clarent is a sword to be used and 'stolen', and where ladies are lavished with kisses yet expected not to point out they're being held prisoner against their will. Even the way he looks is a persona he's built: old and haggard, his face burned by the sun and sporting battle-scars. The highest of kings, full of honor and fair-dealing yet unafraid to get his hands dirty.

Who plays along with him, besides the gaunt companion who waits in the ashen circle? I can't imagine any faery woman pandering to his fantasies, willingly choosing to subjugate herself as his queen. He could make a companion for himself from a human, yet Clarent had said women were rare at court. Even if this High King doesn't personally crave female company, wouldn't he need a queen to complete the Arthurian picture he's created?

I bite at the inside of my cheek, my mind racing. Is it possible that he can't forget himself with the human women he kidnaps? They are stamped with his magic, forever a piece of him; in themselves a reminder of their inferior origins. If he wants a queen, doesn't he need a woman of royal birth? Hermit's words ring in my ears: *Are you a secret faery princess, little Rose?*

He'd been mocking me, of course. I don't glow with inner color the way they do in this gray portal, but if it were just a game of pretense I could play the part. I'm a mystery to this king; not a faery woman, no, but still undeniably full of fae magic and with my lowly origins unknown to him. Any play-acting is a gamble, but with the magic in my fingers I might be able to pull it off.

"My lord!" I launch myself at the High King, flinging grateful arms around his neck. He's caught by surprise, his dark eyes startled, and his hands are too full of Clarent to ward me off. I gaze up at him with a pleading expression, my fingers already stroking the skin of his neck and running through the curls in his hair, dragging my magic along his scalp.

"My lady?" he manages. I can hear the confusion in his voice. Has any free woman ever thrown herself at him like this? Here, Lavender has already helped me; he's pegged her as Clarent's lover, and doesn't imagine that her 'swain' might have a relationship with both of us.

"I'm so relieved you're here," I confess, my voice soft and high and vulnerable. "Please. Please rescue me, my king? You don't know what it's like out here. It hurts all the time; this place feels so wrong on my skin. Please won't you take me with you?"

He blinks at me, taken aback by my words and the part I'm offering to play. Behind him, his gaunt companion frowns. "I should think the silver one is enough, yes?" the tall faery man cautions, suspicion creeping into his voice. "No need for ladies in the smithy, is there?"

The High King tilts his head in the direction of his companion, listening without tearing his eyes away from my face. "Please," I whisper, my lips parted in a soft needy pant. Then I smell Lavender, bless her, helping me in the only way she can. Soft honeysuckle and sweet lavender spread tentatively through the air, chasing away stale anger with the warm scents of hope and love.

"What is your name, my lady?" the faery asks, his voice low and full of gallantry. He hasn't let go of Clarent, but thankfully he has stopped moving to study my face with a soft gaze.

"They call me Rose, my lord," I murmur, my eyes meeting his with a warm smile. I rise up on my toes to embrace him more closely, apparently moved by the depth of my gratitude.

He blinks again and then smiles at some joke I am not privy to. "The romance of the Rose," he muses, then closes the last few precious inches between us to press his lips to mine in a chaste kiss.

Infect him. Kill him. Please! I don't know if the virus within me can hear my commands, but I issue the order with all the ferocity I can muster.

246

Nothing happens. The faery lord holds me and kisses me gently, and still does not release Clarent. Fears bubble to the surface of my mind. Is he one of those few immune to the May Queen's poisons? Is he able to scatter my magic, in the same way Clarent does? Despite Lavender's best efforts, her scent spikes with frightened lemon as the High King holds both her lovers captive and screams rise from the battle that rages around us.

I'm searching for some way to bargain for Clarent's release when I taste warmth in my mouth, salty and bitter. The High King coughs, breaking our embrace, and a thick red stream courses over his lips to coat his neck. His blood is on my face, on my dress, in my mouth. He staggers back at the sight of me covered in his own blood, releasing Clarent and myself in his surprise. My stomach flips over and I fall to my hands and knees, vomiting up the taste of him as Clarent's cool hands steady me.

"Rose!" Lavender drops to her knees with us but keeps her eyes on the High King, determined to defend us. "Rose, are you okay?"

"You... witch," the faery gurgles as he staggers backward, each word causing a fresh gout of bright red blood to spill from his lips. "How did you...?"

He doesn't finish his sentence but stumbles backwards into the ashen circle, falling hard. The tall ginger-haired faery stoops to catch him, his movements quick and nervous. "High King?" His eyes widen as the older man thrashes once and then stills forever.

Burning eyes track up to me then, his thin face suddenly calculating and dangerously curious. "That's a neat trick," he comments, his fingers drumming faster. His voice is a low crackle, like a hungry fire. "Is that how my hunter died? Would you like to replace him, girl?"

I look up at the Fiery Lord from where I kneel. I'm on my hands and knees, covered in blood, my mouth sour with the taste of vomit. Whatever power my lips contain, I've almost certainly exhausted my reserves with that last kiss. I remember the burn of the hunter, how his fire almost killed me, and I have no wish to repeat the experience with his master. And unlike the hunter or the High King, this one is fully forewarned, having just witnessed my powers. I don't think the magic in my fingers and the emotions in Lavender's scents will catch him off-guard.

I spit at the ground between us. "Come and get me," I challenge. "Do you know how many of you I've killed? I can fit another notch on my belt."

He hesitates. His gaze flicks to his father as the ravening creature of earth and vine continues to sweep a path of chaos through the crowded gym, lunging for altereds and snapping at them with jagged stone teeth as large as my head. There is a strong sense that the creature has no interest in parsing friend from foe at the moment. I remember what Hermit said about these monsters eating their children, and one look at the Fiery Lord's face tells me he's well aware of that possibility.

His eyes snap back to me and his fingers drum faster, a blur of motion too fast for my gaze to follow. "I don't think you'd fit in with my household, little flower," he decides, eyes narrowing. Electricity gathers around him, hot and dangerous, and with a crackling flash of light he blinks out of existence, taking his color with him back to the otherworld.

CHAPTER 25

Two faeries are gone, but the worst one remains. I watch the chaos with wide eyes as the stench of the High King's blood clings to me.

Over a dozen fighters have surged forward to challenge the lumbering creature. The monster hurls himself repeatedly into the fray, bowling over warriors with his powerful tree-trunk legs. One of the warriors, a red-haired woman whose name I don't know, leaps forward to stab him in the foreleg with a wicked curved knife. The creature turns to snap at her with his jagged stone teeth, gouging out a chunk of flesh from her shoulder. She falls to the gymnasium floor, bleeding profusely from the deep wound.

Other altereds reach to pull her out of immediate danger, to draw her back to the group of non-combatants huddled in the safety of the northern offices. But before they can grab her, long vines shoot out from the creature's back to wrap around her like hungry tentacles, and she is dragged screaming into the mass of writhing foliage on the monster's broad back. There's a moment when I can see her face, twisted with pain; then she disappears into the lush greenery with a sickening sucking sound.

"What do we do?" Jing crouches nervously beside me, the translucent girl almost invisible in the gray light. "The portal edges outside are closed. That means we're trapped here, aren't we?"

Athena has not bothered to crouch or hide or make herself appear smaller in any way. "You'd think Celia could collapse the portal," she complains. "Maybe that creature is blocking her. Though I suppose she might not want him running loose earthside. Assuming we emerge earthside, of course."

"Celia! Where is she?" I crane my neck, my eyes straining to pick her out of the crowd. She's limping on the outskirts of the fray, pulling back her bowstring for another shot. Her arrows are embedded in the head of the creature, sticking out where eyes and ears should be; yet her attacks haven't slowed him down. "She can't have more than a couple arrows left," I breathe.

"And the ones she's shot aren't doing any good," Lavender adds, the air around her twisting with a fresh burst of sour fear.

Athena considers the creature with her contemptuous gaze, crossing her arms over her chest. "He's very invasive, isn't he?" she observes. "Shall we call him Kudzu?"

Clarent helps me up, steadying me gently with his strong arms. "How are we going to stop him?" he asks, his voice low. "I'm metal. Maybe I could break his teeth? If I could convince him to bite me—"

There's a furious shout from our left. I swivel my head in time to see Dakota rush forward, his glowing skin brighter than ever. He snatches up a folding chair in his hands and slams the flattened makeshift weapon into the creature's gaping maw. The chair bounces off with a sickening clang, the stone teeth unharmed and unchipped. Angrily, the creature makes a retaliating swipe with his huge paw.

Dakota is saved from what would have been a bone-shattering blow by Elric's quick dive, bringing Dakota to the ground. The two men tumble and roll, the massive arm of the faery passing mere inches over them. I hear Elric shouting something incoherent—no doubt derogatory—as they scrabble back to relative safety, away from the worst of the fray.

"I don't think that's going to work," Lavender says flatly.

"But—"

"Clarent," I touch his arm gently, "you were created to be melted and molded. I don't think you're hard enough to break stone."

"Kudzu certainly seems hungry. Did anyone bring any cyanide?" Athena asks, her voice suggesting that to do so would be the most normal thing in the world. "*My* cupcake is already spoken for but, Rose, you could give up yours for the benefit of the group."

I turn to stare at her, blinking as the idea takes root. Lavender grasps my arm hard. "*No*," she says, shaking her head at me. "No, Rose."

I reach up to touch her face, my breath coming in short gasps. "Lavs, this is what I was made for. This is what I'm supposed to *do*."

"It won't work!" Angry tears prick her green eyes, spilling over her cheeks and the tiny dusting of freckles. "You *know* it won't work. It barely worked on Clarent's faery, and you're drained now. You said yourself you need a week to recharge."

I bite the inside of my lip and then whirl to face Clarent, who watches us with grave eyes. "You can make me stronger." My hand darts out to his wrist. "You said earlier that you understand the pattern of my magic. You can make me more lethal; you can give me power!"

My breath catches. I hear Hermit's voice in my head again, haughty and annoyed. *To actually give you magic would require losing some of ours.* I twist to see the High King where he fell in the ashen circle, but the body is gone. His companion, the Fiery Lord, must have taken it—to bury, or to feed on? And when Kieran cut off the creature's arm, the faery had said he would have to eat it later. Does he want the limb for its meat or its magic?

"Rose?" Clarent's voice, confused and concerned, cuts through my thoughts.

"The arm!" I grasp his wrist harder. "Where is it? We can use it!" I turn to look. "There!" The pale plastic-textured limb lies not far from the battle, though too close for comfort. "How can we get it?"

Jing swallows hard, her fingers fluttering nervously against her jeans. "I can get it," she whispers. "I can't do much but I can do *this*." Before I can stop her, to my utter astonishment the translucent girl fades completely away.

"Jing!" I look around wildly, failing to see her anywhere in the chaos.

"I should have asked her to bring my cupcake, too," Athena muses.

I turn my head to stare unblinking at the limb where it lies, wincing whenever the combatants come close. Suddenly it too disappears into thin air. A long moment spins out in silence as we wait, every second seeming longer than the last. A burst of gunshot echoes through the gym as one of the fighters opens fire on the creature; my heart squeezes with fresh fear.

"If they can't see her, they won't know to be careful," I breathe.

"That's true," Athena observes, frowning deeply. "We should have used hooks and fishing line."

There's a roar from the creature, and I twist my head to see a burly giant of a man snatched up in those stone teeth and flung like a rag doll across the room. He collides with something invisible in the empty air, dropping to the ground with a grunt and sliding some way further. At the same time, there is a sharp yelp of pain and the disembodied limb of the Elder Fae materializes several feet away from the fallen warrior.

"If she's wounded while she's invisible, how will we find her?" Clarent asks, his worried gaze turning to meet mine.

"She's still tangible," I breathe, bracing my feet to run. "Maybe I can find her, maybe I can trip over her—"

Lavender grabs my arm. "Wait! There! Look!"

My gaze follows Lavender's pointed finger. Mina stands in the low hallway to the northern offices, a knot of altereds behind her. The area is sheltered from the giant creature, too low and too narrow for him to reach. While the warriors distract him, Mina gestures and four of her group dart out to grab the wounded man and drag him away from the fighting. *They're keeping anyone else from being eaten,* I realize.

"But where's Jing?" Clarent asks.

"Watch the floor," Lavender hisses, and only then do I see the tiny drops of blood coating the slick gymnasium floor, dripping ever closer to us. The limb disappears again, invisible and retrieved, and then she's close enough for us to hear her: a chorus of little "no! no! no!" yelps that hop around the rescuers, trying not to be touched.

As she draws closer to us, I unthinkingly reach out with my hands to steady her, but the blood quickly changes direction to avoid me. "I'm fine," Jing's voice whispers from my left side, a little breathless. "It just grazed me." Slowly, like a drop of ink spreading through water, both limb and girl materialize before us. "It's heavy," she warns, handing over the arm without making contact with my own skin. "Heavier than it ought to be."

My held breath is exhaled in sharp relief. "You did it! Thank you, Jing," I gasp, clutching the severed arm as I anxiously look her over. She's bleeding from a gash on her forehead and numerous scrapes on her hands and knees; the wounds look painful but not serious. "Athena, can you bandage a head wound?"

I turn to face Clarent again, hating myself for ignoring Jing but aware that every second counts. "You can use the magic in this," I urge, thrusting the arm into his hands. "Make me stronger, make my virus deadlier. Pack as much power into me as you can. Hermit said it's possible and you understand how to do it, don't you?"

Lavender's nails grip my wrist in panic. "Rose, you are *not* going to sacrifice yourself," she whispers. "Please! If you care about me, you won't do this!"

Clarent looks equally miserable, his eyes misting with soft silver tears like melted solder. "I don't think I can," he says, his voice cracking.

I can't fall apart now, I think, blinking back tears. My hands reach up to touch them both, cradling our three heads together. My forehead touches Clarent's, and I press Lavender close against my cheek. "Listen," I beg softly. "Nothing else has so much as touched him; not Kieran's blade nor Celia's arrows. But if you can make me strong enough to kill him, I'll survive and we'll all go home." I search Clarent's eyes. "I've always survived before, haven't I? This is just the same."

"You've always kissed people before!" Lavender explodes in a choked whisper. "This time, you want to be *eaten*. It's not the same thing, Rose!"

"Lavs, look at me." I know I'm not being fair to her, but the alternative is to let more of us die. "I'm going up there one way or another. Clarent, do whatever you can to make it more likely for me to survive, but I'm going up there all the same."

He studies my face for a long moment and then nods slowly, his expression grave. Lavender sputters once, frustrated and angry, before falling silent. Clarent reaches for my wrist with his free hand and frowns with intense concentration.

When Clarent had studied the web of my magic before, I hadn't felt anything. Even when he'd begun trying to alter me back to a normal human, the only clue I'd had were the changes my eyes reported in the world around me.

Now whatever he is doing *hurts* and I grit my teeth against the unexpected agony. A sensation of heavy liquid in my veins pushes up from where he grips my wrist, traveling through my arm to my head where a burst of strange babble erupts; voices I can't separate spill rapid words I don't understand. Are those voices mine? Or did they come from the dead limb whose magic is being scavenged? What had Hermit said about their parents giving them memories?

The pain sharpens into a new sensation I can't push away, but it no longer hurts. I still don't 'see' magic the way Clarent seems to, but I can *feel* it in me now, like tiny individual points of light traveling to my extremities. Magic pools in the tips of my fingers, waiting to reach out and coax others to accept me. A deadly virus gathers eagerly at my lips, ready to leap off and infect. Something in the frenzied babble of my mind makes me think I might now be able to will the virus to infect or not as I choose, if only I can focus.

My concentration is broken by a soft gasp. Jing takes a nervous step back from me. "Rose, your eyes are almost glowing," she murmurs. I look down at myself and realize that my green veins are thicker and darker against my skin. The lock of pink hair draped over my shoulder is darker, too; a richer, redder rose.

"How do you feel?" Lavender whispers at my side, studying me with worried eyes.

"I love you," I tell her, reaching up to touch her cheek again. I can feel magic drip from my fingers into her skin; it tells her that I'm a sweet girl, loving and kind and gentle. It's what she already believes fed back to her in a loop, and I only hope it isn't a lie. Quickly I draw my fingers back; I can't afford to waste a drop.

"Don't say things like that," she chokes, fresh tears falling. "It sounds like you're saying goodbye."

"I'll be right back," I promise, shaking my head. "I just need you to know. You're brave and strong and you gave me hope when I hadn't even realized I'd lost it." I wrap her in a tight hug, careful to keep my fingers away from her, and gesture with my wrist to pull Clarent close. "Take care of each other," I whisper.

"Rose, please come back to us," Clarent begs, his voice soft in my ear.

I nod and duck quickly away from them before my tears can spill, sliding through metal arms and soft skin, running as fast I can towards the melee. I scoop up an abandoned knife from the floor; the curved angle of the blade tells me it belonged to the red-haired woman I saw absorbed by the monster earlier. *How appropriate.*

I have to get close enough to be eaten as quickly as possible; if I'm wounded and tossed aside, Mina's crew will pull me away and I'll never get another chance. I launch myself in a leap I didn't know I was capable of, the dagger in my hand slamming inexpertly into the creature's shoulder.

"Rose, what the fuck are you doing!"

Elric's shout is cut short by an angry roar. I cling to the monster's arm, holding on as firmly as possible to the knife I've managed to embed into his flesh. "Eat me," I spit up into his face. I spread my fingers wide and jam them into the foliage of his shoulder, seeking the site of the wound I've opened. Magic flows through me, telling him I'm sweet and good to the taste, full of magic to satisfy his hunger.

Sharp stone teeth as big as my head close on my shoulder, ripping a scream from my throat. Red blood gushes from my wound, mingling with that of the High King on my dress. The shock of pain is enough to make me release the knife, but I don't fall; the teeth hold me in midair. I can hear shouts below—"Let go of her!" and "You bastard!"—but the creature ignores them like so many ants. Tentacles reach out to wrap around my waist and chest, constricting me like a snake.

There's an unexpected flash of steel beside me. Kieran, to whom I will try to be grateful if I manage to survive, has scaled the side of the creature's enormous leg and is hacking away with his blade at the vines that hold me captive.

"No! Get back!" I yell at him. I'm trying to sound like I know what I'm doing, well aware that dangling in the air like a chew-toy, gushing blood, is not the best vantage point from which to project an illusion of confidence.

"You're not a fighter, you little fool," he growls, hacking at another thick tentacle. "I'll get you down and then—"

I don't hear the rest of his plan. The monster growls again, a thick angry sound deep in his throat. His free foreleg comes up and around to brush off the interloper, as easily and with as much force as if he were a spider clinging to a human arm. I hear Kieran hit the ground hard, the crack of bones punctuating his fall. I have only a moment to pray that I haven't gotten him killed before new vines shoot out to replace the cut ones and wrap tightly around me.

The creature opens his mouth, drawing fresh gouts of blood from my mangled shoulder as his teeth pull away. Still I do not fall; instead I'm carried by the vines to his back, settling me against a bed of strangely soft moss that sucks me in like quicksand. There are other bodies here: three desiccated skeletons and the corpse of the red-haired woman, her skin as dry and stretched as a mummy. I feel a moment of panic on seeing the

256

corpses, not relieved by the heady rush of blood loss. Live or die, however, this is what I came here for. I writhe in my restraints—not to get away but to get access. I'm able to wrestle my good arm free and I claw at the creature with my nails, opening a slit to press my lips against.

When I touch my skin to the loamy earth of his back I can feel the virus flowing from me into him. Tiny points of light rush through my body, stampeding to reach my lips, each drop binding to the thick white carrier fluid that seeps eagerly into his monstrous flesh. I should be afraid that this won't work, as I was with the hunter and later with Clarent's faery. Yet I can *feel* my magic, and can hear the excited babble in my mind as the virus flows. I know now how powerful I am. There are so many things I can't do, but I know how to infect this monster. I keep my eyes wide open, mere inches from where my lips stubbornly press, and I watch him weaken. Soft earth dries and cracks like parched summer dirt. A thick fissure opens under me, seeping black oil, and still my virus spreads.

There's a shout from below, different from the angry battle-cries I heard before; it sounds like a warning. The creature beneath me staggers, his movements woozy and uncertain. His black blood bubbles up to mingle with the red that still drips from my mangled shoulder, and I watch the colorful mixture as my vision blurs. I realize I've lost so much blood that we may die together, he and I.

Will they bury us in the same hole? No, why would I think that? Celia will send him back, as she did the hunter. Bodies left to rot in the otherworld don't need to be justified to nosy earthside authorities. *But she won't send me back, will she?* Surely Lavender wouldn't let her. We worked so hard to escape that it would seem wrong to go back.

The world crashes around me with a shuddering blow that rattles my teeth. It takes a long hazy moment before I comprehend that the creature has collapsed to the ground. Then there are hands on me, ripping away dried vines that crackle into dust. *I'm being lifted. Who is lifting me?* A dirty blood-caked face looks down at me, his expression twisted with annoyance and pain. *Kieran.* "I'm so glad you and Elric have each other," I murmur up to him.

"You're delirious from blood loss," he tells me, his voice dry and flat. "That's not a good sign. I need a healer over here," he barks.

"Rose, Rose!"

Clarent and Lavender are here, kneeling over me. Kieran must have laid me on the floor, though I didn't notice him doing so. Am I blacking out? I feel so sleepy. Above me there is the sound of arguments, people rushing to and fro. Someone moves my shoulder, pressing a cloth hard into the mangled wound, but the pain is distant and far away.

"First aid isn't going to help! Where's Joel?"

"I've raised him on his cellphone. Worth is driving as fast as nee can."

"That won't work! Remember? He couldn't heal her before!"

"They did, they just used—"

"—her poison. But he had a whole syringe. Right now she's drained; I don't think he can get any more from her."

"Maybe he can get a little, a few drops. Anything!"

"Clarent!" Lavender's voice washes over me, loud and imperious. "Use it. Make me like her. *Now.*"

I blink up at the riot of colors that whirl around me. Clarent is holding something waxy and plastic in his silver hands while Lavender stands close by, looking up at him as he studies her face. Everything is so bright now with the gray portal gone, but even allowing for that she seems much more intense than before. The green that snakes over her arms is darker, the purple in her hair is deeper. When her head turns to look at me, her eyes are impossibly vibrant; a bright green that instantly grips my gaze.

No!

She throws herself forward, her sharp fingernails tearing at her own lips. White fluid wells out of the cut, dripping on my face and into my mouth; then she's straddling me, kneeling over me to hold me close, her lips pressed hard against mine in the first kiss we've ever shared.

Muscle and sinew knit back together instantly in my shoulder, the wound closing in the space of a breath. My mind and vision clear, fresh blood springing up in my veins to replace all I'd lost. My hands come up instinctively to grab her shoulders, pushing her away, praying that it's not too late to save her. Maybe I don't have enough poison left in my system to hurt her; maybe she'll be sickened but not killed. *Please, don't let me kill her.*

She doesn't want to be pushed away; she fights me for a moment, determined to get the healing fluid from her lips into my system. Then it seems to sink into her that if I'm fighting I must be better, and she pulls away. Kneeling over me, staring down with those impossibly bright green eyes, Lavender giggles. "Rose, I thought you *wanted* to kiss me," she teases, relieved tears welling in her eyes.

My own vision swims in response and I blink rapidly. "Not if it's going to kill you, Lavs," I whisper, slapping her thigh gently where she straddles my waist. "You scared the hell out of me."

She leans down, her lips hovering inches above my own. "Likewise," she whispers softly. Her lips are already healing as I watch, the white fluid working as well on her as it did on me. "But I don't think you can hurt me now, Rose," she says. Her gaze moves to Clarent, still clutching the dead faery's arm; it is dry like an old plaster cast, the skin flaking away in chunks which disintegrate into white dust. "I think we used up all the extra magic, though."

Then she leans forward and kisses me gently. I freeze, old fears seizing my heart, but she's right; I can feel the way the magic moves within me. Little motes of light gather eagerly at my lips, only to turn away when they meet identical magic on the other side. I can't infect her because she's already a carrier of the same disease.

Tears spring up again and my hands wrap around her back, moving up through her hair, pulling her closer into our kiss. I need her, I want her; I don't ever wish to let her go. Then Clarent is beside us, stroking my hair gently, and I pull him down into our kiss; for a long minute there are only her lips and his and my own, kissing without any danger.

"We're here! Where is she?" The doors to the gym burst open, and I hear Worth's warm voice. I jerk in surprise at the sound, banging my head painfully against Clarent's forehead. Joel and Worth stride into the gymnasium, hardly seeming to know what to do with the broken glass, the streaks of blood, and the nearby dead body that looks more like a diseased mountain than anything human.

"We've worked out an immunization plan," Joel rasps proudly, brandishing a thick textbook.

"Is that one of *my* books?" Athena shrieks, her eyes locked on the tome.

He ignores her, too caught up in his triumph to hear. "Now we just draw what we need to heal her, and—" He stops and peers at me. "Well, she looks fine. Celia, you said she was dying."

"She exaggerates terribly," Elric says dryly. He nudges one of the bandaged fighters with his foot. "I don't suppose you could get to work on everyone else? Kieran has broken a few ribs, though he's trying very manfully to hide it."

CHAPTER 26

After that, there is chaos of a different kind: healing and cleaning and arguing and discussing. I ought to help, but Worth brings me a folding chair and orders me in no uncertain terms to sit and rest. Lavender and Clarent huddle close to me, their arms wrapped around my bloody dress. I should feel happiness or relief, but for the moment I'm conscious only of emptiness. I feel I've stepped out of my body and floated up to the ceiling, there to watch the crowd and myself within its noisy center.

We've only lost one person: the red-headed woman whose name, I now learn, had been Russet. The skeletons I'd seen on the creature's back hadn't come from our community; there is loud conjecture between Joel and Athena that they must have been eaten in the otherworld before the portal opened. No one knows how they had been hidden, along with the rest of the creature's gargantuan form, in his human guise; I wonder in a detached way if Hermit could tell us, but Celia does not disclose his existence to the group.

I can't quite believe we didn't lose more people, but I hadn't counted on Mina's ingenuity. After she'd seen the monster absorb Russet, she'd organized rescue crews: clever, fast altereds who could dart into the thick of battle and drag people back to relative safety before they could be captured and eaten. Some of the wounds had been deep and a few lives genuinely feared for, but Joel and Worth managed to patch everyone up. Given what Hermit had told us, I knew it was a miracle we'd only lost one.

Still, she had a name. Russet had a whole life apart from us, now cut short because of us—because Clarent had escaped, even though he hadn't meant to; because Lavender and I had killed the hunter sent to retrieve him. I want to believe we did the right thing, that we'd done the same for him as we would have for any other altered, but I don't feel easy. There's a fresh lump in my throat, and a new face and name to add to my nightmares.

There is argument over what to do with the dead faery, whose body takes up a good fifth of the room. Joel wants to keep it and even Worth looks tempted by the prospect of future research, but Celia argues that storing the corpse of a giant fae-monster for any length of time is just asking for trouble. Athena very helpfully points out that even if anyone had a garage big enough to hold the creature, squeezing it through the gymnasium doors would require an act of herculean strength. In the end, we all agree to send back the dead body to the otherworld.

The sticking point arises over what to do with Russet's body, and those of the skeletons found with her. Celia argues for sending them back with the dead faery, and provides calm persuasive reasoning about neighborhood dogs and why we don't bury people in our backyards. A young man named Rowan—thin, with soft freckles like Lavender and burnished bronze skin—barges angrily out of the crowd at this suggestion. Russet had been close to him and therefore the manner of her burial should be his decision, he argues; furthermore, she was one of our own and should not be sent back to rot in some faery's field.

I don't know how long the argument continues. My body leans into Clarent and Lavender while my mind observes numbly. People nod and murmur in agreement with Rowan, while others share Celia's concerns about secrecy and avoiding notice by the human authorities. Mina expands the discussion by pointing out in her soft way that the skeletons, if they were altered as we are, deserve to rest over here also; whether they were people known to us or not is irrelevant. Ideology clashes with practicality until frustration and grief cause Rowan's wavy red hair to burst into hot flames that lick the air above him.

Elric comes up with a solution then, sending Mina to the church kitchens to scavenge old coffee canisters and Kieran out to his truck to fetch an armful of canvas tarpaulin. We spread the tarp on the floor and lay the bodies upon it. Rowan steps forward, tears in his hazel eyes and his hair glowing like soft coals. He concentrates on Russet's mummified corpse, and under his sorrowful gaze the body grows warmer and then still hotter, burning so brightly that we have to look away. After a long and painful silence, her body eventually collapses into a pile of smoldering ash. Her remains are gently transferred to a coffee canister which Rowan cradles to his chest while he repeats the process, turning his fiery attention to the bones of the strangers. As numb as I am, I can't judge how long the entire process takes, only that the sky outside is dark and the moon has risen high before the last body crumbles.

There is crying, and quiet words spoken over the remains. Celia takes the ashes of the strangers, promising to scatter them in the field behind her house. Then she insists that everyone step outside while she opens a portal to send the body of the faery back to the otherworld. After that, there is sweeping and mopping, and the setting of folding chairs in their places. The shattered windows can't be repaired, but Celia passes the hat for monetary donations to replace them. The most convincing of our sirens is set to work on an explanation involving a broken speaker and very loud music, littered with copious apologies. It will take a little money and a lot of magic, but the humans will be satisfied.

No one feels like having a proper meeting after all that, but Celia gives a quick speech. Clarent stands up to introduce himself quietly, and explains that his faery was the one I'd killed first—and that the second one had seemed wary enough of me to retreat. Wide eyes watch me through his speech; several of the altereds huddling in the safety of the hallways had seen my play-acting, and of course almost everyone had seen me kill the Elder Fae. Without mentioning Hermit, Celia simply says that the monster was a different kind of faery. As we have no way of knowing how the otherworld will react to his death, she urges caution: travel in groups, call in regularly to others, and keep eyes and ears open.

Maybe they'll never bother us again, whispers the hopeful part of my mind. *Maybe they'll wipe us out in retaliation,* suggests the depression. There are other voices too, just on the edge of my perception. These are the ones who tell me what my fingers say, who report on the tiny points of light that mark the virus within me. Am I spiraling further into mental illness? Or did the voices come from the faery whose magic I absorbed? Does Lavender hear them, I wonder?

Rowan leaves soon after Celia's speech, and others trickle out the doors behind him. No one seems to know the right mood to take. Some of the fighters, those who didn't know Russet, are loudly clapping each other on the back; there is talk of finding a bar to get drunk in. Others are more subdued, grappling with tonight's harsh reminder that although we have escaped captivity, we are never safe.

Some of the members of the community avoid our gaze as they leave; others make a point of gently hugging me, Lavender, or Clarent. Jing gives me a lopsided smile before quietly ushering Athena out, who is loudly explaining to anyone who will listen that she is taking tomorrow off, that the bookstore will be closed, and that she cannot be expected to work under these conditions.

Dakota's acknowledgment is more curt: a short nod and a few words. "Good job, Rose. I've got to get back and check on Anwaar. Don't worry about the dress; I didn't like it in the first place." I blink at him as he dashes off, wondering if he means Tox and if he and Elric have sorted out all the paperwork.

Elric punches me in the shoulder, bringing me slightly back to myself if only to feel annoyance. "Jeezus, Rose, can you work on a way to be useful that *isn't* suicidally stupid?" he grumbles. "You keep scaring everyone half to death." He gives Lavender a sly look. "Though *you* made out okay, I see; pun intended."

She gives him her most dignified expression, managing to glare down her nose while looking up at him. "A practical application of magic," she retorts. "I should think Worth and Joel will be interested in my thought process later."

He smirks at her, undeterred by her calm contempt. "I'm interested in your thought process *now*," he offers. "Especially as it pertains to a practical application of Rose's lips."

Kieran interrupts him, throwing a heavy arm over his shoulder. "We're going," he tells Elric sternly, offering me a look that passes for apologetic. "Sorry I got in your way back there. I didn't realize you had a plan."

I shake my head. "It's okay," I reassure him quickly. "You were trying to save me. Sorry I scared you."

He makes a face at the assertion that he was scared but is polite enough not to contradict me. "You're all right, Rosie. C'mon," he adds to Elric, whose expression has reached epic levels of smugness. "Celia says I'm to drive you home before you get into any more arguments she'll have to break up." Elric grins at him and shuffles out with minimal protests, just loud enough to ensure that everyone notices them leaving together.

Only then does Mina bustle over to us, wrapping her arms around my neck with affectionate abandon. "Sweetie, are you okay?" she asks, half-kneeling before me so she can study my face with her worried gaze.

I nod at her, trying to meet her eyes and not quite managing. "I'm fine," I assure her, "just a little overwhelmed. Tired, that's all."

Her eyes soften and she takes my hand gently. "That's normal, sweetie," she says, her voice low and warm. "You've had a long week. I'll talk to Celia and Worth; I think they're ready to let you go home now. Let Lavs and Clarent take you back to the apartment and spoil you with bath and bed and breakfast, okay? Get lots of rest and as many cuddles as you can, then call me in the morning and we'll do coffee." She glances at Lavender and Clarent then, holding their gaze. "That goes for all three of you. I'm always open for one-on-one talking times."

I can't help but smile at her. "I will, I promise. I'll call you."

Mina grins at me. "You'd better." Gently, she reaches to stroke my cheek with the back of her hand. "It's okay to have a lot of feelings about all this," she whispers. "We'll talk it through and have a good cry. You're going to be all right, sweetie." Leaning up, she kisses my cheek softly and turns to embrace Clarent.

She hesitates a moment with Lavender and then giggles. "Is it cheek kisses now?" she asks, her eyes sad though her smile never falters.

Lavender gives her a rueful smile of her own. "I think so," she admits, "at least for a while." She steals a glance at me, her eyes searching mine. "Joel mentioned some kind of immunization plan? And I kind of feel like maybe we might be able to control it with practice. But I think we should test that theory on something less valuable than you, Mina: Joel's lab-rats, or possibly Elric."

Mina laughs at this and leans over to peck Lavender on the cheek. "Call me anytime," she repeats, chuckling happily as she wanders back to the cleaning work.

Clarent squeezes my hand softly, his silver eyes gazing at us with fond affection. "Not that all that didn't sound wonderful," he says, his voice low and kind. "But do you actually *want* me to come home with you? I mean, I'd like that," he admits with a warm smile, a dark blush building under his silver cheeks, "but it's okay if *you* don't. You don't really need me anymore, and it's okay if you two want to be alone; I'll understand."

I stare at him, my eyes widening in surprise. Turning to Lavender for help, I see amused exasperation in her face as she rolls her eyes. "Clarent, of course we want you to come home with us," she protests with a laugh, smacking his arm gently. "If you really believe we only needed you for *that*, why do you think we didn't just opt for the metal dildo? Yes, Rose, we heard you and Mina!"

266

My face flushes and Lavender giggles at the heat in my cheeks. "Well, am I wrong?" she teases, dropping her voice low and wrapping her arms around me from behind. She tucks her chin onto my shoulder to look at me with dancing eyes.

I shake my head, unable to stop a broad embarrassed grin from splitting my face. "No," I admit in a low whisper, "but you could be a little more delicate about it, Lavs."

I turn back to Clarent, my heart melting anew at the delight on his handsome face. Feeling bolder than usual with the strength of Lavender's arms around me, I wrap my own around his neck, pulling him closer and touching my forehead to his.

"I don't know if we *need* you," I tell him, my grin widening, "but I'm pretty sure we both *want* you with us very much. Only if you want that too, of course," I add, my old anxieties creeping back in. Worries I can't express dance through my mind. *I'm a murderer. We cry at night, Lavender and I. There's so much about myself that I still don't know; so much about my past and my heritage that I need to learn. There isn't a single solitary Pop-Tart in the apartment.*

He grins easily at my caveat. "I do," he assures me, his hands reaching up to encircle us both. "Let's go home?" With a sly smile, he adds, "Can I drive this time? I really do think I remember how. It's just a matter of which pedal you press, right?"

EPILOGUE

The Shadowy One watched as the Elder Fae came to collect the body of their own.

He had to watch from a distance, and this was vexing. He would have preferred to hear what they had to say, but the risk was not worth the potential reward. He had yet to meet a human or faery who could detect him as he moved through the portal space between the two worlds, but he would not bet his life that none of the Elders could sense his presence. Their relationship with the portal space was a strange one, and he was not vain enough to believe that the ones who spawned him had no insight into his talents.

So he watched from afar as they examined the body. He had hoped they would consume it, and in this he was not disappointed. His ultimate goal was frustrated, however, when the faint remains of tainted magic failed to spread through the new hosts. He had been desirous of a chain reaction, with each dead Elder slaying the next; instead he was forced to be content with just the one death, which was quite possibly unrepeatable from that vector. The lingering vestiges of the girl's poison meant her taste would now be known to them, marking her as an unacceptable food source. And already her fellow humans spoke of immunization, which meant he had to assume the Elders could develop defenses of their own against the girl. They might even pass those defenses to any new faery born from them.

Another frustrating dead-end. It had taken him over a month to track down the May Queen's prize specimen after she'd stupidly let the girl escape, then another month to arrange to send over the sword from under the High King's nose. The humans had then taken an interminable length of time to consider that it might be worthwhile to make the weaponized girl *stronger*; she'd been willing to lie down and die in front of the child, and the bear had fought his magic so strenuously that his portal had ended up in entirely the wrong place.

Worse yet, the girl had actually asked the sword to *remove* her magic, leaving him scrambling to send over the Fiery Lord's hunter to interrupt them. He'd had more than enough of unpredictable human behavior in the last two days.

Still, he was nothing if not patient. The advantage of living in shadows was the ability to experiment, to set pawns onto the board and watch what transpired. To learn and to adapt; that was what set him apart from his parents and siblings.

Nor had this experiment been a total failure: an Elder Fae was dead, as was that fool of a High King, and he'd had a chance to watch the humans in action. They'd done much better than he would have believed, utilizing their superior numbers and smaller size in surprisingly creative ways. They'd cooperated, which wasn't a tactic his kind were comfortable with. That was something to consider.

He would rest for now, hiding as always in the safety of his shadows. After he regained the strength he'd spent on all those portals, he could begin again.

~

About the Author

ANA MARDOLL is a writer and activist who lives in the dusty Texas wilderness with two spoiled cats. Her favorite employment is weaving new tellings of old fairy tales, fashioning beautiful creations to bring comfort on cold nights. She is the author of the Earthside series, the Rewoven Tales novels, and several short stories.

Aside from reading and writing, Ana enjoys games of almost every flavor and frequently posts videos of gaming sessions on YouTube. After coming out as genderqueer in 2015, Ana answers to both xie/xer and she/her pronouns.

Website: www.AnaMardoll.com
Twitter: @AnaMardoll
YouTube: www.YouTube.com/c/AnaMardoll

Content Notes

Content notes (sometimes referred to as 'trigger warnings') are intended to help trauma survivors avoid being surprised by story elements which may trigger them. These content notes may allude to story spoilers, which is why they have been placed at the back of the book, with a link near the front. The content note system used in this book is the one created by the Fireside Fiction Company, and used here with permission from the owner. This book and the author are not affiliated with the Fireside Fiction Company in any way.

The content notes for this book include:

Animal Abuse • one scene of low intensity
Child Neglect • one scene of low intensity
Sexual Assault •• one scene of moderate intensity
Torture • one scene of low intensity

Made in the USA
San Bernardino, CA
24 November 2017